SPECIAL MESSAGE TO READERS

THE ULVERSCROFT FOUNDATION
(registered UK charity number 264873)
was established in 1972 to provide funds for research, diagnosis and treatment of eye diseases. Examples of major projects funded by the Ulverscroft Foundation are:-

- The Children's Eye Unit at Moorfields Eye Hospital, London
- The Ulverscroft Children's Eye Unit at Great Ormond Street Hospital for Sick Children
- Funding research into eye diseases and treatment at the Department of Ophthalmology, University of Leicester
- The Ulverscroft Vision Research Group, Institute of Child Health
- Twin operating theatres at the Western Ophthalmic Hospital, London
- The Chair of Ophthalmology at the Royal Australian College of Ophthalmologists

You can help further the work of the Foundation by making a donation or leaving a legacy. Every contribution is gratefully received. If you would like to help support the Foundation or require further information, please contact:

THE ULVERSCROFT FOUNDATION
The Green, Bradgate Road, Anstey
Leicester LE7 7FU, England
Tel: (0116) 236 4325

website: www.foundation.ulverscroft.com

Mo Hayder left school at fifteen, and has worked as a barmaid, security guard, film-maker, hostess in a Tokyo club, educational administrator and a teacher of English as a foreign language, before pursuing a career as a novelist. Hayder has an MA in film from the American University in Washington DC, and an MA in Creative Writing from Bath Spa University. She lives just outside Bath with her partner, Bob Randell, and her daughter.

POPPET

The mentally ill patients in Beechway Secure Unit are highly suggestible. A hallucination can spread like a virus. When unexplained power cuts lead to a series of horrifying incidents, fear spreads from the inmates to the staff. Amidst the growing hysteria, AJ, a senior psychiatric nurse, is desperate to protect his charges. Detective Inspector Jack Caffery is looking for the corpse of a missing woman. He knows all too well how it feels to fail to find a loved one's body. When AJ seeks Caffery's help in investigating the trouble at Beechway, each man must face a bitter truth in his own life — before staring pure evil in the eye . . .

Books by Mo Hayder
Published by The House of Ulverscroft:

RITUAL
SKIN
GONE
HANGING HILL

MO HAYDER

POPPET

Complete and Unabridged

CHARNWOOD
Leicester

First published in Great Britain in 2013 by
Bantam Press
an imprint of
Transworld Publishers
London

First Charnwood Edition
published 2014
by arrangement with
Transworld Publishers
A Random House Group Company
London

This book is a work of fiction and, except in the case of historical fact, any resemblance to actual persons, living or dead, is purely coincidental.

A catalogue record for this book is available from the British Library.

ISBN 978–1–4448–1879–6

Published by
F. A. Thorpe (Publishing)
Anstey, Leicestershire

Set by Words & Graphics Ltd.
Anstey, Leicestershire
Printed and bound in Great Britain by
T. J. International Ltd., Padstow, Cornwall

This book is printed on acid-free paper

Invisible

Monster Mother is sitting on the bed when the triangle of light under the door flickers. It moves, dancing sideways a little, then settles.

She stares at it, her heart thumping. Something is out there, waiting.

Silently Monster Mother pushes herself out of bed and creeps to the furthest corner of the room — as far away from the door as she can. She presses herself back into the triangle between the walls, trembling, eyes watering with fear. From the window behind her, electric security spots cast tree shadows across the floor. They shift and bend, fingers scratching across the room, finding and touching the shadow under the door. She scans the place — the walls and the bed and the wardrobe. Checks every corner, every crack in the plaster. Anywhere at all that The Maude can crawl in. Monster Mother knows more about The Maude than anyone here does. She'll never tell what she knows, though. She's too scared.

It's still out there. Not moving a lot — but enough to make the patch of light sway. Monster Mother can hear breathing now. She wants to cry but she can't. Carefully and silently she pushes her shaky hand up under the red negligee and moves her fingers along the skin between her breasts — groping for the thing she needs. When she finds it she tugs. The pain is greater than anything she can remember. It hurts more than cutting off her own arm — or giving birth (something she has done several times). But she continues, pulling the zip down, from sternum to pubis. There is a wet smacking sound as her stomach muscles spring free from her skin.

She grips the edge of the opening and, writhing and weeping, wrenches it outwards. The skin unsticks from her ribs and her breasts and peels down over her shoulders. It tears, it bleeds, but she continues until it hangs from her hips like dripping wax. She takes a few deep breaths and rips it away from her legs.

It gathers in a pool at her feet. A deflated rubber mould.

Monster Mother gathers herself. She straightens — solid and brave — her stripped muscles glinting in the security lights. She turns to face the door, proud and defiant.

The Maude will never find her now.

Browns Brasserie, The Triangle, Bristol

The restaurant was once the university refectory — and it still has a noisy, peopled buzz to it. High ceilings and bouncy acoustics. Except now the students aren't sitting and eating, they're wearing black aprons — slaloming round tables carrying plates, muttering to themselves orders and table numbers. Working off their loans. A 'skinny cocktails' neon blinks above the polished concrete bar, chords from a Gotye song drift out of the speakers latched high in the ceiling girders.

The customers are mostly people who've chosen this place as a venue — it's a high enough price tab to be above drop-in scale. The only lone diners are self-conscious — some cradling Kindles over their borscht soup — some sipping wine and casually checking watches, expecting dates or friends. Out of British politeness nobody stares at them, or even acknowledges them.

Only one diner appears to have any effect on his neighbours. Nearby tables have remarked on him and adjusted their seating accordingly — as if he's a threat or an excitement. A dark-haired man in his early forties breaking myriad unspoken rules. Not just by his attire — a black weatherproof worn over a business suit — the tie removed, the shirt collar slightly open — but by his attitude.

He's eating like someone who wants to eat for no other reason than that he is hungry — not because he wants to be seen here. He doesn't adopt an air or scan the room, he eats steadily, his gaze focused on the mid-distance. It is gross misconduct in a place like this, and there's a kind of satisfaction amongst the others when it all goes wrong for him. Privately they think it's just what *would* happen to someone like him.

It's eight thirty and a table of twenty has come in. They've booked in advance and the tables have been arranged at the rear of the space so they won't disturb the other customers. An engagement party maybe — some of the girls are in cocktail dresses and one or two of the men are in suits. The woman at the back of the group — a blonde in her late fifties, suntanned, dressed in overstitched jeans and a Hollister hoodie — seems, at first glance, to be with the crowd. It's only when they sit, and she doesn't, that it's clear she's tagged along and has no connection with them.

She moves unsteadily. Under the hoodie her breasts are on display in a low-cut T-shirt. She knocks one of the waiters in her transit through the restaurant — stops to apologize, slurring her 'sorry's — resting her hands on his chest as she speaks, smiling confidentially. He shoots a helpless glance at the bar staff, not sure what to do — but before he can object she's gone, bouncing past the tables like a pinball — her eyes locked on her target.

The man in the North Face weatherproof.

He looks up from the half-eaten hamburger.

Registers her. And, as if he knows she means trouble, slowly puts down his knife and fork. Conversation at all the adjacent tables falters and dies. The man picks up his napkin and wipes his mouth.

'Hello, Jacqui.' He sets the napkin down neatly. 'So nice to see you.'

'Fuck you.' She puts her hands on the table and leers at him. 'Just fuck you into next week, you shithead.'

He nods, as if acknowledging the fact he is indeed a shithead. However, he says nothing and that infuriates the woman even further. She slams her hands on the table again, making everything jump. A fork and a napkin fall to the floor.

'Look at you — sitting here just eating. Eating and enjoying yourself. You don't have a fucking clue, do you?'

'Hello?' The waiter touches her on the arm. 'Madam? Shall we try to keep this conversation private? And then we can — '

'Piss off.' She bats his hand away. 'Piss right off. You don't know what you're talking about.' She lurches sideways and grabs the first glass she can see. It's from a neighbouring table and is full of red wine. Its owner makes a futile grab for it, but the woman glides it away and slings the wine at the man in the weatherproof. The wine has a life of its own; it seems able to go everywhere. It lands on his face, on his shirt, in his plate and on the table. Other diners jump to their feet in shock, but the man remains sitting. Completely cool.

'Where the fuck is she?' the woman screams. 'Where is she? You will fucking tell me what you're doing about it or I will kill you — I will fucking kill y — '

Two security staff appear. A huge black guy in a green T-shirt and a headset is in charge. He puts a hand on her arm. 'Babes,' he says, 'this isn't helping you. Now let's go somewhere and have a chat about it.'

'You think I can chat?' She pushes his arm away. 'I'll chat. I'll chat until you fall over. I'll shagging chat until you puke.'

The big guy makes a near-invisible nod, and his staff grab her arms, pin them to her sides as she struggles. She continues squealing at the top of her voice as she is forced back through the restaurant towards the doors: 'He *knows* where she is.' She addresses her fury at the security boss, as if he's going to give a shit. 'He doesn't care. He doesn't CARE. That's what the problem is. He doesn't fucking c — '

The men push her out of the front doors. They lock them and stand, facing outwards, their arms folded, while she squirms on the pavement. The man in the windcheater doesn't get up or look at the door. If anyone asked him how he keeps his cool he'd shrug. Maybe it's his nature, maybe it's from his training. He is police, after all, and that helps. A plain-clothed member of Bristol's Major Crime Investigation Team. Detective Inspector Jack Caffery, age forty-two. He's seen and endured worse than this. Much worse.

Silently he shakes out a napkin and begins blotting the red wine from his face and neck.

Coordinator's Office, Beechway High Secure Unit, Bristol

It's about eleven o'clock when AJ LeGrande, the senior nursing coordinator at Beechway psychiatric unit, wakes from a nightmare with a jolt. His heart is thudding, and it takes a long time for him to reorientate himself and realize he is fully dressed and sitting in his office chair, feet on his desk. The reports he was reading are scattered on the floor.

He rubs his chest uneasily. Blinks and sits up. The room is dark, just a small amount of light coming from under the door. Dancing on his retina is the blurred after-image of a little figure crouched over him. Straddling his chest, its smooth face close to his. Its foreshortened arms resting delicately on his collarbone. He runs his tongue around his mouth, glancing around the office. He imagines the thing escaping through the closed door. Sliding under and out into the corridor, where it will run further and further into the hospital.

His throat is tight. He's not used to wearing a collar — he's only been coordinator for a month and he can't get used to the suit. And the clip-on ties he has to wear for his own safety? He can't seem to get the knack of them. They never hang right or feel right. He drops his feet to the floor and unclips the tie. The tightness in his lungs eases slightly. He gets up and goes to the door. Fingers on the handle, he hesitates. If he opens the door he's going to see a little gowned figure pitter-pattering away down the empty corridor.

Three deep breaths. He opens the door. Looks one way up the corridor, and the other. There is nothing. Just the usual things he's got used to over the years: the green tiled floor, the fire muster point with its diagram of the unit, the padded handrails. No wispy fleeing hem of a gown rounding the corner and disappearing out of sight.

He leans against the doorpost for a moment, trying to clear his head. Dwarfs on his chest? Little figures in nightgowns? The whisper of small feet? And two words he doesn't want to think: *The. Maude*.

Jeeeez. He knocks a knuckle against his head. This is what comes from doing double shifts and falling asleep in a tie that's too tight. Really, it's crazy. He's supposed to be a supervisor, so how has it worked out this is the second night shift he's covered for one of the nursing staff? Completely ridiculous, because the night shift used to be the coveted shift — a chance to catch up on TV or sleep. Everything has changed since what happened on Dandelion Ward last week; suddenly anyone rostered in overnight has been jumping ship like rats, calling in sick with every excuse under the sun. No one wants to spend the night in the unit — as if something unearthly has come into the place.

And now it's even getting to him — even he is hallucinating. The last thing he wants to do is go back into his office, revisit that dream. Instead he closes the door and heads off towards the wards, swiping through an airlock. Maybe he'll get a coffee, speak to a few of the nurses, get some normality back. The fluorescent lights flicker as he walks. Outside the big windows of the 'stem' corridor a gale is howling — lately autumns have been so odd, so hot early on and so ferociously windy mid-October. The trees in the courtyard are bucking and bending — leaves and sticks fly off through the air, but oddly the sky is clear, the moon huge and unblinking.

The admin block beyond is in darkness and the two wards he can see from this vantage point are minimally lit — just the nurses' station and the nightlights in the corridors. Beechway High Secure Unit was originally built as a Victorian workhouse. It evolved over the years — into a municipal hospital, then an orphanage and then an asylum. Years later, after all the 'care in the community' upheaval in the eighties, it was designated a 'High Secure Psychiatric Hospital', housing patients who are an extreme danger to themselves and others. Killers and rapists and the determinedly suicidal — they're all here. AJ has been in this business years — and it never gets any easier or any less tense. Especially when a patient dies on the unit. Suddenly and in an untimely fashion, like Zelda Lornton did last week.

As he walks, with every turn in the corridor he expects to catch a glimpse of the tiny figure, tottering crookedly away ahead of him in the shadows. But he sees no one. Dandelion Ward is hushed, the lights low. He makes coffee in the nurses' kitchen and carries it through into the station where one or two nurses sit sleepily in front of the TV. 'Hey, AJ,' they say lazily, raising a hand or two. ' 'Sup? You OK?'

He considers starting a conversation — maybe asking them why their colleagues keep calling in sick when all they have to do is sit and watch movies like this — but they're so intent on the TV he doesn't bother. Instead he stands at the back of the room and sips his coffee, while on TV the Men in Black shoot aliens. Will Smith is mega-good-looking and Tommy Lee Jones is mega-grumpy. The villain has one arm missing, and there's a half-crab/half-scorpion living in his good hand. Ace. Just what you need in a place like this.

The coffee's done its job. AJ is awake now. He should go back to his office, see if he can finish reading the world's most boring report. But the nightmare is still lingering and he needs a distraction.

'I'll do the midnight round,' he tells the nurses. 'Don't let me interrupt your beauty sleep.'

Lazy, derisory comments follow him. He rinses his cup in the kitchen, pulls out his bunch of keys and goes silently down the corridor, swiping his way into the night quarters. Into the silence.

Now he's been promoted to coordinator he's expected to attend management meetings, do presentations and staff training. All afternoon he's been at a Criminal Justice Forum, a meeting with local community leaders and the police — and this, he is starting to see, is his lot in life. Meetings and paperwork. A daily shoehorning into a suit. He never thought for a minute he'd miss anything about nursing, but now he sees he misses this — the nightly round. There was a kind of satisfaction knowing everyone was asleep. Sorted for the day. You can't get that from a bunch of reports.

The lower corridor is silent, just muffled snoring coming from some of the rooms. He opens one or two of the viewing panes into the rooms, but the only movement is the bend and rush of the trees shadowed on the thin curtains, moonlight moving across the sleeping forms of patients. The next floor up is different. He can sense it the moment he rounds the top of the staircase. Someone is uncomfortable. It's little more than a feeling — an unease he gets from years of experience. Like a vibration in the walls.

This is the place Zelda died last week. Her room is the first on the right and the door stands open, a maintenance warning sign in the opening. The bed has been stripped and the curtains are open. Moonlight streams blue and vivid into the room. A paint roller in a tray is propped up against the wall. At morning and night, as the patients are led to and from the day area, they have to be encouraged to walk past the room without peering in — crying and shaking. Even AJ finds it hard to think about what's happened here this month.

It started about three weeks ago. It was at ten p.m., and AJ had stayed on late to check through some staff returns records. He was in the office when the lights died from a power cut. He and the duty maintenance man rummaged for torches and soon found the source of the problem — a short-circuited dryer in the laundry room. Most of the patients knew nothing about it; many were asleep and those who were still awake barely noticed. Within forty minutes the lights were back on — all was normal. Except Zelda. She was in her room on the upstairs corridor in Dandelion Ward, and the yells she let off when the lights came on were so high-pitched at first AJ thought it was an alarm, jolted into action by the electricity.

The night staff were so used to Zelda screaming and complaining that they were slow about going up to her. They'd learned if she was given time to get it out of her system she was easier to deal with. The decision backfired on them. When AJ and one of the other nursing staff finally went up to check on her they found they weren't the first. The door was open and the clinical director, Melanie Arrow, was sitting on the bed, cupping Zelda's hands as if they were fragile eggs. Zelda was wearing a nightdress and had a towel draped around her shoulders. Her arms were covered in blood and she was weeping. Shaking and trembling.

AJ's heart fell. They'd have been a lot quicker off the mark if they'd known this was happening. Especially if they'd known the director was in the building to witness it. From her face it was one hundred per cent clear she wasn't happy about the situation. Not happy at all.

'Where were you?' Her voice was contained. 'Why wasn't anyone on the ward? Isn't it in the protocol? Someone on every ward?'

The on-call junior consultant was summoned and Zelda was taken to the GP's room next to AJ's office to be checked over. AJ had never seen her so subdued. So genuinely shaken. She was bleeding from the insides of both arms and when the wounds were examined it was found they'd been gouged with a roller-ball pen. Every inch of her inner arms was covered in writing. Melanie Arrow and the consultant went into a conspiratorial huddle under the blinding fluorescent lights while AJ stood, arms folded, back against the wall, shifting uneasily from foot to foot. The consultant had been asleep twenty minutes ago and kept yawning. He'd brought the wrong glasses, and had to hold them about a foot in front of his eyes in order to scrutinize her arms.

'Zelda?' Melanie said. 'You've hurt yourself?'

'No. I didn't hurt myself.'

'Someone did. Didn't they?' Melanie let the sentence hang in the air, waiting for an answer. 'Zelda?'

She shifted uncomfortably and rubbed her chest as if there was a tightness there. 'Someone hurt me. Or some*thing*.'

'I'm sorry? *Something?*'

Zelda licked her lips and glanced around at all the concerned faces peering at her. Her colour was high — spidery veins stood out on her cheeks — but her usual fight was gone. Completely gone. She was bewildered.

'One hundred grams Acuphase,' the doctor

muttered. 'And level-one obs until the morning — two to one please. Maybe bring her down to level two in the morning.'

Now, AJ puts his head into the room and glances around, wondering what actually happened in here. What did Zelda really see that night? Something sitting on her chest? Something small and determined — something that skittered away under the door?

A noise. He lifts his chin. It's coming from the last room on the right — Monster Mother's room. He crosses to it, knocks quietly on her door, and listens.

Monster Mother — or rather, to give her her legal name, Gabriella Jackson — is one of the patients AJ likes best. She's a gentle soul most of the time. But when she's not gentle it's usually herself she takes it out on. She has slashes to her ankles and thighs that will never go away and her left arm is missing from the elbow down. She cut it off one night with an electric carving knife — standing in the kitchen of her million-pound home and calmly using the vegetable chopping board to rest the limb on. She was trying to prove to her dimwit husband how serious, how very serious, she was about not wanting him to have another affair.

This missing limb is the chief reason Monster Mother is in Beechway, that and a few other 'kinks' in her understanding of reality. For example, her belief she has given birth to all the other patients — they are all monsters and have committed vile deeds because they sprung from her poisoned womb. 'Monster Mother' is the name she has given herself, and if you spend long enough talking to her you will hear a detailed account of the birth of every patient in the unit — how long and troublesome the labour was, and how she could see from the first moment that the baby was evil.

The other kink in her reality is a belief that her skin is detachable. That if she removes it she is invisible.

AJ knocks again. 'Gabriella?'

The protocol is always to use the patient's real name, no matter what fantasy they've developed about their identity.

'Gabriella?'

Nothing.

Quietly he opens the door and glances around the room. She is lying in her bed, the sheets up to her chin, her eyes like saucers, staring at him. AJ knows this means she is 'hiding' and that her 'skin' is elsewhere in the room — placed somewhere to draw attention away from herself. He doesn't play into the delusion — though he's permitted to express gentle doubt, he must avoid challenging it directly. (More protocol.)

Without making eye contact he comes in and sits and waits. Silence. Not a murmur. But AJ knows Monster Mother, she can't keep quiet for ever.

Sure enough, eventually she sits up in bed and whispers, 'AJ. I'm here.'

He nods slowly. Still doesn't look directly at her. 'Are you OK?'

'No, I'm not. Will you close the door?'

He wouldn't close the door behind him for

most of the patients in this place, but he's known Monster Mother for years and he's a coordinator now, responsible, so he gets up and pushes the door shut. She shuffles herself up in the bed. She is fifty-seven but her skin is as unwrinkled and pale as an eggshell, her hair a red explosion. Her eyes are extraordinary — the brightest blue with dark lashes, as if she takes hours putting mascara on. She spends all her allowance on her clothes, which would look more at home on a six-year-old at a fairy party. Everything is floaty tulle in a rainbow of colours, tutu skirts and roses in her hair.

Whichever colour she chooses to wear is a reflection of how she sees the world on that particular day. At good times it's pastels: pinks, baby blues, primrose yellows, lilacs. At bad times it's the darker primary colours: dense reds, dark blue or black. Today a red lace negligee is draped at the foot of the bed, and that gives AJ an idea of her mood. Red is for danger. It also tells him that her skin is hanging on the end of the bed too. He directs his attention halfway between the negligee and her face. Somewhere on the wall above the bed. Neutral.

'What's happening, Gabriella? What's on your mind?'

'I had to take it off. It's not safe.'

AJ resists the urge to roll his eyes. Monster Mother is sweet and she's gentle and yes, crazy, but mostly kind of funny crazy, not aggressive crazy. He takes his time answering — again neither denying nor confirming her delusion. 'Gabriella — have you had your meds tonight?

You did take them, didn't you? You know I'll ask the dispensary if they saw you take them. And if they *didn't* see you . . . well, I don't need to search the room, do I?'

'I took them, AJ. I did. I just can't sleep.'

'When's your depot up again? I haven't checked, but I think it's got a long way to run.'

'Ten days. I'm not mad, Mr AJ. I'm not.'

'Of course you're not.'

'It's back, though, AJ — it's in the corridor. It's been running around all night.'

AJ closes his eyes and breathes slowly. What did he expect coming up here? Did he really think it was going to dispel his nightmare? Did he imagine laughter and gaiety and people telling jokes to take his mind off things?

'Look, Gabriella. We've talked about this before. Remember all those chats we had in Acute?'

'Yes. I locked those chats in a box up in my head like the doctors told me I was supposed to.'

'We agreed you weren't going to talk about it again? Do you remember?'

'But, AJ, it's back. It's come back. It got Zelda.'

'Don't you remember what you said, in High Dependency? I remember you saying: 'it doesn't exist. It's just a made-up thing — like in the movies.' Remember?'

She nods, but the glisten of fear in her eyes doesn't go.

'That's good, Gabriella. And you haven't been talking to the others about this, have you?'

'No.'

'Great — that's great. You did the right thing. You keep it to yourself — I know you can. I know you can do that. Now we've got your care-planning meeting in the morning — I'll mention this to the consultant — see what he says. And I'm going to put you on level four obs — just for tonight — OK? I'll look in on you myself. But, Gabriella . . . ?'

'What?'

'You gotta put that . . . that *thing* out of your head, my sweet-heart. You really have.'

Safe

It's funny, to the Monster Mother, how AJ can't see what's happening. He can't even say the words, 'The. Maude.' AJ is kind and he's smart but he hasn't got the extra eye — he can't see the real things that are going on in this unit. He doesn't believe her — that The Maude is out there. Scouting for someone else to hurt.

AJ can't see the lengths Monster Mother has gone to, just to be safe. Maybe if he could he'd understand how serious it is. But he can't see her stripped muscle and tendon. He cannot see the white of her skull or the glinting twin orb eyes without their lids. He is so blind to what is happening. 'Good night,' he says. 'I'll check on you — I promise.'

She slides the sheets back up over her. They rasp at her exposed nerves and skinless muscles. She lays her raw skull on the pillow and tries to smile — using just her cheek muscles. 'AJ?'

'Yes?'

'Please be careful.'

'I will.'

He waits for a few moments, as if he's thinking, then he steps outside and shuts the door. The hospital is silent. She can't close her eyes, she has no eyelids. But at least she is safe from The Maude. If it comes in it'll go straight to her skin on the bedpost.

No one is going to sit on Monster Mother's chest tonight.

Browns Brasserie, The Triangle

DI Caffery knows everyone in the restaurant is monitoring him for signs he's going to react to the woman throwing wine on him. He can sense their universal disappointment when he isn't pulled that easily.

He takes his time with the hamburger — refusing to be harassed or hurried. Occasionally, as he chews, his eyes go casually to the door — to the backs of the two bouncers — legs planted wide, arms folded, facing the glass doors. Beyond them the woman — now on her feet — staggers around on the pavement, hurling abuse at the doormen.

Caffery has spent the dullest lunchtime and afternoon at a Criminal Justice Forum: discussing liaison practices between custody suites and mental health unit admissions ward — he's fed up with talking about stuff he's not interested in, schmoozing and being nice to people he doesn't care about. But this woman — her name is Jacqui Kitson — this woman has, at the eleventh hour, kickstarted an ordinary day into something extraordinary.

Extraordinary. Not pleasant. It's what he's been half expecting for a long time.

She has given up hectoring the door staff and is sitting in the gutter, her head in her hands, crying. By the time Caffery has paid his bill the staff have opened the doors again — allowing in the customers who've had to wait outside. They shuffle in edgily, casting cautious glances at the woman — only pausing to stand aside for Caffery to make his way out.

He puts his wallet in his inside pocket. The bill was forty pounds. Extravagant for a meal alone — but he doesn't have much to spend his money on these days. He's always tinkering around for a hobby to take his mind off work, but it doesn't come naturally and he knows dining alone isn't going to be the answer. Maybe if there was someone to eat with? There's one woman he'd prefer to be with, but the complications there are taller than a mountain. Jacqui Kitson doesn't know it but she is deeply connected with those complications.

'Jacqui,' he says, standing over her. 'You want to talk.'

She turns her head to check out his shoes. Then she raises her face — half blind. Her eyes are swollen and there are long streaks of mascara down her cheeks. Her head isn't steady on her neck. She has been sick in the gutter and her handbag is lying half in the road, straddling the double-yellow lines. She's a total mess.

He sits next to her. 'I'm here now, you can yell at me.'

'Don't wanna yell,' she murmurs. 'Just want her back.'

'I know that — we all do — we all want her back.' He pats his pocket for one of the silver-and-black tubes he's been hauling around for months — V-Cigs — trying to break his old bad habit, which, after years of pressure from the government and friends, he has at last done — replacing it with fake steel replicas. He clicks the atomizer into the battery housing. He is still faintly embarrassed by the gimmickry of the V-Cig. If he was sitting outside himself and watching he'd be tempted to make a scathing comment. The passing motorists and pedestrians let their attention brush briefly over the pair sitting on the pavement. A pink Humvee stretch limo crawls by, the blackened windows open. A woman in a pink cowboy hat and strapped on L-plates leans out and waves at Caffery.

'*I loves you*,' she yells as the Hummer passes. '*I do!!!!*'

Caffery sucks in the nicotine vapour. Holds it and blows it out in a thin stream. 'Jacqui, you're a long way from home. How did you get here — are you on your own?'

'I'm always on my own now, aren't I? Always on my fucking own.'

'Then how am I going to get you home? Did you drive here?'

'Yeah.'

'All the way from Essex?'

'Don't be a fucking idiot. I'm staying here — in a hotel. My car's . . . ' She waves her hand vaguely down the hill. 'Dunno.'

'You didn't drive like this, did you?'

She focuses hazily on the V-Cig. 'Can I have one of them?'

'It's not real.'

'Gimme one out of my — ' She squints,

searching for her bag. Then slaps her hands down — feeling around in panic.

'Here.' Caffery passes her the bag from the road. She pauses, scowls accusingly at him and grabs it — as if he was on the point of stealing it. She starts rummaging through the contents, but every time she lowers her head the alcohol sets her off balance and she has to put her head back and take deep breaths.

'Oh,' she says, 'it's all going round and round. I'm arsed, aren't I?'

'Close your bag, Jacqui. You're going to lose all your stuff. Come on.' He gets to his feet. Holds a hand out to her. 'I'll drive you back to your hotel.'

The Old Workhouse

At Beechway's heart are the remains of the workhouse — extensively redesigned to rid itself of the stereotypical asylum image: the old water tower — a common safeguard against asylums being set ablaze by inmates — was remodelled and given a huge clock, as if to justify the tower's existence. The layout of the wards, which deliberately or inadvertently had been designed to resemble a cross from above, was thought to have religious overtones, so some bright spark on the Trust came up with the idea of turning the cross into a four-leaf clover. *Much more organic*.

Each arm of the cross was extended, laterally, into the shape of a clover leaf to make Beechway the place it is today. Each 'leaf' is a ward, with two floors of bedrooms, glass-fronted communal rooms on one side, and managers' offices and therapy rooms on the others. The windows are large and smooth and the walls rounded. There's a 'stem' — a glassed corridor that leads from the wards in the clover, down through a central garden, known as the courtyard, to the long arced block that contains all the administration offices. Everything — every ward, corridor, room, bathroom — is named after a flower.

It's definitely organic.

When AJ leaves Monster Mother he goes slowly into each leaf, patrols each ward, each corridor — Buttercup, Myrtle, Harebell — checking the other patients haven't been disturbed. Most are fast asleep, or halfway there — off in the clutches of medication. Some he stops and speaks to quietly. He doesn't mention Monster Mother and her skin.

He passes the nurses in their TV room, still laughing at *Men in Black*, and heads back to his office, through the stem and into the admin block. He's about to open his office door when he notices, about twenty metres further down the corridor, one of the security guards. It's the mountainous Jamaican guy they call the Big Lurch. He's standing, hands in his pockets, quite preoccupied with a framed print on the wall. Something in his face makes AJ break step and stop. The Big Lurch glances sideways, sees him and smiles. 'Hey, AJ.'

'Hey.'

'Fraggles asleep are they?'

The Big Lurch is talking about the patients. No one would ever say it to a board member, but the staff call the patients Fraggles after *Fraggle Rock*. 'Oh yes, they're asleep. *The magic is always there as long as we keep looking for it*.' He comes down the corridor. 'What're you up to?'

'Oh, dunno.' The Big Lurch gestures at the print, faintly embarrassed. 'Just checking this out. Suppose I've never bothered to look at it before.'

AJ peers at the framed print. It's a watercolour of the work-house from the mid-nineteenth century, when it was new. These prints are everywhere — they show Beechway High Secure

Unit in various incarnations: copperplate etchings of it as the poorhouse, framed newspaper articles when a new director was appointed in the 1950s, even the 1980s artist's impression of the finished, revamped unit with its wrap-around glass windows. He is drawn into the picture, noting the various recognizable parts of the building — the parts that have survived over a hundred and fifty years. There's the central courtyard, the tower, the axis of the cross which is now the centre of the clover leaf.

'I don't like it in a storm,' the Big Lurch says suddenly. 'It makes me think about the weaknesses.'

'Weaknesses?'

He nods. 'The places those eighties architects didn't really think through properly.'

AJ throws a sideways glance at the Big Lurch. What he sees there is the fear, the same uneasy look that's becoming so familiar in the unit the last few days. He can't believe it, just can't believe it. He has long learned not to get too friendly with staff, but with the Big Lurch he's made an exception. He *likes* this guy. He's been for drinks with him — met his wife and his two little girls — and in all that time he's never taken him to be impressionable.

'Come on, mate. I've got enough problems with the patients without the damned security staff turning into big girls' blouses.'

The Big Lurch half smiles. He puts a finger up to his brow, as if to cover his embarrassment. He's about to give a neat reply when the lights flicker. Both men put their heads back and stare at the ceiling. The lights flicker again. Then they seem to steady, and the corridor is as normal. AJ narrows his eyes — looks at the Big Lurch. There was a power cut a week ago — the last thing they need is another one. That will send the patients through the roof.

'Doo doo doo doo, doo doo doo doo.' He sings out the *Twilight Zone* theme and makes ghost fingers in the Big Lurch's face. 'Come on, Scooby, let's go hide under the sofa.'

The security guy grins sheepishly, bats AJ's hands away. 'See, that's why guys don't *share*. Because of wankers like you.'

AJ sighs. This isn't going to be laughed off. The Big Lurch is genuinely, *genuinely*, not joking.

'Haven't you noticed, AJ? Everyone's calling in sick?'

'Yeah. I did happen to notice. You do a double shift to cover for people and it kind of etches itself on the memory.'

'Yes. And you know what they're saying? The staff?'

'We don't need to talk about this now.'

The Big Lurch shifts uncomfortably. Runs a finger around his collar. 'One of them woke up the other night. He was on Dandelion Ward and he woke up and he says he saw something in his room.'

AJ laughs. Too loudly — the sound echoes down the corridor and back. 'Oh, come on, that was an angina attack. They took him to the doctor and it was an angina attack.' He shakes his head. 'This — this whole . . . thing . . . it's just — '

'AJ, you know what I'm saying. I'm having a hard time getting any of the guys to do night shifts. If I rota them in I know I'm just going to get a call claiming they're sick, or their car's broke down or something.'

AJ puts his hands in his pockets and looks at his feet. He knows where this is leading. Mass hysteria, that's where. After years of silence on the subject of ghosts and haunting suddenly the stories and rumours are all back. Staff calling in sick, Monster Mother panicked, the Big Lurch antsy. And even he, AJ, getting infected. Dreaming about the damned thing.

He looks up and down the corridor. It is still and empty. The only light comes from the knee-level security spots, the only noise is the ticker-tacker of branches and leaves on the windows. The time has come. He's going to have to make it official — speak to the clinical director first thing in the morning. They're going to have to nip this in the bud before the whole unit goes into meltdown.

Hotel du Vin, The Sugar House, Bristol

As they drive it becomes clear that Jacqui Kitson has been trailing Caffery all day. She veers between drunken flirtatiousness, and abusive, furious tears.

'You're so fucking fit,' she says, sucking angrily on her cigarette. 'I'd give you one if I didn't hate you so much. You ugly bastard.'

From what he can piece together she has parked her car near his office in St Philips and has been following him on foot ever since. Tomorrow she's got an interview with a national newspaper. They are paying for her hotel and probably she's planned it so she could accost Caffery at the same time. She started drinking at lunchtime.

Jacqui Kitson, being who she is, has chosen the Hotel du Vin — because celebrities occasionally stay here and it's got a bit of boutiquey glamour to it. The staff give pained smiles when she arrives, dishevelled and smelling of vomit — escorted through reception by someone who has the demeanour of a security guard — except for the red stains on his shirt and collar.

Her suite is in the attic — a feature wall papered in bronze-and-black repeat patterns, low comfortable leather chairs and everywhere the painted cast-iron pillars that remain from the time this was a sugar warehouse. Her room looks out over the city centre — at eye level St John the Baptist church, lit up at night, rises into the sky.

Jacqui immediately pours herself a vodka and orange from the minibar. When she goes into the bathroom Caffery empties the drink out of the window and fills it with orange juice. He sets it on the bedstand, then stands at the open window. It is freezing out there — he can hear the tinkling laughter of drinkers coming and going from the bars down in the streets.

He's been in this part of the country for over three years, and is slowly getting to learn the geography of Bristol as well as he knew the geography of his native South London. He knows all the bars and the crimes that have taken place at street level — can scroll back through the pub brawls and the murders. The barmaid in a place a few hundred metres away, stabbed to death eight years ago by the customer who waited until the place emptied so he could be alone with his victim. A fight that ended with an eighteen-year-old having his face slashed a few metres further down the road. A takeaway next door to that, busted one day nineteen months ago for serving not just kebabs but also crack cocaine and ketamine.

It is Caffery's job to ferret out the secrets hidden under the veneer. His unit — MCIT — is the one that gets all the murders and difficult cases. The cases that need high-level attention. Like the one that's making Jacqui so angry.

The toilet flushes and she comes out again. She ignores the drink and throws herself on to the bed, face down.

'You OK?'

She nods into the pillow. 'I took a sleeping pill.'

'Is that a good idea?'

'It's the only idea.'

Caffery checks his watch. It means he's going to have to wait with her — make sure she doesn't throw up and choke herself. Or go into a coma. He glances around the room. There's a plush brown sofa with gold scatter cushions he can rest on. He draws the quilt over Jacqui then goes into the bathroom. Puts the plug in the basin and turns the taps on. While the sink fills he hunts through the various pill packets she has scattered around. There are no prescription drugs, just over-the-counter things — stomach-acid tablets and paracetamol and some slimming aids. Also a packet of Nytol, which he opens. One has been removed from the blister pack. He checks the bin and there are no empty pill packets. She hasn't overdosed then.

He hunts through all the designer toiletries — finds a shower gel which he squirts into the sink until he can make a lather. Then he pulls off his shirt and drops it in the sink. He rubs the soap into it, scrubbing at the collar where the wine has soaked in. He rinses it, then hangs it over the huge rain-shower head.

He goes back into the bedroom, drying his hands on a towel. Jacqui is exactly where he left her, on her front, her arms wide apart, her face turned to one side. He stands alongside her, head tilted, waiting and listening. Her eyes are closed and there's already a faint snoring noise.

He sits on a low animal-hide chair and surveys the room. There's a TV but he'd wake her up. A couple of magazines. He leafs through them — nothing much to see. An article about a designer hotel on the outskirts of Bristol that holds his attention for a moment, because he was at the same hotel this lunchtime — attending the killer-boring Criminal Justice Forum. He recognizes the downlit beaten-copper sinks in the gents, the sweeping poured-concrete reception desk. He spent a few minutes at that reception desk, with a pretty, very professional woman — a blonde, who had some top-drawer position in a local health trust — talking shop, all the while his primitive brain conjecturing in a vague, theoretical way whether or not he could get her into bed. She was the only interesting thing about the event. Otherwise it was eminently forgettable.

He tries to read a little longer, but can't concentrate. He drops the magazine and looks around the room again. There is a lavish hand-tied bunch of flowers shoved into an ice bucket on the drinks table. Caffery gets up, goes to the flowers, and reads the card. It's from the newspaper Jacqui is supposed to be giving an interview to. Misty, her twenty-five-year-old model daughter, walked out of a rehab clinic on the Wiltshire border a year and a half ago. She was a drug addict and having relationship problems with her footballer boyfriend, but neither of those things was sufficient to explain why she was never seen again. Every avenue has been searched over and over — and there are still no clues. She was simply there one day, not the next. Thousands of people go missing each year and if they're ordinary, adult and competent, the police time spent on them is embarrassingly little. But Misty was a celebrity of sorts; young, pretty. The media has kept the interest going long after police would normally have given up. Jacqui Kitson has been a regular face in the tabloids — pictures of Jacqui in the last place Misty was seen, on the sweeping white steps of the clinic, gazing pensively up at the building where her daughter spent her final days. Posing with a photo of Misty and a handkerchief clutched to her face. She dishes every insult about police incompetence she can muster.

Each of her words is a knife in Caffery's side. He is the Senior Investigating Officer tasked with finding Misty and the case has been haunting him for ages — it has been bounced back and forward between MCIT and the review team until Misty's name has burned a hole through his head. But truth is stranger than fiction and the world is never what it seems: for over a year Caffery's been hopscotching over the issue, he's been guarding the case like a hound, appearing to be working on it while simultaneously leading the unit away from what he really knows about Misty's disappearance — which is more, *much* more, than any cop has a right. It's a big fat secret he's been hiding. Something he can't do anything about.

He replaces the card gently amongst the gaudy blooms. Can't? Or won't? Or is he just not quite ready? There's one more bridge to cross, the one he's been avoiding for months.

'I know,' Jacqui says suddenly from the bed. 'I do know.'

Caffery thought she was asleep. He approaches slowly. She doesn't open her eyes, but nods, as if to acknowledge him. She hasn't moved, her eyes are closed, her voice muffled.

'I do know.'

'Know what, Jacqui? What do you know?'

'I know she's dead.'

That Misty is still alive hasn't realistically crossed the mind of any of the officers on the case — not for months and months. It shakes Caffery a little to realize that it's taken time and work for Jacqui to come to the same conclusion.

'And I'm OK with it,' she continues, her eyes still closed, only her mouth working. 'I am OK with her being dead. There's just one thing I need.'

'What's that?'

'I just need her body back. You don't know what it's like, not to have a body to bury. It's all I want.'

The Maude

Legend has it that Maude is the ghost of a matron from when Beechway High Secure Unit was a workhouse, back in the 1860s. Born a dwarf, she'd risen to a position of authority in the workhouse through sheer determination and single-mindedness. It was a position she abused. It is said that children who misbehaved would be subjected to Sister Maude straddling their chests, spooning 'medicine' into their mouths until they choked. That she would make the children write out biblical texts — line after line until their fingers bled. Some versions of the myth say Sister Maude had something under her robes she kept private: that she wasn't really a 'sister' at all but actually a male dwarf dressed as a female.

Four and a half years ago, just before AJ first came to work on the unit, an anorexic patient named Pauline Scott had convinced herself something was coming into her room at night. She claimed it would sit on her chest, would try to suffocate her. She'd showed the doctor where her thighs had been slashed. The words *Be thou not one of them that committeth foul acts* had been gouged into her leg. Two unfolded and bloodied paper clips had been found in Pauline's bin — which she denied all knowledge of. No one much liked Pauline, they thought the engraving on her legs was apt. She'd been returned to Acute Assessment, where they'd monitored her for three weeks.

When AJ arrived, shortly after the incident, it was all the staff could talk about. At night in the nurses' station there'd be whispers and jokes, people trying to spook each other hiding in dark doorways. A few took it seriously — an agency nurse on a midnight shift swore she heard the scratches of fingernails on a windowpane and refused ever to set foot inside the unit again. One of the more highly strung social workers claimed she'd once looked out of a window and seen a dwarf sitting on the lawn, wearing a white Victorian gown. The dwarf was doing nothing. Just watching the unit. Its face was smooth and shining in the moonlight.

AJ was one of those who found it little more than entertaining — a bit of a diversion. Then The Maude paid another visit. And this time it wiped the smile off everyone's face.

Moses Jackson was a long-stay patient — a grizzled grey guy with thin limbs and a nasty attitude. A downright, whole-enchilada, nasty little shit. He was vicious and deceitful and rude. He would call the female staff 'Splits' and was always pulling down his pants to show them his penis. Female staff couldn't be alone with him, which complicated his care and made him even more time-consuming. Of course if any of this was pointed out to Moses he'd scream racism and demand that the Trust's top brass came and met him to explain what they were going to do about it.

AJ was still a nurse in those days. He'd arrived

for the early shift that morning to find the place in chaos: nurses were rushing around from ward to ward, grabbing notes, grabbing phones, council workers traipsed in and out carrying toolkits, and an unearthly screaming was coming from Buttercup Ward. The allocated 'Control and Restraint' nurses were in another ward — so eventually, when AJ couldn't stand the noise any more, he decided to go and attend to it himself. Moses was standing in the middle of his room. He was stripped naked from the waist down, and was hugging himself and crying — staring at the walls. Every inch had been scribbled on in red felt-tip. Hundreds and hundreds of words — on the walls, the skirting boards, even the ceiling.

AJ had seen the worst and the weirdest in various institutions before Beechway, but this was a different level of bizarre. He was silent for a moment, gawping at the sheer extent of the damage.

'Moses.' He shook his head, half wanting to laugh, half to cry. 'Moses, mate, what did you do this for?'

'I didn't.'

'Have the doctors changed your meds?' AJ studied Moses carefully. He couldn't recall seeing a note in the care file — usually the nursing staff were given clear instructions if anything changed. Especially with medication. 'Did you have something different last night? Yesterday?'

'I didn't do it!'

'OK,' AJ said patiently. The room smelled, the vaguest undertone of something like burning fish, so he cracked one of the window vents. He glanced down at the old guy's genitalia, which dangled in front of his scrawny, grey-haired legs. 'How about putting your drawers back on, mate? The doctors will need to check you over — you don't want them seeing all your man stuff hanging out.'

'I never took them off.'

'Well, how about you just put them on anyway?' He handed over the pyjama bottoms. 'There you go.'

While Moses was putting them on, AJ wandered around the room, his head canted on one side, reading the words:

Anyone who looks at a woman lustfully has already committed adultery in his heart.

On other sections: *If your right eye causes you to sin, gouge it out and throw it away*.

The lines were repeated dozens and dozens of times. They'd have to be scrubbed out, or painted over.

'Moses,' AJ said calmly, not drawing attention to the writing, 'shall we go to breakfast?' There was nothing in AJ's long experience of psychiatric nursing more effective at changing the subject or distracting a patient than the mention of food. 'They're doing waffles and syrup for dessert.'

Moses went along willingly to the dining room, though he had the appearance of someone moving further and further away from reality. The drugs, which he usually tolerated with few side effects, seemed to have started to work against him. There was a wet patch on his trousers and lines of drool hung like pendulous beads of pearls from his mouth. The other patients gave him a wide berth. He was withdrawn, standing quietly in the queue, one fist jammed into his right eye socket, which he kept rubbing at like crazy.

Isaac Handel, a runty long-stay patient with a pudding-basin haircut, was the first to notice when things crossed over into the serious.

'Hey,' he said to one of the nurses. 'Look, look.'

The nurses looked. Moses had separated from the queue and turned his back on the room. He was bending slightly at the waist, head down, and seemed to be struggling with his face. AJ was slow off the mark. Instead of responding instantly, he meandered across the dining room, a half-smile on his face — more curious about what Moses was doing than anxious.

'Moses, mate? You all right there?'

'A spoon,' Handel said. 'He's got a spoon.'

The patients were allowed spoons on the pre-discharge wards. It had never been seen as a danger or a threat. AJ approached Moses from behind. He was about to put a reassuring hand on his back when he noticed something dangling from the guy's jaw. Or rather, not dangling but dripping. It was blood and it was coming in such a steady stream he'd mistaken it for a cord hanging there.

'C and R!' he yelled, automatically tugging out the ring on his panic alarm. 'C and R, dining area. Paramedics.' Three other nurses came running, trying to grab Moses and get him on to the ground to the supine position. But he had the strength of ten men. He wrenched away from

AJ and continued struggling with whatever it was he was doing to his face.

'I'm on the head,' one of the nurses yelled. 'Left arm, left leg,' yelled another. 'GET EVERYONE OUT OF HERE,' yelled AJ.

More staff came running and the panic alarms shrieked through the building. From Moses' face came a strange, crisp popping sound — quite compact and clear, considering the mayhem around. Later, when AJ was writing his report, he had to think about the best way to describe that sound, and reflected that it sounded like the snap of tendon and movement of greased white-bone socket when a barbecued chicken leg is pulled apart (he won't eat chicken again from this day hence). Of course it was no chicken joint responsible for that noise. Instead a stringy globe, like an egg with bloodied albumen, fell out on to Moses' cheek. The spoon clattered to the ground and he dropped to his knees, then keeled on to his left hand, half fainting.

'*Paramedic*,' AJ bellowed. 'Get a fucking paramedic. *Paramedic. Paramedic, Paramedic* . . . '

Average Joe

The night shift seems to go on for ever. AJ's tried to keep working as normal, completing his reports and doing more rounds of the wards, checking on Monster Mother three times, but he's hated every minute of it. Especially being alone in his office. It is overheated and the windows make clicking noises as they expand and contract with the changes in temperature. Every time he tried to doze, words echoed like sonar through his head. *Paramedic. Get a fucking paramedic* . . . Boing boing boing. *If your right eye causes you to sin, gouge it out and throw it away* . . . A vortex of images crawling over the walls. Gristle and blood on the canteen hotplates. Sizzling and mingling into the waffles.

The paramedics came quickly, but they couldn't save Moses' eye. He was returned to the unit after two weeks with an optical prosthetic and a changed, humbled attitude. People avoided him, tiptoed around him. Whispers went through the patient community about what Moses had seen that morning to make him spoon out his own eye. And what about the writing on his walls? They remained only whispers, until Pauline, who had been permitted to rejoin the graduated-rehabilitation cycle and worked her way back to pre-discharge, disappeared one day during 'unsupervised ground leave'. The police were involved, search teams came and went, an inquiry was set up. To the Trust's extreme embarrassment it wasn't until several months later that her decomposed body was discovered, under leaf litter in one of the remotest corners of the grounds, just outside the search team's parameters. The decomposition was too advanced for the postmortem to pinpoint what had killed her, so the Trust and the police and the pathologist and the coroner decided on 'unknown causes'.

At that, the whispers went viral. Hysteria spread like wildfire, everyone was talking about The Maude and the hauntings. Hitherto stabilized patients went into crisis, screams rang out through the wards, Control and Restraint teams raced through the corridors. Half the pre-discharge patients got hauled back up to Acute, the rest were denied communal time, leave and privileges. There were staff shortages, long and involved cross-departmental meetings, new directives and general mayhem.

The clinical teams got involved. They had a battle to put a lid on it but, slowly, by targeting individual patients in therapy sessions, gently reinforcing that The Maude was nothing more than a delusion and a rumour, they eventually managed to restore the calm. The unit went back to running smoothly. Four years went by without a murmur. Not a solitary soul mentioned the haunting and it was starting to seem that the legend of The Maude would disappear without a trace. Then three weeks ago Zelda Lornton woke up screaming, her arms covered in writing. And bam — the hysteria took hold again.

The kettle boils. AJ scoops two heaped spoonfuls of instant coffee into the cup, tops it up with water, milk and sugar. He carries it to the window and stands there, sipping thoughtfully, watching the day creep into the courtyard. The storm has passed and the garden is sodden. The spot where the social worker reported seeing the dwarf all those years ago is now covered in broken branches and leaves. To one side, barely visible beneath the trees, is a gravestone — the resting place of a child who died here in Victorian times. An unknown philanthropist at the end of Victoria's reign put up money for this memorial to 'an unknown child of God'. It's the only stone left — the other graves were dug up and moved when the 1980s remodelling took place. That reinterment — according to the mythology in the hospital — is when The Maude's tomb was moved. Her ghost was disturbed and eventually, years later, found its way back inside the unit.

So, AJ thinks. Time to start the whole process of putting Maude back in her grave.

He gets the tie he discarded last night and clips it back on, using the computer screen as a mirror. He takes a deep breath and runs his hands down the lapels of his cheap suit, studying his reflection. The name on his birth certificate is not AJ at all — the name was given to him years ago by some cocky consultant who used to come in and snap his fingers at the nurses when he wanted something on a patient's drugs round changed; if AJ didn't respond, he'd yell across the ward: 'Hey, you — yes, you — average Joe

— AJ — I'm talking to you.'

Average Joe. AJ. The name stuck. He is Average Joe. Average height, average age (forty-three), average salary. AJ LeGrande. It sounds like the name of some rapper. Actually, he has got a little black in him, from his grandmother, though you wouldn't know it: his dark hair hasn't got a kink in it, his skin isn't even coffee-coloured, more of a Mediterranean olive, and he's got one of those straight European noses. The one thing he'd have really liked is black-guy legs — long, strong footballer's legs, the kind Big Lurch has got — the sort of legs that make you look forward to summer so you can show them off. But he hasn't — he's got ordinary, hairy white-guy legs. What's the point in having a black ancestor if you didn't get any of the cool shit passed down? Sometimes people tell him that if he resembles anyone at all it's Elvis Presley — from some angles and in certain lights. AJ wishes it were true — if he had a tenth of Presley's looks, talent or magnetism he wouldn't be employed here. And he certainly wouldn't be working up a big anxiety about having to explain to the clinical director, in the calmest, most rational of terms, that there's a ghost in the unit. That he, as senior nursing coordinator, has failed to put a lid on the mania.

Tired and heavy, he makes his way down the corridor, swiping through the various airlock doors. The director, Melanie Arrow, has ruffled everyone's feathers by insisting that her office space be moved out of the admin block into the clinical area. She has commandeered a room on the mezzanine overlooking the central hall between the wards. It has been renovated and knocked through to provide her with a bathroom and a kitchen, and is equipped with a trestle bed that she often spends the night on. This is a hideous abuse of the unspoken rules, because it means the nursing staff have an eavesdropper in their midst. One who has a habit of appearing at the most unexpected moments to catch them dozing or watching porn.

At the foot of the stairs he hesitates. There's a light coming through the bottom of her door. He doesn't know if it means she's spent the night in her office on the trestle bed, or if she's just come in mega-early. If there is one person guaranteed to make him feel inadequate it's Melanie Arrow. She is the only staff member who's been at Beechway longer than him, and she is notoriously hard-arsed and professional. 'Ice Queen' is the name that gets whispered behind her back. Funnily enough, in the days when he was still a nurse, AJ never had a problem with Melanie; he didn't need to deal with her directly at work and his only face-to-face encounters were at office parties when everyone's guard was down — there was even a best-forgotten drunken night when he convinced himself she was flirting with him. Now that he's a coordinator, however, he has to liaise with her a lot more. He's definitely starting to see where she gets her Ice Queen reputation from.

He climbs the stairs slowly and knocks, a little irritated with himself for his nerves. There's a long pause, then 'Yes?'

'AJ.'

'Come in, AJ.'

He opens the door and steps inside, smiling confidently, his eyes focused on a point about a foot in front of her face so he doesn't have to make eye contact. She is at her desk, the computer screen lighting her face, her tiny wire-framed glasses perched at the end of her nose. He knows that she put in a twelve-hour day yesterday — she was at the Criminal Justice Forum with him and went straight to a Trust meeting afterwards — but she shows no signs of tiredness. She's a cool, cool blonde — ordered and contained. AJ may have African blood in him, but Melanie definitely has a touch of the fjords in her — her hair is liquid silk and her skin is so pale, ethereal, that the sprinkling of freckles over her nose stands out like face paint. As always, she is wearing a simple white blouse and a sensible schoolmistress skirt, giving her a clinical, authoritative look. There is a great body under the clothes — AJ and probably most of the male staff are fairly certain about that — but no one would mention it, even in an off-guard moment. Lightning would strike them — it would be like passing comment on the Virgin Mary's figure.

'Yes, AJ?' When he doesn't speak — tongue-tied as always — she slides the glasses further down her nose and studies him over the rims. 'Did you want something?'

She's not fierce or arrogant or impatient — she doesn't yell or bark orders like some directors of psychiatric units — in fact, she has a soft, understated voice. It's more her crispness that makes her seem brisk and professional. She says as little as she needs to get information across, then she stops. For someone as woolly and generally undisciplined as AJ, that's incredibly intimidating.

'There's a problem,' he says. 'Regarding Zelda Lornton.'

Melanie nods but otherwise doesn't react.

He shakes his head, doesn't know how to put it. 'It's the heart attack. People are saying . . . ' He rubs his neck in embarrassment. 'People are saying it's odd — can't be natural, someone that young, just dying.'

Still Melanie doesn't react. This is how she always is — she carefully considers everything before she speaks, never worries how long the other person is kept waiting.

Eventually she says, 'We don't yet have the results of the postmortem. At the moment heart attack is only what the paramedics told us. In due course the review process will tell us how odd or natural her death was.'

'But I take it you know what everyone is thinking. You do know the rumours are back?'

'The rumours?'

'Yes. About the . . . well, the supernatural things the patients sometimes entertain ideas about.'

This time, although her face is absolutely motionless, a tiny spread of colour comes to her cheeks. The last time The Maude came to the hospital it proved a long, stressful and complicated process to get things back on track. Melanie was at the helm of that initiative. 'The delusions, you mean.'

'Yes. They're back and the effect is spreading — to the staff. There's been forty per cent absenteeism on nights this week. It's a whole repeat process of what happened with Pauline Scott and Moses.'

'So, AJ, what do you propose to do?'

'What do *I* propose to do?' He opens his hands, helpless. 'Well, I don't know. Maybe I should just look it up in the protocol — the 'Ghost Stalking the Corridors' protocol. Probably it starts with 'Include in weekly board report'. Then I guess it's 'Fill in requisitions in triplicate to the council's Trust-related ethics committee with special reference to subsection 17.' Then I guess it's — '

'I didn't ask for sarcasm.' Her eyes are as clear blue as the sky. 'I asked you what you propose to do about the spread of a delusion.'

AJ is silent for a moment. She's so curt. Her professional mask is genuinely scary, and in her mouth the word 'delusion' rankles for reasons he can't quite define. Maybe it's the way it seems unfair on Monster Mother to dismiss her fear so lightly. Or maybe it's his own dream which still feels so real. Little hands, little face. His eyes stray to the window, the trees stark and old, forking up from the frosty ground. Then over to the window where Melanie's trestle bed is tucked in a gap between the shelves. He wonders if she sleeps well when she's here at night. If she has dreams.

'I thought you might tell me,' he says at last. 'That's what I was hoping.'

She taps her finger thoughtfully on the table, taking in his face. It's like being inspected by the headmistress. 'OK, OK.' She pushes the glasses back up her nose and makes a note on the large pad on her desk. 'Leave the clinical route with me — I'll deal with the consultants. We'll do what we did last time — target each individual during therapy — no group meetings. In the meantime I'll leave it to you to deal with the nursing staff. Fair?'

'Thank you,' he mutters. 'Thank you.'

'You're very welcome.'

He has his hand on the door to leave the office when he thinks he hears Melanie's voice behind him. He turns. 'Yes? Sorry?'

She is studying him. There is something in her face he's never seen before — something he can't read. It's as if she wants to speak but doesn't know how to begin.

'Yes?' he repeats.

'Do *you* find the unit spooky?' Her eyes flicker briefly. They go to the bottom of the door. Then just as quickly she averts them, and clears her throat. 'By which I mean I hope you don't ever feel the need to call in sick?'

'Of course not.' He gives his shoulders a small, dismissive shrug. 'I mean, what's to be scared of?'

'Exactly. Nothing.' She turns back to the computer and taps in a few words. 'Just keep me informed of what happens.'

The Bridge

When Caffery wakes after five hours' sleep, Jacqui Kitson is still snoring on the bed. He rolls on to his side and watches her. He can't go on for ever telling the lie about her daughter's disappearance. Not for ever.

'Hey,' he whispers across the room. 'You were right. I am a shithead.'

She doesn't react, merely carries on snoring. He sits up, aching from a night on the cramped sofa, ties the hotel robe he's slept in. He can see the headlines if he gets up undressed: *Missing Misty: Senior Detective Gropes Mum in Sleazy Hotel Romp*.

He crosses to the bed and watches Jacqui — monitoring her breathing. She's going to live. He pads into the bathroom. He showers, makes coffee, tries to shave with the hotel razor, cuts himself and has to use Jacqui's perfume to seal the wound. His shirt is just about wearable, a little creased and damp on the collar. He checks his reflection. He looks, frankly, like someone who has spent the night on a sofa. Smells as bad too. As he leaves, he books an alarm call for nine in case Jacqui sleeps through, then he slips out — closing the door silently. Outside, the streets are quiet. A bus appears — a moving light cube of empty seats, two middle-aged women in the back, both fast asleep, their heads jiggling gently with the movement. He waits for it to pass then crosses the road to the White Lion, where beer crates are piled in the doorway. The high, sweet stench of alcohol, honey and acid reminds him he didn't drink last night. The first time in months. It must be that holier-than-thou thing kicking in. Seeing Jacqui so wasted. Feeling righteous drinking Badoit.

There's a grille in the pavement which most people don't realize leads to an underground river that flows endlessly beneath the streets. He imagines the long swish of water under there — what it carries in it. He knows because he's seen. Broken plastic chairs, dead cats, crisp packets, floating cans. They all fetch up a few hundred metres on, in the teeth of the grille that lets out into the harbour. Like a great baleen whale — holding back the filth. The things that are hidden. The things we walk over. Under. Past. Every single day of our lives, and never notice. A hundred places a body could be hidden for ever.

He could tell Jacqui Kitson exactly where her daughter Misty is. He could and he hasn't. Because he's protecting someone. Someone who needs a little slack. A *little* slack, he tells himself. As opposed to a lifetime of leniency. Does thinking this mean it's time to act? To cross the bridge he's been avoiding?

He pulls out a V-Cig, clicks the cartridge, and sucks in the fake smoke. He takes it out of his mouth and inspects the thing. Shit. It's really shit. It still makes him feel he's being poisoned. He uncaps the cartridge and drops it through the grille. Feed the whale.

No point in driving home — he'll go straight to work. He turns in the direction of the place his car is parked. Over the roofs daytime is bleeding in — thick and milky. Another day. The church is lit by floodlights, one or two dead leaves are whipped in a spiral around the steeple. He stops in his tracks. Turns slowly to look through the gate into the graveyard. He can see waste baskets and dog-shit bins and chewing gum spotting the path. He can see plastic flowers on graves, all grimed from the city fumes. Two marble-sided graves with those glassy green pebbles they all seem to use. Beyond them is a Victorian grave — an angel praying on it — mossed and crumbling.

Jacqui says Caffery has no idea what it's like not to have a body to bury. That's where she's wrong. He knows exactly what it's like. In fact he's a past master. When Winnie Johnson, mother of the missing Moors victim, died not knowing where her son was buried, Caffery took the day off work and sat in his kitchen, staring out of the window. He's lived in the same hole as her and Jacqui for years. And years.

In Caffery's case it isn't a son or a daughter — it's a brother. Maybe that's why he keeps it so close to his chest. The rest of the world understands that the loss of a child can never be overcome, but the loss of a brother? After thirty-five years? He should have got over it by now. There have been plenty of clues, plenty of avenues he's nosed up, but none of them has led him to that tangible evidence — the body. Maybe if he had a body to bury he'd get rid of that itch. That constant, plaguing voice. He understands Jacqui so much better than she knows.

He stares at the angel. For a reason he can't define he knows it's the grave of a child. He half raises his hand to open the gate, then stops himself. He stands, stock-still, his heart thudding.

Cross that bridge, Jack. Just fucking do it.

Patience and Stewart

Usually when AJ leaves the unit he can forget about the place. Not today. Today as he drives home, through the drizzle and morning rush-hour traffic, he keeps going back there in his head. Keeps seeing that smooth face from the nightmare, the constriction in his chest. Keeps re-enacting the later conversation with Melanie.

He wonders, not for the first time, what Zelda Lornton's postmortem report is going to say. Any death in the unit has, by law, to be investigated by the police and an external review team. The superintendent who took the job admits there's been a bit of a fire in the coroner's office over who's going to do the autopsy. Zelda's death didn't strike the coroner as being odd enough to warrant an expensive full-scale post-mortem by a Home Office pathologist, but the ordinary hospital doctors have been reluctant to take on the responsibility of cutting open a patient who has died unexpectedly on a psychiatric unit. The examination has been a hot potato that bounced around the Flax Bourton mortuary like a ping-pong ball until someone put their foot down and insisted one of the pathologists did it as a coroner's 'special' post-mortem — something, apparently, halfway between an ordinary PM and a forensic PM. That was three days ago and they're still waiting to hear.

Maybe the coroner is right. Zelda was young, but she was very overweight — over twenty stone — and inactive. Considered from that perspective, she was an unsurprising candidate. Enormously lazy, she was pushed everywhere in a wheelchair though she was quite capable of walking. Her clothing strained at the seams and the staff had to rub Vaseline into the folds on her legs to stop her getting sores. Her clothes consisted of seven red T-shirts and seven grey pairs of joggers and seven pairs of red socks. She would wear nothing else, even when she began to outgrow them and they'd been stitched so often they were more darning thread than fabric. Anything beyond eating and watching television was an abuse of Zelda's rights. She was a habitual blamer of the system; the staff lost track of the times they were accused of abusing/molesting/raping her. No one argued with her, though many would have liked to. She could tip the mood of the entire ward on its head — everyone responded to her. Everyone walked on a knife-edge.

AJ cannot, will not, ever pretend he liked Zelda. But as he gets to the end of the narrow country lane where he lives, he finds he can't get rid of the image of her that night with her arms bloodied. All the rebellion taken out of her. And the words, 'Someone . . . some*thing*.'

He pulls on the handbrake and switches off the engine. Lets the silence leak in. There's not much to look at here — only the spread of the Severn flood plain, Berkeley Castle, the glorious view of the decommissioned nuclear-power station to admire at sunset. No neighbours, just the cows. This is Eden Hole Cottages — the place he was raised — right out in the middle of nowhere. Brought up by his mother, Dolly Jessie LeGrande, and his aunt Patience Belle LeGrande — two sassy half-Jamaican women from Bristol. Mum has been dead three years, but Aunt Patience is still going strong. Stronger and stronger.

'Where the hell've you been?' Patience yells from the front room as he lets himself in. '*Daybreak*'s finished — it's nearly time for damned *Cash in the* goddamned *Attic*.'

Aunt Patience is so badly named. She yells at everyone, slams the phone down at the merest provocation and doesn't believe in queues. She's an irascible, tetchy, eccentric force of nature — she exudes the gravity of a planet; everything falls into her orbit. When she is in a bad mood objects fall off shelves and strangers' babies cry; when she's happy it's like the sun has come out. People smile, couples kiss, and arguments cease. Some days he'd happily throttle Aunt Patience — put a pillow on her face and suffocate her. Put arsenic in her tea, sell tickets for people to watch. Except he knows that life would have been impossible without her. And without Stewart, his mongrel dog. Patience and Stewart are all he's got left of his family.

'Working late,' he calls back. Stewart has raced out of the kitchen and is turning circles with excitement to see him. AJ hangs his jacket on the hook and bends to scratch the dog behind the ears. 'Remember that thing called work? Things are hard at the unit.' Beyond hard, he thinks, beyond hard. That word 'delusions' Melanie Arrow used keeps niggling at him. It's as if she knows exactly what he dreamt last night — as if she's worked out that he's just as susceptible to the eeriness of Beechway as anyone else.

'Come on, mate.' He goes wearily into the living room with Stewart. Patience is sitting there, her feet up, her arms folded stubbornly, a cup of tea at her elbow. The room is so comfortable, a big warm fire and stacks of wood he's cut piled up alongside. Squishy familiar sofas and chairs, hodge-podge patchwork cushions his mum made. Aunt Patience watches him sink into the settee, exhausted. She knows him so well. This is where he comes to re-set his head.

'Breakfast's in the oven,' she says. Breakfast in this house is a moveable feast — it happens whenever AJ arrives home, regardless of what his shift is — two in the afternoon or two in the morning — food is there, ready for him. The kitchen is always filled with aromas that could make a grown man cry. 'I cooked it and cooked it and I got to the place where I thought I was wasting my time.'

'I'm sorry. I should have called.'

'You sure you haven't got yourself a lady friend, AJ?' Even Aunt Patience calls him AJ these days. 'Me and Stewart don't mind — we'll be fine on our own for a night or two.'

'No lady friend.'

'You sure?'

Patience is always going on about him finding a girlfriend. Something about her obsession with it makes him wonder how she would actually react if he did. Whether she'd be more threatened than pleased by it.

'I don't know, Patience, but you must think I work at a dating agency. Or location-scouting for a lingerie photographer or something.'

'I know where you work.'

'Well then. It's not exactly Girl Central.'

Patience purses her lips. 'If you'd rather be out there romancing a tree.'

'Please.' He folds his arms, looks at the ceiling. 'I can't take a tree-hugger lecture today.'

For two years in a row he's belonged to a club that makes cider. They brew and compete with each other to get the best cider possible. And it just so happens that one of the traditions associated with cider making is wassailing. It's an old West Country tradition in which the trees are thanked for their year's yield and asked to produce another yield in the coming year. Then there's a bit of dancing and yelling to scare away bad spirits from the trees, and, because he and the lads thought it was a nice way to pass the time testing their brewing skills, Patience has got it into her head he's a hippy, bypass-protesting eco-terrorist — prepared to spend his life in a culvert if it means saving a single crested newt. She's got some neck giving him a hard time about it — like she can talk. If she's not in the betting shop she's out in the fields collecting sloe and damson for her big illegal stills in the garage, always rooting around for fruit to make her non-stop jams. The cottages have land — oh, land aplenty — but no garden whatsoever.

Outside, it's lines and lines of labelled furrows like Beatrix Potter's Peter Rabbit watercolours. Patience is in perpetual turmoil over what the deer and the muntjacs have eaten, and whether the rabbits are going to get at the vegetable patch this year. She knows exactly what food is in season at any given time — if he asked her right now she'd reel off a list: pumpkins, artichokes, medlars, cabbage. He never calls her a tree hugger.

He gets up and goes through to the kitchen, where he gathers breakfast. Mountains of Patience's scrambled egg and fennel. A pile of sauteed chestnut mushrooms. Three thick rashers of bacon. He adds tomato ketchup and a big wedge of home-made bread and sits at the table to eat.

He was the one who found Zelda dead. It was just after he'd come on shift. She was lying on her back, her mouth open slightly as if she was snoring. Her arms were still bandaged from the self-harm episode twelve days before. AJ hasn't told Patience about it; he doesn't want to say the words: *I found someone dead*. Because he knows the sentence that comes after it would be: *That's the second time in three years*. He and Patience talk about Mum, they have her picture everywhere, but they don't really talk about how it happened.

Out of the window, beyond the monster power-station towers, he can see the daylight catching the River Severn. Slowly, slowly, the unit slides away from him and he's just a man again. An ordinary man in his ordinary kitchen, eating an ordinary breakfast at his ordinary table.

The Man from the East

The land surrounding Bristol's so-called 'feeder' canal was once the city's hub for coal-gas generation, an industry which left long tracts of the land unusable due to high levels of cyanide. In spite of an expensive urban-regeneration programme in the 1980s it remains a speckled and bitty landscape, home to derelict churches blitzed in the war, car showrooms and industrial units. The old bonded warehouses that line the canal have been largely bricked up. It is to this bleak corner of the city that the Major Crime Investigation Team has moved its operations, into a cast-concrete 1970s building which once served as offices for an electricity company.

Caffery is one of the few people in MCIT, aside from the superintendent, who has managed to carve out a personal space in the vast open-plan offices. His has a view of the Spine Road flyover and the cream-and-orange tower blocks at Barton Hill. The room contains a desk, chairs, a small red Ikea sofa, a coffee- and tea-making station with a tiny portable fridge that can barely accommodate a six-pack of beers and a carton of milk. There are no personal photographs or certificates or press clippings, just a large photograph of Misty Kitson and the filing cabinet with her case papers in it. He wheeled it in here when there wasn't enough space in the incident room for other, more active operations. On the wall next to Misty's photo three laminated OS maps bristle with pins of different colours. Each has a significance to him — locations connected to Misty's disappearance. Other locations remain in his head. They are the ones that haven't yet been brought to the attention of his colleagues.

He spends the afternoon considering and analysing those pins — trying to get to a place where he can decide how to go forward. He's had several months to think about this problem and he's got a long-game walking around his head. A solution. But for the solution to work he needs the cooperation of one person. A woman — a fellow cop. The person he's protecting. She is the only obstacle. And he still doesn't know how to make that approach. It could go so badly wrong.

He stands a pace away from Misty's photograph, studies her, hoping for some guidance. Her face is a little bigger than life-size — her eyes are on the same level as his. She was a pretty girl. Whatever the cynics say about her they can't take away her prettiness. He tries to get his eyes to focus on hers, but the spacing's not right. The proportions are wrong: He stops trying and lowers his chin. Leans forward, his forehead resting against hers.

A knock on the door. Caffery steps back from the picture. He moves to the desk and sits down. Groping for something to seem occupied with, he clicks the computer out of standby and drags the keyboard over.

'Yes?'

The door opens. The superintendent puts his head through the gap. 'You free?'

Caffery checks his watch. 'Thought you'd gone home.'

'You wish. We need a chat.'

'A chat? An ominous chat?'

'No — a spot of box-ticking.' He holds up a file, gives it a shake. 'Review team report.'

Caffery gets up and pulls out a chair. The superintendent comes in and sits in it. He is a big sandy-haired man — an ex-CTIU terrorist-squad guy who got moved when something that no one speaks about happened with one of the unit's weapons. He doesn't beat about the bush.

'So — the news is this. The search for our friend' — he nods at Misty's photo — 'is going to be scaled down. It's haemorrhaging money.'

'Meaning?'

'Meaning I can't be wasting one of my few inspectors on something that's going nowhere. I'm giving it to a DS. It's not a category-A any more.'

Caffery picks up a pen and slowly taps it on the table. 'Sorry,' he says. 'You can't do that.'

'Here, let me just write that down so the review team can read it: *DI Caffery apologizes but says we can't do that*.'

'I mean it — you can't move the case. I believe in finishing what I start.'

'And the Home Secretary believes in deficit reduction. The HR department is on the Atkins diet — we are starving. We are lean. We cut corners, we axe, we tighten belts. It's not a question of what you want me to do — it's not even a question of what I want to do — it's a question of what we've got to do. There's been no new intel since the day she disappeared and now I need you somewhere else. You can spend tomorrow morning briefing one of the DSs and then you pick up the first job that comes through the door — I don't care if it's a category-A bells-and-whistles serial killer or a cat-D domestic. It's yours.'

'No. It's exactly the *wrong* time to be doing this. Jacqui Kitson's in town.'

The superintendent pauses. 'I beg your pardon?'

'She's got interviews lined up. The press are going to be crawling all over us. It's not a good moment to be shuffling the case down the ranks. We need to address it. At least give the press something to chew on — draw attention away from her.'

The superintendent considers this for a short while, scrutinizing Caffery's face, trying to decide if he's bluffing or not. The superintendent's always struggled with this inspector who chose not to climb the ranks when everyone knew he could have. This city guy who walked in one day out of the East with a bunch of London ways and attitudes, the one who joined the unit in person, yet never really in his heart. Not a team player — a bad-tempered, lone wolf, who won't take orders yet invariably manages to nail a case. He's got the best detection rates in the unit, and that makes the superintendent furious and proud and pissed off and insecure all at once. He's forever trying to find ways of reasserting his authority over Caffery.

'It's already decided. You're SIO on the next operation. End of.'

'Then I'll do both jobs — the next job and keep Misty's.'

'I need my DI to be a hundred per cent there for whatever gets assigned to us.'

'Watch me. I'll deal with whatever comes through that door and I'll get the press off our backs over Misty.'

'What are you going to give them? Another reconstruction? Her walking down the steps of the clinic? Because that worked wonders last time. Lost count of the leads that gave us — not.'

Caffery taps the pen a little harder. He's been thinking about this all day; the superintendent is right, the reconstruction didn't work. He's sure the best way to keep the press happy, at the same time as moving his private long-game forward, is to instigate another search of the area she went missing. But if Misty's disappearance loses its category-A status the open-ended budget will dry up.

'Give me three more weeks. I'll get you results.'

The superintendent sighs, resigned. 'OK — give the press what they need. But whatever job comes through the door gets your full attention too. Are you hearing me?'

'Loud and clear.'

'That's what I like about you, Jack,' he mutters sarcastically. 'Just love the way we're always on the same wavelength.'

Caffery doesn't get up and hold the door

when the superintendent leaves, instead he stays where he is, tapping his pen on the table. He senses Misty's eyes on him, but he resists turning to face her.

'Don't look at me like that,' he murmurs eventually. 'It's all in hand.'

The Dream

At lunchtime AJ gets a call on his mobile to say two night staff have gone sick again — that if there is to be any cover for that night it'll have to be him. He has to change everything, all his plans. Instead of having twenty hours to adjust, he now has precisely six. He goes to bed with a mask strapped to his face. He falls asleep thinking about Zelda Lornton. He dreams, not about the unit, but about a place his dreams have taken him before. It's a cramped, enclosed room or cave with shining, carved walls. Small faces seem to be sunk into the surfaces around him, watching him thoughtfully. But they're not threatening faces. If anything, they are peaceful. Somehow he knows he is safe here — it's a place where only good can happen. He gets thinner and thinner to the point he feels he's going to stop breathing altogether and become so insubstantial that he will slip through a pinhole. He will emerge in a place of perpetual sun, where all the fruit on the trees is sweet and ripe, where the pathways are pale gold, the grass is green. He's sure Mum is there, somewhere among the rolling hills.

It's always at the point where he is about to go through the pinhole that AJ wakes. He lies there, breathing hard, feeling something beautiful has just been snatched away from him.

He's at home. There is a very dim light coming

through the thin curtains. He rolls over and looks groggily at the clock. Five fifteen. Wearily he throws back the covers. Drops his feet on to the floor. He's got to be at work by seven.

He showers, shaves and drinks lots of Patience's coffee. Then he heads off, stopping in Thornbury to do some comfort shopping for the night — stuff like crisps and chocolate and little-kid treats. All the staff do it — easy comforts to push them through the tedium of a night in the unit. The shop's got Forager's Fayre jam on the shelf — it's a locally made line and the only store-bought preserves Patience will allow in the house. She actually takes inspiration from Forager's Fayre instead of scoffing at it. He throws a few jars into the basket to give to her in the morning.

It's an ordinary late-autumn evening in a rural town — a couple of express supermarkets still open, the pharmacy and a gift shop. The off-licence and the Indian and Chinese. But as he's leaving the supermarket loaded down with bags, he notices something out of the ordinary. On the opposite side of the road two or three people have gathered around someone who is kneeling on the ground.

The Good Samaritan in AJ died a death many moons ago — he's so used to picking up messes in his job his instinct is to walk the other way — but he's got basic first-aid skills, so morally he can't pretend not to see. He crosses the road. As he gets nearer, he realizes the person on the pavement is a woman. She is apparently unhurt, apart from her hand — which she is pressing hard with a white handkerchief. She is wearing the white lace blouse she wore this morning, and lilac leather Mary Janes, from which rise her delicate ankles and her strong calves. He recognizes the calves instantly — God knows he's studied them often enough. It's Melanie Arrow. Ice Queen.

'Really,' she is saying to the onlookers, 'I am absolutely fine.' Next to her is a carrier bag surrounded by a pool of clear liquid — a few pieces of broken glass lying amongst it. 'I mean it — I'm absolutely fine.'

'You don't look fine,' someone says. 'You're bleeding.'

She is indeed bleeding — the handkerchief is already soaked. A woman is rummaging in her handbag, pulling out handfuls of tissues that drop like petals on the ground. AJ puts down his shopping and nips across the street to the pharmacy. It is quiet and the assistant hurriedly pulls out all the bandages she can find. He pays and trots back outside.

The group of people is still there and so is his shopping, but Melanie Arrow is gone.

'What happened?' he calls to them. 'Where did she go?'

The woman with the handbag nods in the direction of the car park. 'Said she was OK.'

AJ turns and crosses back over the road. The car park is small — quite empty at this time of day — and he spots the familiar black VW Beetle immediately. It is perfect — the alloys sparkling, the sun glinting off it. It's a few years old, but the bright plastic flower that was the finishing touch when it rolled off the production line still sits perkily in its holder. In the driver's seat is Melanie Arrow. She sits with her head bent slightly, her hair covering her face. Her hand is bleeding copiously; it is running down her wrist and the tissues aren't containing it.

'Hey.' He taps on the window. She looks up, shocked to see him. He rolls his hand, miming the action of undoing the window. She shakes her head.

'I'm OK,' she mouths. 'I'm fine.'

'You're not fine.' He tries the door handle — it's locked. He knocks on the window again. 'You're bleeding.'

'I'm fine,' she yells. 'Honestly. It's nearly stopped.'

'Bollocks. Open the door.'

'I'm *fine*.'

AJ doesn't know what takes over — maybe a memory of the look she gave him in the office that morning — but instead of walking away he pulls out his phone and jabs in the numbers 999. He doesn't press call but holds the phone up to the window. Melanie looks at it and he raises his eyebrows at her.

'OK? Now open the door?'

She shakes her head, resignedly. The central-locking system clunks and AJ goes round to the passenger side and gets in. The car stinks of alcohol. On the back seat is the carrier bag that was earlier on the pavement — a little blood on it. It's got one bottle of vodka in it and the remains of a second, smashed.

'AJ, I'm absolutely OK. I tripped coming out

of the shop, that's all.'

He tugs the bandages out of the packing and reaches for her hand. She flinches when he touches her. Pulls away, her expression defensive.

'Come on.' He shakes his head. 'You are an adult. Aren't you?'

She sucks in a breath to reply. But instead of speaking she holds the breath, holds it and holds it as if she can't decide what to do with it. Then she lets it all out at once and relinquishes the hand, the bloodied tissues falling into her lap.

'Oh God,' she mutters, staring out of the window. 'Just get on with it.'

Maybe AJ is too well trained, or maybe he finds a long-forgotten empathic spark, because while he is inspecting the damaged hand and wrapping it, he hears himself saying, almost confidently, as if this is a patient and not the super-organized, mega-sorted clinical director: 'You know, Melanie, it seems to me, as an outsider, that you've got a really tough role. A *really* tough role. And if you want me to be honest, it looks as if the world is asking an awful lot of you at the moment.'

The comment provokes a shiver. She turns her head away, her uninjured hand pressed hard against her mouth. AJ holds the wounded hand and stares at the back of her head. He can't quite believe this — that she hasn't smacked him in the face — that he's forced his way into the car — that he's daring still to speak.

'No,' he continues. 'I can see it's not easy — not easy at all.'

She drops her head then. A faint current runs

through her muscles — a contained spasm, but he can't tell if she's actually crying or not. His memory opens suddenly on the drunken night years ago, and he wonders again why he didn't respond then to her come-on. At the time he had a girlfriend, but there was something else stopping him. Melanie somehow seemed in a different world — as if she belonged to a grown-up league of dating he had no right to trespass in. She was just too . . . too *sensible* somehow. Serious. When he and the girlfriend separated a few weeks later and he made a tentative approach to Melanie she froze him out, saying something short about the Trust and its dim view of relationships between staff. Since then their only interactions have been the cool, professional ones. Like this morning. Now he concentrates on bandaging her hand. It should stop bleeding if it's dressed properly. He's glad he didn't dial 999; they don't need a hospital visit.

'You know what,' Melanie says quietly, 'I spent five hours today talking to the review team. Five.'

He glances up, surprised by her tone. Her face is still turned away, her blonde hair covering her expression. 'About Zelda, you mean?'

'It's like they're accusing us of doing something to her. Her post-mortem has finally been done. Did you know that?'

'What did they find?'

'Nothing.' She shrugs. 'At least, nothing you can hang a hat on. It said she died of heart failure, but they couldn't pin the cause on anything, except possibly her weight. So now the review team can't make up their minds whether to walk away or to keep on at us. They've gone over and over everything — the staff logs, her care plan. Every time they turned up as much as a spelling mistake in one of the meds logs they looked at me as if I had horns.'

For the first time it dawns on AJ that Melanie's feelings about the unit run really deep. Yes, it's her professional reputation on the line, but she actually seems to care. Really care. In his experience genuine commitment beyond a pay cheque is thin on the ground in Beechway.

He clears his throat. 'You've carried the can for the rest of us. We wander around whingeing about overtime and night pay, but at least at the end of the day we can walk away from it.' He finishes tying the bandage and gently pushes the hand back at her. 'There you go. You'll live.'

Melanie fumbles up one of the blood-stained tissues from her lap and blows her nose noisily. She lets the hand sit in her lap and stares at it blankly. She *has* been crying, there are mascara trails on her face. 'Everyone's going to say I'm suicidal. They're going to say I cut myself. What's the expression? Eventually the system will turn in on itself?'

'I don't know.'

She sniffs again and looks at him. 'AJ?'

'Yes?'

'I'm sorry about the professional-bitch demeanour this morning.'

'That's OK. You've got a job to do.'

She gives a small, tearful laugh. 'Sometimes it's the only way I know how to be.'

'Like I said, it's OK. It's fine.'

There's a short pause. He wonders where this is going. Then she says, 'We've known each other a long time. Tell me honestly. This delusion they have — the you-know-what.'

'The Mau — '

'Please don't say it.' She looks at him with a watery smile. 'Sorry — it's just, I . . . AJ — you've never seen anything, have you? Something you couldn't explain.'

He gives a scoffing laugh. 'Oh, all the time. People walking through walls.'

'Seriously. What *is* it about this delusion?'

'That depends,' he says, 'on whether I'm Scully and you're Mulder.'

'I'm definitely Scully.'

'No — you can't be. 'Cos I'm Scully.'

'Then it'll have to be two cynics. Two cynics in a Beetle. They should make a film about us.'

They both give a half-hearted laugh. AJ sits back and stares out of the windscreen to where a drunk woman is picking a fight with an equally drunk man in camouflage trousers. There's a long silence, then he says: 'You've got to admit, she was a bloody nuisance.'

'Who?'

'Zelda.'

'No, no — AJ, you can't say that. Every person on the unit has a right to our care. We shouldn't let anyone down.'

'But she was a nuisance. I know it's taboo to say it, but out of all the people it could have happened to, aren't you glad it happened to Zelda? I certainly am.'

There's a pause. Melanie keeps her eyes on the two drunks. Her mouth is moving slightly — as if she's suppressing a slight smile. 'We never had this conversation,' she says, not meeting his eyes. 'I never heard you say that and you never saw me nod. OK?'

'What conversation?'

'And last but not least, you never saw . . . '

'What?'

She tilts her chin over her shoulder at the vodka bag on the back seat. 'You never saw what was in that carrier bag either.'

The End

Suki's breathing slows. The rapid in and out — the frantic panting of the last few hours — deflates into something slow and thoughtful. A measured surrender. To Penny this is the first sign that the end really is coming. It's going to be soon.

She looks at her watch. Five o'clock. Evening. So it will be evening when Suki goes. It can't be much longer. She hitches up the duvet which makes a tent over her and Suki — here on the floor in the office where Suki lies curled on the tatty old bed that she has had for fifteen years — ever since she was a tiny puppy. Penny has been here all last night and today. She's not tired, not sleepy. Not at all.

'Don't be scared, Suki.' She strokes her face. 'Don't be scared. I promise there's nothing to be scared of.'

Suki takes another breath. Almost pensive. She lets it out. Penny rests her hand on Suki's ribcage — very lightly, because the skeleton is so tiny, so feeble. It seems a ridiculous insult to expect it to rise one more time. This little old dog — small and shrunken as a walnut. Even as a youngster Suki was tiny. Not a proper breeder's dog — she was a rescue puppy, a cute hairy-faced mutt. All her life no one has ever noticed or paid attention to Suki — not the way they'd whoop and ooh over the glamorous red setters and Weimaraners. Of course, Suki has never minded. She's always been content to trot along next to Penny, quite happy with the world and the way it was. No one is really going to notice when she's gone. Only Penny.

Another breath comes. A slow release. Penny watches the ribcage — expecting another.

She waits, and she waits.

'Suki?'

No response.

'Suki? Is that it?'

Her chest doesn't move. Penny presses her hands into it, her fingertips gently searching between the ribs for the last flutter of heartbeat. Nothing. The little dog's chin is down and the whiskers around her mouth are curled and brown where they touch her front leg.

'Suki?'

Penny looks at her watch again. Five minutes go by. Then another five. She makes herself count the seconds out in her head. All the way to a hundred and eighty. Three more minutes. Nothing, no one, can exist without breathing for this long. It is definitely the end.

'OK.' She rocks back on her heels. 'OK.'

She cries. Just a little, and has to hold up her sleeve to soak up the tears. There'd be more, but the heavy ones passed through yesterday morning, when the vet told her the end was coming.

'I'm picking you up now.' After a long time she bends at the waist and lifts Suki up on to her lap. The dog doesn't move or resist. Her legs flop down. She weighs nothing — no more than a small wicker basket. Penny hunches down, puts her face against the old muzzle. Rocks her. 'It's all right, my girl. It's OK. You've been so good. Such a good girl. Thank you,' she tells her. 'Thank you so so much. For everything.'

The Nobel Peace Prize

AJ is in that place again. The cave, its walls as smooth and warm and glowing as polished walnut. The hole is there too, slightly to his right. There's a slender strand of something — gossamer, or spider silk maybe — reaching into the hole, almost as if it's pointing the way. He is certain that if he tugs on the strand every miracle on earth will be revealed to him, all in one cosmic white blast. But this time, just as he's about to grip the strand, the babble of infant laughter comes to him. He jerks round to the cave opening. Something is out there. A familiar pitter-patter of feet. A shadow crosses the ground.

He wakes, gulping in air. Breathing hard, his heart galloping, hands groping for something to hold on to.

'Shit shit *shit*.'

'AJ? You all right there, mate?'

He blinks. The Big Lurch and one of the nurses are staring at him from the other sofa. He opens his mouth, struggles up on his elbows and stares blankly at them. He's in the nurses' TV room. The digital clock on the wall says nine forty-five. The TV is on. A woman wearing nothing but thigh-high boots is gyrating her pelvis, throwing her long blonde hair around like a whip.

AJ groans and turns away into the damp-smelling sofa, his face in his hands. He shakes his head. He is so tired now it is beyond a joke. He wants to sleep but he can't. He is going slowly, very slowly, mad. The lunatics are taking over the asylum, the system is feeding on its own young. He wishes he could wear a *You don't have to be mad to work here but it helps* T-shirt. Why is he stuck on this highway to hell of a career? There was a time he'd deluded himself he was going to change the world by caring for the patients, he even thought he was doing it to make Mum proud — make her believe her son was caring and thoughtful. Now he looks back at those rose-tinted days and thinks, without any humour, he should have gone to Specsavers.

He's seen the worst of human nature in this profession. He's seen guys who've stabbed random little kids to death in the high street, he's nursed a woman (long dead now) who killed her disabled husband by pouring a kettle of boiling water over his head and leaving him in his wheelchair for three days until he died of the burns and the infection — AJ's heart used to gallop every time he saw her holding a cup of coffee; she was only allowed that after ten years on the unit. Then there was the guy who'd hacked up, cooked and eaten his neighbour's pony because it was 'looking at him strange'. And the AIDS sufferer who put his used needles pointing upwards in the sandpit at the local children's playground. And so it goes, on and on.

At some point he decided he didn't want to know what someone was in the can for. He reckoned he'd nurse them better if he was none the wiser about the things they'd done.

Technically, he's supposed to know it all — the staff need to be aware of the offending history — but he's found ways of learning only the bare minimum. He prefers it this way — his patients are to him like strangers in a pub or on a train — no illusions or preconceptions. There are simply some he likes and some he doesn't, but he always tries to give them the same care.

'You should be nominated for a Nobel Peace Prize,' says Patience. 'For that and for your work with trees.'

He doesn't feel like a Nobel Prize winner. Anything but.

'Right.' Now he rolls his feet off the sofa. Tilts himself forward and sits for a moment, rubbing his face. There's a strange, almost fishy smell in the room — maybe something they've been eating. 'Right,' he repeats. 'I'm going to do a walk-through.'

No one acknowledges him. The woman on screen is, evidently, in the middle of a drawn-out orgasm. She is yelping and squealing and acting her heart out. Massaging her breasts. The Big Lurch and the other nurse are agog. AJ hopes he's never fallen for a fake orgasm in his life. The odds are, he supposes, pretty high.

'I said, I'm going to do a walk-through.'

Neither of the other two men break away from the screen. '*Hey!*' Suddenly he's irritated. 'Hey. Look at me.'

Both of them turn, startled. The Big Lurch fumbles with the remote and clicks the TV off. Holds his hands up. 'Sorry, AJ, my man. I'm sorry.'

'OK — well, now I've got your attention, can I enquire what that fucking disgusting smell is? Have the bins been emptied? Has the washing-up been done? You aren't being paid to sit around here all night.'

'It's the kettle — it fused.'

'The kettle is fused? Then what do you do about it? Do you a) ignore it and watch more porn? b) ignore it, hope it will go away, and then watch more porn? or c) try and fix it?'

The Big Lurch gives a long sigh and gets up. 'Don't worry — I know the rest. If we can't fix it, then we put in an order to Accounts. I even know the right forms.'

'Great — that's a result. Gold star, mate.' He shakes his head resignedly. Puts his hands on his knees and pushes himself painfully to his feet. 'Now I am going to walk the wards — actually work for a living.'

'Jesus,' murmurs the Big Lurch as AJ walks past him. 'Who puffed sand up your backside?'

He ignores that comment, trudges out of the room, to the staircase, his mood getting progressively worse. He doesn't want to be here; he's tingly and amped, but at the same time he's tired and he's fed up with it all. He passes Zelda's room — casts a quick glance in there. Everything is exactly as it was last night, paint roller still up against the wall. *Plus ça change*. That's just the way things happen around here — at a snail's pace.

He goes first to Monster Mother's room and opens the observation hole — peers through. The room is quiet, she is asleep in bed. The curtains are closed and on her chair hangs a dark kimono-style dressing gown, the light reflecting off its fat folds. While it's impossible to know if Monster Mother is skinless tonight, at least she is sleeping. He closes the hatch and goes quietly back down the corridor.

On Buttercup Ward something isn't right. It's just a small noise, a creak of a bed, a breathing pattern that's fallen out of sync. He crosses the corridor to room 17 — Moses Jackson's room — and turns the little spigot in the pane. He sees immediately this is where the noise is coming from.

Moses is sitting on his bunk, rocking himself to and fro, holding his head. He's a completely different person from the arrogant one The Maude attacked. Ever since his 'auto ennucleation' he's been nervous and self-effacing. He is so changed. Tonight he's dressed in his vest and underpants and he hasn't noticed AJ because he's too caught up in his own internal battle. Batting his face, and screaming silently. Rocking and rocking.

AJ opens the door. 'Moses. Moses, it's me.'

Moses instantly stops moving. He freezes, lowers his arms.

'Moses? It's AJ. You OK, mate?'

He blinks with his one good eye. 'AJ?'

'I'm going to come in.'

'Yes,' he mumbles. 'AJ, help me.'

AJ closes the door and comes into the room. On Buttercup Ward the colour theme is, unsurprisingly, yellow. Even in the dim light you can't get away from the yellow — the curtains are yellow with grey diamonds and the floor is a sickly yellow linoleum flecked black. It is one of the rehabilitation wards reserved for patients who are considered to be less of a danger, and the rooms have some movable furniture. AJ goes and sits on the very edge of the bed. You're not supposed to sit on the beds — it opens you up to all sorts of possibilities of abuse accusations. But Moses is shaking like a leaf.

'Moses? Hey, hey, mate, come on. What's up?'

'AJ, AJ AJ.' He grips his curled hair tightly. 'AJ, help me.'

'That's why I'm here. Now let's take deep breaths. You've had your meds, haven't you?'

'Yes.'

'Usual time?'

'Yes, yes, yes.'

'Good. So what's the problem?'

Moses shakes his head. He moans and tightens his hands against his scalp. When he speaks his voice is almost inaudible. 'I'm scared, Mr AJ. Moses is scared.'

'Hey, hey.' AJ gently untangles his fingers from his hair and holds them. 'Moses, old man,' he says, keeping his voice well modulated, 'calmly now. Some more of those deep breaths. That's the way . . . '

Moses nods. He takes a long shaky breath, lets it all out.

'Don't make me say what's scary, Mr AJ, or mention that name. I bin told I ain't supposed to say it so I ain't even going to whisper it and you'll excuse me for that, but though you are my deep and most respectful of friends, I am just going to keep my piehole shut at this moment in time.'

He nods to himself, as if to confirm those were the exact words he meant to use. He says nothing more. The doctors spent a long time putting Moses back together, working on his eye implant, but if you know what to look for you can still see his face is misshapen. What actually happened to Moses that night? AJ wonders. They can go on putting The Maude down to hallucinations and fantasy, but *something* happened that night. And whatever it was was powerful enough to make Moses gouge out his own eye.

An Apple Tree

When Suki has been dead for so long that she's cold, Penny starts to move. Outside, everything is ready — she has lived with herself for forty-two years and she knows herself well enough to have already prepared what she's going to do next. She's been out already this morning and dug the hole. It's under the apple tree, the one that Suki as a baby — not much bigger than a guinea pig — used to chew at. Growling and leaping at it. Her own play-monster.

Dressed in the same sweater and skirt and socks she's been wearing for almost two days, Penny carries the dog out into the main part of the mill — her home for the last sixteen years. The lights are all low, just a faint glow from the big log burner in the centre of the floor. Even wrapped in the old chewed blanket she used to drag around the house, there's nothing of Suki — she's no heavier than a feather.

At the back door Penny realizes she needs her boots on. Instead of putting Suki down on the mat — she doesn't think she can bear that — she leans her shoulder against the door frame and jams her feet into the wellies, wriggling her toes around. It's sort of comic, this middle-aged woman with all her scarves and her coloured hair and her jingly bracelets, standing there like a drunk in the doorway with a dead pet in her arms. She has to smile. Suki would be laughing. Wherever she is now. Up in the dark slipstreams.

It's very, very dark. Very cold. Her breath is in the air. Winter is moving in. It has moved in. She gets to the bottom of the garden, in spite of all the slippery terraces. It would be better to be drunk or stoned or high, but there hasn't been the chance. It would be better to have washed and changed — she'd like to feel cleaner and prettier for something this important, but she's not young and no one is going to watch.

She crouches and lowers Suki into the hole. She's lined it with dried flowers and fruit and blankets and Suki's tennis ball — covered in dog spit and hair. The dog seems to sigh as her body settles, as if this is a relief. Penny moves her hands out from under the blanket — takes a step back, closes her eyes and rests her hands in a light clasp at her waist. She drops her face and tries to be respectful. She tries to wish good things and think about where Suki is going to go, but she can't do it, so in the end she just takes the shovel and pushes frozen earth into the hole. Quickly, before she can change her mind.

Power Cuts

Something is bothering AJ, but he can't quite put his finger on it. Instead of finishing his walk of the wards he goes hunting down the Big Lurch. He has to go into the nurses' station and out into the admin block and through all the toilets and the kitchens until he finds him in the security guards' control room — a giant futuristic glass pod in the reception area of the unit. He is sitting on a swivel seat in front of a bank of monitors. His feet are up and his arms are crossed, his head floppy as if he's sleeping, or on the point of sleeping.

'Amazing.' AJ stands in the doorway, arms folded. 'You're where you're meant to be. The last place I'd have looked.'

The Big Lurch lifts his head a little. Frowns.

'AJ? You look all crazy — like one of those people they lock up in a loony bin. You ought to see a doctor about that — it's not a good look.'

AJ rubs his eyes. He comes into the room and sits on one of the chairs, running his hands over the soft suede of the armrest. He's always liked this place — it's got a comfort to it yet it's not claustrophobic. You can feel warm in here, and look out on to the world: see the moon or the sun, the city and the trees, the cars and the clouds. It's like being on the bridge of a ship. The Starship *Enterprise* maybe. The glass shield between here and the outside world is bulletproof. A lot of money has gone into this operations room. A lot of money and power and wealth. The Trust can find finance for this sort of thing, but they can't stop people like Moses ripping out their own eyes in the breakfast queue.

'What do you think?' he says. 'Do you think our director knows how unhappy we are? Hmm? Does she think we're happy, or does she know we're unhappy? What do you sense?'

The Big Lurch lowers his chin and scrutinizes AJ with hauteur. 'Honestly?'

'Honestly.'

'She's too unhappy herself to care what's going on with us. A person can only see suffering when they're not suffering themselves. Caring? It's a luxury, if you want the honest truth.'

AJ nods slowly, appreciatively. The Big Lurch doesn't speak much — but when he does, his words are premium-rate gilded.

'So? What's making her unhappy?'

'Don't you know?'

'Am I supposed to?'

The Big Lurch turns and faces AJ full on. Surprised. 'You really don't know?'

AJ stares at him, mystified. 'What? What am I supposed to know?'

'About Jonathan?'

'*Jonathan?* Jonathan who?' He fumbles around in his head for a face to connect to the name. A patient? No — no Jonathans in the unit. The only person he can think of is Jonathan Keay — an occupational therapist who left the unit last month. 'Jonathan Keay, you mean?'

'Of course Jonathan Keay.'

'The ocky therapy guy who left? What about him?'

The Big Lurch gives AJ an amused half-smile. He lets a puff of laughter come out of his chest. *Aha aha aha*. 'AJ, *seriously*, my man! For a switched-on person, you occasionally lack perspicacity.'

'Then tell me, for Christ's sake.'

'Melanie and Keay? You didn't notice?'

'Are you serious?'

'Oh please, mate. Please.'

AJ lowers his eyes to the smooth arms of the chair — moves his hands up and down, up and down. Melanie and Jonathan Keay? Seriously? Until now he's always imagined he was the one who knew the secrets. That *he* walked around with the knowledge of the world on his shoulders. Apparently not, though. Apparently he is the last to know. OT staff giving it the old jiggety-jig with top-drawer management? If it's true, that's fairly scandalous stuff — the biggest taboo, like incest, or staff sleeping with a patient. Montagues and Capulets. Melanie herself said it — the Trust takes a dim view of it.

And meanwhile her and Keay? Jonathan is someone AJ has never given much thought to. A normal enough guy — late thirties, a lot of experience under his belt. If AJ recalls rightly, Keay and Melanie had worked together in another unit in the north of England before they came here. They'd both started on low grades and had worked their way up the ranks. No one quite knows why he left Beechway last month. Word had it, he'd left on medical grounds. It was all very sudden, he didn't even say goodbye — one moment he was there, the next he wasn't. AJ vaguely remembers a card arriving — written in very formal handwriting — from his mother: *Thank you for being such generous colleagues to my son — he will miss you all*. It had a kind of funereal aura to it.

AJ had always assumed, without particularly focusing on it, that Keay had some sort of secret private life he didn't want to talk about. At the time, AJ hadn't much cared, but now he's combing through every word the guy ever said — putting it in the context that Keay's secret may have been an affair with Melanie. Maybe her frantic little episode with the voddy had something to do with him. Everything AJ thought he knew about Melanie jack-knifes and amplifies and turns itself somersault over somersault and his estimation — and jealousy — of Jonathan Keay takes a quantum leap.

His attention is dragged away from his speculation by one of the CCTV monitors. He wonders what it was that brought him down here — it certainly wasn't to speculate about the love lives of the other staff. It was something that was bugging him about the camera system in the unit. But what?

The monitors show nothing. Empty, motionless corridors. The outdoor-training Astro court. The pinch point in the stem corridor. Even a view of the security pod from behind and above — him and the Big Lurch sitting there, the backs of their heads barely clipping into the bottom edge of the frame.

And then it hits him. He sits forward a little, peering at the images. He thinks he knows what it is. The thing that's been bothering him, the reason the word 'delusion' has always seemed so inaccurate. He stays where he is, staring at the screens, his thoughts turning slow cartwheels. The smell in the nurses' station earlier — the burning-fish smell of a fused kettle. The smell in Moses' room that morning. Something in the building had fused that day too.

'Hey,' he says slowly. 'These cameras — you log the footage you take, don't you?'

The Big Lurch throws him a sarcastic look. 'No — they're there for show. I use them to play my porn on the long dark nights. Of course we log it, bro. I mean, it only stays on for two weeks, but we log it.'

'The night Zelda self-harmed — when she did her arms — you lost that because of the power cut.'

'Uh huh.' He nods. 'I told you there's something weird going on in this place — the power cutting out all the time, and it's always some different reason.'

'And the night Zelda died?'

'Yeah — same thing that night. And the — ' He stops. He takes his feet off the desk with a bang. Twists the chair to face AJ. 'You know what — you're right. Every single time there's been a power cut.'

The Secret of Flying

Fartlek means 'speed play' in Swedish. It is a training method designed to place stresses on the aerobic and anaerobic systems, stimulating the heart and discouraging it from falling into a steady rhythm. It can be adjusted to suit the individual, and is therefore ideal for anyone wanting to recoup their fitness after a long period of inactivity.

The football ground behind Avon and Somerset police's northern operations centre has its own mini-'Fartlek hill', a man-made mound at one end of the pitch with three polyurethane tartan track lanes snaking up and over it. At seven a.m., just as the sun is rising above the city, thirty-year-old Sergeant Flea Marley pushes herself up the hill. She passes the bases of the three wind turbines mounted along the crest, runs down the other side. Keeping her pace hard and fast, she executes a speed turn at the foot of the hill and races back up it. Her black, wicking force T-shirt — 'POLICE' embossed on the deltoids — is saturated with sweat. It evaporates off her in clouds. With Fartlek you have to push through the lactic-acid build — the bleed of pain in the long muscles. The nausea. You have to want to do it.

Flea wants to do it. She wants to get back to fitness. She is sergeant of the force's Underwater Search Unit — the police diving team. A woman in a man's world and above everything she needs her body to be in tune. Over ten months ago she was hurt in an explosion in a tunnel which left her with muscle injuries to her thigh and a burst eardrum. It's been a long haul getting fit again. But she's made the most of it — she's worked it and worked it. She is, quite simply, a different person from the one she was last year. In control — and things in her head are nicely spaced. It's all been about putting things in boxes in her head. Closing lids. That's the secret of flying — you never look down or over your shoulder.

She abandons the hill and enters the pitch, moving into the easy running phase. She pounds along — the ground dry and cold underfoot. The turf pitch is unlit — the only luminance comes from the floodlights over on the Astro where a youth-alliance football team are doing morning training. The compression sleeve she had on her thigh for months is off now, and the air on it feels good. The burst eardrum got infected and held her back longer than she expected — she's been at work but on restricted duties for eight months — she probably won't be able to dive for another three weeks, after a visit to the barotrauma specialists in Plymouth to be formally ticked back into work. But her body feels organized, and for the first time in ages she thinks she looks nice too. She's gained weight and her skin is healthy.

As she transitions into the final minute of fast pace she realizes she's being watched. A man is sitting on a bench in the arbour that leads to the car park — under a sweep of autumnal branches.

She circuits the full five hundred metres, monitoring him with small glances as she does. The leaves are on the ground around him, and he wears a dark-blue gabardine jacket, the collar up, his elbows on his knees. His face is hard, set — he has a wide neck, intense blue eyes and thick dark hair kept very short. If he got up it would be a calm movement — one that people, especially women, would notice. Flea knows this because she knows who it is. It's DI Jack Caffery.

She hasn't seen or spoken to him in almost a year — and she doesn't acknowledge him now. Instead she executes a sixty-metre sprint along the eastern edges of the pitch, dropping the pace as she comes round the corner. He'll be able to watch her uninterrupted, and that's fine. For the first time in ages she likes her body — she doesn't mind people watching it. She's got a lot to be proud of.

As she rounds the top end of the pitch, her airwaves radio in the black holster around her bicep gives a familiar warble. It's the unique sound of a point-to-point contact — someone wanting to speak to her directly. She slows her running to a long loping gait, pulling the radio out of her holster. Maybe this is his way of contacting her. But when she sees the ID on the handset it's not Jack Caffery but Wellard, her acting sergeant.

She bends over, one hand on her thigh, panting. Then, almost recovered, she straightens and holds the radio to her mouth.

'Hi, Wellard — wassup?'

'Tried your mobile. No signal.'

'No — I'm on the football-club track. I think it's the turbines.'

'Can you get back then? A job's come in.'

'A job?' Flea digs her fingers into her stomach muscles, where they ache. 'A diving job?'

'No — it's a search. MCIT.'

MCIT — Jack Caffery's unit. She resists an urge to look over her shoulder to where he's sitting. 'What do they want?'

Wellard sighs. 'A search. Misper. I'm guessing it got kicked up by the review team because it's one we've done before — Misty Kitson.'

'Misty Kitson.'

'That's what I said.'

Flea takes her finger off the button. She breathes in and out — dragging the air down into the bottom of her lungs. Her heart rate, which should be slowing, has picked up at the mention of that name. Misty Kitson.

'Boss? You there?'

She coughs. Hits the button. 'Yeah, yeah — I'm here.'

'I was saying — Misty Kitson — they want us to search near the clinic again. They're going to extend the parameters.'

'Yeah, I heard you.'

'Can you come back to the office? Start thinking about staffing?'

'I'm on my way.'

She snaps the radio into the holster and stands for a minute, her heart thudding. Misty Kitson. A search for Misty Kitson. The only officer at MCIT who would have issued a request like that is the one who was the Senior Investigating

Officer on the case. DI Jack Caffery.

Slowly she turns in the direction of the shaded pathway where he sits.

But this time the lamplight shines on an empty place. Caffery — if it was him — has disappeared.

Mulder and Scully

AJ has surprised himself by managing another two hours' sleep. The night shift are going home now, but he's stayed in his office, drinking industrial-strength coffee, trying to wake up. By seven a.m., when Melanie arrives at the unit, he is buzzing and alert. He stands at his window and watches her cross the car park, the security lights picking out the silvery bullets of rain sweeping past her. Dressed in a beige raincoat and red wellingtons, she holds a newspaper over her head and ducks as she hurries towards reception. As soon as she's inside he withdraws from the window. Scratches around trying to keep himself awake with coffee and paperwork — giving her twenty minutes or so to get her head together.

At seven twenty he gathers himself. Straightens his clip-on tie and walks resolutely down the corridor. Knocks on her door.

'Yes?'

'AJ.'

There's a pause. A slight sound of something moving in there. Then: 'Come in.'

He opens the door. She is sitting at the desk behind a pile of papers, her glasses on. She's taken off the wellies and rain-spattered coat, and now she is wearing a blouse with drooping, lace-embellished cuffs that make her look like something from the court of Louis Quatorze.

The reason for the cuffs, of course, is the bandaged hand. Putting the lid on the rumour mill.

'AJ?' Her smile is kind, but reserved. 'Thank you for yesterday. You were a marvel. Have you been working all night?'

'Can I come in?'

'Of course.' She nods at the seat in front of her desk. 'Please.'

He comes and sits — feeling again like a pupil in the headmistress's office. *She was sleeping with one of the OTs, mate. Don't forget that. Getting down and dirty with one of the great unwashed. Not quite as professional as she seems . . .*

'I've got some results from the Home Office on those tribunals last week,' she says brightly. 'Good news — we've got a free bed on pre-discharge tomorrow.'

'Oh?'

'Isaac Handel. We thought he'd be going — they've rubber-stamped it. So I guess we'll want to be thinking about who's coming out of Acute and where the next referral will come from, so I . . . ' She breaks off. Tilts her head to one side. 'AJ? Is that what you were here about?'

'No.' He clears his throat, uncomfortable. 'No — actually, I, uh, I wanted to talk about — you know — about what we were talking about yesterday. The delusions — among the patients. The M-word.'

She lets out a long sigh. 'Oh, OK.'

'We — I mean, the unit — we've always taken a middle-of-the-road attitude to it. We've reached our conclusions and stuck with them. Easy conclusions to reach if you're dealing with this population: mass hallucination, hysteria, etcetera.'

'Are there any other conclusions to reach?'

'Yes. There are.'

She lowers the paper she's holding and stares at him, her cheeks suddenly red. Her eyes are magnified behind the glasses. 'AJ,' she says levelly. 'Or Mulder, should I say? Is this you crossing over to the dark side? Jacking in your sceptic credentials? Are we now a Maude believer?'

'No. In fact the ugly sceptic in me has just drunk a case of Red Bull and carjacked a Ferrari. I'm Scully, Scully to the hilt. More Scully than Scully is. Scully could have been based on me.'

She takes her glasses off and lays them carefully to one side. She clasps her hands together and leans forward, looking at him like a judge. Eyebrows raised, waiting for an explanation.

'A power cut,' he says. 'Every time The Maude appears, there's been a power cut. There was a power cut the night Zelda self-harmed and the night she died.'

'I know. Sometimes I watch *Ashes to Ashes* and think, Wish I could do that — rewind to the eighties when the unit was being built. There are a few people I'd have a full'n'frank with. The electricians, to start with.'

'And I think there may have been a power cut when Moses wrote those things on his walls. I remembered he said he smelled burning fish.'

'From the kitchen? I don't remember that bit.'

'Well, I thought about the kitchen — but have you ever smelled a fuse blowing?'

'Yes, it's like . . . ' She frowns. 'Like burning fish.'

'Some of the security staff think there was a power cut when Moses had his episode. Do you remember?'

'I wish. I can't remember my own name these days — let alone back that far.'

'Who has records of things like that?'

'Maybe maintenance — except, no, their records get cleared every year.' She shrugs. 'Christ knows. Ask Moses?'

'Have you tried asking Moses about anything that happened that day? It's as if this is Guantanamo, and you're going to waterboard him.' She shrugs again and reaches for her glasses, as if she's about to lose interest. He sits forward and says, 'A power cut equals no CCTV — the emergency generator doesn't feed the CCTV, I've checked with central security. Delusions, hallucinations and fantasies? The Maude? That's Mulder's world — independent of the nuts and bolts of reality. But cruelty and power cuts? That's Scully stuff. My camp.'

Melanie sets the glasses down again, leans forward, her ridiculously blue eyes locked on his. 'AJ,' she says calmly, 'I have absolutely no idea what you're talking about.'

'No CCTV — no evidence.'

'I still don't get it.'

'Well, duh, Melanie, sorry to be rude, but think about it. Moses was a nuisance — so was

Zelda and so was Pauline. They pissed people off. What I'm saying is — could it be the delusions aren't delusions? Could it have happened the way they said? Could it be someone in the unit — a real live *human* — one of the other patients, or the staff even, trying to shut them up?' He pauses, letting the implication settle on Melanie. 'I mean, Moses? Zelda? Pauline? Who wouldn't?'

'No, AJ — what crap, if you'll excuse the expression. They would have told us.'

'It was dark — how could they see who came into their room? And what if someone had titted around with their medication? They're already dosed up to the eyeballs anyway — what if they'd been given even more sedative than they usually had? Have you not thought about that unattributable heart attack? Secondary to obesity — was that what it went down as? I'm sure the pathologist wasn't looking for crush injuries to the heart, because who would have said anything?'

'Crush injuries?'

'Yes — like someone sitting on her. And I don't mean a ghost sitting on her, I mean a person. A *person*.'

'They would have checked, wouldn't they? That's the first thing they look for: signs of injury from restraint.'

'Maybe. But it could have been a stress-induced heart attack. Stress because someone was tormenting her. Did anyone check whether the writing on Zelda's arms was actually *hers*? The writing on Moses' walls — Pauline's legs?

We all assumed they'd done it themselves, but who checked? I certainly didn't. *Be thou not one of them that committeth foul acts? Anyone who looks at a woman lustfully has already committed adultery in his heart? Avoid idleness and intemperance?* Moses might have committed adultery a hundred times, but would he know that word? And where did Zelda learn a word like intemperance? *I*'m not even sure what it means.'

'Greed. It means greed.'

AJ raises an eyebrow. 'Impressive.'

'I looked it up. I saw it written . . . somewhere. On one of the pictures, I don't know . . . ' She peers up at her etching of the workhouse, as if groping for a memory. She shakes her head. 'Anyway — whatever — I looked it up. It means greed.'

'Sort of fits then, in Zelda's case.'

Melanie puts the glasses on, frowns tolerantly over the rims. 'AJ, remind me — what was Zelda's DSM classification again? I can't remember.'

'She was . . . probably schizophrenia, axis 2? BPD, I guess and — '

'Basically, she's suggestible. Has auditory and visual hallucinations?'

'I'm asking you to keep an open mind, that's all.'

'I have got an open mind, AJ. In fact, I am about as open-minded as they come in this job. And I will promise you this: it didn't happen. It's impossible. I'd rather that freaky little dead dwarf came and sat on my chest than have to believe what you're suggesting.'

'I think we should look into it. Speak to the police even.'

'The police have been here all week. They're as fed up with it as we are, they won't want us digging it all up again.'

'I meant a different part of the police? One of the specialist teams. Remember those detectives we met at the Criminal Justice Forum the other day? Major Crime? You were speaking to one of them — you could give him a call, talk in confidence.'

'AJ, I understand your concerns, but dragging the police back in? Especially when we don't know what happened. At the moment it looks as if it's all going to drift, and I for one am *more* than happy to let that happen, to let the unit slowly settle back to normal. Forgive me — I just don't think I can handle the police coming back. Not with everything else that's going on.'

AJ sighs. Sits back and massages his temples. Maybe she's right — maybe he's just exhausted and saddled with an overactive imagination. He's spent far too long in this place over the last seven days — he has time in lieu backing up to next month. He's got to get some time off.

'I'm sorry,' he says. 'Sorry. You're right.' He pauses, looks at her hand. 'And you? How's your hand?'

She glances down at it. 'It's fine. But I suppose you think I'm an alcoholic now.'

'No. No — like I said, I think you've got a lot on your plate. And Jonathan going? That must be hard.'

The words are out before he realizes what he's said. But it's too late. Her chin jerks up and a small hint of the emotion he saw in the car yesterday evening creeps into her face. Like cochineal dropped in a lake. 'I'm sorry? I beg your pardon?'

'Yes — I, uh — nothing. Nothing.' He begins to get to his feet. 'I'm going — forget I said it.'

'No. Wait. Did I hear you right?'

Now it's AJ's turn to feel the colour rising in his face. He stays where he is, half standing half sitting, not knowing where to put himself. 'Yes — I was only checking you were OK. That's all.'

'Does everyone know?'

'Not exactly *everyone*.'

'Jesus.' Melanie drops her injured hand on the desk and shakes her head. 'Oh Jesus, Jesus, Jesus. What a bloody awful mess.'

The Great Grand Power

For the first time in years Penny doesn't wake at the crack of dawn and get to work. Instead she sleeps late, alone in the bedroom at the top of the mill. When she wakes it is light outside — grey ice clouds slide lazily across the sky. Suki used to be allowed on the bed — in the dead of night Penny would reach out and feel her comforting warmth. Would get a happy lick on her hand as reward for her effort. Today the pillow in the empty space is cold.

She lies there and looks at it. Suki is gone. She is at one with the great grand power. Now she will feed and nurture everything that grows. Her spirit will float and move like smoke — find its way into each tree, each blade of grass, each bird and each mushroom. Penny is thankful of nature, of the generous and non-judgemental way it orbits and replenishes itself, regardless of humanity and the stupid shit mankind tries. She sings to the trees after she's borrowed their fruit. In the dead of winter she returns to the plant, bringing a little of whatever it is she's made — be it jam or cordial or preserves or sloe gin. In these parts everyone used to do this with the apple trees — they'd come in January and anoint them with the young cider of last year's crop. There are still some groups that do it, though Penny has never joined one. They call it wassailing, this blessing of the tree with its own produce; Penny just calls it plain old 'thanking'.

'Thanking trees'? 'Borrowing' fruit? Singing to them? No wonder you haven't got a boyfriend, she thinks. You're a crusty old hippy. There are wind chimes in your garden, and crystals in the windows, for God's sake. *Crystals*. One day you'll stop washing altogether and grow a luxuriant beard that small creatures will nest in.

She looks at the phone on the bedstand and wonders if there is anyone at all she can talk to about Suki dying. Her brother lives in the next village, but she hasn't seen him in years, and she doubts he'd care anyway. Who would be interested? The lady in the corner shop, maybe? The neighbours? Probably not.

She pulls up the home-made quilt from the bottom of the bed and holds it to her face. It's still got a faint dog smell. She breathes it in, rubs it against her face. She made this quilt herself, five years ago, sitting by the fire like an old granny, Suki at her feet. She'd saved up the fabrics from clothes she'd worn out, faded cushions, there's even a tea towel in here somewhere. It's loved and worn and threadbare — falling apart.

'Oh, quilt,' she murmurs, with a sad smile, 'you need some TLC. A little repair. Time to rest. Just like me.'

Long Johns and Boots

So, the Big Lurch was right — Melanie Arrow and Jonathan Keay were an item. AJ stands for a while in the staffroom looking at a photo of Keay that's pinned on the board half lost under various notices and postcards and flyers. He's with the other nursing staff at some long-forgotten Christmas party in some long-forgotten pub. He's wearing a paper hat and a checked shirt with the sleeves rolled up. AJ studies his eyes, hunting for a hint, a trace of evidence of what was happening between him and Melanie. He can find none.

He's not at all sure why he went into her office just now. Does it matter to him what happened to Pauline and Moses and Zelda? Was he trying to show her that he cares what goes on in the unit? Stand proud, little soldier. Or was it because he wanted to find out the truth about Melanie and Jonathan Keay?

He's still asking himself when he leaves the unit, wondering about her. The thoughts would get lurid if he let them, but he's old enough not to let them go that route. Instead he kids himself it's natural professional concern for a colleague's mental well-being. At home, Patience doesn't complain that he's late. She's mellow, and especially forgiving when he gives her the Forager's Fayre jam she likes. She clicks a jar open, sniffs and gives an approving cluck.

'Like, like, *like*. Whoever it is makes this stuff uses good ingredients. I take my hat off to her.'

'How do you know it's a *her* and not a *him*?'

'Please,' Patience says tolerantly. 'Don't make me say something sexist.'

Breakfast is ready. On days when Patience has no produce from the garden to fry, poach or broil, she shops in Thornbury and does the sort of cooking her mother taught her — half Caribbean, half Deep South. Sometimes it's saltfish and fritters, pancake towers with maple syrup and four miniature buttermilk scoops melting on top. Today it's banana porridge followed by soft biscuits, gravy and link sausage. There's Patience's home-made lovage brandy too. Two or three thimblefuls in a ceramic flask with a steaming mug of black coffee out of the espresso pot on the Aga. He can drink coffee by the barrel load — even before he goes to sleep.

He sits with Stewart at his foot and eats, using the biscuits to mop up the gravy. Biscuits. He's always been a bit split-headed about biscuits: are they cookies or are they, like these, a kind of savoury scone? He doesn't ask Patience because she's fretting over the form on the Cheltenham Showcase. She and Mum had the betting habit — they both claimed it was passed down in the genes from their mother. AJ recalls the many long afternoons he spent as a small child, waiting outside the bookies' in Thornbury while his mum and Patience went inside, armed with their purses and newspapers. He was too young to join them inside, so the two women would come out to compare the form with him, asking him what he thought. 'You're our lucky mascot,' they'd laugh. Lucky, lucky.

'So much for my inheritance,' AJ says as he moves the sausages around the plate. 'You put it all on Rude Boy to win at Wincanton.'

Patience dumps the skillet down with a bang. He likes winding her up because she is fabulously tetchy on this subject. 'Yes, and what's your point?'

'I dunno — I suppose you could have put it each way? At least you'd have covered your ass.'

'There's not enough money in the world to cover my butt,' Patience says, straight-faced.

'Stop being such a stereotype, Patience. You're behaving like something out of *Gone with the Wind*. Talking like it too. You're half white.'

'So? Why should I stop? Give people what they expect, it makes life a whole lot simpler.'

'Yes, but you're only perpetuating negative images of your race.'

'My *half* race. And that — what you just said — it's all psychobabble. You got that from that place you work.'

'It's not psychobabble, it's a vernacular far more rooted in the sociological sciences than in psychology,' he says loftily. 'And I didn't get it from the unit. You can pick up a comment like that on any street corner.'

Aunt Patience can't answer him when he starts talking that way, so she gives a big stage yawn, and turns away to check her texts. That's how her tips come in these days. Not from the biroed circles on the back pages of a newspaper, the way he remembers as a child, but from bookies who have her phone number on their lists and text her.

As much love and company as Patience provides, there is a price. She's as bad with money as Mum was. AJ's convinced that, if he wasn't around to keep an eye on her, this home and everything in it would have long since been gambled away. Not that it's much, a funny old place made up of three tiny cottages tacked together. There are three staircases — and that suited him and Mum and Patience. The communal space was downstairs, while each individual had their own bedroom and bathroom on the first floor. Mum's bedroom was the centre one. He and Patience could use it as a storeroom or something now that Mum was dead, but neither of them want to raise the subject so the room sits empty. A hole above them. They don't mention it because then they'd have to talk about Mum's death.

Yes, he thinks, feeding the rest of his link sausage to Stewart, when it comes to the way Mum died there are some things that will probably never get said.

He is inked in to work tomorrow morning so he's got to readjust his sleep patterns (for the millionth time). He goes to bed at two p.m., hoping the lovage brandy will help him sleep until maybe four the next morning, but the whole thing with Melanie keeps nagging at him and, although he drifts off by two fifteen, and although it's a deep, dreamless sleep for a change, four hours later he's wide awake.

He lies there for a while, looking out of the

window at the countryside. He misses Mum. He misses her so much. But he takes a very special comfort from the countryside, and his place within it. His neighbours are the local wildlife; when he's shooing the deer away from Patience's pink roses, he can recognize each individual from its markings, height, scars. He likes the solitude. He likes the fact that his clothes can smell of a bonfire without people wrinkling their noses. It's so remote out here that on days when he's really tired he doesn't have to bother getting dressed — he'll walk around the garden in long johns and boots like a character in a cowboy movie.

He's not lonely. But he's not sure that's good enough any more — the simple state of not being lonely. Maybe this means mourning Mum has moved into a different phase — maybe he's ready to start being with people again. Maybe it even means he's ready to be a proper grown-up, have a proper adult relationship? At the spring-chicken age of forty-three? It's a big, big step. Not something he is going to do lightly.

He glances at his watch. Six twenty. He yawns and gets up and goes into his bathroom and showers. As he's shaving he notices a measuring spoon on top of the medicine cabinet doing a silent balancing act, as if it's hovering on the edge. He puts down the razor and goes to it. The plastic double-ended spoon is only sitting there upright because it has become lodged in the sticky, unwiped residue of some ancient cough linctus. As a coordinator, he's responsible for compiling weekly reports on the hygiene of the wards. Now that's a laugh.

He gets a bin bag and sweeps everything into it, using a rag to mop up the crystallized green syrup. He drops empty cartons of paracetamol dated 2009 and a carton of Q-tips he remembers having when he got his first job aged twenty. What sort of woman would put up with this, he thinks impatiently. Really. What sort of lunatic would buy into this dump? Certainly not a mature, sensible woman.

Melanie Arrow probably lives in one of those Scandinavian houses — walls of perfect white, furniture of driftwood and linen. He imagines row after row of exquisitely tailored blouses hanging in dry-cleaning bags. And — if he's honest — he imagines silk knickers too.

'Hey,' he tells his reflection. 'You can stop it there. Wrong. All wrong.'

His reflection blinks back at him. He holds its gaze for a long time. Then he puts a hand up at the mirror. To hell with it. He's going to do something about it.

The Truth About Misty Kitson

Eight hours searching for Misty Kitson's body and Flea Marley's diving unit, which is here because it has a remit to assist with any search, land- or water-based, has worked hard, using scientifically formulated patterns. They have been given a hundred-metre band which encircles the area covered a year ago when Misty first went missing. This search is an extension of the original two-mile radius around the rehab clinic — an austere, white Palladian building that sits high on a hill. It is going to take a week to complete and as far as any of the searchers can tell it's based not on new intelligence but on MCIT's urgent need to prove to the media they are still doing something. By mid-afternoon the team has found nothing and the light is dying. They drive back to the offices in their white Mercedes Sprinter van, their spirits low. Some of the men jump straight into their cars and head home, others take time to warm up — brewing tea and showering — letting the hot water dig out the cold in their bones.

Flea is the last one left in the building. She stands in the shower with her eyes closed, the water thrumming on the back of her neck, thinking about the day. A full-on, rapid-edit montage of all the places they've searched unreels in her head. *Smash cut*: the clinic perimeter; *match cut*: electricity substation; *jump cut*: a B road. Jack Caffery standing silently, watching her, the same way he watched her running this morning. Not speaking.

She hasn't let his scrutiny bother her — she's searched the locations painstakingly, acting her heart out. Only she knows it's a waste of time. Misty's bones aren't lodged in a hedgerow. Or scattered in a field, or buried in a shallow grave in one of the copses near the clinic. They are several miles away from the clinic — on the other side of the county.

Flea Marley knows this because she is the one who concealed the body. Almost eighteen months ago. It's one of the things she's been working to keep locked in a box inside her head. One of the things she can't look at unless she wants to lose the secret of flying. Crash and burn.

She switches off the shower, steps out and towels off. The offices are empty now — it's just her and row after row of diving suits hanging like ghosts in the kit room. The masks in the locker room. The dead-body bags in the technician's room. No one to check on her or ask her what she's doing. She wipes steam off the mirror with the towel and stares at her reflection. Yes, she's fuller in the face — her skin is healthier — but now MCIT is reinvestigating Misty's disappearance, there's a thin, scared tightness around her eyes again.

She has been faintly desperate all day — thinking at any moment she was going to cry.

It's weird no one has noticed it. Even now she has to count to ten, until she's sure she's not going to start blubbing like a baby. Then she sprays on deodorant, pulls her sports clothing out of her rucksack and dresses slowly. Lots of layers — it's cold out there. She pulls waterproof trousers on over her leggings, and a big force-issue Montane jacket. She stuffs nitrile and Thinsulate gloves into her pocket, turns off all the lights, checks all the computers are switched off, and heads out to the car park, her face down.

Rush hour has died, but it still takes more than an hour to wind her way across the north of Somerset. She passes close to her house, close to the clinic — the key places on the vast storyboard of what *really* happened to Misty Kitson all those months ago. When she stops, it's on a small C road a mile south-east of the clinic, at the bottom of two huge fields that sweep down from the woods around Farleigh Park Hall.

All day while the team have been searching she's surreptitiously monitored this location on the map — sliding her secret attention over to it on the dashboard — calculating how long before the planned search would come round to this road. It's just outside the area searched last year, and it's slated to be covered in this new sweep. Probably it'll be late the day after tomorrow, or the day after that.

She opens the car door and drops her feet on to the tarmac. It's so quiet this far out in the countryside — real live things live out here — like deer and badger and rabbit. Somewhere an owl is hooting — up in the trees at the top of the slope. Even concentrating, she can't hear a single engine — not a car or an aeroplane. Nothing. She hauls out her rucksack and shoulders it. Kicks the door closed.

This road is a small, rarely frequented route — a few farmers' fields on the left, forest on the right. She knows it well. As she walks, high up beyond the trees ahead, the faint glow of lights from a hamlet appear. There was a murder in that hamlet not so long ago. All the American and Chinese and Japanese tourists who come round here and make goggle eyes at the pretty cottages and thatches and village greens . . . they don't know the half of it. The unzippered ugliness of it all. The killings, the rapes, the wife beatings, the jealousy, the hit and runs.

Yes, the hit and runs. People never spare a thought for all those hit and runs.

The road takes an abrupt bend to the left, then continues in a straight, roman line for the next half a mile — flat and opaque, until it dwindles into the night a hundred metres ahead. Above the clouds the moon is full and it sends down a scattered, diffuse glow that's sufficient to navigate by. She walks, pacing out the steps, counting in her head. Fifty metres down she stops and turns to face the fields, surveying them with her razor-sharp knowledge. She turns to the hamlet and does the same. The bearings are slightly wrong, so she continues a few more paces and repeats the exercise. This time she gets it straight away. Yup. This is where it happened.

She lowers her rucksack to the ground and

clicks the head torch on. It has to be angled down so it's illuminating the tarmac. The area needs to be searched in the finest detail. Things need to be removed before the team comes through here. One slip and she will be in the deepest shit. If she has to put half the hedgerow into her rucksack, she's going to. There mustn't be anything — anything at all — to connect this location with what really happened to Misty Kitson.

She pulls on the nitrile gloves and sets to work. It's no different from any other fingertip search she's done — a regular grid pattern to make sure every inch of the road is covered. She collects everything she finds — regardless of what — and puts it in the rucksack. A crisp packet, two beer tins, some toilet paper. A ring-pull that looks about fifty years old and an old CD. Maybe none of it is relevant, maybe all of it.

When she's a hundred per cent sure there is nothing left here except the dead leaves and the naked blackberry bushes, she pulls the torch off her head and uses it to inspect the road itself — the tarmac. The skidmarks are still here but they are so, so faint. She has to sink to her haunches and rest her hand on them to believe they still exist. A year and a half ago they were like a deep scar on the road — but nearly eighteen months of rain and sun and English seasons have leached the rubber away.

The sound of a car engine grows in the distance. A few seconds later headlights — from the direction she's parked. She gets up and steps smartly into the verge, clicking off the head torch as she does. As the car appears round the corner she presses herself tightly against a tree. Puts her hands in her pockets and drops her face, presenting as few reflective surfaces as possible.

The car passes. And almost instantly slows. And then, just fifty metres away, it stops. Her heart sinks. The engine is killed, and in the sudden silence comes the clear click of a door closing. Footsteps.

A crunch of gravel. Whoever it is they're close, really close. Slowly, furtively, she rolls back into the shadows, her shoulders tight. She slides down the tree until she's sitting and pulls the hood of her coat over her face. Like an ostrich. Head in the sand. She stays absolutely still, monitoring the footsteps. Just her and the thick drumbeat of her heart in her ears, greenish commas of light pulsing behind her eyes from the headlights. No reason for someone to stop out here in the middle of nowhere. No reason whatsoever. This is no-man's-land.

The noise stops and she dares to glance sideways. There — about a yard away, are two feet in walking boots. The lizard part of her brain scurries over them — knows they're familiar — can't quite connect to why they are and what it all means.

She raises her eyes. DI Jack Caffery is standing there. Dressed in black all-weather gear. His hands in his pockets, looking down at her.

High Street

AJ only has to wait for ten minutes, feeling like a stalker or a nervous teenager outside the girls' school gates, before Melanie appears at the off-licence, same as last night. He loiters outside, watching her speak to the sales assistant. Nodding. Concentrating on putting her pin number in the terminal.

Moments later she emerges, the long sleeves of her blouse peeking out of her raincoat, bouncing with each step. She is so close, almost two metres away, when she sees him.

'Oh no,' she groans, bringing herself up short. 'You caught me again.'

'It's not what it looks like — I wasn't following you. I always do my shopping here.'

She smiles tiredly. 'Well, this isn't what it looks like either.' She opens her carrier bag and shows him two cartons of orange juice. 'To go with the vodka at home.'

AJ peers up at the darkening sky, then over at his car, then up and down the street. He wishes he knew which angle it is that makes him look like Presley because he'd adopt it right this second. Instead he says:

'Vodka has its limitations, in my humble opinion. I wonder if you've ever ventured into the wild-and-woolly world of cider drinking.'

'Wild and woolly?'

'Yes — we're, uh, tree huggers. Most of us

have beards and wear Fair Isles — I'm the exception to the rule.' He nods up the street to the old pub, beloved of the local cider connoisseurs. 'But if you did ever want to risk the hairy element — that would be the place to start.'

She turns and glances over her shoulder at the pub. She stares at it for a long time. His heart sinks — she's formulating a way to say no. But when she turns back she's smiling. She puts a hand over her eyes to shield it from the overhead street light so she can meet his gaze.

'I dunno,' she says. 'You sure I'm not a little overdressed?'

The Ostrich

'Hi,' Caffery says, as if he's just wandered in on Flea in her office. 'Think you've got time for a chat?'

She can't do anything now except respond. Get her big ugly ostrich head out of the sand.

'Yeah.' She stands casually, straightening her jacket and brushing some of the mud from her hands, as if it's the most normal thing in the world to be sitting behind a tree in the middle of nowhere on a freezing-cold night. She gives him a tight, teenage grin and a wave. 'Hi. How're things?'

'Fine. You?'

'Freezing.' She comes out and stands in front of him. Wraps her arms around her — shivers. 'One of the boys left a GPS unit out here today. They're too lazy to come back and get it, so who's the obvious monkey who has to do it?' She makes bunny ears on her head. 'The sergeant — because that's what we're here for. A few extra hundred quid a month in return for taking all the shit, all the responsibility. I'd go back to being a grunt like' — she snaps her fingers — '*that*.'

He nods, silently. His eyes are very dark and very steady. He's not having any of it.

She holds up her hands, to say OK, whatever. 'But how the hell did you find me?' She gestures around at the empty road stretching into the darkness. 'Out in the middle of — ?'

'A guess.'

'A *guess*? You *guessed* I'd be here? Seriously?'

'Yes.'

'Explain.'

He laughs ironically — as if to say, *The explanation is so long, so embroidered and ornate and convoluted it would take a thousand years*. Then his face sobers. 'I ordered the extra search. You know that.'

'Yeah.' She gives a grim smile. Shoves her hands into her pockets. 'Look, I hope this won't come as a surprise to you, Jack, but everyone's thinking WTF about this search — why you ordered it. The only answer we can come up with is you're doing it to keep the press happy.'

He inclines his head in assent. 'You'd be right. There's no new intel — it's to distract them from the attractive prospect of Misty's mum being in town. It's a waste of time. We're not going to find Misty's body. Not here.'

'Aren't we? What makes you so sure?'

There's a pause, then he turns his eyes to hers. He shakes his head. His expression is so serious her confidence curls up and dies.

'*What?*' she murmurs. 'Why're you looking at me like that?'

Again he shakes his head. He looks so sad. So very sad.

'What?'

He shrugs apologetically, then says, 'I know what happened.'

Cider Drinking

The grass in the beer garden is still spotted with rain but the landlord has lit the chimineas and it's warm enough to sit outside. They choose a gnarled old table next to the hedge that divides the garden from the street. The hedge is a dense evergreen laurel, but pedestrians can just be glimpsed passing on the other side.

AJ has lined up four glasses of different ciders on the table between them. Three are almost empty — Melanie is peering thoughtfully into the fourth.

'You can see the bottom, can't you?'

She nods. 'And bubbles.'

'Now, don't take this the wrong way, but if I'm honest I'm going to say this one will appeal to you more than the other three.'

She looks up at him. 'What — because I'm a woman, you mean?'

'It does tend to be more of a lady's cider. Sparklier. Sweeter — sort of golden, isn't it? Appealing to look at. Not enough tannin in it for my taste.'

'In that case . . . ' She pushes it away. Folds her arms petulantly. 'In that case I'm not interested. You drink it.'

'I can't. I can't possibly. I've got a reputation to protect — anyone could wander by and catch me drinking it. That'll be my cred right out of the window.'

'Misogynist.'

'Dungaree wearer. I should have known it when I saw your car — Beetle — dead giveaway.'

'Ewwww.' She wrinkles her nose and peers at him as if he's a cockroach just scuttled out from under the table. 'A fascist.'

He nods happily. 'And the worst sort of fascist. The liberal who got mugged — we make the nastiest conservatives. We're as bad as ex-smokers when we meet a liberal — want to kill them. Attila the Hun was dangerously and irresponsibly liberal.'

She laughs. She's got a sweet laugh. He's surprised he's just said that and wonders if he's half serious. 'I don't really mean that,' he says. 'I'm not really a fascist.'

'I don't care if you are. It's a tough system we work in. It's tough to see the way it's abused.'

'A waste of taxpayers' money. And we're dancing to Brussels' tune most of the time.'

'I know it. And I also know that if I hadn't been a woman I wouldn't have done half as well. I was up against three men for the job — I was maybe as good as two of them, not as good as the other, but what panel member was going to give him the job ahead of me?'

'You're being modest.'

She gives a rueful smile. 'Maybe. I don't know. But I do still care. I do care about them — every last one of them. From Zelda to Moses to Isaac Handel to Monster Mother. I care about them all.'

AJ presses his lips together. He decides not to answer that. Zelda? He's just not going to lie on that issue.

'So.' He changes the subject. 'Have I made you into a cider drinker? Do you like it?'

She beams at him. 'I love it!'

'Another? I'll get you a man's cider this time.'

Her glittering smile doesn't change. 'No thank you. I'll have a vodka.'

'You hate cider, don't you?'

'Yes. I'd puke if I had any more.'

He shakes his head. 'You're so adventurous. Open to new possibilities — flexible.'

'I know. Make the voddy a double.'

AJ gets the drinks. When he sets them on the table he finds he can't keep up the humour.

'What is it?' Melanie says. 'Has something happened?'

'No,' he says. 'Nothing.'

'Then what?'

'Nothing.'

'Don't tell me nothing. It's a lie. And I'm your boss.'

AJ's trapped. He can't say what he's really thinking — it would be the cider talking — so he says the first thing that pops into his head that sounds vaguely funny. 'Oh, you know. Just I found my first grey pube today. Forty-three and already I've got grey pubes.'

Melanie begins to open her mouth — all ready to answer that comment — then she realizes what he's said and her mouth freezes as if her jaw has seized up. Her eyes open a little wider. AJ's heart sinks. It was meant to be funny but he got it so, so wrong. The first rule of basic human psychology: never assume intimacy and ease too early on. He wants to defend himself, but of course it's too late. Not only could this cost him any chance he might have had with her, she could accuse him of sexual harassment — he could get fired — he could be blacklisted.

But Melanie grins.

'What?'

'That,' she says, 'is the best answer I've ever heard.'

'Is it?'

'Yes. Is it true? Because I've had two since I was thirty-six. They glint at me in the bathroom mirror every time I have a shower. Sometimes I think they're mocking me.'

Usually AJ can come back with something, but now he hasn't a clue. For four years he's thought Melanie was off limits — that she was too serious and strait-laced ever to be interested in him. But, in the last twenty-four hours, he's learned she's completely different outside the unit — a natural, lovely human being with problems like the rest of the world. She's struggling with her job, she likes a drink, she's been having an affair with someone she shouldn't, and she's got two grey pubic hairs. Which glint when she gets out of the shower.

He wishes she hadn't said anything about the pubes and getting out of the shower. Too much — too much. He does that thing old-fashioned guys do when they're nervous. He slides a finger into his collar and moves it side to side as if he's struggling with his Adam's apple.

'Anyway,' she says, 'you're lying. I can tell from looking at you it's not true.'

'Well, OK. It's not true.'

'Good.'

'Actually, I noticed them two weeks ago.'

She shakes her head and smiles. 'I mean you're not worried about pubic hairs. It's more than that.'

He feels defeated. And tired. He blinks. 'OK, I'll tell you the truth. I'm just thinking about what happened — remember our misunderstanding at that party?'

'I do. And I don't think it was a misunderstanding.'

He lowers his chin. 'I didn't misunderstand you?'

'No. I flirted with you. I was single — I'd just got divorced. I was on the lookout.'

'And,' he says slowly, putting the pieces together, 'by the time I came back and asked you, you were — ?'

'With Jonathan.'

'With Jonathan,' he echoes, thinking, What a twat, what a lame wanker he's been. He puts his head in his hands and groans. 'I can't believe it. You mean, all this time — all this time, you and I could have been . . . ?'

She smiles a little shyly, holding his eyes. And then she gets half to her feet, puts her hands on the table, leans across and kisses him full on the mouth.

Hit and Run

Flea's face is drained and white — as if all the moonlight is bouncing off it. Her eyes are locked on Caffery's.

'*You what?*' she murmurs. '*What did you say?* Say it again.'

He stands in the hollow night and repeats it — almost guiltily. 'I know what happened to Misty. I know what happened and where. It was here. On this stretch of road.'

Flea stares at him, incredulous. He imagines he can see a little buzz of light zipping round behind her eyes — the evidence of her brain working, formulating an answer. But she ducks the question — lowers her face, shrugs and says offhandedly, 'Yeah, well, I don't know what you're talking about. Seriously — I have absolutely no *idea* what you're talking about. I mean, you're more insane than I ever suspected — and that's saying something.'

She begins to gather up her rucksack. She hikes it on to her shoulder and turns away, in the direction of the car.

'Frankly, Jack, I can hear the sounds of someone losing the plot, and I don't have to hang around to . . . Hey!' She stops. He's grabbed the dangling strap of the rucksack. 'Let go!' She struggles with him, leaning back and pulling on the bag. He holds on tight. 'What're you doing — let it *go*.'

He answers her pull — using two hands. She's strong — surprisingly strong — it takes all his effort to keep the bag level. 'Stop this,' he says. 'Stop this and sit down. I know what's going on — now keep still and listen to me. I know what he did.'

'What *who* did? WHO WHO WHO? And WHAT WHAT WHAT? WHO did WHAT? See?' She yanks the bag. 'You can't even answer. You can't even answer me when I — '

'Thom,' he yells. 'Thom, your *fucking* brother.'

The breath goes out of her. She stops shouting, stops pulling, and stands there — glaring at him, head jutting forward, sinews on her neck standing up.

'I know what happened. The whole thing. Get used to it.'

A long moment passes. Somewhere, on a distant, invisible jet stream in the west, a plane changes course. Whines high and thin and lonely. Flea's eyes glisten. And then, just when he thinks she's going to spit at him, she releases the bag and sinks to the ground. Bone-weary — she drops her head between her knees, clasps her hands around the back of her neck.

He stands a pace away, breathing hard. More than three years ago Flea Marley lost her parents in a horrific diving accident. Since then other things have gone wrong in her life — badly wrong, she hasn't had it easy. Because of that he's protected her role in Misty's disappearance. But enough time has elapsed. Now it's time for Flea to return the favour and help him. When he imagined this encounter he'd half imagined she'd be so grateful to him that she'd cry, throw her arms around his neck or something. He certainly didn't anticipate this. But then, when someone's kept something like this inside for so long it's crazy to expect it to be a painless operation.

He calms himself, pushes the hair off his forehead. He takes five paces, stops in the centre of the road and twists round.

'OK,' he says. 'I'm going to give you a demonstration. A lesson. About hit and runs.'

She lifts her face, bewildered. Her eyes focus hazily on him.

'A car comes from this direction.' He points off to the east, away into the distance. 'It's a silver Ford Focus and it's going fast. Too fast. The driver — Thom — is drunk. He thinks it's an open road, a straight road. At the same time a woman is coming down from that field over there. She's drunk too — and high on heroin she's smuggled into the clinic. She's disorientated. She gets to the road, and either she doesn't realize it's a road and walks into it without looking, or she knows it's a road and she steps out deliberately, trying to flag down the car. Wanting a lift maybe. Either way, Thom doesn't notice her until he gets here.'

Caffery digs a finger down to indicate the place he stands.

'He slams on the brakes, but he's going so fast that he doesn't stop until he reaches . . . ' Caffery takes fifteen strides along the road, then stops and opens his hands ' . . . here. Too late.

Misty goes up over the roof and ends up — well, right about where you're sitting.' He pauses. There's a long silence, interrupted by an owl screeching somewhere above the hamlet. He clears his throat, embarrassed. 'Anyway, Thom doesn't report it. Somehow he gets the body away from here. And you, Flea, *you*, in your infinite wisdom, you protect your brother. You cover the whole thing up for him.'

He stops. She is getting to her feet. She's a little unsteady, still disorientated and shaky. But she keeps her balance. She drags her bag up, hoists it on to her shoulder. She turns on one heel and walks stiffly away. After a few seconds he follows, only he's left it too long. By the time he rounds the corner she has broken into a jog and is almost at the car. Before he can catch up she has jumped inside, started the engine and is screeching off into the road.

He puts out a hand to stop her, but she executes a tight U-turn, guns the engine and within a few short seconds is gone. Then it's just him and the night — the whiff of exhaust and burnt rubber like a handprint in the air.

Strawberries and Marshmallow

They end up taking a taxi to her house, which turns out to be not a million miles from his — but quite different. Melanie lives in a very sparkly, clean new-build three-bed maisonette on the outskirts of Stroud. She has an overrun garden which, she explains to AJ, she doesn't have time to venture into, a view of the surrounding hills on one side and a view of the city lights on the other. There's no driftwood furniture — in fact she doesn't have any discernible style. It's clean and straightforward and not as perfect and grown-up as he thought it would be.

She pours more drinks — vodka and orange — but they sit untouched on the glass coffee table while he and Melanie get down to some heavier kissing on the sofa. AJ is lost, his head turning crazily. She is soft and smooth and silky. She smells of all the things he imagined she'd smell of: strawberries and lemon and marshmallow. And she is making up for lost time — devouring him — holding him by both ears and pulling his mouth hard on to hers. He runs a finger down her spine — feels the soft nub of her bra fastening between her spine and blouse.

'Mmmmmmm,' she murmurs, not resisting him at all. 'Nice . . . '

'Melanie . . . ' He has to pull away from her. He puts both feet on the floor, elbows on his knees, head dropped. His thoughts are racing.

There's a pause, then she sits up. Pushes her hair back. 'AJ? What is it?'

'It's been a long time. That's all.'

'Well . . . ' She gives a small, nervous giggle. 'That's OK, isn't it?'

'No, I . . . '

'Oh no — ' She clamps her hands over her mouth. 'You're gay.'

'I'm not gay.'

'You're impotent.'

'No! No — none of that. I'm just . . . ' He swallows. Rubs his hands hard across his face, trying to bring a little sobriety into the equation. 'I'm . . . ' He turns and looks at her. Her make-up is all smudged. 'Christ, you're so fucking fanciable.'

'Am I?'

'God yes.'

'Then . . . ?'

He sighs. 'Don't freak out when I tell you — it puts some girls off.'

'OK,' she says cautiously. 'Hit me with it. HIV? Herpes?'

'No. Worse. I'm old-fashioned.'

'Old-fashioned? In what way? Kinky? Or sensitive?'

'Not kinky.'

'Sensitive then? And that puts women off?'

'Can I explain?'

'I'm sorry. I won't interrupt.'

'OK — three years ago I was with this girl, this woman — '

'You're still in love with her?'
'Are you going to let me talk?'
'I'm sorry.'
'OK — the answer's no. I definitely am not in love with her and I definitely *wasn't* at the time. In fact, I can't even remember her name. But that was sort of common for me in those days.'
'Racy.'
'Yes — racy — but kind of pathetic and empty. So I'm in bed with this nameless, faceless girl, knowing that after the sex I'll probably pay her cab home then avoid her phone calls, because that's the sort of person I was in those days. Girlfriends came and went. It's afternoon — y'know us shift workers have to get it when we can — and my mum's out in the garden.'
'You live with your mother?'
'Yes — I mean, no. It's not like it sounds. It was good the way it was. Anyway, I'm in the bedroom and mum's outside and . . . ' He trails off. He still doesn't quite get this part right when he tells it to people — it never comes out as smoothly as he wants. 'And Mum had a convulsion — she used to from time to time. Epilepsy. I used to take her to the neurology clinic at Frenchay to keep her medication checked — they said it was under control, except, no, the drugs weren't working. So she's having this convulsion and as she's going down she hits a rock in the garden.' He taps his temple. 'Here.'
'Nasty.' Melanie sucks in a breath. 'One of the worst places.'
'She'd have survived if she'd been taken to

hospital. But I'm so engrossed in what's happening on the end of my dick that I'm not thinking about my mother. I can hear my dog barking outside, but I ignore it. There's no one else at home and so Mum lies out there. There's a bleed on her brain and before you know it . . . '

'Christ. Christ.'

'I know . . . Christ.'

A long dulling silence comes down on them as they both go over this in their heads, Melanie maybe trying to picture it more clearly and AJ trying to picture it less clearly. Then, after what seems like for ever, she rests a tentative hand on his back. 'Look, if it helps at all, my dad died — he had brain cancer, so I learned a bit about the brain. I used to go with him when he went for radiology. So you and I? We've got something in common.'

AJ remembers the radiology department — he used to walk past it with Mum. All the living dead, their perspex radiology masks in their hands, waiting to have their heads blasted. So her dad too? He feels stupid. 'I'm sorry. I know I'm not the only one — I'm being selfish.'

'No no! You're not. Not at all — I completely get it, I promise. And I get the guilt thing too. But listen — let's picture this: you're at work when it happens. Or at the shops, or at the pub . . . '

'I know, I know all that — I know the logic — and I know the reality. I'm not saying I'm a born-again Christian or anything, but it's made me a bit more . . . serious. Grown-up? That zip-up-and-move-on stuff? I just don't do it any more. And it turns out that is the biggest turn-off for lots of girls. Turns out women are more ruthless than men when it comes to sex.'

'Sluts,' she says, her eyes hooded. 'What awful, shallow little sluts.'

He gives a sad laugh. 'Yeah, well. I dunno why I had to come out with that speech now, I just did. That's what I mean: I'm old-fashioned.'

'Well, thank God for that.' She stands and pushes him back on the sofa. Straddles him with both legs. 'I thought you were going to tell me you couldn't get it up.'

Under the Flyover

Life has just taken exactly the slow, unstoppable flip of fortune Caffery hoped it wouldn't. He's got it wrong — so wrong it is spectacular. He imagined Flea would at least recognize what it's cost him to keep her secret, if not actually thank him and call him a hero. But life has a way of not behaving. And anyway, saints and heroes aren't in the spectrum of colours Caffery plays. He has to look at things afresh.

He drives back to the offices slowly, through the streets of Bristol, where the last wave of drinkers are trailing home. This town was built on the slave trade — all the spindly town houses grown up from the money of that trade, unabashed by their finery. He's tired. He's hungry and he wants a drink. He holds his pass to the automatic barrier and slides into the car park. The place is almost empty, just one or two Scientific Investigations vans and a scatter of vehicles belonging to civilian staff. He parks under the flyover, nose into the railway line, pulls on the handbrake. He's about to get out when he senses he's not alone here. There's someone else.

It's Flea. Sitting in her Renault four lanes away, half concealed behind the green shipping storage container that sits amongst bushes in the middle of the car park.

He gets out of his car, pulling on his jacket. He clicks closed his door and stands for a moment. Her silhouette doesn't move. He approaches the Renault and tries the door — it's open. He knows he's supposed to get in, so that is what he does, no apologies or pretence. She is sitting with her elbows on the steering wheel, her face in her hands. She's still wearing the waterproofs. Just the curve of her ear is visible, peeking out from her tangled hair.

It smells in here of the polyurethane bags the support group use to carry their kits, and a faint, feminine perfume. Shampoo or body lotion. He waits.

'OK,' she says eventually. 'OK,' she says, not looking up at him. 'I don't think I have ever felt so ashamed in my life.'

'You were protecting your brother. For some reason.'

'Yes.' She lets a small silence elapse. She taps her fingers on her forehead. 'Will you tell me how you found out?'

'Someone saw the accident.'

'Someone who is . . . ? You?'

'No.'

'Then?'

'My friend.'

A pause. He thinks she's going to turn to him, but she doesn't. 'Your friend?'

'Yes.' Caffery considers the word 'friend'. The old vagrant who saw Thom hit Misty? Is he strictly a friend? Caffery doesn't know for sure. He gives a small cough. 'He's no one you need to worry about. I promise.'

'You promise? And you tell the truth? Always?'

'Not always. But in this case, yes. Trust me.'

'I don't think I've got a choice.' She taps a little harder. 'Next question — how long have you known?'

'A year and a half. Give or take.'

'And why haven't you said anything?'

'Some days I ask myself the same question.'

'But you've said something now.'

'I've been waiting for you to recuperate — from the accident. And suddenly I've got sharks snapping at me.'

'We all have sharks.'

'Yes. But I'm tired of mine. And I need you to help me get rid of mine. See, though I don't know how Thom talked you into it, I *do* know what you did with the body.'

Her fingers stop tapping. She tilts her face sideways and one eye appears. It is smudged with the remnants of mascara. It blinks. 'Say that again.'

'I saw you, Flea. I saw what you did. Elf's Grotto. The quarry. I saw you putting the body in the water.'

She raises her face and stares at him, her mouth a little open. He can almost feel the heat of her brain labouring, the glucose it is eating up to get all the information into the right slots. Absorbing that comment.

'It's true. I'm sorry.'

Her mouth moves soundlessly. Then she drops her head, shakes it. 'I can't believe this,' she says. 'You know *everything*? You've known *all* about me, *all* about Thom and you've known *all* this time. And you've kept it a secret? *Why?*'

'I don't know. Maybe the same reason you covered for Thom.'

She starts to answer, but seems to think better of it. She presses the heels of her hands into her eyes, as if she's trying to blot an image out. She's small and delicate compared to the men in her unit — it's difficult to picture what she did with the body. If he hadn't witnessed it, hiding himself in the darkness, he wouldn't have believed it was possible. But it happened. He's checked the quarry schematics and worked out that Misty could be almost sixty metres underwater at the bottom of the quarry. The thought makes him cold — the quarry is one of the nastiest, freakiest places he's ever been. Isolated, disused and flooded, it's got a mean, supernatural drag to it. A suicide mecca — he's lost count of the number of people who've ended their lives there. Sometimes the body has come back, sometimes not.

'If they ever drained that place,' he says, 'it would be like wading into hell.'

'Yes. But if they did, they still wouldn't find Misty.'

'I'm sorry?'

'She's not at the bottom of the quarry.'

Caffery lowers his chin and scrutinizes her. This doesn't click with what he saw. Not at all. 'You took her into the quarry. I saw you — you did *something* with her.'

'Yeah — I did something. Certainly I did something.' Flea pulls her jacket tight around her, sniffs. 'Are you going to tell anyone?'

'No.'

'Then why the search? You ordered it — you must be doing it for a reason.'

'Yes. I've got a . . . a way for us to sort it all — make it go away. I've thought about it from every single angle. It can't go wrong.'

'Nothing can go wrong now if we leave it as it is. She'll never be found. I might be ashamed but I can at least sleep easy at night.'

Caffery stares out of the window. The rust stains on the flyover struts, the flickering of headlights on the highway up there. He feels a weight of water — a million tonnes of it. A freezing black quarry, a giant ice heart. He doesn't believe Flea when she says she sleeps easy at night.

'I need her remains back.'

A sharp intake of breath. She turns and stares at him. 'I'm sorry. Did you just say what I think you just said?'

'For it to work, I need whatever is left of her. I can't do that — only you can. And . . . ' He trails off. Her eyes are so frozen with shock he knows he's gone too far. He's going to lose her. He gives a small, embarrassed cough. 'Tell you what — I'm going to leave this now. Let you sleep on it.'

She doesn't answer. Just continues staring.

'Are you going to be all right?'

She gives him a tight, barely controlled nod. 'Yes. Yes.'

'Do you want some coffee? A drink?'

'No thank you. I think I'd better go home.'

'OK,' he says. 'OK.'

He waits for a little longer, wondering whether to say anything else, but when she doesn't speak or move he gets out. Zips up his jacket. He watches her start the engine and swing the Renault out of the car park. It pulls out into the feeder road and soon is swallowed up amongst the buildings. He waits for almost five minutes before he realizes she's not going to come back.

He turns his collar up and heads back to the offices.

Frost

AJ dreams about the cave again. And this time there's a woman there too. She is standing at the entrance to the cave, but her face is turned away. He thinks it's Melanie. He calls her, but she doesn't respond. *Melanie?* This time she stirs a little, but just as it seems she's going to turn, the dream dies and crumbles. He wakes, reaching into the cold air.

It takes him a moment or two to remember he's in Melanie's bedroom in Stroud. And then he realizes she's awake too — sitting next to him. The curtains are open and the moonlight streams through the window, lighting her blue and almost supernatural.

She is bathed in sweat, staring in disbelief at the window.

'Melanie?' He props himself up on his elbows. 'Melanie? What's up?'

She points at the window in a trance. He can't tell if she's awake or asleep. 'It was wearing a — ' She bites the sentence in half. Shakes her head and holds her knuckles up to her forehead. 'No. I didn't see anything.'

'Melanie?' He puts his hand on her back, leans forward a little to get a view out of the window. He sees the trees beyond the garden moving slightly in the moonlight. 'What do you think you saw?'

'Nothing. I was . . . I don't know.' She gives a

long shudder. 'I must have been dreaming.'

'Yes, but what do you *think* you saw?'

'Nothing. Nothing at all — I just — '

'Just?'

She swings her legs out of bed, grabs a pillow to hold in front of her naked body, and goes to the window. AJ gets out and comes to stand next to her, looking over her shoulder at the garden. The ground is frosty — and a clear dark slash extends from the treeline to about halfway down the garden. Exactly as if someone has walked into the garden, stopped to look up at the bedroom window, then turned and gone back the way they've come.

He snatches up his T-shirt and jeans and begins pulling them on.

'What're you doing?'

'Someone's out there.'

'No — there's no one there. I dreamt it.' She sounds panicked. She is shaking, bewildered. 'AJ — don't go outside — please don't.'

'Have you got a torch?'

'Please. I'm scared now.'

'Have you got a torch?'

'Oh God.' Moving clumsily, she goes to a chest of drawers and rummages through, dropping things in her hurry. She pulls out a torch. It's big and reassuringly heavy. He weighs it steadily in both hands.

'That'll do.'

He goes down the stairs. She comes trotting behind him, pulling on a kimono. 'There's no one there — there can't be, please stay in here with me.'

The back door is closed and when he tries it he finds it's unlocked.

'Shit,' she hisses, tying the belt of the kimono. 'I forget to lock it — I never think about it. This is such a safe area.' She cranes her neck to see past him into the garden. 'Don't go out — please. Don't leave me.'

'Put some shoes on.'

She obeys, jamming her feet into wellingtons. He pulls on his shoes — no socks — and together they step outside, closing the door behind them with a soft click.

It's very quiet. Distant traffic sounds from the town float over the roof from behind them, but from the direction of the garden is nothing but the slight rustle of wind in the branches. They stand on the doorstep, listening to the night, hardly breathing. Overhead a security light has come on, but it isn't strong enough to reach the front of the garden.

AJ switches on the torch. It's got a strong beam that illuminates the trees down there.

'There's no fence,' Melanie whispers. 'The builders walked off site — never finished the garden.'

Nothing in the trees is moving — there's no eye gleam, nothing suspicious. AJ runs the beam into the grass. He takes a few steps into the garden — the frosty ground crunches underfoot. He stops at the place the dark slash from the woods finishes and shines the torch at his feet. Nothing. He's not a tracker — some Navajo or scout — he's only pretending to know what he's looking for. A ghostly blur on his imagination

— a nightgown and a patter of small feet. More likely an animal. He thinks about the muntjac that wander from the forests through Patience's lettuce rows. Better to fix that in his thoughts than anything else.

'Anyone there?' he calls into the trees. 'Something you want?'

Silence.

'Let's go inside,' Melanie hisses. She's trembling now. 'I want to go back in.'

AJ stands a few minutes more — trying to put some width into his silhouette. It's probably nothing, but if there is someone wandering around in the trees he wants them to know there's a man here. But there's still no sound. Eventually he switches off the torch and silently re-enters the house. Melanie locks and bolts the door. They check all the windows, then, shivering and cold, they go back to bed.

They lie together trying to get warm, but Melanie is strange. She turns away from him and although she is silent he knows, without looking at her, that she's wide awake, not likely to go to sleep. 'Hey,' he whispers. 'What did you see? What did you think it was?'

She shakes her head. 'I didn't see anything. I was dreaming.'

'What did you dream?'

'I don't even remember now. Something — stupid.'

They lapse into silence. A long time passes and AJ is just falling off to sleep again when Melanie says suddenly, 'AJ?'

'Mmmmm?'

'Do you believe that if you worry about something long enough you can make yourself dream about it? Or even hallucinate it?'

'Of course. I'd say it's very likely. What were you worrying about so much that you dreamt about it?'

She shrugs. 'I don't know — can't remember.' She gives a big fake yawn. 'Night night, AJ. Night night.'

Someone Must Know Something

Flea gets to bed at two but doesn't sleep until four. She leaves the TV on for company, playing silently in the corner. It's a bad night; she turns and fidgets and cannot get comfortable. From time to time she half wakes — thinking someone has walked into the room. Sometimes it's her parents, sometimes it's Jack Caffery. Once she sits up straight and sees, reflected in the TV screen, a skull — half woman, half horse, the teeth long in the front, gums drawn up. Her hair is blonde and her eye sockets are empty.

Misty? she says.

Yeah, hi, what? she says. *Have you got a couple of wraps for me, or is that too much to ask? And why did you put me there? They'll find me — he'll find me if you don't do it for him.*

Flea reaches out her hand, but the face dissolves and she's lying on her bed, her heart carumph-carumphing along in her chest. She stares at the TV, still working away in silence. Fake tans and strutting, angry women in big heels. A woman appears, perched, solemn-faced, on a blue sofa. Short skirt, tanned knees together, turned demurely to face the presenter, who has adopted a serious, sympathetic expression. Flea fumbles for the remote. Turns the volume up.

' . . . someone must know something,' says Jacqui Kitson. 'Someone must know where she is . . . '

Flea hits the off button. The TV whines and dies. She rests her elbows on her knees, uses her thumbs to massage her temples. Did last night really happen? Really and truly? Jack says he saw her at the quarry. It has to be true. There's no other way he could have known.

Outside the window the breaking sun creeps up the long scrape of the valley. The lights of the city of Bath wink out one by one. The city is slowly raising itself out of the monochrome mist. She drags herself out of bed, pads to the bathroom, along the corridor with its wonky floors. On the left is the room where she stores the cardboard boxes that have been taped down. This straggly old house is home — the place she grew up. Mum and Dad are dead — a scuba-diving accident years ago — and the house is so empty without them. A shell. Recently she's finally got round to packing away their belongings. All part of her healing process — a kind of fartlekking for the spirit. The way she can go on flying.

She cleans her teeth, splashes her face and gets straight into her running gear, sitting on the edge of the bath to lace the trainers. She can't do what Caffery wants — because it means opening boxed thoughts that have been packed away as neatly as the crates in the other room — stored in the dark edges of her memory. She's got to keep herself together. If she thinks about it, or lets it in, it's going to cut her down at the knees.

Reduce her to nothing. And that will do no one any good. Not her, not Caffery. Not Jacqui Kitson.

She jumps up, trots fiercely down the stairs.

You can put things back in a box. Yes, from time to time they might pop out and wriggle, but you can make them go back if you try hard enough. The idea is to keep moving. Don't look down. She gets her running jacket and her keys from the hook. Opens the door to the freezing mist.

The Bracelet

The next morning Melanie and AJ make an unspoken pact to brush off what happened in the night. To make light of it. She cracks a bad joke about ghosts. He gives a small laugh, ricochets a joke back — something about stalkers, and about how she's going to turn into one of the patients and wander around with dinner down her clothes and drool coming uncontrollably out of her mouth. She tickles him, and swooshes her hair over his chest. He makes play grabs for her breasts, and she curls up, squealing with laughter.

They make love with the curtains wide open. The bare branches in the forest at the bottom of the garden are frosted and motionless. Afterwards she lies on her front, her head resting on her arms, and talks.

It turns out Melanie has her own bundle of sensitivities and inadequacies. It's not only about losing her dad, it's more a case of the girl losing the guy from her dedication to the job. In the fallout from the Thatcher Years Melanie's unit in Gloucester got closed and she was moved around the country. She fetched up in Rotherham, where she climbed the ranks to ward manager, then director. Five years ago the hospital closed and she and Jonathan Keay both relocated to Beechway. In those days Keay and Melanie were just friends; in fact, she was married to someone else, a tax lawyer from Oldham. The marriage lasted ten months into her time at Beechway — roughly the time AJ arrived at the unit — when her husband decided she was more dedicated to the unit than to cooking for him and filed for divorce.

'So this was at about the time of our party encounter?'

'Uh huh,' she murmurs into the crook of her arm. 'The divorce nearly killed me. That night was the first night of me trying to bounce back.'

'Shit. Why didn't I step up to the plate?'

'I don't know. Why didn't you?'

He gives a sorrowful laugh. 'I think you know that. We talked about it last night. You didn't seem like the sort of woman who'd be interested in the dating world according to AJ.'

It's difficult for AJ to accept what he's been missing all these years, but he also understands that he was a different person back then. He wasn't like Jonathan Keay — who was canny and confident enough to pick up the baton he'd dropped. Keay and Melanie kept the affair from anyone in the unit secret for a long time. It was almost four years before he walked away.

'It took him that long to work out I wasn't going to quit, I wasn't going to give up looking after the clients and stay at home baking him cakes. Mind you,' she says thoughtfully, 'I might have been through hell but at least I'm losing weight for the first time in living memory. So maybe it's not all bad — silver linings, etcetera, etcetera.'

Melanie is getting more and more human by the second — coming more and more into focus for AJ. He is amazed by how relaxed he is in her company. It's like they've been doing this for ever — chit-chatting about their pasts. Admitting their flaws.

They drink coffee together and eat toast, which she has burnt. A muntjac stalks through the frosty grass in the garden, and AJ watches silently, thinking it could have been a muntjac last night. Maybe. And if it *was*, then isn't it a kind of benediction? Like a little of his countryside creeping all this way into town as if to say, It's right. It's perfectly right. The bewildered exhaustion he's felt all week has evaporated like Scotch mist and instead he's wildly invigorated — as if this is the first day on Earth. The first sunshine, the first blue sky, the first bed, pillow, carpet, window known to man.

He has so much energy that he finds himself doing a few DIY jobs around the house as Melanie gets ready for work. As if he owns the place already. A broken handle in the kitchen and the panel of the bath has come loose, so now he's fixing that — feeling like the first guy on Earth — muscled and worthy, as if he's got those black-guy footballer's legs he always wanted. He lies on the floor in his boxers and T-shirt, trying to make Melanie's girlie pink-handled toolset do something useful other than look cute. Meanwhile Melanie is in the bedroom putting on make-up — also looking very cute. She's wearing a short pink kimono in satin that would be cheap on anyone else. On her it's stunning.

'What?' she says, catching him looking at her. She opens her arms and looks down at herself to check the kimono isn't showing anything. That's the funny thing about women — they let you do all sorts of incredible things to their bodies then they'll suddenly, out of nowhere, get self-conscious. 'Am I fat?'

'Huge. I wonder how you live with yourself.'

'What?' she says, panicked. In fact she's got a tiny tummy on her, just one little roll of fat which he thinks is unbelievably sexy. She spent a lot of last night worrying about that roll of flesh, putting her hands over it, pleading, 'Don't look at me — please don't.' 'Seriously?' she says. 'What can you see?'

'Melanie — it's nothing. I'm looking at you, and if you want the truth, I'm not thinking about your thinness but about how much I'd like to fuck you again.'

She relaxes at that. Gives a giggle, a wave of the hand. 'Oh, honestly.'

'I'm serious.'

Her face colours, she opens her mouth — seriously considering this option — then seems to remember work. She checks her watch. 'Awwww, AJ . . . ?'

'Tonight then? After work?'

'I can't see why not.'

'It's a deal.'

He goes back to wrestling with the bath panel. It's not that straightforward — one of the screws looks as if it's been forcibly pulled out — ripping at the fibreglass. He wonders how it happened — it's sort of violent, he thinks. Jonathan Keay's face comes into his head. He's surprised Jonathan didn't get busy around Melanie's house. Maybe he wasn't much of a DIY guy.

'That's strange.'

He stops what he's doing and squashes his chin down so he can see Melanie in the bedroom. She's got her handbag open on her lap and is frowning. Puzzled.

'What's strange?'

She glances up at him. 'I don't know. My bracelet. It was in here. It's gone.'

'Bracelet?'

'Yes, I . . . ' She rummages in the bag. 'I put it in here yesterday morning — I took it off at work — didn't want it to draw attention to this.' Grimly she raises her bandaged hand. 'Thought it would make everyone stare more.'

'What sort of bracelet?'

'It's a little thing, just a little thing. Jonathan gave it to me.'

He shuffles out from the bath and props himself up on his elbows so he can see her properly. She is genuinely anxious, hurriedly pulling things out of her bag. 'Damn,' she says. 'Damn.'

She catches him watching and stops. She composes herself and gives him a weak smile. 'Oh well.' She rubs the back of her neck wearily — as if to say this is all to be expected. 'It wasn't worth anything. Nothing at all.'

AJ thinks she's lying. He thinks the bracelet wasn't 'nothing at all' to her. He thinks it meant a lot. An unexpected spasm of jealousy gets him. He has to swallow it down. He shuffles back half under the bath and carries on fixing the panel.

Zelda's Locker

One of Beechway's long-term residents was discharged yesterday — and ordinarily that change in dynamic would have made the remaining patients unsettled. But today, if anything, the opposite seems to happen. In fact the unit seems far calmer than it has for months. There are no alarms going off, no crises, no ambulances, no threats or tears or episodes of incontinence. The unit drifts in a dreamless state of tranquillity.

AJ's office is so different in the daylight. He can't understand why he hadn't wanted to stay here the other night. What's to be nervous of? Darkness brings fear — the most basic human instinct. Was it the same fear that conjured the track in Melanie's garden last night? No — the track was there. They didn't imagine it. It's just that the atmosphere in the unit — all the crazy ideas and rumours — has made his and Mel's imaginations work overtime.

He tries to find the maintenance records for when Moses spooned out his eye, but Melanie is right: they've either been destroyed or buried so deep in the great bureaucratic engine that they won't be found again. Some of the paperwork associated with Zelda's death is in his office — so he turns his attention to that. There are forms to be filled in, letters to be written, her belongings to be dealt with, and when her body is released by the coroner the unit is going to have to make a show of involvement with funeral arrangements. Probably Melanie will attend the service, out of respect. AJ could accompany her, but it would be hypocritical — he couldn't stand Zelda. He can't go to her funeral and act sad for her family.

There's a folder on his desk containing all Zelda's rehabilitation papers. The in-house social workers have left it here with a note: *Found this in Zelda's therapy centre locker. Does it need to go to the inquiry team? Family? If not please destroy — no further use*. He leafs idly through it: endless tasks she's been set, including theoretical CVs for theoretical jobs. Lists of things she thinks she has to offer the world (she has written: *attractive, a peoples person, always ready to lissen*). Recipes she's copied from the Web, artwork, drafts of complaint letters detailing marauding patients, staff and demons raping her every night. One is to Barack Obama. AJ shakes his head. He imagines the White House having a dedicated team to deal with the crank mail — men in suits and Brooks College girls, like in *The West Wing*.

AJ is about to drop the lot into the bin when something about one of Zelda's paintings makes him stop. He sits back in the chair with the folder on his lap and unfolds the huge picture on the desk. In his experience, artwork produced by the mentally ill is either highly intricate — obsessively so (people constructing the London skyline inside a perfume bottle sort of thing) — or numbingly childlike.

Zelda's work falls into the second category. It's the kind of thing a year-four primary-school student would be proud of. There are crudely drawn horses ridden by something that is possibly meant to be Heathcliff thundering across the moors, but could be Dracula too. What's drawn AJ's eye is something in the top corner. It appears to be a second figure, watching the scene from a distant mountain. It is mostly human in form, except for the face, which is eerily smooth and featureless. It is wearing a white dress. It has hair that bushes out to the sides, and the arms are striped orange and brown. In both hands it's clutching what appear to be small puppets.

AJ drops the paper hurriedly. He stands up quickly and walks two or three paces up and down the office, wiping his hands, shooting uneasy glances at the drawing. Eventually he pulls the reading lamp across the desk and studies it more carefully. Now he sees that Heathcliff resembles Dracula because his tongue has been drawn bright red and swollen in his mouth. His arms are bleeding. AJ drags his eyes back to the gnome-like figure on the horizon. Squatting? Or simply small? Like a dwarf. Anyone who has ever described The Maude has said it has a smooth, almost featureless face.

He's angry with it all. Just as his mood was getting good, just as he was hoping to stop thinking about The Maude, *this* has to come along.

Peach Stone Cave

The room is small and low-ceilinged. Its walls are like a polished peach stone, the floor is soft underfoot. It smells of pine and it is dark — so dark that Penny should be afraid. But she never is. She is sure that this blackness will pass, and that somewhere in this tiny cramped place is a doorway, a wormhole that leads to something greater. She feels around blindly, certain the entrance is hereabouts. Sometimes in the dream she imagines she's searching for a cork lodged in the wall which needs unstoppering. Sometimes it's a small doorway leading to a minuscule passageway that she will be able to squeeze into. Other times it's a plug on a chain. Tugging at the chain will open the hole — it will ignite stars and suns and whole solar systems.

The dream always fizzles and dies at the moment she believes she is about to find the gateway. The image peels away, winds race by, and then it's just plain Penny — lying on her back, blinking at the ceiling in her bedroom at the Old Mill. Her heart thumping loudly.

Instinctively she puts her hand out, reaching for Suki on the other side of the bed. And then she remembers. Ah yes. That part of her life is over. All gone. She lets her hand trail across the quilt, sure there is a faint warmth — as if something living has been there. But it's her wishful thinking. Her ghost dog.

Again she notices how ragtag the quilt is. There's a piece missing, she sees — a piece from a dress she used to wear — she remembers it well: a purple, flower-sprigged design with twined leaves. Bell sleeves and an asymmetrical hem. The piece has come unstitched and disappeared. It makes her think of a boy — a boy she knew years and years ago. He used to steal people's clothes. Tiny scraps: a snip of a blouse here, a thread from a coat there. Poor boy. Poor sick boy. So dangerous and so sad. Penny puts the quilt down and gets out of bed. There's no time for self-pity — no time to mourn and complain, to cry and regret. This is her busiest time of year, and after two days of nursing Suki the work has piled up.

She throws open the shutters, quickly showers, dresses and pads down the stairs to the ground floor. Her business, Forager's Fayre — which has been going since before the divorce, before the affair with Graham — operates from this floor. There are two huge industrial cookers at the far end and the brick walls are covered with shelves on which are stacked the tools of her trade. Jam jars, chutney jars, boxes of labels, files containing details of all her customers. The mill was built in the early nineteenth century when the area was thriving on the profits from the wool industry — there's a whole additional lower storey that has never been modernized; the stream racing down there was harnessed to drive the mill, wash the fleece. She could expand into it, but Forager's Fayre has worn itself into a comfortable groove in this room. She hasn't the energy or the desire to make it bigger.

Breakfast is a hunk of bread dipped into the cooled, jellied froth she skims from the tops of her jam vats. Most people throw it away; she saves it in little earthenware bowls in the fridge. Things in this house get reused, recycled.

She goes into the prepping room. Three days ago she took delivery of twenty kilos of medlars. Already semi-bletted, they will need to be turned this morning to rot them thoroughly, ready for jam making. Then there are two dozen straining muslins to be boiled, labels to be printed. She's not in the mood — not without Suki to keep her company. Nevertheless she ties on her apron, fixes her hair up in a cap, and sets to work.

It's the muslins that jolt the memory. She has boiled them and is hanging them out in the drying room when a memory of what happened at Upton Farm comes back to her in such a rush it makes her legs weak. It's something to do with the smell and the distinctive ginger-wine colour on the strainers. She realizes then that this was exactly what she was doing that morning fifteen years ago. The medlars are early this year, just like that year — and that day they were bletting in the drying room, just like they are now. There were muslin strainers hanging out to dry too. It's the stained cotton and the whispery scent of iron that gets to her. Like dried blood.

She has to go back into the kitchen. She stands there in shock, conscious of how similar it all is — the jars piled up, the lids, the circular discs of wax paper standing by until it's time to set them on the surface of the jam. In the boot room she can see the steaming mash of seeds she's dumped ready to take to the compost heap. The same sugar and bubbling-syrup smell is in the air.

On a far shelf, in a gap between the stacks of 'Penny's Christmas Chutney' and the 'Four-Lane Forgotten Crab-apple Jelly' is a calendar. She hand-made it one cold December weekend when she'd no orders to fill, no one to see, and nothing better to do — carefully colouring the top panel in the colours of that month, using an old calligraphy pen to hand-letter the days of the week. She crosses to it now and frowns. It's October. October, the month to collect crab apple and sloe. To start her gin infusions. She goes to it, lifts the page and looks at November — just a few days away. The second of November is All Souls'. The day human beings truly understand the pointlessness of their bodies, and recognize where they really exist — in their spirit. The ancient and mystical day of the dead.

It is fifteen years — almost to the day, since Isaac Handel killed his parents.

Isaac Handel

As AJ goes down the corridor towards Melanie's office, Zelda's painting in his hand, it strikes him that maybe it's not just the chill he got from this picture that's driving him, but more his need for an excuse to speak to her. To be in her company. As he climbs the stairs to the mezzanine he's thinking of the way she turned her back to him in bed last night — and how it made him want to protect her. He wonders about Jonathan Keay and his strong arms and whether he protected her. The patients used to call him 'Throw away the key, Keay' for his surly manner. He had an arrogant, upper-class accent, as if he had grown up playing polo. AJ considers whether Keay was ever surly with Melanie. If so, she didn't deserve it.

He knocks, out of decorum, and there is a long pause. Then a groggy 'Yes?'

'It's me.'

'AJ?'

'Yes.'

Another pause. He hears footsteps and the key being turned. It's only now he realizes the door was locked. When she opens it and he sees her face he understands. She's sleep-creased — her hair mussed. She's been catching up. Instantly he wants to kiss her.

'Oh.' She rubs her face. 'I'm sorry. I was . . . '

'I know.' He comes in and closes the door

behind him. 'Hey,' he says, holding out his arms. 'Come here.'

She smiles and falls against his chest. He squeezes her and kisses her on the head. She is so warm and so soft. If he knew the words and had the confidence, he'd propose marriage to her here and now. Just so he could go on smelling her messed-up hair for ever.

'I didn't sleep last night.'

'I know,' he murmurs. 'Me neither. Shall I make you some coffee?'

'Oh God. Yes please.'

Melanie has an annexe to her office with a bathroom and a kitchen area equipped with a microwave, a hob, a sink, a fridge and a state-of-the-art coffee-maker with lots of very bright enamelled cups the size of thimbles. While she goes into the bathroom and splashes her face with water, he makes three cups — two for her and one for him. He knows how she likes her coffee now they've had breakfast together. Strong, black and full of sugar. He thinks it's great she has sugar instead of sweeteners and lots of milk — it's exactly the way Mum and Patience drink their coffee; not American, very European. Melanie might be contained and strict at work, but when it comes to pleasure and passion she gives it free rein.

She goes back to her desk and he brings the cups over. She picks up hers, sips and raises her eyebrows at him. 'So?'

He unrolls Zelda's painting and holds it out. Melanie stares at it for a while, then puts on her glasses and peers at it more closely. Eventually she shakes her head.

'Sorry, no. I'm a *dummkopf*. What am I looking at?'

'Zelda painted it.'

'And? It's Dracula. Or a bat — it's hard to tell.'

'I think it's her running away. And here? See it?'

He puts his finger on the face of the figure on the hillside.

'What about it?'

'It's you-know-what. The M word.'

Melanie peers at the painting. After a while her face falls. She rubs her eyes wearily. 'Oh, AJ, please God, not this again. It's all done and dusted — '

'Is it?'

'Yes. I got a call from the review team this morning. They can't say anything on record, but they gave me the nod things are going to be OK — there won't be any further inquiries. Zelda will be buried with the dignity she deserves and everything will go back to normal. *Normal*.' She emphasizes the word. 'And you showing me this? AJ, seriously, the words 'hornets'' and 'nest' are coming to mind. Also the word 'poke'. Poke in a nonsexual way.'

'Hear me out, please . . . '

She gives a long groan. But she doesn't get up from the desk. She props her head in her hands and rolls her eyes. 'Go on — hit me with it. I'm all ears. The eyes, though? They're a different matter — no control over them. If you think I'm drifting — blame the eyes.'

He sits down opposite her.

'Look at this.' He rests a finger on the figure. 'Doesn't it make you think of anything? Anyone?'

Melanie is silent for a moment, staring at the image. She doesn't dismiss it — she actually is studying it — giving it some thought. 'Yes,' she admits, taking off her glasses. 'OK, yes, it does remind me of someone. It looks like Isaac Handel. It's the pullover — his favourite pullover. And the hair — and his toys, of course.'

'Isaac.' AJ takes a long, controlled breath. 'Exactly. Isaac.'

'He's gone. He was released yesterday.'

AJ nods. He doesn't say anything about the garden last night but he's thinking it. He wonders if she is. 'Melanie — looking back, do you remember him sometimes talking to Zelda?'

'Maybe.'

'Why would she draw him like this?'

'I don't know, AJ. I honestly don't know.'

'Isaac was a patient at the same time that Pauline died — do we know if they spent time together?'

'I can't recall things like that. It was years ago. And aren't we going above and beyond our remit here? Losing Zelda — the whole bureaucratic nest of vipers it's stirred — I thought it was all calming down, tying itself up.'

'Think about it — it's too much of a coincidence — the power cuts, the writing. And Isaac wearing the . . . ' He gestures at the picture, groping for the right words. 'Him painted with this face. Can we call one of those cops — the ones we met at the forum? They deal with stuff like this. We don't have to make it official, just ask to meet them casually and — '

'AJ, *please*.' Melanie covers his hand with hers. '*Please*, I know I'm not perfect, but — just let me be a slob on this? Let it lie, eh? Keep the unit moving in the right direction. No scandal, no police ferreting around. The Trust hates that sort of thing.' She bites her lip, her head on one side. 'Please, AJ. This means a lot to me.'

He is silent. He looks at her fingers on his hand. She loves this unit so much. If he's going to get into the proper world of relationships, these are the things he has to shut up about.

'Something else,' she says, while he's still waging his internal battle. 'I was going to ask, if it's not too rude, whether you had plans for tonight?'

He glances up. She's smiling at him, those clear blue eyes like summer sky. She raises her eyebrows. 'Well?'

It's as if she's flicked a switch, releasing a stream of endorphins that surges through him. He shakes his head, sighs. 'Yeah yeah yeah — OK. I'll need to see to Stewart first though. I'm going to have to walk him — I leave him with Patience too long and he turns into a butter ball.'

'It's a shame you can't bring him to my place. The lease is pretty dogmatic about animals.' She pauses. '*Dogmatic*.'

AJ laughs. She's everything he thought she wasn't — she's funny and sweet and silly and he's falling in love with her. After less than twenty-four hours he's actually toppling over the cliff he never thought he would. 'How about after I've walked him? Say yours at eight?'

'Sounds like a date to me.'

He walks on air out of the office. On the next floor down the Big Lurch happens to be crossing the hallway. AJ hesitates — wondering whether to back up on to the gallery and wait for a moment when he won't be seen, but it's too late. The Big Lurch glances up — sees him, sees his face. Maybe AJ's expression speaks volumes, maybe it's advertising to the world that he wasn't in the director's office on plain business, because there's a pause, during which neither of them seems to know how to react, then a sly, understanding grin creeps over the Big Lurch's face. He goes on his way, his clenched fist held up to AJ, throwing him a gang sign.

He's saying, *Congratulations*. He's saying, *Respect*.

The Plan

The day passes slowly in the grey outdoors. The sky is low and furred. The trees in east Somerset reach down and drop bright wet leaves on to the men and women in black all-weather gear who move painstakingly and agonizingly across the steaming forest floors. It's the Avon and Somerset support group on their second day of deployment to find the remains of Misty Kitson.

At the RV point, the place all the search teams have parked their vehicles, Jack Caffery sits in his car, radio on to some chat show or other, window open to the bracing air. He wears an RAB fleece over his suit and is slowly puffing a V-Cig. He didn't sleep last night — even half a bottle of Scotch couldn't stop his hamster-wheel head shuffling away. Trying to decide how to work this — how to place himself in a flawed scenario he's created. He thought he'd waited long enough for her to get into the place where she'd see the situation. But he hasn't. She's shocked and combative and reluctant; it's up to him to deal with that.

He looks out at the skyline — leafless, spindly trees against a boiled-white sky. There aren't many days left for him to put his long-game into action. To add to the weight, first thing this morning the superintendent was waiting for him at the office, telling him grudgingly he was lucky — no new cases had come in. Reminding him that the moment a job did come up, things would change.

It dawns on Caffery now that the person speaking on the radio is Jacqui Kitson. He clicks out the cigarette cartridge and closes the window, turns the volume up.

'The police are doing everything they can — and I, you know, I want to say I think it's about time too.'

He taps the cartridge on the steering wheel as Jacqui continues.

'Of course I pray my daughter'll still be found alive. Even after all this time, I'm not giving up hope.'

He clicks off the radio. Sits for a minute, head lowered. His mother was a Catholic; she'd say he's committed an original sin. She'd search around for the name to the sin and what had led him to it: cowardice or lust. Not greed. That's one thing she'd never be able to point at him.

Knock knock knock. He jolts up straight. Blinks. Flea is staring through the passenger window at him, her breath fogging the pane. She's still wearing her Tyvek search suit, hood rolled down. He hesitates then leans over and unlocks the door. She opens it, climbs in, and slams the door.

'Right,' she says. 'What's going on?'

'Going on?'

'We searched the road once and now the POLSA is saying we've got to do it again. You've directed that, haven't you?'

'I had to make sure you hadn't missed anything.'

'Bullshit. It's the only place you've chosen to have re-covered. You did it to put pressure on me.'

He closes his eyes. Counts to ten. 'OK.' He puts his elbow on the steering wheel and turns to face her. 'I've protected you for a long time — and in return I get rudeness.'

She takes a long, levelling breath. Her face is ruddy from the cold. Her hair is tangled. 'I'm sorry. Tell me what you were going to say last night. I might not agree with it but at least you'll be done with it.'

He puts the cartridge of his fake cigarette into the pocket of his fleece. Takes a few moments to get the words into his head. He's gone through this before, rehearsed it, but he's never done it in the face of this hostility.

'I'm going to give you a scenario of what *could* happen. Picture this. You are searching the area we omitted to search last time. You find skeletized remains, say — oh, I don't know . . . somewhere, anywhere out here and — '

'Wait, *wait*! Are you saying what I think you're saying?'

'Think about it — how often have you dealt with a situation like that? Someone's gone missing — you search, but you draw the search area a fraction too tight . . . Usually the remains are so decomposed it's impossible to identify them or give cause of death. And in Misty's case? She was an addict, depressed, her marriage was falling apart, she was in the press for all the wrong reasons. Maybe she found a quiet place to fix herself up, got a bit lost, lay down to sleep and didn't wake up. It was May but it got cold that night — I've checked the temperatures. That night was a blip on the average. In her state she could have got hypothermic quite quickly, disorientated. It's so common it's almost a cliché. We scatter the bones the way animals would — a pathologist's nightmare. And let's not forget one salient point. The person who directs the forensics: the SIO. And in this case the SIO being . . . '

She turns away. She knows that as Senior Investigating Officer he has control over where the forensics budget is concentrated. He could guide the pathologists in any direction he wanted.

'And,' he pushes home the point, 'if I was there when you found the remains, any trace evidence we'd overlooked would just go down as a contaminated-evidence trail. We're covered every which way.'

She stares out of the window. In her holster the radio makes a low crackling noise. Outside, all the teams are coming and going, stopping to speak in the car park. The earnest faces of people who don't know they're on a wild-goose chase.

When eventually she speaks it's in a quiet, controlled voice. 'I can't dive. My ears are shot. And getting to the place you want to go is impossible. Even if you knew exactly where to go, you'd have to be a brilliant diver. An exceptionally brilliant diver.'

'Is that a yes?'

'What will you do if I say no?'

'I haven't thought that far ahead.'

She sighs. Pinches her nose. 'I'm sorry, Jack. I thank you for what you've done, but no. I've thought about it and thought about it — gone through and through it in my head and really this is the best way. The safest way. I'm really, really sorry.'

Starbucks

Isaac Handel was the pudding-basin haircut guy who alerted AJ to what Moses was doing with the spoon in the breakfast room that day. Until yesterday morning when he was released into a halfway house, he had spent all of his adult life in Beechway High Secure Unit. He was admitted to the acute ward as a referral from a juvenile unit seven years before AJ arrived, and according to all the stories from that time he didn't start off as the easiest patient.

He was eighteen years old. Acned, greasy, and disorientated. He smelled awful — everywhere he went the smell trailed around with him. He also insisted on carrying two doll-like figures he called his 'poppets' tucked in the crooks of his arms — ugly things that smelled as bad as he did. He wouldn't be parted from them — not ever.

The smell got worse and the staff had to employ physical tactics to get Isaac to wash. Three orderlies took him to the shower and managed to undress him. But when they tried to prise the poppets away from him they were rewarded for their efforts by having Isaac urinate liberally on them. After that they never again tried to take the dolls away from him.

Slowly, as the medication and therapy began to take effect, Isaac calmed. He started showering and stopped being so smelly that no one would sit near him. His collection of dolls grew — he bought materials with his allowance and in art-therapy classes with Jonathan Keay he was always sewing and painting the damned things. Keay used to help him a lot, in fact AJ often wondered if Keay favoured Isaac above some of the other patients. The poppets were freaky, with individual little teeth and lifelike eyes in woollen-crocheted faces. Or faces moulded from porcelain fired in the therapy-centre kiln, eyes outlined in red. But Isaac would not be separated from them. He'd carry as many as possible with him, the rest would be in his room, piled on the bed — distorted, lolling, squished together like miniature corpses.

AJ can't keep still. Despite his promise to Melanie he can't stop thinking about Isaac Handel. Weird little Isaac. He waits until one of the office secretaries gets up to take a bathroom break and calls after her retreating back, 'Can I use your station — check a rota?' When she waves a dismissive hand, he slips into her seat.

AJ has never known — never wanted to know — what put Isaac in Beechway in the first place. By the time he arrived at the unit, Isaac was a different person — silent and pliable and non-confrontational — he took his medication without fuss. In fact, in a weird way, AJ got on with the guy. The only thing he didn't care for was the way Isaac behaved whenever Melanie made an appearance. Sometimes he'd stop and stare at her when she passed him in the corridor, like a horny dog watching a bitch — as if she was leaving a hormone trail. He'd ask AJ inappropriate questions about her: *Where does she live?*

How old is she? Is she married? AJ's used to the male patients reacting this way to Melanie — she's a conundrum that their drug-pickled brains can't decipher. In the grand scheme, Isaac wasn't much more intrusive about Melanie than the rest of the patients. AJ had no other good reason to dislike him.

The secretary whose desk he's sitting at is the appointed MHA administrator on the unit's review tribunals. It's her job to transcribe the tapes of the meetings. AJ finds Isaac Handel's transcript on her desktop instantly — she's extremely organized and neat — and he swiftly downloads it on to a gimicky memory stick Patience was given as a loyal customer by the betting shop. It's in the shape of a horse's head. AJ is old enough for it to bring to mind the dead horse's head in the *Godfather* movies — but the stick serves its purpose, and he pockets it.

He can't read this here in the unit — he imagines Melanie coming in and catching him. If she finds out he's not letting this go it will be the last time he's invited back to her house in Stroud. He knows this. He sends her a text: *Got to disappear bit earlier babe, Patience just called — Stewart acting up. See you later xxx. PS you look beautiful on no sleep. Must be good genes*.

He drives to the nearest Starbucks, orders the first thing on the menu — which turns out to taste more like a heated-up coffee milkshake than a proper coffee — and sits in the corner, his back to the rest of the customers, his laptop open. He calls up the transcript of the tribunal:

Isaac Peter Handel v MHRT
Wednesday, 10 October
Beechway Psychiatric Unit
Chair: Mr Gerard Unsworth, QC

AJ was at this tribunal. He's been to hundreds of these over the years and there wasn't much about it that made it memorable. Ancillary staff had set up and cleaned the conference room on the admin block and provided a slew of sandwiches and Thermoses of tea and coffee. AJ was only there briefly as a witness to present the Patient Nursing Report to the panel. It was all routine shit: he talked through Isaac's response to his meds, the logging of his behavioural markers, his level of engagement with therapy and his relationships with other patients.

Most reviews that recommend discharge are little more than a formality; usually an informal decision has been made in the routine tribunal six months previously. Isaac and his solicitor were therefore already primed: as long as he'd toed the line since the last hearing he'd be recommended for discharge. There were a few hoops to jump through, the usual protocols to be observed, but it was all routine.

With the exception, AJ realizes in hindsight, of Mrs Jane Potter.

On every tribunal panel there must be a lay person — someone responsible but objective. Jane Potter is part of a pool of lay people and AJ has seen her on panels before — she's president of the local Women's Institute and is an Ofsted inspector. This time he recalls noting, briefly, that her posture was different from how it usually was. She sat stiffly, her hands clenched, as if she was angry — or shocked.

Now he wonders what had made her so tense. He takes a sip of coffee-flavoured froth and skims the transcript for the sections before he came into the room. He wants to see if something had happened to make Jane Potter react like that. His lips move silently, fast-forwarding through the usual stuff:

> . . . panel will consider an application for conditional discharge of Isaac Peter Handel . . . appellant present, and Ms Lucy Tripple, appellant's advocate . . . panel consists of chair Gerard Unsworth, QC; Dr Brian Yeats, consultant psychiatrist, responsible clinician to the appellant; Ms Melanie Arrow, clinical director; and Miss Bryony Marsh, Mental Health Act Administrator; Mrs Jane Potter . . .

In the transcript each panel member is given an acronym: IPH, LT, GU, BY, MA, JP. There is the usual stuff of people introducing themselves: The QC explains who he is — that's a laugh because they all know Unsworth. He's chaired numerous tribunals, and before he rose to the bench he prosecuted a number of high-profile cases against hospitals on behalf of patients detained under the Mental Health Act. With Unsworth in the chair everyone who worked on the unit was on high alert. Melanie in particular must have been stressed. Was it just after she and

Jonathan separated, AJ wonders? That would have made it worse.

Unsworth gives a little introductory spiel, noting that Handel has been on the unit for eleven years, that he was previously detained elsewhere under the Children Act between the ages of fourteen and eighteen, then transferred to Beechway under Section 37 of the Mental Health Act. AJ wasn't aware of any of this — he's never heard Isaac mention a word about his childhood.

The QC takes time to outline some of the basics — for the benefit of the lay person, who may not be familiar with the law.

> Mrs Potter, I realize you've been with us before, but just to remind you: Section 37 is used by the courts to send an offender to hospital for treatment instead of prison. Mr Handel is s37/41. A Section 41 is a restriction order imposed to protect the public from serious harm. Any applications for leave or discharge must be formally approved. Today we can recommend Mr Handel's discharge, or decline his application — but the final decision rests with the Home Office. Now, there has been a non-disclosure request on parts of the report because there are aspects of this case that might cause harm to Mr Handel if he were to read about them or be reminded of the particulars.

AJ frowns at the screen. This is something else he'd forgotten — when he came in to give evidence he'd noticed several pages of the tribunal bundle — the reports and medical documents collated by the MHA administrator — had been stamped with the words: '*Not to be disclosed to the patient without the express permission of the tribunal.*'

Put simply, Isaac could not, for his own protection, be reminded of the acts that put him into the mental-health system fifteen years ago. It isn't the first occasion AJ's come across the wording; at the time it didn't seem unusual or noteworthy, but maybe Jane Potter had seen whatever was in the reports of Handel's sectioning and that's what had distressed her.

He skips down the page, stopping at the point where the panel were going through the Clinician's Report.

GU: Mr Yeats — can you give us a snapshot of where the appellant is with regard to medication.

BY: Yes, of course. Isaac has had a range of adverse reactions to antipsychotics over the years, but last year he was put on new meds which he tolerated well. He's suffered mild cognitive impairment as a result of his illness, however his recent IQ scores on these meds are ten points higher than any previous measurements — for him, these meds simply don't cause what the patients usually term 'brain fog'. Added to that, the method of administration was changed to depot injections — which ensure compliance.

GU: Because a patient can't forget or refuse to take the meds, once the depot is in place?

BY: Exactly. Now if you turn to page 33 of my report you'll see I've outlined his response to the anxiolytics and antidepressants used to lower his anxiety. Also his history of responses to a range of antipsychotics — and we've tried many. Haloperidol, droperidol, Stelazine, flupenthixol, and chlorpromazine, which are first-generation antipsychotics, also called typical antipsychotics —

GU: I know what antipsychotics are, but perhaps for the benefit of us all you would . . .

BY: Yes, of course, they're a quite commonly used medication — their purpose is to . . . Their purpose is . . . Mrs Potter?

GU: Mrs Potter, are you . . . ? A drink for Mrs Potter perhaps? Can someone . . . some water . . .

JP: I'm sorry — sorry — I just . . .

GU: Please, will someone get Mrs Potter a . . .

JP: I'm fine.

MA: Bryony, open a window. Are you OK, Jane? Here — take a sip . . .

JP: Thank you.

GU: Should we adjourn this . . .

JP: Please, no — keep going. I'll be fine. Please keep going.

GU: Are you sure?

JP: Yes — it's just — looking at Mr Handel's original sectioning — what he did — what the pathologist said about it is . . . well, a bit . . . I didn't know any of it. I shouldn't have read it — I realize it's not relevant.

GU: Yes — the clinicians want to keep certain aspects from the patient. Perhaps they should have extended the same concern to the panel members.

LT: Is this entirely necessary? There's a reason for a non-disclosure clause and —

GU: I think it's time we adjourned this meeting I . . .

JP: Please, I mean what I say. I'm fine. It's just that I used to live near Upton Farm . . . I don't remember seeing it in the papers. They never reported the details.

LT: My client was a minor at the time. It's a shame it wasn't noted that you, Mrs Potter, had some personal connections that might affect your position on the review panel.

JP: I DON'T have personal connections. I happened to live nearby, that's all. I'm fine now. Please continue.

GU: Thank you, Mrs Potter.

LT: Well, with your permission, I'd like to remind everyone present that the details of my client's sectioning are provided for context only, and that your deliberations should and must be focused on Mr Handel's current state of mind.

GU: Absolutely. Absolutely.

MA: Naturally.

LT: So, do I have everyone's agreement — we concentrate on that?

GU: Yes yes — now, where were we? Doctor Yeats, I believe you were giving us an overview of antipsychotics . . .

Sitting with his cup of froth in Starbucks, AJ cannot drag his eyes from the screen. Like Jane Potter, he knows Upton Farm. It's only about four miles from Eden Hole Cottages. He's known for years that something happened up there, but he's never been sure quite what. And he's certainly never connected it to Isaac until now — he didn't even know that Isaac was local.

All these years he's never wanted to know what his patients have been in the unit for. Now he's starting to wonder exactly how smart a decision that was.

Elf's Grotto

The Mendips is a range of limestone hills, running east to west, about twenty miles south of Bristol. The hills have been mined for two thousand years, until the late nineteenth century, mostly on a small scale. Less than a fifth of the original sites are still quarried and many of the abandoned workings, now flooded, shelve steeply twenty metres from water's edge to clifftop, and up to sixty metres more below the teal-blue surface of the water. One string of quarries is connected via underground channels to a network of natural caves known as the Elf's Grotto, featuring pillars and curves and twisted ceilings — like the catacombs of an ancient cathedral — carved not by man but by the water that floods the entire system.

Quarry number eight sits at the end of the chain of quarries. Situated deep in the woods, it is largely forgotten and rarely visited. There is no public road leading down here — only a rutted and potholed limestone track so seldom used that wildlife have adopted it as their own. Tonight, however, they scurry into the shadows as a car appears, its headlights bumping and flashing off the undersides of the overhanging trees. It's a small car — a Renault Clio — a city runabout, designed for metalled roads and tight parking spaces, not for off-roading. The branches squeal as they scrape over its roof. It jerks out of the lane and on to the track that circles the quarry. Near the base of a towering mound of hewn rock cubes — abandoned here for so long that trees are growing in their crevices — the car stops. The engine dies. The headlights dwindle to twin glow-worms reflected in the water.

Flea Marley opens a window and sticks her head out — listening for any sign of movement: a cough, a shuffle of feet, a tell-tale patter of stones tumbling from the rock face. The quarry is silent. It's bitterly cold out here — freezing. She uses her binoculars to scan the horseshoe-shaped amphitheatre of rock. At the distant end of the quarry mounds of powdered limestone seem to give off their own faint glow. The stars and the clouds reflect in the motionless water.

Over forty-five metres below this surface — an unimaginable depth, equivalent to a twelve-storey tower block — in the lightless, frozen water, there exists an unmarked and unrecorded hole in the cliff face. It does not feature on any of the quarry schematics; this opening can be found by memory and blind instinct alone. Once entered, it leads to a passage that travels three metres into the sheer rock then dog-legs back upwards — a natural, water-filled bore hole. One metre wide, the tube ascends forty-six metres vertically — opening into caves that cannot be accessed any other way. Part natural, part burrowed into by ancient Roman workings, the caves are unstable and impenetrable — except by this one clandestine entry route. For a diver inside the rock chimney there are only two directions to go — up or down. It's too narrow to change your mind and jack-knife back — once you've decided to go you're committed. With the immense water pressure, you have to be extremely skilled to ascend safely.

Caffery can't dive. And he hasn't got Flea's connections. All he knows is that Misty is somewhere here. He's been patient so far, but he's a determined bastard when he gets the bit between his teeth, and it's not beyond him to mount some insane diving job — maybe privately, maybe with a unit from another force. He's senior enough to be able to work it if he wanted — he'd only have to come up with the flimsiest of pretexts. Flea can't afford to take that chance.

She wears an ordinary fleece on her upper half; on her lower half is a dry suit — rolled down to her waist. She gets out now, drags her kitbag from the back seat and closes the door gently. The click, which in most settings would be virtually inaudible, seems to echo like a gunshot over the silent water. She unzips the bag and begins to dress. This is the part she hates. In the water she's fine — it doesn't matter how big or small she is — but out of the water she is at a disadvantage. She struggles to carry all the equipment — the cylinders, the weight belt.

At the edge of the quarry she sits and pulls on her fins. From this point a rusted ladder leads into the water which she scans again, looking for some ripple or change in the mirrored surface. There is only one other person in the world who knows about this place — only one person skilled enough to enter, and he is long gone, Flea has no idea where. He won't give the secret away

— she can be sure of that. He was one of the shadow people — on the wrong side of this country — and it's no surprise he didn't stick around. Maybe he's dead. She's been back several times to check; the place has been deserted for months. She is on her own.

She makes her final checks. Weights, releases, air. That jaw-aching bite of rubber as the regulator goes in her mouth — the sudden Darth Vader suck and whistle of breath. The entrance to the cave is far beyond the safe fifty metres authorized by British diving safety associations. It's not something to be attempted on compressed air — let alone by a diver who's yet to be signed off as fit by the barotrauma experts. Flea's ear is the weak point — her left ear. The signs she's got to look out for are nausea and a pain that radiates across the side of the face. Vertigo and confusion can come at around the time the eardrum shatters. She can't afford for that to happen. If she bursts the eardrum again, this will be her last dive. Ever.

She places one hand flat against the regulator to pin it to her face for the descent, in the other she holds the inflator tube for her buoyancy vest. Then she plops, straight into the water, dropping through the dark.

Jam-Making Season

AJ trails thoughtfully back to his car. He drives home with the radio turned off because he wants to keep his head clear. The business cards of the cops who were at that conference are in the big folder in Melanie's office — but AJ doesn't need their names. If he wanted to, he could just bell the unit they work for: the Major Crime Investigation Team, if he remembers rightly. It can't be that hard to find. If he was sure his suspicions about Handel were justified, he might do it. Yeah right, he thinks, as he turns into the rutted track to Eden Hole, like it's entirely because you're not one hundred per cent certain. And absolutely nothing to do with the fact you'd upset Melanie if you did. Coward.

He gets out and stands for a moment in the cold, his back to the car. From here the land rises up to a plateau that runs across the top of an escarpment at the beginning of the Cotswolds. The escarpment is bleak and wind-blasted, with skeleton trees dotted along the summit.

Upton Farm is less than four miles away, on the other side of the escarpment. He's never been there, but he knows where it is, because people locally whisper the name. Until now, with his usual philosophy of seeking only necessary information and nothing more, AJ hasn't wanted to know what went on there. Or what Isaac did that weirded Jane Potter out so much.

Inside, the cottage is warm, with a fire lit and good smells coming from the kitchen. It's jam-making season, which means the kitchen's overrun by a constant succession of bubbling cauldrons, spoonfuls of jam smeared on frozen plates in the freezer and sticky jam thermometers on every surface. Patience mocks AJ for his wassailing, tree-hugging ways, but when he comes home from a walk laden with blackberries from the hedgerow and the pink-streaked Kingston Black apples that fall in the abandoned orchard at the end of the forest, she's delighted. She rolls up her sleeves and starts sterilizing jars.

Today she has an apron on and is clucking around the place with skimmers and piles of sealing discs. Breakfast is set — banana fritters and toast and coffee and one of the Forager's Fayre jars he bought her. He takes off his jacket and greets Stewart, then he sits and butters toast, spreads some jam on it. Stewart watches him from his bed next to the Aga.

'Turns out your dog was born under a wandering star,' Patience says tightly. 'Maybe he's like his daddy — got himself a lady friend.'

'Why? Where's he been?'

'I dunno — sowing his wild seed, I guess.'

'He's neutered, Patience.'

'Doesn't stop him disappearing. Maybe we should neuter you too.'

There's a little barb in there, and AJ wonders whether to explain to Patience where he was last night and where he's going tonight. He decides not to. She's a grown woman, she can work it out. He butters another piece of toast.

'Have you ever been up past that orchard?' he asks. 'The one I get the Kingston Black apples from. It's up in The Wilds. Between the church and Raymond Athey's land.'

'I know where it is, thank you. But you won't catch me up there. The place on the other side of it is haunted.'

'Haunted?'

'Things happen up there.'

'Upton Farm, you mean?'

Patience doesn't answer. Her mouth forms an irritated moue as she busies herself, clattering around with the jam pots, lining them up on the table where he's eating.

AJ's not ready to let it go though. 'We were living here fifteen years ago. Something happened at Upton Farm. Do you remember what?'

'I remember a boy went mad — killed his parents. Is there more I need to know?'

'Killed his parents?'

'That's what I said.'

AJ's been in the mental-health system so long nothing should shock him any more — he's known serial killers who've had a far higher body count than two. Even so he still can't quite imagine Isaac Handel doing it. And so nearby too.

'Why're we talking about it?' Patience says. 'Hey, Stewart, your dad's come home, but instead of walking you he's sitting around eating and talking about ghosts. What do you think about that?'

AJ shakes his head resignedly. He finishes his

toast then takes his cup and plate to the sink, washes them and sets them on the draining rack.

Imagine — little pudding-basin-hair Handel killing two people. How does it work that someone can do things like that and there's no sign of it left on their faces for the world to see?

AJ gets his coat and the dog lead. 'Come on, Stewie. Let's get some fresh air, eh?'

Outside, it soon becomes obvious that, although Patience might be in a strop, she is at least right on one count: there's definitely something odd about Stewart. AJ stands in the rain, hood up, throwing a stick into the field, but Stewart is hesitant to run after it — as if he's suddenly grown cautious about his surroundings.

'Go on, boy, go on,' AJ urges.

Eventually the dog goes into the field, but AJ knows something is wrong. Sure enough, Stewart doesn't pick up the stick but wanders around sniffing. Then he trots to the edge of the field where a stile leads into a patch of woodland.

'What're you doing? Come here.'

Stewart is reluctant to come back. He turns in a little circle, then sits. When AJ approaches with the lead, he begins to whine.

'Stewart, you headcase — what's up?'

The stile where Stewart has stopped is a single slab of stone with a crossbar above it. AJ leans over and glances left and right into the wood. A path leads away from the stile, meandering off into the trees. A faint mist hangs in the air. He can't see what's bothering Stewart. In all the years he's lived here and with all the rambling he's done he can count on his fingers the number of times he's been along that path — there are far nicer and easier paths to take. He can't quite recall its exact route, but he does know it leads up to the edge of the plateau. And he knows that if you followed it far enough it would drop down on the other side, down through the place they call The Wilds, and ultimately, if you let it, it would lead to Upton Farm.

Isaac, he thinks. You killed your mum and dad in that farm.

He glances down at Stewart. He wouldn't put anything past this dog. It's not hard to believe that Stewart picks up on people's silent preoccupations, but to the point of being psychic?

'Not even you are that special, Stew. Sorry, mate — there's nothing there. Now come on — let's get you home. Your dadda's got a hot date.'

Diving Beyond Qualifications

It is colder than the Arctic. So cold Flea's lungs are pressed by it and she has to concentrate hard on keeping her ribs lifting and lowering. She descends, like a stone, down down down into the blackness. This is the way Mum and Dad died, nearly four years ago. Except they probably went head first. No one is sure how much of it they were conscious for.

She checks her wrist. The dive computer she has strapped there is her private, clandestine unit — it is kept under lock and key when she's not using it. If it got into the wrong hands the records of the illicit dives she's logged on it could cause serious trouble.

She gets to the first milestone — the fifty-metre mark, and dabs a little compressed air into the vest to slow the descent. Get her neutral buoyancy back and level out. Her ear is good. So far at least.

It takes a bit of searching with her underwater torch to find the gateway. A net emblazoned with warning signs: DEPTHS EXCEEDING 50 METRES. DO NOT DIVE BEYOND YOUR QUALIFICATIONS AND CAPABILITIES. Set there to discourage recreational divers from pushing into uncharted depths. This is the threshold. The doorway to hell. You cannot and must not predict what happens past here.

The cold is going to slow her thinking, so she

works methodically, rigidly adhering to the routine, taking her time: using a torch to check depth, air supply, duration — comparing it religiously to her dive plan. There's the slightest pain in her ear, spreading over her temples into her eye. It might just be the tightness of the mask, which hasn't been used in months, but if the pain gets any worse she'll have to head to the surface. There's no nausea yet, and that has to be a good sign.

Two short snaps on the valve. Automatic. Then she tips herself forward until she is prone, suspended in mid-water, one hand on the net to steady herself. She pushes it aside, squirms her legs over it, and lets herself sink even further, feet first, her hands at her sides.

The rock face comes at her suddenly out of the gloom. She grabs on to it and, rotating ninety degrees, so her body is flat against the rock, feels her way, crab-like, down the quarry, examining the rock wall with one gloved hand, skimming over the moss and lichen.

Below her the quarry continues to drop. What she's looking for is halfway between here and the quarry floor. Every metre she must descend, the greater the pressure on her ear — the more the chance of disaster.

At sixty metres she stops. There's just blackness and the magnified sound of her own breathing. You never think about the amount of water overhead — if you did, you'd go mad. The entrance is somewhere here. She hangs on tightly, keeping those breaths steady. She studies everything in the beam of her torch, trying to recall the secret striations and signature formations. Her heart is thumping but she slows her breathing wilfully. Panic is the prime reason people die at depths such as this. Breathing consistently is everything.

Her hand finds it before her dive torch does: a small crevice that marks the upper edge of the hole. The entrance is sufficiently wide for two divers in full gear.

It's only further in that it gets really narrow. No one would find this if they didn't know what they were looking for. No matter how skilled.

A *wah wah wah* noise pounds in her ears. Maybe the first sign something's going to go wrong. She ignores it. This is the deepest she will go tonight — from here on it is upwards. Even if someone did, in the unlikeliest of scenarios, happen on this entrance, they wouldn't dare to go further. The ascent through the chimney is ragged with danger — toppling boulders, sweeping debris and clay into the shaft, trailing roots that could hook the cylinders right off your back, shards of rock that could puncture a buoyancy jacket. But at least it's upwards all the way; it will give her body a chance to recover from the extreme pressure.

She knocks out a few more shallow breaths to make herself sink further, then uses her fingers to propel herself inside the cave. She moves on, following the slope of the floor, torch pointing up, until it locates the next opening overhead: the entrance to the narrow chimney. The bubbles from her regulator shoot upwards in a silvery haze — collecting in the various overhanging crags and ledges above her. When they get big enough, they spring away from the walls, racing up the chimney after the others. Disappearing. She knows where they will eventually break the surface, forty-six metres over her head. If only she could get messages from those bubbles about what's up there. Whether anything has changed. What is waiting for her.

The dive computer on her wrist now says sixty-three metres. A bad bad depth. She positions herself so she is standing at the foot of the chimney, raises one hand over her head, and releases a jet of compressed air into her vest. Slowly she begins to rise, following the gas bubbles. It's a strange feeling of lightness — as if she's heading for the sky.

Forty-five metres. Her first scheduled decompression stop. She halts, hands braced against the rock. The pain in her ears has lessened. She's through. She's through. She's done it. Her ears have held up and she's past the first hurdle.

Sliding Into Each Other

It's four in the morning when the security light comes on outside Melanie's window.

AJ is already awake. He'd had that dream again — the one where he was about to slip down a rabbit hole into heaven — and was lying on his back, eyes open, listening to Melanie's soft breathing. His mind was rambling — he was thinking about so many things. About Isaac. About what he did at Upton Farm, killing his parents. And only a few miles away from Eden Hole.

Life was wonderful, but it was also deeply weird. He glanced down at Melanie, fast asleep. He still couldn't believe how easy and obvious the decision was — how simply they'd just slid into each other's existences. He wasn't alone any more. Maybe he never would be again.

Then the light came on.

At first he doesn't move. He can see insects circling in its beam, all juiced up and busy now the rain has stopped. It's like summer has come back, seeing those flies. Not late autumn.

Silently he throws off the covers and pads barefoot across the room. As he reaches the window the security light clicks out. But not before he catches a glimpse, just a split second, of a figure in the garden.

It's over so quickly it's like a mirage — a burst on his retina. He blinks, trying to adjust to the suddenly dark garden. Not sure what he saw. Has he made it up or did the figure have a smooth white face? No facial contours. And a hint of laced gown.

'AJ?' Melanie murmurs sleepily. 'What is it?'

'Nothing.' He opens the window and leans out. In the gardens the shadows are beginning to coalesce, turn into something recognizable.

'AJ?'

'Shhhhhhhhhh!'

He holds his breath and leans out further, listening to the garden. He can hear little noises in the trees but nothing specific — maybe a rustle of leaf, a tiny snap of twig. Or maybe it's just the drip drip of last night's rain. The dark path in the grass from yesterday is still there — he can't tell if it's been made afresh.

'What did you see?' Melanie comes to stand next to him. She stares out into the garden, her eyes watery with apprehension. 'What was it?'

'I don't know.'

She looks up at him. 'You don't know?'

'I don't know.'

He crosses to the bathroom and switches on the light. He puts his head under the tap and lets the water fall over him. He doesn't want to speak to her for a moment. The doors downstairs are all locked. He double-checked them before they came to bed. And he made sure the windows were locked too. The torch — the heavy thing that he could swing at someone should he need to — is next to the bed.

He wets a flannel and runs it over his hair, around the back of his neck. He's remembering

Isaac staring at Melanie, saying '*Where does she live? Where does she live?*'

He turns off the tap and pulls a towel off the rail, putting his face in it. When he lowers the towel he sees she has moved to the bed and is sitting there, watching him silently through the doorway.

'AJ?' she says, and this time he can't get away from her. 'AJ?'

'Mel — how much do you know about why Isaac was in Beechway?'

'I know everything. I'm the clinical director — it's my job to know.'

'You're not scared?'

She blinks. 'He was ill when he offended, we successfully rehabilitated him. Why would I be scared?'

'It hasn't occurred to you it might have been Isaac in the garden just now? That he might know where you live?'

She swallows. 'I didn't see what you saw.'

'No, but you saw something last night.'

'I was dreaming.'

'No, you weren't. I'm sorry — but we both know what I'm talking about and it's beyond crazy now. I want to go to the police.'

'AJ, please.' Melanie makes a pained face. 'You're talking about something that is going to lose me my job. And I just can't let that happen. I'm sorry — I fought for my job. I had to . . . ' She sighs. 'I really had to fight. I can't lose it. It's all I've got.'

AJ doesn't answer. He drops the towel and goes downstairs. Checks all the locks. When he comes back upstairs Melanie is in bed with her back to him. He lies beside her, listens to her breathing. Eventually it slows. She's either asleep or pretending to be. AJ stays awake, alert for every sound, every creak in the woods outside.

Crash and Burn

Flea can't afford to ignore any of the safety stops. Especially diving alone and deeper than she's qualified. She climbs the chimney, monitoring herself rigidly. It's been such a long ascent a lot of the nitrogen has seeped out of her muscles and joints. This, the last decompression stop, is only five metres below the surface, but it's the most important of all. She wedges herself in the tube and wills the minutes away, impatient to be moving again. After a hundred breaths — each one counted with the concentration of a Zen master — she opens her eyes and clicks on her torch.

Above her the chimney widens. A faint hiss as her jacket inflates, and she begins to rise. One hand is raised, as it always is on an ascent, to protect her from unseen obstacles above, the other is on her regulator, held at an angle so she can see her wrist computer clicking off the last few metres. Her cylinders scrape briefly against the rock wall. Two more metres, then the chimney opens and she bobs like a cork to the surface of the water.

It's a massive cave, twelve metres high; part of the complex of Roman lead mines.

She lifts her dive torch up out of the hole and plonks it on the cave floor. She's tested the air before and knows it is safe to breathe, so she pulls off her mask and rests, arms on the edge, head on her hands, breathing hard. She's done it. No problems with her ear — she puts a finger in there and wriggles it. Mr Doctor, I can tell you before I even see you — the ears are perfect. Epic, in fact. Good to nearly sixty-five metres — beat that!

When the strength returns to her arms she boosts herself out of the hole, her chest and legs screaming after the long minutes braced against the shaft of the chimney. Quickly she strips off her weight belt and cylinders, picks up the torch. It has been battered in the ascent, but it's still working. She shines the beam around the cavern. The black walls glitter like anthracite: lead ore and galena, mined from the Mendip Hills since the first millennium. The one person who knew about this place has long gone — it's as silent and undisturbed as it was the last time she was here.

She bends to take off her fins.

A high squeak comes from behind her; she snatches up the torch and pivots, sweeping the beam over the northern wall of the cave, sees twin circular reflections. A rat. It sits back on its haunches, contemplating her, then turns and ambles away — flowing off into the darkness. An answering squeak and patter of paws. Impossible in the echo-chamber of the cave to say which direction they're coming from, but from the different pitch and tone she's sure the place is teeming with them. There are bore-holes the rats can come through — they've been here since she can remember. Their presence means nothing at all. Nothing has changed.

Jamming the dive torch under one arm, she rips off her second fin and in her thin dive boots picks her way deeper into the cave, the torch out in front of her. Glinting dully in the beam of light, she finds a long narrow ridge of blackish stones, like a keloid scar. You wouldn't notice this unless you knew exactly what you were looking for — unless you were combing the place from top to bottom. Under this unremarkable scatter of stones are Misty's remains. Flea crouches and digs with her hands until she finds the edge of the dirty plastic sheeting. Her heart gives a little relieved skip to find it's exactly as she left it.

The plastic is dirty. She pulls it away and shines the torch on what is inside. In life Misty Kitson was a well-fleshed, well-tanned and high-lighted young woman. A beauty, according to some newspapers. Body of the year, according to *Nuts* magazine. Time, though, has boiled her down. It's stripped her of skin and features and fat and muscle. Her golden hair is now a few scraps pasted to a crackling yellowing skull. Her bones have accordioned in on themselves. Her shin bone lies on the right of her skull and her ribcage has toe bones resting on it. Amazing that a full-grown woman could be parcelled up so small — just a tiny package. A human.

Flea examines the plastic. It's been gnawed in places where rats have got in. Caffery obviously hasn't thought this part of it through. Misty's bones are going to have a completely different forensic signature after being left here, wrapped in plastic, than if her body had decayed out in the woods. He's overlooked the artefacts left by animals on the body. Animals can change a human corpse into something utterly unrecognizable — it doesn't take long.

She turns the torch in the direction of the chimney — then back to the remains, measuring the distance. She could parcel this up, make it watertight, and take Misty to the surface. Open a box that doesn't need to be opened. She could, but she's not going to. It's OK. No one is going to come here — no one is going to find this. She can keep on flying.

She refolds the plastic and begins to pile the stones on top.

I am so sorry, Misty. Sorry for you, and sorry for your mum. I know what it is to lose someone and have nothing to put in a grave, but for now I can't. It's not my time to crash and burn.

Not now. Maybe never.

Yellow

Melanie and AJ have reached an impasse. So early in their relationship and they're as wary and mistrustful of each other as divorcees. They are wooden at breakfast, hardly speaking. He's surprised and taken aback at the way she has pulled down the shutters, and he believes she's embarrassed by it now. He's known a lot of women who've risen through the ranks to a position of power; many find staying there incredibly difficult. It's as if they are so surprised to have got there at all that they cling on harder than they need to.

He loads his breakfast stuff into the dishwasher and goes into the garden again — just to see it in the daylight. He doesn't know what he's searching for, so he kicks around a bit, trying to look important, then goes back inside. He keeps catching her watching him, and when he thinks her attention is elsewhere he, in turn, studies her. Searching for any hint she's going to tell him she doesn't want to go on with this — that she wants to cool things. He won't be surprised when it happens. It'll be because she's embarrassed — the worst reason, but she has her pride.

By the time they get to work AJ is wrung out. He is exhausted, and the memory of whatever it was in the garden won't leave him alone. Flashes of it come back to him when he closes his eyes: a face covered in something — a stocking mask maybe. Its absolute stillness and lack of urgency — so motionless that he still can't quite believe it was a human being — are the worst things. The image won't stop pressing at him, and eventually he gives in. He lets it take him the first place it will. He isn't surprised to find himself outside Monster Mother's door.

Monster Mother sits in the window as always. She is holding her stump high above her head. There seems no particular reason for her doing this; she neither tires of it, nor refers to it when AJ comes in, but smiles graciously, half rising to give him a tiny bobbing curtsey, twitching the hem of her floaty yellow lace with her good hand, the stump still raised aloft.

'Gabriella.'

'Hello, dearest AJ. The world is extremely yellow today.'

'Yellow as in . . . ?'

'As in sunny.' She settles down, beaming. The arm stays up in the air, cheerfully revealing the huge thatch of gingery hair in her armpit. 'The world is happy.'

'Happy because . . . ?'

'Because it's gone. The Maude will leave us alone now. We're safe. Ohhhh, AJ.' She turns her amazing eyes to him. They are eyes that could light up the world. 'It's all because of you. You are so lovely. You're the favourite of all my children. You grew up the straightest — the straightest of them all.'

AJ gives a wan smile. Isaac Handel has gone from the unit and now Monster Mother is happy. It's too much of a coincidence to ignore. 'Can I sit down?'

'Of course, my lovely son.' Monster Mother still hasn't lowered her arm. 'Sit, sit. Do you want some tea? Some cakes? Strawberry is nice.'

Monster Mother has the wherewithal to make neither tea nor cakes in her room, but AJ inclines his head politely. 'That's OK, Gabriella. I've just eaten, thank you.' He sits. Takes a breath. 'Gabriella? Do you think Isaac knows something about The Maude?'

Instantly Monster Mother's mood changes. A cloud flits across her face and she lowers her stump.

'Gabriella?'

She moves her tongue around in her mouth, as if she's having an internal argument with herself. Her eyes flicker from side to side.

'Gabriella? I asked, do you — '

'I gave birth to him — how am I supposed to forget? I don't forget any of you. I still cry because of Isaac.' She pauses and mutters to herself, her eyes lowered to a point on the floor, as if there is something or someone there she is speaking to. Finally she jerks her head up and looks hard at AJ. 'Where is he?'

'I don't know. He's left us.'

'Where is he now? Is he coming here?'

'No. He's not coming back. I promise you.'

'A promise?'

'Yes, a promise.'

Monster Mother lowers her chin and frowns. Her eyes close halfway. She mutters to herself again, words AJ can't hear.

'Gabriella? Tell me something else. Our clinical director, Miss Arrow — do you remember Isaac ever talking about her?'

Monster Mother glares at AJ, her breathing suddenly picking up speed.

'Gabriella?'

In reply she jumps up from her chair and turns away so she's facing the window.

She sways, muttering under her breath, massaging her arm stump the way she does when she is anxious.

AJ rubs his eyes tiredly. He has gone as far as he can. Her silence is the answer he wants.

Enough is enough.

Triumph

Caffery has slept badly again and wakes aching all over. He drinks coffee, takes paracetamol, showers, dresses and drives through the Bristol traffic, hearing police sirens and car horns, drive-time on the radio. No mention of Misty Kitson this morning. She's there, regardless, somewhere behind the headlines and the jingles and the music. Misty is always going to be in the public's consciousness.

Flea says the body isn't at the bottom of the quarry. That it's more complicated than that. Is that the truth? Diving is outside his experience, it's an intricate and highly technical world, but there have to be other people who would be able to tell him. He digs his fingernails into the leather-covered steering wheel, considering this — seriously considering it. There are other police diving teams. And commercial divers too. Where do you start? The irony isn't lost on him — if he's prepared to involve someone else then why has he kept this a secret up until now?

He wonders who he's more fucked off with — Flea? Or with himself for carrying around this tiny remnant of faith that eventually she'll change her mind.

When he arrives at work the superintendent is waiting for him in reception. From his smug expression it's clear a new case has come in. He's waiting under the framed photograph of the late chief constable, one hand resting nonchalantly on the water cooler, a patient, faintly triumphant smile on his face. Next to him stands a dark-haired guy — mid-forties, dressed in a suit that seems to be making him uncomfortable. Caffery recognizes him vaguely from somewhere.

'Jack — allow me to introduce Mr LeGrande. He'd like a word with you.'

Caffery offers his hand. 'Nice to meet you, Mr LeGrande.'

'Mr Caffery.' They shake.

LeGrande has already been given a visitor's pass, hanging from one of the new-issue MCIT lanyards, decorated comically with silhouettes of Sherlock Holmes and Isambard Kingdom Brunel. 'Call me AJ. We met at the Criminal Justice Forum?'

'Yes — I recognize you.'

'Jack!' The superintendent has the air of a well-polished political campaigner as he touches both men on their arms, encouraging them. He's riding this triumph like the wind. 'Why don't you take Mr LeGrande on upstairs? Let me know how it goes?'

They make their way to his office, and as they walk the corridors, in his head Caffery is going through the probabilities of what AJ wants. Please, not some jobsworth: *Mr Caffery, good of you to see me. I wanted to follow up the discussions we had at the forum. I've written up a proposal for you on implementing smoother transitions from the custody suite . . . blah de blah . . .*

In his office he makes them each a cup of

coffee — AJ looks as if he needs it almost as much as Caffery does, maybe more — and they sit, AJ on the sofa, Caffery at the desk.

'So, AJ, what can I do for you?'

AJ puts his hand to his mouth and gives an embarrassed cough.

'Well, uh — before we go any further — this has to be in confidence.'

Caffery raises an eyebrow. 'In theory that's OK. But no promises until I know what we're talking about.'

'It's extremely important no one knows I'm here.'

'Someone's threatening you?'

'No, it's not that — it's . . . ' He hesitates, then says in a rush, 'Something's going on where I work. Or rather, it *was* going on. We're a high-secure unit, if you remember, and things have been happening that don't feel right . . . I'm uneasy.'

Caffery takes off his glasses and rubs his eyes tiredly. 'Just for future reference, Mr LeGrande, 'I'm uneasy' is not a phrase cops are fond of. Don't expect to be welcomed if you go bandying it about. Has an unwelcome ring. But go ahead anyway.'

'OK. This is going to sound a bit nuts — but there you go, I work in a nuthouse, so what can I say.'

'Are you allowed to call it a nuthouse?'

'I am, you're not. You're on the outside. On the inside we have special privileges. Believe me, we deserve them.' He gives a brief smile. 'It's a loony bin. And in our particular loony bin, ever since I can remember, there's been an even loonier myth doing the rounds. It's a . . . ' He sighs, half embarrassed. 'A *ghost* story that kind of circulates amongst the patients from time to time. They're suggestible — you can imagine. We try to keep a lid on it where we can. But it's popped up a few times, and at least three times I know of, what's ended up happening has been a bizarre cluster of DSH cases.'

'DSH?'

'Sorry — deliberate self-harm. People cutting themselves, that sort of thing. A few years back it escalated to a death — maybe a suicide, we don't know for sure. Then a week ago there was another death — a heart attack, according to the doctors. But it doesn't feel right.'

Caffery taps his pen thoughtfully, studying AJ's face. It's a sad story, one he's heard before. Suicides in a secure unit always make the senior staff unhappy — deeply unhappy — but they rarely turn out to be anything MCIT needs to be interested in. Maybe this can be moved through the system quickly.

'One guy put his own eye out.'

'Nasty.'

'Nasty, though not that uncommon in a, you know, loony bin. But he had the same hallucinations — just like the patient we lost last week. Her heart attack was after delusions. And it was the same a few years ago, when the other patient died. She'd convinced herself she'd seen The Mau — Sorry, I didn't explain: they call this thing 'The Maude'.'

'The Maude?'

AJ shakes his head. 'It's a long story. But whatever was going on in this one patient's mind was so bad that one day she walks out of the unit and no one sees her again. Not until months later when they find her body in the grounds. The autopsy never did say for sure how she died — I think everyone had it in the back of their head it was a suicide, but it got moved on down the tracks.'

'What was her name?'

'Pauline Scott.'

It rings vague bells for Caffery.

It was before his time, but he's fairly sure it's a case Flea mentioned, notable because it was embarrassing for everyone concerned: Beechway, for letting a vulnerable patient wander out, and the police search advisor, the POLSA, on Flea's unit, who was tasked with the search and didn't quite extend the parameters far enough. So easy to miss someone a few metres outside. He doesn't move his eyes, but his attention trails across the room to Misty's face. A search like that? Metres, even centimetres, can count.

'Except,' AJ says, 'I think it's a case of the Scooby-Doo ghost.'

'A case of the what?'

'Scooby-Doo. You know — Scooby and Shaggy and the gang always catch the ghost, pull off its mask and turns out to be . . . I dunno, the local property developer or something? Wants to make people believe the place is haunted so the land prices drop? That's what I call a Scooby ghost — something that's real but it's made to look supernatural. I reckon we've got one haunting the corridors of Beechway.'

'And you're Shaggy — '

'No, I'm Velma. I'm the brains. And I'm Scully, by the way, because sometimes I get asked that too.'

'Velma. Scully. The stage is all yours. Hit me.'

AJ nods. If he had nerd glasses he'd push them up his nose.

'OK. I can't find out for certain, but I'm pretty sure every time it's happened there's been a power cut.'

'Uh-huh.'

'Power cuts put the CCTV system down.'

'Have a lot of power cuts, do you?'

'No. Two, maybe three — that's all I can remember in the four years I've been there.' He puts his rucksack on the floor and unzips it. 'I've got something I want you to see. It won't mean anything to you, but to me . . . ?' He gives a small, pained smile. 'Well, it frightened the daylights out of me.'

The Grief Calculator

Flea stands in her low-ceilinged kitchen and makes breakfast. Standing so close to the stove at last a bit of warmth begins to crawl back into her bones. She's showered and scrubbed, but it's taking for ever to get the cold of the quarry out of her.

She stares blankly at the eggs and bacon sizzling in the skillet, turns them automatically. The bacon is the Old Spot stuff from the local farmers' market and the eggs are from a neighbouring family who, in spite of her insistence, are trying to say thank you for two hours she spent fixing a manifold pump on their underfloor heating. As a diver she knows about pumps, it wasn't a difficult job, but they keep leaving eggs at her back door. Eggs, eggs everywhere. Eggs coming out of the walls.

She slides breakfast on to a plate and plonks it down without ceremony on the table. A heavy mug of strong coffee and a jar of sugar with a spoon stuck in it. She's a proper support-group sergeant — likes her breakfasts fried and unfussy. The ketchup is in a squeezy bottle. No airs and graces here. Mum and Dad would have both fallen down in a flat faint if they'd ever caught the faintest whiff of pretension.

'So,' she murmurs as she pulls up a chair and begins to eat. 'Just as well you're not here then, isn't it.'

She chews with concentration — elbows on the table. She doesn't look up, doesn't look to either side. It's better sometimes not to remember where you are. Especially when it's the house of your dead parents. Dad would know what to say to her now — he'd put his hand on her shoulder and answer her questions. She'd say: *Dad, is it OK to just let things be? And if it is then what do I tell this guy — how do I explain it to him, because one thing's for sure — he's not going to leave it be.*

Dad would kiss her head, talk to her gently, reasonably. He'd know the answers. And if he didn't know what to say, he'd talk to Mum. They'd go into the room at the end of the house, switch on the light over the piano and sit in facing armchairs. They'd speak in low voices — talking until they had a solution to her problem. They'd close ranks and Flea would be safe.

She has to stop chewing then. She pauses, and, with an effort, swallows the mouthful. She picks up the mug and gulps a few swigs of coffee to wash it down. Then she sits for a while, her head lowered, staring at the eggs and bacon.

There must, somewhere, be an equation for how long grief lasts. A calculator like they have for currencies online: you'd jab in things like your age, your gender, your job, your social life. You'd divide it by how close you were to the person who's gone, you'd have to add lots of points for the fact you haven't got a body to bury, and you'd get a number — a finite quantity — a guarantee that after exactly 573 days the pain would stop. Christ, if you can convert the Pakistani rupee into zlotys, if you can map the human genome and work out what Martian soil is composed of, why can't you calculate when the hurt will be over?

She gets up and chucks the food in the bin. Washes the plates. She's got a long day ahead of her. If she's lucky, by the time Jack Caffery arrives at the search site she'll have got an explanation together. If she's unlucky it's going to be the coldest, wettest day of the year and she'll end up crying in the shower at the end of it.

Parking Tickets

AJ remembers Caffery well. At the Criminal Justice Forum he overheard two of the female delegates whispering about Caffery as he left the hotel. They were giggling and blushing, and from that AJ understands the inspector is attractive. Probably for the very reasons that AJ doesn't have women giggling and blushing: Caffery exudes something — a brand of confidence or carelessness — AJ doesn't know exactly, but he wishes he had some of it.

Now, sitting in his office, AJ sees the inspector hasn't got any less good-looking, the bastard. He's maybe early forties, going slightly grey at the temples in the way some women find madly attractive. There is something about the way his eyes move, a bit too quick, but AJ guesses that's intelligence and determination at work and not dishonesty. There's no hint of a personal life in the office. No framed photographs or certificates — just a couple of OS maps of the Avon and Somerset district covered with coloured pins, and a giant photo of a woman AJ recognizes vaguely. He thinks she's the celebrity that went missing last year, Kitty someone? He can't remember the details.

'Zelda Lornton — the one who died a week ago from a heart attack . . . ' From his rucksack AJ pulls out the painting Zelda did and puts it on the table in front of him. Caffery leans over to study it. 'She'd had an episode of self-harm about three weeks previously. She said this — this ghost thing, The Maude, did it. It wrote on her arms — a lot of biblical stuff. The sort of thing it's hard to believe Zelda would have come up with on her own. Two weeks later she was dead.' He runs his fingers over The Maude's smooth face. 'I found this amongst her OT work. This weird little bugger here? It fits exactly the way the patients describe The Maude. And this — the sweater, these dolls in its hands?'

'Yes?'

'That fits one of our patients. It can't be a coincidence Zelda did this.'

'One of your patients?' Caffery looks at him over his glasses. AJ can't tell whether he's mocking or taking this seriously. 'One of your patients is the Scooby ghost?'

'When I say one of our patients, I mean one of our ex-patients. He was discharged two days ago. Which kind of puts him' — AJ nods at the window — 'out there somewhere. And I'm not sure that's a good thing.'

Caffery picks up a pen and begins to jot some notes. He writes today's date. 'Name?'

'Isaac Handel.'

'Isaac . . . ' Caffery stops writing. He raises his eyes to AJ. 'Isaac Handel? Is that the Upton Farm Isaac Handel?'

'You know him?'

'I know of him. The case was before my time, and the Senior Investigating Officer retired a while ago. But Handel and what happened at Upton Farm? It gets talked about a lot around this place.'

'Because what he did was pretty memorable?'

'Memorable.' Caffery nods. 'Yes, you could call it that. *Memorable*.'

'I don't know much about it. I've nursed him for years, but I've only just worked out he was connected to Upton Farm. And even though I grew up not far from there, and I know he killed his parents, the *exact* details of what happened are . . . well, you know, it's all rumour and people doing that hush-voice thing?' He wonders briefly if Caffery would give him the minutiae of the case if he asked. But, no, he's decided he doesn't want to find out. It was something out of the ordinary — something particularly nasty, and he's happy just to know that sketch, rather than get all the close-up pictures. 'You get the drift, reading between the lines, that he didn't get locked away for a parking ticket.'

'I can assure you it wasn't a parking ticket.'

'He was fourteen? Is that right?'

'That's right.'

'He killed his parents. Some schizophrenics can be unnecessarily . . . *violent*. Under the wrong circumstances?'

Caffery nods, as if agreeing. 'I don't know the full story — I'd have to get the case called up. I remember there was some problem with the post-mortems. It took a long time for the pathologist to be given access to the bodies. Something odd about it.' He moves papers around on his desk as if he's uncomfortable. Then he clears his throat, picks up his pen and begins to write again. 'So you're connecting him to a death, a possible suicide? And two . . . no, three episodes that were put down as self-harm?'

'Yes.' AJ watches him writing. He says, 'Can I just reiterate, I'd like this to be confidential?'

'Confidential from whom?'

'Anyone in the Trust.'

Caffery glances up. 'That's going to limit what I can do. If you want me to look into this, I'll need to pay a visit to the unit.'

'Do you have to? Can't you just, I don't know, find Isaac Handel? Find out what he's doing out there? Speak to him. I mean, I can't be here. Seriously — if this comes out, I could lose more than just my job. And if you have to come out to the unit I'll have to . . . ' He waves his hand vaguely in the direction of the door. 'I'll have to make like I wasn't here. I just can't be seen talking to you.'

Caffery gives a small, non-committal shrug and puts down the pen. Opens his hands as if to say, *Fine. No skin off my nose if we don't pursue this*.

'Please — I'm sorry,' says AJ. 'It's awkward, that's all.'

'Maybe if you were more specific about who we're keeping this from?'

'Some people in the Trust. They're protective — they wouldn't be happy, knowing I was here. The clinical director in particular. Melanie Arrow.'

'I think I met her. At the conference? Blonde?'

AJ is caught by surprise hearing the word 'blonde' in Caffery's mouth. He knows they talked, but for how long? Caffery remembers she's blonde, what else does he remember? He wonders whether Caffery flirted with Melanie. And worse, whether she flirted back.

'Yes. Blonde. And she would definitely not be pleased to discover I was opening up a can of worms. Not because she is bad. Or wrong. Just because she wants to keep her job.'

'We'd all like to keep our jobs. In an ideal world.'

'Are you going to take me seriously?' AJ says. 'Are you?'

There's a long silence. Then Caffery pushes his chair back. 'Leave it with me, Mr LeGrande. I'll see what I can do.'

The Avonmere Hotel

Caffery wasn't looking forward to the superintendent's new case, but now he's not so sure. Maybe there are benefits. They say the watched pot never boils — it might be good to keep himself occupied while Flea has time to let the shock work through her system and decide what she's going to do. And maybe by then he'll have a plan B for if she says no.

He reports back to the superintendent, sits through the inevitable lecture — how much longer will the teams be out searching for Misty Kitson? How he can justify the spend? Surely the press must be satisfied by now? — and then announces his intention to check out the Beechway case. Just have a sniff.

The superintendent isn't easily won over. 'OK,' he says. 'But I want to know tomorrow at the latest how we're going to categorize it. And if it's a case for us then I want you full throttle on it.'

The first thing Caffery does is get the three grand spend for a forensic post-mortem OK'd by the scientific investigations co-ordinator, then he calls the coroner's office to put a snatch on Zelda's body, stop it going to burial. She's still in the mortuary at Flax Bourton where all the post-mortems are done now the hospitals in the area have closed down their facilities. He gets put through to his old friend Beatrice Foxton, the on-call Home Office pathologist. He's lucky she didn't do the original PM — he'd be embarrassed to ask her to do it again — nevertheless, she's still a little uncomfortable about it. Firstly the conclusion on the current PM — heart attack secondary to obesity — is a new syndrome which is only just finding its way to death certificates. Secondly she hasn't seen the deceased yet and is concerned the incision to open the body might be the one used for ordinary hospital PMs which can interfere with the neck area she'd want to examine. But Beatrice promises to do her best, and to make Zelda a priority.

Next he sends one of the civilian investigators out in the van to get the hard copies of the Isaac Handel case from the archive. It's going to take most of the day, so in the meantime he studies the case outline in the HOLMES database. Then he puts in phone calls to a couple of the force's old warhorses who've been around long enough to remember the Upton Farm killings. They fill in the details Caffery wouldn't find in HOLMES. They're not pretty.

As he works, Misty's eyes seem to follow him. Every time he looks up from his desk, it's as if she's saying, *What about me? Have you forgotten me?* He almost holds a hand up to deflect the glare of her attention. He'd turn her to face the wall if he didn't think that would be worse.

He checks his blank phone screen, wondering whether to call Flea. He starts to compose a text message, but thinks better of it, pockets the phone and sits for a while swinging his hands at his sides, not sure what to do with himself. If this thing ever gets resolved it will be on Flea's terms, and in her own good time.

Irritated now, he pulls on his coat, heads down the stairs to the car park and gets in the car. It feels good to be moving. It feels good to be thinking about something else. Even Isaac Handel — a teenage psycho who killed both his parents and did unspeakable things to their bodies.

He drives out through the west Bristol suburbs wondering how much faith one should put in the mental-health and justice systems in the UK. The answer is, of course, that one can never be one hundred per cent confident. How often does a person secretly torment fellow patients? And how often does someone like that get away with it? Even get released from the facility, unchecked and unmonitored?

Ordinarily, Caffery would ride roughshod over anyone who had the nerve to ask for a favour then slap conditions on it. But, strangely, he likes AJ. Besides, after what Caffery's heard he's happy not to go to Beechway unit, and instead to go directly to Isaac Handel. At the very least, he wants to be sure Handel's sticking to the terms of his discharge. To find out who's keeping track of his movements.

His supported-living placement is the Avonmere Hotel, overlooking the muddy riverbanks. Caffery pulls up outside a little after midday. The exterior is fitted out to look like a standard B&B, though the sign in the sitting-room window probably always reads 'no vacancies'. Caffery knows places like this. The clientele won't look much like visiting businessmen or tourists, either. In fact they'll all be addicts and s37/41 discharges.

No one stops Caffery walking in or peering into rooms. The ground-floor accommodation is set up for group socializing — a sitting room, dining room and games/TV room; the upper floors are probably divided into bedsits. He finds a door marked 'Office' at the end of the hall and opens it. Still no one has stopped him. The manager is with a client, but one glance at Caffery in suit and tie, and he bends to the client and murmurs, 'Can we finish this later?'

The client swivels in Caffery's direction, his movements slow and slightly jerky. His eyes don't seem to register anything, but he shoots to his feet so fast he nearly topples over.

'No rush, mate,' the manager says.

The guy nods three times, looking at his feet. Bringing his hand up to the crown of his head, he swats his hair with the palm of his hand, smoothing it forward so that it lies flat on his forehead. Caffery stands to one side, holding the door open. The guy lumbers out, not making eye contact. Caffery waits until he's gone before showing his warrant card.

'Detective Inspector Jack Caffery.'

'Yes,' the manager says. 'Been looking forward to meeting you.' He must be in his late thirties, but his face has a childlike quality that is heightened, paradoxically, by his baldness. He has shaved what little of his hair remains, giving him the appearance of an ageing cherub. He wears a black stud in his right ear and a

Celtic-knot steel ring on the middle finger of his right hand. Behind his desk is a poster of The Smiths, Glastonbury 1984. He offers his hand.

'Bill Hurst.'

Caffery shakes his hand. Notices that as soon as he releases it, Hurst brings his hand straight to the back of his neck.

'I'm here to speak to Isaac Handel.'

'Yes — yes.' Hurst stands awkwardly — scratching his neck — avoiding meeting Caffery's eyes. 'Yes, you did say.'

'So? Is there somewhere private I can chat to him?'

'Thing is . . . ' he begins sheepishly. 'About Isaac . . . '

'Yes?'

'Well, it's a bit embarrassing.'

'What is?'

'He's kind of not here at the moment.'

'Beg pardon?'

'Not here.'

'That's what I thought you said. So where, kind of, is he?'

'Ummmmm . . . not a hundred per cent sure, to tell you the truth.'

'When I phoned, you said I could speak to him.'

'Yes — I thought he'd have come back by then. You've got to understand, this isn't a secure hostel. Clients are required to sleep here, but they're free to go wherever they want during the day as long as they're not breaking any restrictions in their discharge papers.'

Caffery takes a moment to rein in his

impatience. He counts to ten in his head. 'OK, OK. Let's start from the beginning — when did you last see him?'

Hurst begins to fidget. 'Ummmm . . . '

'Come on, spit it out — this morning?' Hurst doesn't answer. He scratches his neck harder. 'Jesus!' Caffery exhales. 'Yesterday?'

'I think so.'

'You *think* so?'

'It's not a perfect system. I'm short-staffed, just had two phone calls from people calling in sick. It's the uncertainty about what the government wants to do to our jobs.'

'Fantastic. Outstanding.' Caffery shakes his head, weary. The more he sees, the more he's wondering why Handel was ever released into a flimsy place like this. 'He must have slept somewhere last night?'

Hurst shrugs.

'You've reported him missing?'

'This morning. The Community Mental Health Team will take it from here.'

He still can't look Caffery in the eye. Christ, what a spectacular jerk this guy is.

'Anyone here he talked to? Anyone who might point me in the right direction?'

'Not really — Handel was a bit of a lone wolf from what I saw of him. Didn't talk to anyone that I saw, just listened to his iPod, kept himself to himself.'

'And he was compliant?'

'Mostly. A bit agitated. He was always playing 'All Souls' Day' on his iPod. You know?' He gives Caffery a faintly hopeful look. 'The Ataris? Best pop punk to come out of the States in decades?'

Caffery sighs. Shakes his head.

'It's only a day,' Hurst protests. 'Not that long.'

'You know how lame that sounds? Even as it's coming out of your mouth, a part of you must be thinking: this is lay-ayme.'

Hurst dips his head. 'Point taken.'

'When's his depot due?'

'The day after tomorrow.'

Two days before the antipsychotic depot injection is due. From the little Caffery knows about mental illness, Handel's stability will disintegrate rapidly if that appointment is missed.

'I need to see his room.'

Hurst's eyes widen a fraction. 'Awww, mate, I'm sorry — I can't allow that. Everything in this place is based on trust — the staff's trust for the clients and the clients' trust in the staff. I can't go letting you into someone's room without a really, really good reason.'

'He's on an s47 conditional discharge — and staying in the hostel every night was one of those conditions. He's not complying, which is a criminal act, dah de dah. I won't patronize you by reciting the spiel, you've been here before, you know the drill. Rooms are upstairs, aren't they?' Caffery is already out of his chair. 'Maybe I'll just knock on every door till I find the right one.'

He is out of the room before Hurst has time to make it around to the other side of his desk. The manager catches up with him in the hall. He's breathing hard.

'OK,' he hisses. 'All right — but can we please keep it low key?'

'After you,' Caffery says.

Hurst edges past him. 'Low key — yeah?' he repeats.

'Of course.'

Caffery follows him up the stairs to the first floor. Two doors open within seconds of each other; the first tenant steps on to the landing — strung out, the front of his sweatshirt stained, his trousers hanging half mast. When he sees Caffery he makes a quick U-turn back into his room. The second door slams shut before Caffery can get a look at the occupant.

All of the rooms are secured with Yale locks. As Hurst pulls out the key to the door of number five, he seems to be having misgivings.

He turns his back to the room and raises both hands. 'I don't know, man. I should probably wait till I get the all-clear from the mental-health team.'

Legally, Caffery can't go in without an invitation, but it will take time and useless paperwork to obtain a warrant. He fixes the manager with a stare. 'Aren't you curious what Handel did that got him locked up for fifteen years?'

'No — and I don't want to know.' Hurst's ears flush red. 'We're not given details on patients' mental health, just guidance on what to look for in case they become unstable. We're here to rehabilitate, not judge.'

Caffery leans back against the handrail. He examines the cherubic face from the pale, shining forehead to the dimpled chin. 'Maybe it's a good thing you don't know the nuts and bolts of how your 'clients' end up in the system. Sadly, I do know. And in Handel's case let's just put it this way — 'sick' isn't even ballpark.'

Hurst fingers the bunch of keys attached to the key reel on his belt, but he's still undecided.

'And that was when he was only a kid,' Caffery continues. 'I don't think any of us know what he's capable of as an adult. A paranoid schizophrenic, out on licence, missing for twenty-four hours?'

Hurst's eyes fix on the door number, and a pink patch of colour spreads from his ears to the dome of his head.

'And you have only just reported him missing?'

'OK, OK,' he mutters, dragging the keys from his belt. 'I can manage without the lecture.'

Pompom Socks

The Trust is far from perfect, but even AJ has to admit the sports facility they've given their employees discounted membership to is pretty damned splendid. Situated on the outskirts of Thornbury, Tarlington Manor boasts a twenty-five-metre swimming pool and a gym packed with the latest fitness gizmos — suspension trainers, Core-texes, and vibrating power-plates. There's a sauna, a laconium, twenty tennis courts and an outdoor hot tub with a log fire next to it where middle-aged women sip champagne at lunchtime.

Three days a week Melanie leaves work early, comes here and knocks the hell out of a squash ball on her own for an hour. AJ has to check at least six viewing galleries before he finds her court. She is soaked with sweat but still thrashing the ball, her ponytail bobbing like mad. Her T-shirt is pink with a black puma above the left breast and she's as sexy as hell in her lycra training shorts, blinding-white trainers, and little white pompom socks like the ones he remembers the girls wearing at Wimbledon when he was a teenager. In those days he used to spend a lot of time watching the ladies' tennis — much to Mum and Patience's amusement and ridicule.

It wouldn't be that difficult for Isaac Handel to figure out where Melanie lives. The image of the figure in the garden flickers around AJ's head. And DI Caffery, and the way he was so uncomfortable talking about the murders at Upton Farm.

He makes his way down to the next level and opens the door to the court. Melanie stops when she sees him — gives a surprised yelp and flaps her hand. 'AJ! Go away, for God's sake, don't watch. You'll make me self-conscious.'

'Self-conscious? After what you let me do last night?'

'Oh, stop it.' She crosses to her kit in the corner and pulls out a towel, which she holds up to her face, letting it hang down in front of her body so he can't see her full length. She's wearing wristbands too — another retro detail that takes him straight back to the eighties. 'Go away — I'll have to stop if you don't go away.'

'We need to talk.'

'Need to talk?' She lowers the towel from her face. Sweat has smeared her mascara. 'Oh-oh. That sounds ominous.'

'Mel, let's not pretend. You saw something in the garden the other morning. And last night I saw it too.'

'No.' She shakes her head seriously. 'We didn't. It was our imaginations — we were half asleep. No sleep, too much sex, too much booze. I can smell it on me.' She lifts her arm and gives her armpit a dubious little sniff. 'It's coming out of me. Christ — lucky I'm playing on my own here.'

'I wasn't drunk last night. And even if we were both drunk the night before and we *imagined* it

— the fact we imagined the same thing says we're worrying about it. And we're worrying about it because we know on some level Zelda, and Pauline and Moses may have seen something similar. And I'm about as sure as I can be that I know who was behind their 'hallucinations', 'delusions' — if that's what we're going to call them.'

Melanie's eyes open even wider. 'Not Handel again — please. I really think we — '

'It's not just Zelda's picture, it's not just what he did to his parents. It's . . . I've got a bad feeling about this. Please, you need to believe me.'

'We've talked about it.' She puts a hand out, making to leave the court, but he stands his ground.

'Melanie — I read the tribunal transcript.'

Her face changes at that. Her eyes tighten a little, like cooling metal, and she drops her weight back on to her heels. 'I'm sorry? You read the transcript — what does that mean?'

'I read your statement to Handel's discharge tribunal. I never realized you'd been so involved with him.'

'*Involved?* What the hell are you talking about?'

'The way you talked, it sounded as if you'd spent every day with him. You said things like: 'he was always cooperative', 'absolutely no problems with compliance', 'understands the nature of his illness and the importance of daily contact with the team to maintain that stability post-transfer', 'gave me the impression that he understood the severity of his crime, and also deeply regretted it' . . . Shall I go on?'

Melanie's face is burning. Her nostrils have dilated slightly and she's sucking air in very slowly to calm herself.

'Shall I go on, Melanie? Because I read it all and it's bullshit — you never spent any time with Isaac. I never once saw you speak to him.'

'I don't get you,' she says bitterly. 'I don't get you at all.'

She pushes past him to the door, jabbing him with her elbow as she does. She slings the bag over her shoulder and walks away in a very straight, precise line.

'Melanie?' he says to her retreating back. 'Melanie — I'm sorry — I don't want an argument.'

'You could have fooled me.'

'No, honestly, I didn't mean to sound . . . '

He trails off. She has reached the ladies' locker room. Without a backward glance she goes inside and slams the door behind her.

Carrier Bags

When Caffery thinks about it, he can't imagine how Isaac has survived a cold October night with nowhere to stay. The patients receive an allowance while they're on the unit and, according to AJ, Isaac had saved a lot of cash; nevertheless Caffery reckons he'd struggle to get a room. A confused schizophrenic would be shown the 'no vacancies' sign, no matter how much cash he had on him. An image comes: a warm bed, food. Someone helping Handel? AJ mentioned power cuts in the unit that coincided with each episode; it's hard to believe that a patient would have the kind of access to pull that off on his own.

Someone else involved. Caffery parks the idea in the corner of his head. He'll come back to it later.

He stands in the room at the Avonmere Hotel, absorbing it all. It's just big enough to squeeze in a single bed, a bedside cabinet, chest of drawers and wardrobe. The curtains are thin; the carpet, a hardwearing cord, looks as if it has been cleaned recently. Everything is neat, well ordered: the bed is made, there is no clothing on view except for a pair of slippers. The chest of drawers is piled high with magazines. Caffrey flicks through them: *What Hi-Fi, Computing, Computer Weekly*, two Maplin catalogues, and one from Screwfix. There is no TV in the room, just an iPod docking station.

Caffery opens the bedside cabinet and takes out a brown pharmacy bottle. Seroxat — it's in Handel's name. He shows it to Hurst and gives it a shake to demonstrate it's empty.

Hurst spreads his hands wide. 'Don't look at me — speak to the mental-health team.'

'Yeah, we've got a department like that in the police. The SEP unit.'

'What?'

'Someone Else's Problem.'

Hurst narrows his eyes. He's beyond disgruntled now. 'I don't get a cop's salary,' he says. 'No early retirement and a pension either — index-linked or otherwise.'

Caffery puts the pill bottle back in the cabinet. He checks under the bed, pushing his hand up between the slats and the mattress. He runs his fingertips along the top of the curtain rail and then across the empty coat hangers in the wardrobe, making them clatter. He has absolutely no idea what he's looking for — he doesn't even know why he's doing this, except to prove a point to Hurst. How many people like Handel slip through the net, he wonders. In places like this it's probably a daily occurrence.

He stops. In the bottom of Handel's wardrobe is a stack of folded carrier bags. He squats down and presses his hand against them. They're all from Wickes. A hardware store is not the most reassuring place for someone like Handel to be shopping — particularly in the context of what he did to his parents.

Caffery pulls the bags out and carefully shakes

each one. They are all empty, except for the fifth, which contains a receipt for the iPod dock and the box it came in — now empty.

'Most of our clients spend their allowances on sweets and crisps.'

'I'm sure that's exactly what they spend it on,' Caffery says drily. 'Mind if I keep this?'

'He might want it for the guarantee.'

Caffery gives him a long look.

Eventually Hurst shrugs. 'Be my guest.'

Fred Astaire

It's seven fifteen. AJ sits on the bench outside the ladies' locker room, feeling shittier and shittier by the second. He has drunk two cups of coffee from the machine and eaten a Mars bar and now all there is to do is stare at the notices on the board and rub his toe against a piece of chewing gum that clings resolutely to the floor. It's been forty-five minutes, and although plenty of women have come and gone in that time, giving him surreptitious looks that make him feel like a prize pervert, none of them has been Melanie. Either she can sulk for Britain, or she's climbed out of the locker-room window.

He regrets what he said, the way he said it. He's texted her three apologies, but the signal's not good down here so there's no knowing whether they've arrived, or if she's ignoring him. He's about to fish the phone out and try again when the door opens and Melanie comes out.

She's changed into a simple white wool dress and furry suede boots. Her hair is still slightly damp from the shower. She's got no make-up on and she's so lovely his heart almost stops.

'Melanie — ' he begins, standing up. But she puts a finger to her lips, shakes her head. She drops her bag and sits on the bench about a foot away from him, studying him intently.

'AJ.'

'Melanie, I'm sorry.'

'That's not for you to say — I'm the one who should be sorry. I did lie. It's just . . . sometimes you look at the patients, who've sometimes made just *one* mistake, a mistake they've paid for over and over again by being in the unit, having to jump through all the hoops we set them, and you know they *deserve* a chance to get out and live a normal life. But at the same time there's one vital piece of the jigsaw missing — a box ticked in the wrong-colour biro or some tiny detail that will make the great bureaucratic engine spit out their application and refuse discharge. Through no fault of their own, the patient will be back to square one, facing the prospect of being run through the spin cycle all over again.'

AJ rests his hands on his knees and taps out a drumbeat. He doesn't agree with Melanie that every patient, no matter who, deserves a chance. A lot of the people in the unit have taken away someone else's right to life; in any other facility they'd be called murderers. Some of them are beyond rehabilitation. Especially the ones whose crimes are as memorable as Isaac Handel's.

'AJ? Have I said something wrong?'

'No, no. I don't blame you. Especially not with the amount of pressure the Trust are heaping on you over performance targets.'

He's talking about the 'intractable' patients, the long-stay patients, the bed blockers. Those that can't be recycled out into the community because relatives are unwilling to accept the patient back into their lives. Or those who have no desire to leave the unit and start facing up to the responsibilities of the real world, so they throw obstacles in the way of their own discharge. Such patients form a giant plug in the pipes of the system, and in an effort to clear the blockage, the staff at Beechway are bombarded with directives from above reminding them of the need to lower the ALS — the average length of stay. Melanie, most of all, must get hit with it constantly.

'Believe me, we all feel that pressure, Melanie. There isn't a nurse or therapist in the unit who wouldn't be tempted to take part in a little off-the-rule-book activity if it meant patients moved faster through the system. And you — well, you must be feeling it harder than any of us.'

There's a pause — then Melanie lowers her head. 'Oh God,' she says miserably. 'Honestly, I just looked at Isaac and . . . ' She laces her fingers into her hair, as if she's got a headache. 'Shit — OK, I'm just going to be honest. I thought he hadn't been any trouble for years and years, he'd completely toed the line — he'd be a good candidate. Fuck.' She digs her heels back into the grille under the seat. 'Talk about shooting yourself in the foot. You're right, AJ — it was Isaac in my garden. Two nights in a row. I couldn't bring myself to admit it before.' She gives a long sigh. 'There — I've said it. I suppose this means curtains for our little dalliance. You must hate me now.'

'Hate you? Christ!' He lets out a short, ironic laugh. '*Hate* you? Jesus, if you only knew . . . '

'Knew what?'

'Melanie,' he says, shaking his head. 'Come

on, beautiful woman — I am *insane* about you. I'm like Monster Mother on a lilac day all the time just thinking about you. I'm like Moses when he hears it's sausages for breakfast. I am like Fred Astaire dancing — I am NUTS. About. You.'

'Seriously?'

'I told you — I'm a wimp around you, pathetic.'

She gives a hopeful little smile. A quick sniff — as if tears had been close. 'I'm sorry — it's all driving me mad.'

'I know.'

'And I'm scared. If that was Isaac in the garden — then why? What does he want?'

AJ doesn't answer. A memory flashes up in his brain like a giant billboard — Isaac watching Melanie walk down the corridor.

'There's always the police,' he says tentatively.

'We *can't*,' she says wearily. 'Maybe Isaac will just . . . you know, *vanish* into the ether. But whatever — we can't speak to the police. Can you imagine what would happen to someone in my position if it came out I'd been lying to the tribunal? *Lying?*'

AJ colours when she says the word 'lying'. She has no way of knowing where he's been today, but he's defensive nonetheless. He coughs loudly. Taps his fingers harder on his knees.

'OK, let's say he doesn't vanish into the ether. If we can't go to the police, I'm not about to sit back and let him hound us. I reckon it was him in your garden. Probably the first thing he did when he was discharged was to find out where you live — he'll have made it his business. Your house is a bad place to be right now. This might sound a bit forward — and please don't misinterpret me, but . . . '

'But?'

He hesitates. He doesn't know how to say it. And he doesn't know if it's the right thing. All he knows is he wants Melanie where he can see her.

'I live — well, I live closer to Upton Farm than you do, but Isaac hasn't got a clue where I am. So I was thinking . . . why don't you come stay at my place for a while? Give it some time for things to settle down, see where everything lands? No — it's a crazy idea, I know, forget I said it, I was just thinking aloud, but at least check into a hotel somewhere — just to get you away from your — '

'AJ!'

He stops talking. A smile has broken across her face, revealing her small, perfect teeth.

'AJ, it's fine. It's not crazy at all. In fact, it's a fabulous idea. I've been dying to meet Patience.'

Wickes

The days are short this far into autumn and it's pretty much dark when Caffery gets to the shop at the north end of Bristol. CCTV cameras are trained on the entrance, the tills, with three or four more above the aisles. The store is divided into Decoration/Plumbing/Electrical/Tools. At least two of those categories sit uneasily with Caffery. Even without reading the full report he knows that the things Handel did to his parents involved objects purchased from a place like this.

'Manager.' He flashes his warrant card to the security guy. 'Please.'

He is shown to a small office piled with paperwork. Kieran Bolt is small and clean-shaven with eyes reddened through tiredness. He's getting ready to go home, and doesn't look pleased to see Caffery. He squints at the receipt for a few seconds. 'This is for cash. I can't give you a name from this.'

'I don't need a name,' Caffery says. 'I've already got that. I'm interested in what else he bought.'

'What makes you think he bought more?'

'Seven empty carrier bags.'

Bolt looks at him, startled, then at the receipt again, examining it as if he thinks he must have missed something. 'Where did you say you were from?'

'Major Crimes Investigation Unit.' Caffery

watches the manager run through the reasons a police officer might be asking questions about purchases at a hardware store. When he finally looks up again, the wariness behind Bolt's eyes says he's thinking National Security, terrorist threat.

'We just sell the stuff. We don't ask people what they're going to do with it.'

'Nobody's accusing you of anything. I'm making inquiries, that's all.'

The manager is easy to read; he's anxious, he's going to bend over backwards to help. 'I can check the till receipts — if he used a credit card for anything else it should come up. But if he paid cash . . . '

'That's OK. We'll find him on the CCTV.'

Bolt clasps a hand to his forehead.

'Problem?'

'No. No — absolutely no problem. It's just . . . ' He checks his watch. 'No — I'll make a quick phone call and you're fine. I can stay with you.'

Bolt is saying it's going to take for ever to trawl through the footage. There are eight cameras dotted around the store, they keep twenty-one days' worth of recordings, at a guess, and they're open seven till eight, Monday to Saturday — and six hours on Sunday.

'It's OK,' Caffery says. 'You will get home tonight. I promise.'

Eden Hole

When AJ and Melanie get back to the cottage, Stewart is barking like crazy. He doesn't even seem to recognize AJ when he opens the door, he just sits in the hallway, head back, yapping at them.

'Hey hey! Stewie? What's up — it's only me.' AJ crouches beside him. 'What's up, Stewie?'

Stewart stops barking and sniffs AJ's hands sullenly, his eyes rolling suspiciously up to Melanie. She regards him warily, holding her bags high out of his reach.

'He's . . . he's lovely,' she says uncertainly.

'I swear he's not like this usually.' AJ gives the dog a scratch behind the ears. He's panting and his heart is racing under his ribcage. 'He's been weird since yesterday. He disappeared for the day and now he's acting like a nutjob — I don't get it. What happened, boy?'

Stewart does a small, agitated circle on the floor. Then, reluctantly, he sits, tongue hanging out. AJ is mystified. 'I'll take him out later — run him until he's too knackered to be neurotic. Come on — come and meet Patience.'

They carry Melanie's bags through into the living room. AJ has called ahead and warned his aunt Melanie will be staying. Patience's only comment was: *Tell the poor girl she'll have to like my cooking. I don't want any of your mincy little food Nazis in my house. If she wants to live on lettuce and air, she can go live in a warren.*

AJ has noted the way Patience says 'poor girl'. As if any woman crazy enough to be involved with him must be a truly miserable specimen. Or very slutty and self-obsessed. When Melanie walks through the door in the simple white wool dress, her honey hair falling around her face, Patience's face falls a mile. This is not what she was expecting. AJ can't help smirking.

'Well now,' she says, getting to her feet. 'Melanie. It's good to meet you.'

She shakes Melanie's hand, letting her eyes go slowly from her feet all the way up to her face and down again. Then she releases her hand, steps back and folds her arms, appraising her, eyebrows raised like question marks. She makes a loud tut in the back of her throat, tosses her head and sashays into the kitchen, hips swinging imperiously.

'God!' AJ scratches his head, embarrassed. 'I'm sorry. She obviously didn't expect me to be with someone who's as . . . you know . . . nice as you.'

'Okaaaaa-aaay.' Melanie drops her hands. She surreptitiously wipes the palm Patience touched against her skirt. 'That's fine — I understand.' She smiles waveringly, glancing around the room. It's in a state of chaos: Patience's jam jars on every surface and clutches of wildflowers in milk bottles on the windowsill, the water going brown. She shoots a look at the kitchen, then back at the hallway where Stewart is sitting moodily watching them.

AJ's spirit sinks. This isn't going well — not well at all.

'Melanie, listen — you're so welcome here. We're not exactly conventional, I know. Patience takes a bit of getting used to — '

'I heard that,' Patience hollers from the kitchen. 'I'll have to get used to her is what you should be saying.'

AJ shakes his head, gives a small smile.

'Like I say, you'll have to get used to my *lovely aunt,* but we want you to be comfortable. If you need somewhere private — somewhere you can be yourself — you can have Mum's old room.' He jabs his finger at the ceiling. 'There's a bedroom above here and a bathroom — completely private. And clean — I promise — in spite of what it looks like down here, it is clean up there — I did it myself.'

'I heard that too. Do you want your breakfast or not?'

'*Breakfast?*' Melanie whispers. '*Breakfast?*'

'It's a family tradition — when I come home from work. Don't panic.' He jabs a finger at the stairwell that leads to his section. 'I've got the same thing up those stairs — mirror image. Only a wall separating us.'

Melanie raises her eyes to the ceiling — to the oak beams. 'Is there a doorway?'

'No.'

'So to get to you from there I've got to . . . what? Come down here and go up?'

'Yes. Or you could just throw your chips in and stay with me.'

The One They All Avoid

The coffee is from a little sachet like a teabag and has grounds floating in it. But it's dark and strong and exactly what Caffery needs at this time of day. He loads it with sugar and eats four biscuits in the over-bright, fluorescent-lit staffroom at Wickes. Lately he's been having to remind himself to eat. When he forgets, he'll catch sight of himself in a window and see a stranger's face that his inbuilt pigeon-holer immediately categorizes as: *Forty something. Stressful job. Not married*.

Bolt, who clearly *is* married and anxious to get home, has done a till-receipt search but turned up nothing under the name Handel. Now he's setting up a laptop linked to the CCTV's external drive. Caffery hangs his jacket on the back of the chair, sets his coffee down, and fishes out his phone. He blows up the photograph of Handel that AJ messaged him earlier and props the phone against the monitor.

There are fifteen hundred hours of video footage loaded on the drive, but he can narrow those hours down. Handel was released only fifty-four hours ago. The goods must have been purchased between then and last night, when he was last seen at the hostel. That info alone cuts out a huge wad of data. Also the receipt for the iPod dock is time-and-date stamped for five p.m. Tuesday and, though it's a gamble, Caffery's willing to bet Handel didn't come all the way here from the hostel twice. Either he bought the dock and then remembered something and went back into the shop, or vice versa. More likely vice versa, since you don't 'forget' seven carrier bags of hardware.

He quickly skips to the Tuesday-evening section of the till-camera recording and, sure enough, there is Handel standing in the queue, waiting to be served. Caffery compares it to the photo on the phone. Stained sweatpants and the stripy orange-and-brown sweater AJ talked about. The haircut is seriously random too — a bit like a monk's. He is staring intently at other customers, making everyone uneasy — standing too close to the woman ahead of him. She steals nervous glances at him over her shoulder.

No — there's no way he'd be able to walk into a hotel and book a room.

He is holding several carrier bags. Bulging. In fact he has to put them on the floor as he pays for the docking station. As he does, the assistant glances anxiously past him a few times. Probably trying to catch the eye of the security guard in case something kicks off. But Handel just picks up his bags and then walks out of the shop. The waiting customers exchange relieved glances.

Caffery skips back through the footage — the hurried blurs of customers, staff zipping in and out, stopping for milliseconds to talk to cashiers, customers, then equally quickly vanishing. Then, just ten minutes ahead of his iPod-dock purchase, Handel appears in the cash queue. This time he has no carrier bags but a trolley loaded with goods.

Caffery freezes the picture. The boxes and reels and tins in the trolley are unidentifiable from the image. He unpauses the video and lets it run real time.

Handel is as unsettling this time as he is in the later footage. Small though he is, something in his face makes people around him uncomfortable. One or two other customers push trolleys to the end of the queue, but within seconds of being in Handel's vicinity they change their minds and steer their trolleys to another counter. One begins to unload goods on to the conveyor belt then changes her mind. She actually packs things back into her trolley and heads off, trying to appear casual, as if she's forgotten something.

Caffery watches closely as the cashier runs Handel's items through the till. Again he freezes the picture. He has nothing to write on so he rolls up his shirtsleeve and jots down the time code on his arm. He gets up, goes to Kieran Bolt's office door, and knocks.

An Angel

Sometimes things are so beautiful you can tie yourself in knots trying to explain them or capture them. Maybe it's Mum's death, and the way he remembers her, or maybe it's simply that AJ is a grown-up now — whatever, he's learned to accept beauty when it comes his way, appreciate it, and believe it will come to him again. He doesn't care that it's a bit new-age, wisdom-of-the-universe stuff. It's the way he's learned to view the world.

Except there's one problem with it. Because — while it's easy to look out of his window at the acres of green, at the boundless cloudy horizon — and accept and believe in it all and its continuity — he finds he can't accept the fact that Melanie Arrow is sitting here at the old kitchen table, eating Patience's nine p.m. breakfast. He simply can't believe it and he can't help wanting to own it and contain it. Wishing he'd done it earlier yet at the same time being glad he waited until it was right. It's as if Mum is sitting in the corner smiling contentedly at Melanie — proud and glad that at last he's done the right thing. Because an angel may as well have plopped down in their cottage. Someone to transform him — make him a better person.

'More?' Patience stands with her hand on her hip, the skillet in her hand, looking down her nose at Melanie, who has just, generously, consumed a pile of sausages, eggs, coconut 'bammy' cakes and fried pumpkin. Apparently the pumpkin patch is going crazy and Patience seems determined to feed every last one to Melanie. Not to mention the lovage brandy she keeps slopping into her glass. 'Don't you want to eat more?'

AJ digs his teeth into the mug he's sipping coffee from, vowing not to speak or interfere. If Mum was still alive she'd say that Patience has really got her sass out tonight. Melanie is the biggest challenge Patience has had in years. Probably since the 50–1 she backed at Kempton Park. She is all scrutiny, subjecting the first girlfriend her nephew has brought home in years to a stewards' inquiry. The giveaway fail for Melanie will be any food cowardice. For AJ, Patience wants big, child-bearing women with huge breasts and hips. The slightest hint of a food hater will turn her into a mean-eyed bitch from hell.

'Some dumpling? Haddock? I've got haddock poached in milk — I can do you a bowl with a dumpling and a bit of toast to soak it up? Some more of my lovage brandy?'

The breakfast Patience has provided is the most elaborate to have graced this table in living memory. Melanie has been appreciative to a fault, but there has to be a tipping point.

'I was supposed to be on a diet,' she tells Patience. 'But honestly, you've got *diet saboteur* written across your forehead.'

She's trying to humour Patience, but instead of a smile she's rewarded with more food ladled on her plate. Patience turns away, unimpressed — still challenging. Melanie eats dutifully, her eyes on Patience's back. She casts AJ the occasional brave glance and he nods encouragingly. He wants to explain in more detail — *this is your initiation ceremony, Melanie. You're doing well, it won't always be like this* . . . But maybe she's already worked that out, because she applies herself to the task with a ferocity he's only seen her use in the clinic.

She finishes the plate. Delicately dabs her mouth, then hands it to Patience, who takes it without a murmur. She doesn't offer Melanie any more food.

It means the test has been passed.

The Inventory

The transaction at Wickes was in cash and itemized by the superstore. It took Kieran Bolt just two minutes to find it. He and Caffery stood in silence and read through the record of what Handel bought fifteen minutes before he paid for the docking station. To anyone else the list might have seemed innocuous. To Caffery, knowing what he did about Handel, it read like a bullet-point inventory of warning signs:

Copper wiring
Crocodile clips (seven different colours)
Hacksaw blade
Stanley knife
Pliers

Mercifully, back at the MCIT offices, the superintendent has gone home — so no big self-justification exercises needed. The building is almost empty. Caffery closes the blinds and clears the desk. In the corner are six green transport crates: Isaac's paperwork up from Archives. Caffery lifts the first on to the desk. He opens a folder and begins to read.

Handel lived at Upton Farm from the day he was born. At twelve he was already coming to the attention of the school for his increasingly withdrawn behaviour and bizarre outbursts. He was moved to a school for the learning disabled. Everyone knew Isaac was troubled, but evidently neither his teachers, social services nor his parents realized how dangerous he was. Not until it was too late.

Next to Caffery's mouse mat is the copy of the Wickes receipt. It connects so blatantly to what happened next it's almost surreal. Like a joke. He takes a pen and begins underlining some of the items on the list. The first is:

Stanley knife

On 2 November, when Isaac was fourteen, he took a Stanley knife to his parents' throats in the master bedroom of their house. Isaac's father fought back, but he had the beginnings of heart disease and was no match for his adolescent son. Isaac incapacitated him by running the blade under his chin, opening up his windpipe and damaging the oesophagus. He did the same to his mother. For a while both victims were still breathing through the holes in their necks. It was blood loss that would eventually kill them.

Pliers

After cutting their throats, Isaac really went to town on them. He stayed with them for hours. While they died he carved their faces and cut off their ears. He cut out their tongues and removed several of their teeth, using, the pathologist speculates, a wrench. Like the one on the Wickes receipt.

Nothing Handel removed from the bodies was found at the scene. And to this day none of the body parts has been traced. Some of the investigating officers speculated that he threw them out of the window and they were eaten by wildlife. Others insist the only way Isaac could have feasibly removed the things from the scene was to have ingested them. There is, however, no record of Isaac being examined or X-rayed. Teeth at least would have shown up in his stomach on an X-ray, Caffery thinks. But with a CSI's dream of a crime scene — with a defence of insanity — no police force in the country opens its piggy bank to dig deeper in an investigation. That only happens when a Misty Kitson goes missing.

Wire and crocodile clips

Graham and Louise Handel were discovered positioned on their backs, their mouths wide open. That may have been the result of the muscles spasming when their son wrenched their teeth out. The remaining sockets are black and blood-streaked in the photographs. In the report the pathologist notes time and time again he was unable to make an accurate examination due to the delays encountered because of 'circumstances' at the crime scene. Without immediate access to the bodies a lot of his conclusions were leaps of faith. He could only estimate that it took Mrs Handel in excess of thirty minutes to die, Mr Handel a little less — maybe eighteen to twenty minutes. Nor could he say whether their open mouths were a result of rigor mortis — or whether Isaac managed to position them like that in death.

The 'circumstances' preventing the crew getting to the bodies are logged by several parties: the forensics investigators, the first attending officer, the SIO. And they make Caffery even more uneasy.

At a place exactly equidistant to the door and

to the bodies, Handel had placed a length of wire. The first attending was canny enough to spot it and instantly called in military bomb-disposal experts. It took them ninety minutes to travel from Salisbury and make the scene safe. They explained that anyone entering the scene unwittingly would have triggered a chemical explosion that would have ignited the entire room. A booby-trapped crime scene. It's so clever.

When Caffery's finished reading he turns the last page of the CSI report face down in the box, closes the lid and contemplates it. There's something awry here — an inconsistency or anomaly, something he can't quite put a finger on . . . He sits with his thumbs digging into his temples, trying to concentrate. But he can't quite nail it.

He drags across the photograph of Isaac Handel. Many people claim that they can see evil in a person's eyes, and Caffery sometimes wonders if he's missing a vital component, because in all his years in this job, with all the killers and rapists and child murderers he's met, he's never *ever* been able to look into the eyes of a killer and see evil. In Isaac Handel's eyes he sees nothing. Nothing at all. It's as if there's an impenetrable barrier slotted down there behind the irises.

Again he wonders what was missing from the report. And when he can't come up with an answer he leans back in his chair, hands folded across his stomach, and lines up his thoughts in a row.

Assume, he tells himself, because all the signs are there, that Handel is not rehabilitated and that he is a danger to himself and to the public.

Assume that what happened in Beechway High Secure Unit is secondary.

Assume finding Isaac Handel is primary.

Assume that the superintendent won't raise the budget on this to a homicide until Zelda's post-mortem is re-done, and that he certainly won't be interested in a ghost in a psychiatric unit.

All of which means Caffery has to do things the hard way — finding Handel on his own.

And, as with most things in life, assume the best place to start is at the beginning.

Stewart and the Wandering Star

Melanie is still loaded down with food and slow moving. The sex she and AJ have that night is the sort that belongs on a desert island, lazy and leisurely and un-showoffy. It takes for ever; it's speechless. Afterwards she amazes him by curling up next to him, holding him tightly, as if she's clinging on to a life raft. He drifts off to sleep in the middle of studying her — mapping every detail of her face. He's in the same position, on his back, arm pushed out to the side, when he wakes.

She's still lying on his arm but she's wide awake, prodding him.

'*AJ?* AJ?'

'Yeah? What?' He rubs his eyes, props himself up on his elbows and looks around groggily. His first thought is Isaac Handel, but the curtains are closed. 'What's up?'

Mel kisses his ear. She smells of warm orange and shampoo. 'Don't take this the wrong way, sweetheart. Don't think I'm being rude, but would you ask Stewart to go out on to the landing?'

Stewart is in his usual place next to the door, lying down. He's wide awake too — eyes fixed on AJ and Melanie. 'Stewart? Why? What's he done?'

'Nothing.' She gives a little shiver. Dabs her nose with a tissue. Sniffs. 'Maybe he's been out in the grass — I don't know — it's just my allergy's kicking in.'

Even through the pall of sleep AJ knows her sniffs are fake. He sits up now, peers seriously at her. 'Melanie? Allergy? Are you sure? It's autumn.'

'Yes — I'm sorry, I think it's dear old Stewart and I . . . '

AJ looks from Stewart to Melanie and back again, perplexed. But he gets up anyway and takes Stewart out on to the landing, closes the door and returns to bed.

'Thank you.' She cuddles into him. She's cold and covered in goosebumps. From her breathing he knows her nose isn't bunged up at all. 'Thank you.'

'What's really the matter?' he asks. 'You haven't got an allergy.'

She stops her wriggling and goes still like an animal caught in a trap. He can feel her ribcage rising and falling very gently.

'Melanie? What is it? Did you see something?'

'No — I promise. It's an allergy.'

'Please. I'm honest with you.'

There's a long silence. Then she shakes her head. 'No. You'll think I'm crazy.'

'Try me.'

'I couldn't sleep — '

'Not surprising. And with everything you ate last night too.'

'No — every time I opened my eyes Stewart was awake. I just kept thinking what you said about how something happened — how he . . . ' She swallows. 'How he disappeared. AJ? What do you think he saw?'

AJ frowns, looks down at her to see if she's serious. Melanie Arrow, the hard-headed, no-nonsense workaholic. It's actually getting to her.

'Hey.' He kisses her on her forehead. 'You're safe here. I promise.'

She gives a weak smile. 'Promise, promise, pinkie promise?'

'Pinkie promise, cross my heart. Now go to sleep.'

Eventually she does go back to sleep. AJ does too. It's a dreamless, deep sleep — and they are both so tired that they snooze on through the alarm. It's only Stewart scratching at the door and whimpering that wakes them. They jump up hurriedly, and race around trying to organize themselves. Patience is still asleep but she's been up in the night and has left coffee brewing for them on the stove. AJ pours a cup for Melanie and drinks his mug standing in the doorway watching Stewart doing his thing in the fields.

He wonders what on earth is going on with the dog. Mel's right, something is really askew. When Stewart's had a pee, instead of trotting back to the cottage for his breakfast, he turns and looks in the direction of the woods.

'No.' AJ shakes his head. 'No, Stewart, not again. Come on, come here. Now.'

Stewart can't make up his mind whether to obey. He gives the woods a longing look, then glances back at AJ.

'I said *now*, Stewart.'

Finally Stewart's stomach gets the better of him and he trots obligingly back inside. If he resents being thrown out of the bedroom last night it doesn't show as he tucks into his breakfast. AJ watches him thoughtfully for a few moments, then he washes his coffee mug and heads back upstairs.

Melanie has showered and is already dressed and sitting in the chair next to his bedroom window, delving into her handbag. She's wearing a white blouse with a sailor collar and little black bow and silver earrings dangling around her jawline. When he comes in she hurriedly takes her hands out of the handbag. But not so quickly that he hasn't seen what she was doing.

He looks at the bag. 'Still haven't found your bracelet?'

'Oh,' she shrugs. 'No — no, I . . . Never mind, it's not the end of the world.'

'It's hard, when you lose something that precious to you.'

Melanie blinks and continues smiling at him. But he can tell it's an effort. She's fighting to stop something under the surface cracking open.

'Melanie?'

'Yes,' she says brightly. She jumps up and turns her back on him, begins shovelling things into her bag. 'Gotta get going, AJ, we've gotta get going — people to see, hospitals to run. Come on.' She holds up her hand and clicks her fingers, still not looking at him. '*Vamos, vamos, vamos, babbbeeeee!*'

The Bath

AJ's head is misbehaving — leaping all over the places he doesn't want it to leap. If he's not thinking about whether Melanie's still got feelings for Jonathan Keay, he's wondering why DI Caffery hasn't called. Not that AJ expects him to, but he'd like some sort of contact. And an update. That conversation they had keeps plaguing him: *Do you really not know what happened at Upton Farm . . .*

The moment he and Melanie get to work, AJ makes an excuse and goes straight to Handel's room. It still hasn't been turned round for the next admission off the acute ward. He unlocks the door, goes in, and locks the door behind him before anyone sees. The rooms in the pre-discharge ward are designed for low-risk patients ready to move either out into the community or to be referred on to medium-secure units. The patients have furniture and can put up posters. Some risk-evaluated patients even have baths in their en suites. Handel was allowed a tub and coat hangers and a spotlight above his bed for reading.

A start has been made on preparing the room for the next occupant. The cleaning equipment has been brought up here and left in the corner. There are two bin liners full of rubbish sitting under the window. AJ squats and starts going through the contents. Nothing too odd: the usual assortment of sweet-wrappers, a mouldy apple, magazines and old underwear.

The patients are very good at hiding things away — and it's rarely the sort of things one might expect, like cigarettes or drugs. Quite often it's food. AJ's lost count of the number of treasure troves of mouldering cake and pizza he's found tucked away in pillowcases, in the backs of wardrobes, even stuffed into trainers with the laces tied neatly over the top. Sometimes it's dirty clothes they've attached a random significance to. Once he found an old-fashioned ceramic sewing thimble that had been packed to the brim with a thick sticky substance. He'd put the tip of a biro into it and dug around for several seconds before he realized it was the patient's collection of ear wax.

It's a charmed life this, working at Beechway.

Having gone through the contents of the bin bags and found nothing that means anything to him, AJ sits on the mattress and glances around. The walls are bare apart from a few dabs of Blu-tack where Isaac's posters have been taken down. The curtains are torn in one place — he must make a note of that and get a works requisition into Maintenance. The door to Isaac's shower room is open, and AJ's attention is drawn to the tap in the basin, which is dripping steadily.

The bathrooms are designed to be indestructible, with no 'ligature points' — i.e. nowhere the patient can hang him or herself. All the taps and handles are curved down towards the floor. These bathrooms are black holes of dread to the nursing staff. It is rare to go into one and find the toilet unused. And then there is the usual careless detritus of human functions — tissues glued together with snot, and, in the case of the men, other bodily secretions. Pubic hair, scabs, vomit. Even the most fastidious OCD patients seem to have a blind spot when it comes to bathrooms.

He stares into the room for a long time, the cogs in his head turning slowly. Then he gets up and crosses to the bathroom door, switches on the light.

Thankfully the cleaning crew have been through already — it smells of bleach and the light reflects off the newly cleaned sink. The window looks out over to the admin unit, where one or two lighted windows can be seen. The skies are clouded and low, threatening rain. It's as dark out there as if it was evening. AJ uses his toe to give the bath panel a quick push. It bends then bounces back with a loud *whoomp*. He crouches and runs his hand around the edge where the plastic meets the bathtub. His forefinger finds the breech — up in the top-right-hand corner, at the end where the taps are, the panel is missing a bracket.

He fumbles his keys out from his trouser pocket and, using the passive security fob, which is a rigid slab of plastic, he carefully pries the top corner of the panel away from the bath and peers inside. The fibreglass bottom of the bathtub is visible, but not much more. He gets out his mobile phone, and opens the torch app. Pushing his right hand in between the panel and the bath, he uses his arm to increase the space, then shines the torch into the dark.

Something is wedged down there. A large holdall with 'Adidas' written on it. He grits his teeth — stretches for it, catching the handle on the tip of his finger and dragging it closer. He won't be able to pull it out intact — he'll have to open it and empty the contents while it's still behind the panel. When the bag is close enough, he shifts position so he can keep the phone light shining on it and get leverage on the zip.

He pulls the zip back, feeling the soft tick tick tick of the slider bumping along the teeth. There's a smell coming out of the bag — a smell of old laundry. You only have to work in a place like this for one day to learn that patients will store the strangest of things in the strangest of places — you never put your hands anywhere you can't see first. So he nudges the phone closer and squints through the gap.

What he sees makes him hurriedly pull his hand out. The bath panel snaps closed with a loud crack and he sits back, breathing hard.

A Holdall

The phone wakes Caffery. It is morning and he is lying on the sofa in his office. He jerks upright, thinking it's his mobile, thinking it's Flea. It's not. It's the office phone. He rolls over, reaching across to the desk for it. It's reception — AJ's here again — something he wants to talk about.

'Give me five. I'll be down.'

He loosens his tie and sits for a while rubbing his face, reorientating himself. Isaac's report is scattered on the floor around him — he must have fallen asleep reading. In the incident room there are three civilian officers already at their work stations. He's slept through it all. The first proper night's sleep he's had since Jacqui Kitson walked into Browns Brasserie five nights ago.

He fishes his mobile out and checks for texts or calls or emails from Flea. Nothing. Now there's a surprise. After a while he gets up. He avoids looking at Misty's photograph — as if he's ashamed to have been thinking about something else. He finds his spare toothbrush in the top drawer, has a quick, make-do wash in the men's, then goes down to meet AJ, who is standing shyly in reception, holding an enormous Adidas holdall. Is it just Caffery or is he a little paler than he was yesterday?

'Thank you for letting me come up,' he says when they get back to the office. 'Everything OK?'

Caffery shrugs. Pulls a seat out for AJ. There's a briefing on another case going on in the CCTV viewing suite — he has to close his door on the noise.

'I had a word with the pathologist last night — they're going to take a second look at Zelda.'

'So you are going to follow up on it?'

'I've already started. Yesterday I went to the hostel Isaac's supposed to be staying at.'

'And?'

'He's not there. Hasn't been since the day before yesterday.'

'Fuck.' AJ sits down with a bump. 'Fuck.'

'I know.' Caffery checks his watch again. He didn't mean to sleep this late — it's set him back. 'We don't know where he is but I've got some leads I'm going to follow.' His eyes travel down to the holdall. 'I take it there's something important in the bag?'

'Yes, I . . . or rather, I don't know. I don't know if it's important, but I found these. Hidden in Handel's bathroom.'

He lifts the holdall on to the desk, unzips it and spills out the contents. Caffery puts his glasses on and shuffles his chair forward for a closer look. He gets a whiff and covers his nose with his hand. 'Jesus. They stink.'

'I know. I'm sorry. I don't even know if I should have them — if they're stolen property — or evidence or what. Maybe I should have left them where I found them — but I didn't.'

'I wish you had.' Caffery pushes his chair away from the desk and gets to his feet to open the window.

‘I thought you’d want them.’
‘Why would I want them?’
AJ shifts uncertainly. He shoves his hands in the pockets of his jacket and looks at his feet. ‘I don’t know,’ he says lamely. ‘I suppose I thought you might get Handel’s DNA from them? Maybe?’
‘Right.’ Caffery fastens the window open as far as it will go. The chill morning air comes in. ‘Right.’
They stand together in silence and stare at what is on the desk. A pile of dolls. Nightmarish things, made from a variety of plastics and fabrics. Most have awful, lifelike eyes — tiny plastic things from a hobby shop. Like frogs’ eyes they blink open and closed when the dolls are moved. A few have stitch marks where the eyes should be. One has a normal eye on the left and a red boiled sweet in place of the right one.
Each is different and unwholesome in its own way. Some seem to represent females — they have long string hair and crude breasts sewn from sheets of knitting. Others are males with tiny appendages of hobby-shop felt or dangling, crocheted sacs. Some have miniature strips of masking tape placed over their eyes and mouths. Others have their arms tied behind their backs with lengths of garden twine. Some have horrible little sets of teeth — made of maybe shells or fake pearls, Caffery can’t tell. Some are enshrined on pink satin cushions, their hands crossed on their chests, the way medieval saints and warriors are often depicted on their tombs — brave, sacred and martyred.

'They were in his bathroom?'

'Uh-huh. Hidden behind the bath panel.'

'They stink. No one noticed the smell?'

'You'd have to put it in context. You know, of the overwhelming completely unavoidable, completely constant and disgusting smell that is normality in the unit. Don't tell me you've never been in a place like that?'

Caffery inclines his head. 'Not pleasant, I grant you.'

'And everyone was used to Isaac smelling. Especially in the beginning. These — ' He waves a hand over the dolls, as if he's struggling to find the words to describe them. 'These *things* he made. It was all he ever did with his time. He'd always carry one or two around with him — couldn't be separated from them. Not ever. We gave up trying. If you'd spent most of your time sandwiched under Isaac's armpits you'd smell too.'

He unfolds a piece of paper torn from a ring binder and holds it out to Caffery. On it have been written several lines in a very small, neat hand. Caffery peers at them. He can make out one or two phrases that sound biblical in origin.

AJ runs a finger under a few of them:

Be thou not one of them that committeth foul acts.

Avoid idleness and intemperance.

'This is what Pauline wrote on her thighs. And this is what Zelda wrote. And this . . . ?'

He locates a line at the bottom and taps it.

Anyone who looks at a woman lustfully has already committed adultery in his heart.

'That is what Moses wrote on his walls before he pulled his eye out.'

Caffery nods slowly. He raises his eyes and finds AJ looking at him steadily.

'If I had any doubt at all before — when I saw this I thought . . .'

'I know what you thought.' Caffery wants to be going and he wants to be going now. 'And for the record? I'm thinking it too.'

Upton Farm

Moments after AJ leaves the building Caffery gets a call from Beatrice Foxton, the pathologist. She's done the second post-mortem on Zelda and hasn't been able to reach any further conclusions. Sometimes, she explains, we just have to hold our hands up. And say we don't know for sure.

Caffery decides it doesn't matter. He's seen and heard enough about Handel to keep going anyway. He puts on a pair of nitrile gloves — as much for the sake of cleanliness as from a fear of contaminating evidentiary material — and packs the dolls into the holdall. He seals it in a bag he gets from one of the CSIs, then carries it to the car. Throws it in the boot and climbs into the car. He lets the engine run for a few minutes then sniffs. No smell coming from the dolls. Good. He puts the car into gear and heads out of the car park.

In the nineties when Handel murdered his parents, there was still such a thing as policing in villages. If the place was too small for a station, there would be a single cop who lived in an authority-owned police house, a cop who stepped out of his front door straight on to his beat — who knew not just the locals in the village itself, but the inhabitants of every lane and every farm in the area. He would have known Isaac and his parents. The photocopied transcript of the police notebook on the day of the murders states that a call from a nearby phone box went through to the village police station. That the cop, Sergeant Harry Pilson, was on the scene within ten minutes.

Upton Farm has changed hands three times in the years since the murders. The present owners, a couple who live two miles away, bought the place five years ago and let it out as a holiday home. Caffery stops off at their house to pick up a set of keys. The husband's out, but the wife is there. She's a forty-something woman with angry eyes and defiantly city hair; it's clear country living is an aesthetic choice and not what she was born to. Every inch of the place is filled with the sort of country living that townies aspire to: oilskins and designer wellies. Paintings on the wall that are self-consciously artisan in their appearance. She probably hopes he'll admire it, but he's known women like her before and is too old to waste his time lying. He declines her offer of coffee and asks for the keys to Upton Farm.

'You've always rented it out?'

She gives a short laugh. No humour. 'We've always *tried* to rent it out. If anyone would take it. This area is supposed to be a popular holiday destination, but I've only had six rentals this year. And two of those changed their mind after the first night there. Walked out and demanded their money back.' She shakes her head. 'I'd put it on the market, but who would want it? Only some London idiots like us who don't know its history.'

Outside, it's a cold, damp day. Wisps of vapour streak up from the red-and-orange forests that line the valleys and cling to the cliffs like low cloud. Caffery has the heating on full blast as he drives, along back lanes wide enough for one car, with passing places at intervals — and God help the traveller who meets a tractor coming the other way. On the passenger seat is Sergeant Pilson's report from the day of the murders. One of the DCs at MCIT is checking whether Pilson still lives in the area. If he does, they'll message Caffery his contact details.

In the nineties there were phone boxes deep in the countryside where the big telecommunications companies hadn't yet got their signals. The call to Sergeant Pilson came from a phone box just to the south of Upton Farm — a woman driving past the farmhouse realized something was wrong. She drove on, got to the phone box and called. She gave her name and address, but when the investigating team tried to trace the witness her address turned out not to exist. Either she had lied, or, in Pilson's own admission, he might have written it down incorrectly. Police press releases urging the person to come forward amounted to nothing. Ultimately it was the only loose end in a very tight case.

Upton Farm is about as high as you can get in this part of the world and as Caffery gets nearer clouds gather. The air turns whiter and his visibility dwindles. He skirts west of the dark Forestry Commission pine forest before heading northward. As he nears the farm, a few spots of rain begin to fall. It's like crossing into the Himalayas. A sign at the roadside reads: *Upton Farm Cottage — holiday lets available*.

It's similar land to where Caffery lives — but it's higher, more lonely. He turns on to the driveway and the house comes into view. It's a handsome three-storey Edwardian dwelling built from a blueish-grey shale. There's a newly fitted slate roof and the windows are freshly painted. The sparkling panes reflect a perfect image of the surrounding conifers. Two large barns, constructed of wood which has been treated in pitch, stand on the opposite side of the concrete courtyard. Beyond them clouds have closed in; where distant hills should be visible is an impenetrable wall of shifting white.

Caffery parks in front of the house. A section of the concrete has been dug up and replaced, incongruously, with York stone flags. A couple of potted bay trees stand either side of the front door. An Edwardian-style boot scraper to the left of the doorstep completes the picture. Elegant rusticity.

He unlocks the front door and steps inside. The house smells of furniture polish and air freshener — everywhere are dotted dried-flower arrangements. The staircase has a polished-oak handrail and a hardwearing cord carpet runs up the centre of the risers. He's transferred the crime-scene photos to his phone, and he opens the ones taken in this hallway and compares them to what is in front of him. In the nineties the staircase had an enclosed banister, wall-papered in stipple paint effect. Where he's standing now, the wall was daubed with bloody handprints.

The handprints were an exact match. Handel was responsible for torturing, killing and mutilating his parents — no doubt about it. That's not what's wrong here. It's something else. Caffery has no idea what. He goes slowly up the stairs, opening his mind and his ears and his skin to everything this place can communicate.

The room where Graham and Louise Handel were found is along the landing to the right of the stairway. When Isaac lived here this corridor was dark — carpeted in green Axminster with a leaf-swirl pattern. Now there are bare boards, stripped and waxed. The photos on Caffery's phone show seven framed prints on the wall, all hanging askew from the violence that had taken place. Now the walls are bare. Painted grey.

He opens the door to the room slowly. The curtains are open, the light is chalky and flat. Here too, everything is as different as can be. An oak box bed with a scrolled leather headboard replaces the divan; a thick sheepskin rug at the foot of the bed covers the place Isaac's parents died.

The trip-wire was between here and the bed. The bomb-disposal team had to work only inches from the mutilated bodies of Graham and Louise. The men should have been accustomed to carnage, but the experience evidently got to them — one of the team resigned his position the following day and became a teacher. Apparently he never explained his reasons to anyone.

Caffery comes in and squats, lifting a corner of the rug. The boards beneath it are as smooth and polished as the rest, but there is a slight tonal difference, a darker patina in the grain. A succession of new owners hasn't been able to get rid of all the bloodstains.

He holds up his phone in front of the modern image of the room and zooms on the photo of Louise, pictured from this angle. She wears jogging trousers and a Dunlop T-shirt, and lies on her back, her mouth wrenched open. Blood trails from the corners of her mouth to her jaw. Her ears and some teeth are missing.

Caffery glances up and around — tries to picture the minimalist room with curtainless windows as it was in the nineties: old lumpy furniture, heavy curtains against dark windows. He closes his eyes and spins himself through the years. It's not much of a leap for him to imagine that era, and it doesn't bring him any closer to the nudging point of what is wrong with the whole scenario.

No. He's not there yet.

He takes one last look around the room, then starts along the corridor and back down the stairs. Outside, the clouds have cleared briefly; pale sunshine floods the farmyard, glancing off his windscreen. He wonders about the woman who reported the murders. What could she have seen to alert her?

Caffery turns and gauges the distance from here to the road. That's wrong to start with — the bottom part of the house isn't visible from the road. The crime-scene report says Pilson responded to the call and he arrived at six forty-five p.m. That he followed a blood trail that led from the house to the barn. The fence and the paved area are new — fifteen years ago, the house and barns would have stood on the same concrete courtyard. A cop responding to a triple-nine call would pull up outside the house, and his first instinct would be to look for casualties. According to the report, the front door was open. The distance from the house to the barns is approximately twenty-five metres. So why didn't Harry Pilson go into the house first?

Caffery crosses to the right-hand barn. It was in this barn, the larger of the two, that Handel was cornered and arrested. The large doors are padlocked, so Caffery tries the small access door. It's bolted but not locked, and it swings open. The barn is still being used to store straw and hay. Inside, it is surprisingly warm, a little dusty, and all the sounds from outside are muffled. He blinks — his eyes adjusting to the gloom. A shaft of grey sunlight from the partly open door falls at an angle to his right, catching motes of hay dust and casting a small square of light on the floor of the barn. There's a sound — a *churr, churr* rising in pitch, again and again, and ending on the third *churr*, with a decisive *cluck*. Hens — half a dozen of them — stalk out of the shadows, into the small square of light and begin to scratch and peck at the floor, searching for insects and spilt grain.

Caffery looks at the picture on his phone. Pilson said he spotted Handel in the hayloft — right from this spot. The hayloft is almost directly above him, and Caffery cranes his neck, trying to find the correct line of sight. All he can see is planking overhead; he can't see the edge of the loft. He steps inside the barn, keeping his palm flat against the door to prevent it slamming closed and cutting off the light. The hayloft rim is still out of his line of sight.

'And that's just not right,' he murmurs. He jams his ASP baton between the door and the frame to keep it open, and takes a couple more steps inside. The hens scatter noisily into the dark. Again he stares at the hayloft.

He stands there for a long time — thinking about the phone call, the blood trail, and the rest of the bullshit in the report. Yup, he thinks, bullshit.

That's what's been bugging him all along. Sergeant Harry Pilson's report is all lies.

Poppets

The Jams are all potted and now need time to cool. Penny lies on the sofa, a blanket pulled up around her. She's weary — she didn't sleep well and when she woke this morning she was in no doubt. The quilt next to her was warm. She felt it all over, trying to understand how this quirk of temperature had happened. The shutters weren't open for the sun to come in and she hadn't been lying on it — the blankets were still tucked around her. There was no explaining it. It was just as if Suki had been there.

She sighs and lifts her hands behind her head, staring at the ceiling. Her breasts chafe at the underside of the blankets — a sudden, crackling reminder of what it was to be sexual. Sensuality has been Penny's undoing. Over the years she's eaten too much and drunk too much and loved too much, in all the wrong places. You get told as youngsters that a type of emotional incontinence, a stray hedonistic streak, will lead to no good. You never believe it — until, lo and behold, it leads to no good.

Fifteen years ago Penny was married. Not happily, but respectably and without rancour. Not much sex, but equally no fighting and no poison. Then her hormones sabotaged everything. She met the Handels at a village party and soon she and her husband became friends with the attractive couple from Upton Farm. Graham in particular was good-looking — tall with a touch of danger about him that pricked Penny's senses wide awake. Graham, for his part, took one look at the pretty cook who had moved into the Old Mill and knew exactly where his life was going to take him. Penny didn't stand a chance.

The affair evolved slowly, almost under the noses of their respective spouses. Louise Handel travelled away on business a lot and that allowed Graham and Penny to spend more time together. She grew to know a lot about the Handels and their lives. More than she wanted to know. She found they had a son who didn't attend the local school but was taken out of the county to a 'special' school. Isaac definitely had needs. Introspective and unable to look anyone in the eye, on occasions when Penny encountered him with his parents she tried to get through to him but failed.

Sometimes when Louise was away Graham would send Isaac outside to play while he and Penny locked themselves in the spare bedroom on the top floor. Penny worried about Isaac outside — his silence was disturbing — maybe he suspected what was happening. Maybe he would tell his mother. After sex, she would look out of the window under the eaves and watch Isaac playing — always solitary and a bit too intense for a thirteen-year-old who should be out kicking a football with his friends. Usually he would be squatting, completely absorbed in some private task. Making something.

One day, during school hours, Penny happened to be passing Isaac's bedroom on her way to get a glass of water. Ordinarily she'd have walked straight past — she'd made a pact with herself never to pry into the life of Graham's family. Today, however, Graham was showering, Louise was away on business and Isaac's door stood open. It was too tempting. On his bed was a small tin. Curious, she crept inside, sat on his bed and opened the tin. Inside she found a collection of odd little dolls made from scraps of leather and pieces of stick. One wore a crudely made track suit, fashioned from scraps of fabric Penny recognized as belonging to Louise. The other doll was male. It wore trousers of brown cord — similar to a pair Graham had in his wardrobe.

Penny chose not to mention the dolls to Graham. She wasn't sure why — was it because they were so disturbing? Or was it because they felt like a subtle key to her lover's private world? Over the following weeks she increased the times she went into Isaac's room and from what she found and the snippets of information she got in conversation from Graham, began to piece together what was happening to the boy. She decided that anyone or anything who had upset or angered Isaac would have a doll made in their likeness. These strange mini-representations of people and creatures populated the adolescent's world. A neighbour's notoriously bad-tempered cat — who had once scratched Isaac — was depicted with a toilet roll as the body, real hair stapled to it, eyes glued on clownishly. Its paws, Penny noticed, were bound, and the hair seemed to be real cat hair. She stole a few strands and the next day secretly compared it to the cat. The hairs appeared to match.

Graham told Penny that at Isaac's school there was a little girl who had a habit of stealing. She must have been driven by the thrill, because the purloined objects followed no logical pattern — sweets and toys and money and clothing and pencils and pieces of paper and socks. She stole the pencil shavings from someone's sharpener, just to prove she could. The day Isaac's football disappeared from his show-and-tell shelf was the day he came home and made an effigy of the little girl in a torn blue gingham that exactly matched the girls' uniforms at Isaac's school. It had long black hair made of wool and one hand tied behind its back. The stealing hand, forever disabled.

Penny went to the local library and browsed several books on voodoo. The books explained that a voodoo fetish, or 'poppet', must contain an object close to the person represented — ideally something taken from the body: fingernail clippings or hair. Excretions too — urine, faeces, semen, mucus, sweat, blood — could be collected and used. Even clothing. A shaman or medicine man would then chant spells which had the power to transfer physical acts committed on the doll to the person or thing it represented.

'Mrs Handel has these books out on loan all the time,' said the librarian with a sniff. 'Makes you wonder, doesn't it? You know — the way the boy's turned out.'

Louise was doing an OU history course, and

when Penny dug a little deeper she discovered Louise had indeed chosen voodoo and the slave trade for one of her papers. It was clear to Penny that Isaac had somehow seen the books, or been influenced by Louise's interest, but when she questioned Graham about the books he made light of her unease. This marked the beginning of her loss of faith in her lover. Slowly, over the next few months, she began to suspect he wasn't serious about her. She even began to wonder if she wasn't the only lover Graham had known during his marriage, and whether Louise's 'business' trips were actually getaways to visit her own boyfriends. Penny's anxiety and guilt about her husband — her quiet, unargumentative, unadventurous, unsexy husband — exploded.

That month Penny and her husband were invited to the Handels' Halloween party. Graham insisted it would seem odd if they didn't attend. Penny can still remember it in vivid detail — she spent most of the night in the kitchen wearing her gypsy blouse and patchwork skirt, clutching her handmade witch hat in one hand, bemused by all the strange women dressed in green wigs and suspender belts who smoked and laughed and swallowed champagne in gulps and outlined their mouths in red gloss.

To her husband's bewilderment, Penny went home crying. Her error had been exposed in the clearest light. Graham was a different person from the one she'd believed she was in love with. She made up her mind she would end the affair with Graham — whatever the cost.

Now, sitting on the sofa in the mill, her

attention goes to the windows. They open out on to the bottom of the valley. On the other side of the stream the forests slope up and up — ending where the mists at the top crowd around Upton Farm. Maybe it was her punishment, the world teaching her a lesson, but she never did get the chance to tell Graham it was over.

Ironically, the day she chose to do it — All Souls' Day — happened to be the day Isaac Handel had decided to end his parents' lives.

Job

Harry Pilson still lives in the police house he worked from for thirty years. He retired at fifty to avoid a move out of the village to Chipping Sodbury police station and purchased the house under the right-to-buy scheme.

Pilson has just got in — he delivers ready-meals to the elderly in his area. He's a lean and healthy sixty-year-old dressed in a pullover and corduroys. He glances at Caffery's card, then shows him through to the back room, past his wife, who stands in the kitchen drying a plate and gaping at them. 'Job,' he murmurs to her, pulling the door closed on her disapproving frown. 'Won't be long.'

If Caffery knows cops, it's probably been this way for years in the Pilson household — Harry's job taking him away all the time, his wife always abandoned in the middle of something in the kitchen, wondering when it's all going to stop.

Pilson closes the living-room door behind him and leans against it for a second. It's one of those very ordered rooms — a cabinet full of crystal and figurines, the TV remote set neatly on top of today's folded newspaper. DVDs shelved in alphabetical order.

'What can I do for you, Inspector?'

'Can we talk? Properly.'

'Isn't that what we're doing?'

'No — I mean, *properly*.' Caffery sits at the

small dining table and places the case file in front of him. He nudges the chair opposite with his foot. Looks up at Pilson. 'Not fucking-around talking, not job talking and not canapé talking either.'

Pilson hesitates. He sits down obediently, but there's a chink in his expression that warns Caffery not to push it. He folds his arms.

'Go on then.'

'It's about Isaac Handel and what happened at Upton Farm.'

Pilson's face sags visibly. Caffery has opened a wound. A hatch into the past. 'Why now, after all this time? Why MCIT?'

'Can we talk or can we not?'

'Yes,' he says. 'We can talk.'

'You must have known the family. What were they like?'

'What does your intel tell you?'

'Not much.'

Pilson taps his fingers on the table, as if he's considering his options. 'OK,' he says eventually. 'And I'm only telling you this because it's so long ago. I did know them. Graham Handel — the father — he was the start of the problem. Playing away from home like an addiction. He never tired of it. His wife? She gave up waiting for him to change and followed suit — ended up almost as bad.'

'The report says people in the village used to talk about them dabbling in voodoo?'

Pilson snorts. 'Nah — Louise did a course and had some books out from the library — that's all. You get a double murder like that and the local grapevine goes sonic — two plus two becomes a hundred.'

'Talk me through what happened, after you got the call.'

'It's a long time ago — my memory's not what it was.'

'I'm sure you can remember taking the call.'

'What I can remember is in the file.'

'Is it?'

Something in the room shifts at Caffery's tone. Pilson's attention narrows and hardens to a point. 'Of course. Why wouldn't it be?'

'I've been up to the farm — it's not the kind of place you just happen to be passing and notice something odd. So your tipster must've gone out of their way to get up there.'

Harry rubs his forehead distractedly. 'I wouldn't know — I swear. So many years have gone by it's hard to recall details.'

Caffery shakes his head, opens the file. 'Just so you know? The poor-memory thing? It isn't working for you.' He finds Pilson's report, pulls it out. 'It's very detailed — exemplary, in fact. Except some of the details don't make sense when you stand them up against each other.'

He slides out the crime-scene photos, placing them on the table.

Pilson becomes quite still. Stiff. He averts his gaze from Graham and Louise's faces, their mouths pulled open. 'Do we have to?'

'We do. I like to get things very clear in my head. And thinking about what you went through, I can kind of see how the facts might have got a bit scrambled.' He leaves the briefest of pauses. 'How some details might have slipped your mind.'

Caffery has just given him the chance to own up and keep his reputation intact. Pilson doesn't take it. Instead he shoves the photographs back across the table to a place he can't see them.

Caffery folds his arms. Sighs. 'OK — we'll do it the hard way. So let's see . . . you arrived at the house at six forty-five p.m. — ten minutes after the call? The front door was open, but you didn't go into the house — you went straight to the barn. Now why would you do that?'

'I don't remember.'

'Says here that you saw a trail of blood leading into the barn.'

'Well, then, that must have been it.'

'You're not sure?'

'Like I said, it was a long time ago.'

Caffery stares at him. 'You're really not in a position to lie any more. Let's talk about the blood trail.' He finds the photograph of the farmyard and barn. He makes a show of peering closely at the photograph. 'I can't see any sign of a blood trail. Can you?'

'Maybe it doesn't show in the photos.'

'It doesn't show in the CSI report either. There's some blood in the downstairs hallway, but Isaac would need to have been dripping with it for you to see it on the ground outside. Graham and Louise had been dead three hours — their blood would have been mostly dry by then anyway.'

'I can't remember what I saw. I just knew he was in the barn.'

'The front door to the house is wide open, and yet, for some reason, instead of going into the house, you go straight to the barn?'

Pilson doesn't answer. Caffery tries a different tack. 'OK — for the sake of argument, let's say it's something — copper's nous maybe — leads you, against all evidence, *away* from the house and over to the barn. And then . . . ' Caffery locates the section of the report, reads: '*The access door to the big barn was open. I looked around the door frame and saw Isaac Handel in the hayloft. He appeared to be covered in blood.*'

Caffery runs a thumb along the folder, so that it will lie open at the page. 'You want to modify your statement, Mr Pilson?'

'What? You expect me to remember it *better* after all this time?'

'No, I expect you to remember it accurately, to tell me the truth. I've just come from that barn. It's pitch-dark in there. You can't even see the hayloft from the access door — you've got to be a good six feet inside the barn — and still you'd have to bend backwards to get a good look.'

Pilson is shaking his head, but he doesn't look like an ex-cop any more; he looks like anyone who's been caught in a lie and won't admit it.

'Fine,' Caffery says. 'So you're trying to work out how much trouble you're in. Why not let me fill in the blanks for you? You're protecting some-one — I don't know who, but I'm going to find out. OK?' He pauses, giving time for that to sink in. 'And when I do, I'll be coming back here to charge you with obstruction. And if Handel does anything else in the future, it'll be on your head.'

Anxiety crosses Pilson's face briefly. 'Handel can't *do* anything, He's inside. High Secure.'

'That's right. High Secure — which, every six months, whether the patients ask for it or not, holds the statutory MHA discharge tribunals. And this time . . . ta-dah!' He gives a flourish of the hand, like a magician. 'Isaac Handel was discharged. I guess that's why they go through the whole rigmarole — to make sure the ones who need to be kept in are. And the ones who don't need to be kept in get let out.'

Pilson's mouth closes. You can almost hear his teeth dancing one against the other. 'They've let him *out*? Are you having a . . . ? Aren't they supposed to tell us when they let people like that out?'

'Our unit was informed, as is the protocol. Though most relevant parties are retired now, like yourself. Besides, what's to worry about? The doctors say he's stabilized. The tribunal reckons he's safe to live in the community.'

There's a pulse beating in Pilson's temple. He glances towards the kitchen where his wife is.

'Would you like me to get her to lock the doors?' Caffery says. 'Would that make you feel better?'

'They don't know what they've done. Letting him out.'

'But you do. Who called it in? Who were you protecting?'

For half a minute, Pilson says nothing, just keeps taking deep breaths, shaking his head every so often. He reaches across the table and with trembling fingers he turns the crime-scene photographs over so they are face down.

'My sister,' he says miserably. 'I was protecting Penny.'

The Old Mill

The story Harry Pilson has to tell is old, and sadly familiar to Caffery, who has heard every imaginable tale of adultery over the years. Every possible combination, every conceivable twist. Still he can't help feeling sorry for the guy. The more he talks, the more Caffery understands why he lied.

Fifteen years ago Pilson's sister, Penny — who was married at the time — was having an affair with Graham Handel, Isaac's father. On the day of the killings she went up to the house to see him. She intended finishing the affair. By the time she arrived, Graham Handel and his wife had both been dead some hours.

Penny knew she had to report it, but she had no excuse to give her husband for her presence up at the house. So Harry agreed to cover for her. Together they conjured up the phone call. The fake woman. Fake name, fake address.

'She's drifted away from me,' Harry says. 'Or I've drifted from her. I think she's ashamed, even now — it was a bleak spot in her life. When you see her, will you send her my love? Tell her I still think about her. Ask her how that mongrel dog of hers is.'

Penny is now divorced from the husband she wanted to protect, and lives in the last house in the village. The Old Mill. Harry has told Caffery it's the house with grass growing on the roof, and he sees it immediately, even in the dark: a green froth on the old clay roof tiles. At the windows are Swiss-style shutters — a heart cut in each centre — and there's a hand-carved business sign above the porch — *Forager's Fayre, Home-made Preserves*.

He has to rap loudly to get an answer. When the door opens, he sees Penny is quite different from her brother. Much younger — probably mid-forties — and very pretty, with heavily kohled eyes and bright henna-red hair cut pixie-style. A faint, quizzical smile.

'Yes?'

'Penny Pilson?'

'That's me.'

He holds up his card. 'Have you got a moment? Just some routine questions.'

Penny's face falls a little. But she doesn't ask him what the routine questions are. She holds the door open and lets him in. The hallway is narrow with bare stone walls, the floor tiles also stone — worn in clear twin grooves by centuries of foot traffic. Penny beckons him to follow and heads away down the corridor. She's small and voluptuous. She wears a falling cascade of bracelets on her arms, battered jeans and beaded leather thong sandals on her dainty feet, which are bare, in spite of the cold.

It's a high-ceilinged building — brick-walled, but warmed by a huge wood burner in the centre of the floor. At one end of the space is what looks like a commercial kitchen, where industri-alsized pots simmer on a huge catering-style stainless-steel cooker, filling the air with the smell of stewing fruit. There are pyramids of freshly picked apples in the corner, and a trestle table at the far end of the room houses a range of jars — all hand-labelled, and tied with hemp or raffia. Every wall is covered in shelves similarly piled with jars.

Penny clicks on the overhead light and takes a pile of paperwork off a chair for Caffery to sit.

'Tea? Coffee? Something stronger?'

He smiles. 'I'd love a Scotch, but under the circumstances . . . '

'I make the best plum vodka. I'll get you some.'

Caffery tilts back in his chair, his head turned to watch her moving around the kitchen. 'Can I just say that you're a bad woman. If I was an alcoholic — which I probably am on some level — you'd have *co-dependent* or *enabler* stamped on your forehead. Not to mention I'm driving.'

'I'll make it a small one. Just to taste. Just to leave you wanting more.'

He shakes his head. This is the sort of woman who can spell trouble for men. Earthy and sexy. Knows how to feed the senses. Obviously her appeal wasn't lost on Graham Handel. She fills a tiny glass with a ruby-coloured liquor. It catches the light and reminds him Christmas is not far off. He sniffs and sips. It's the taste of a hundred different berries, a hundred different spices.

'Forager's Fayre? How come I've never heard of you before?'

'I dunno. Welcome to wild-and-woolly Gloucestershire. The crusties. Note my attire? Every piece of fruit I use has been foraged — or donated by friends. You walk around these days and see apples rotting on the ground. People just don't bother to pick them. Ever noticed that?'

'Now you mention it.'

'People'd rather go to the supermarket and buy stuff grown thousands of miles away than eat what's growing in their back garden. Go figure. Want to know my best-selling variety?'

'It was the first thing I was going to ask you.'

'Church Car Park Crab-apple Jelly.'

'Car Park Jelly?'

'Yup.' She reaches to a shelf and grabs a jar. 'A church car park in Wotton and ten crab-apple trees just drop their fruit every September. What was the diocese doing with the fruit? Not sending out a work party to collect them, I can promise you. Instead they were partitioning off that side of the car park so no one could park there. Didn't want complaints from the congregation that their cars were getting sticky. Here — '

She comes to the table and opens the jar for him. The vacuum makes a reassuring *thwock*. He leans over and smells it. 'Mmmm.'

'Tastes even better — there you go, all yours.'

'Thank you.' He takes the jar, recaps it, and sets it in front of him on the table. Folds his arms. 'And now, I think we should talk.'

'Do we have to?'

'We have to. Even though you're doing everything you can to avoid the subject.'

She gives a grim half-smile. 'And in my position? A cop turning up on your doorstep? It means bad, bad, bad. I can only think it's Harry

— and I don't want to.'

'Harry's fine. He says to send his love.'

She gives a small frown. 'Not Harry?'

'He sent me here, but he's OK.'

There's a tiny pause. She sits at the table, meets his eyes head on. 'OK — then what?'

'Upton Farm. Harry told me the truth.'

She is silent for a long time, her eyes roving over his face. Then she shakes her head. 'So, tell me. Am I in trouble? That was years ago — in the end I don't know how what we did could be seen as obstructing the police — I mean, I did report it, and . . . '

The sentence dies. Caffery is shaking his head. 'It's not about what you did back then. It's what's happening now. It's Isaac.'

'Isaac. What's happened to Isaac?'

'He's out.'

That knocks Penny's expression in half. She pales. Her mouth opens slightly, but she doesn't speak. In the corner a grandfather clock ticks the seconds out, as if emphasizing the way time is stretching. And then she leans forward, elbows on the table.

'He's *out*? Really?'

'Really.'

'OK, OK. OK.' She pinches her nose tightly. 'This is insane. I was only thinking about him this morning . . . And he's out, you say? What happened? He escaped?'

'No — he had a tribunal — he was discharged. He's rehabilitated.'

'*Rehabilitated*? No — oh no. Someone like him doesn't . . . ' She lets the sentence drift off.

'Where's he been released to?'

Caffery doesn't answer.

'Not back *here*? You are kidding me, aren't you?'

'I need you to help me fill in the details. I'm trying to get an idea of what Isaac was like. The sort of things that preoccupied him. Things that interested him.'

'Why?'

'Because it might help me pin down the places he's likely to gravitate to.'

'You've lost him, haven't you? He's gone.'

'I'm not here to alarm you — there's nothing to suggest he presents a danger. I'm trying to get a feel for what he's like, that's all. Take me through what happened.'

Penny scrapes her chair back. She stands for a few moments, nervously unbuttoning and buttoning the front of her cardigan, her eyes darting around the room. She crosses to the windows that face out over the valley. The trees on the far side have turned purple in the failing light. She opens the window and stands for a moment, looking up the valley in the direction of Upton Farm.

Then she pulls the shutters closed. She locks them. She goes to the next window and locks those shutters. And the next. She circulates the entire room — locking every window. She disappears into a side room where he can see fruit piled and he hears her locking and bolting the door there. A moment later she crosses the living room and goes to the front door, which she also locks.

'Jesus.' She grabs a glass and comes back to sit at the table. She fills it with the plum vodka, knocks it back in one. Then a second. She wipes her eyes and makes an effort to calm herself. 'I'm sorry. I suppose it serves me right. If Harry had put my name on the report — if we'd been honest — then I'd have been warned, wouldn't I?'

'Possibly.'

'Lost my little old dog the other night too. It never rains, eh? All my fault. I know — all my own fault.'

Caffery watches her drink more vodka. He watches the colour come slowly back to her face.

'November the second,' she says suddenly. 'That's when it happened. It was a horrible November — a bad year for the fruit. We'd had a wet summer and some of the trees were empty. I remember worrying that the wildlife was going to starve — all the birds and the squirrels. The business had only just started, so that was a worry too. And I was trying to work out how to end it with Graham. As it turned out that was the last thing I should have been worrying about. They told me later Isaac had been with the bodies for three hours. Doing things to them. I suppose if I hadn't arrived he'd have gone on and on.'

Caffery nods silently. 'You know about the trip wire, don't you?'

She looks up. 'The explosives? Yes. They said it was meant for whoever found the crime scene — but Isaac told Harry he'd planned on setting the bodies alight remotely. He could deal with all the things he'd done to their bodies, but he couldn't stomach seeing them burn. He'd got some sort of device to start the fire — he was always clever with his hands. Electronics and things like that. Second nature.'

Caffery clears his throat. Clever with electronics?

'So what happens now?' Penny asks.

'That's what I'm here to ask — what do you think happens now?'

Car headlights shaft through the heart-shaped holes, finding the rows of glass jars with their multi-coloured preserves. Honey gleams gold, blackcurrant jam a deep amethyst. Penny taps her foot a few times, seems to be considering whether to continue. When she does, it's in a lower, more confidential voice.

'He'll be off out there in the wilds, living like an animal. But he'll be back. He hates this world — he hates it. The warning signs were there all along. I could have predicted what he was going to do — if I'd known how to read the signs.'

'Meaning?'

'His poppets. The ones of his mum and dad. He'd sewn their eyes shut. I should have known what he was planning.'

'I beg your pardon? His what?'

'His poppets, his dolls? You *do* know about his poppets?'

'Yes. I just never heard them called — '

'He was holding them when he came out of the house. One in each hand. I knew what he'd done just from the way he was clutching them.

Eyes stitched closed.' She gives him a curious smile, as if he's stupid. 'Don't you know what the poppets are for? Don't you know about Isaac and why he makes his dolls?'

Thom Marley

The dive unit have spent their day searching and bitching, hunched against the cold and the wet. They've continued to scour the wide band, Flea alongside them, dragging her empty body from hedge to hedge, field to field. It's been the longest two days she can remember. She hasn't caught up from diving all night then going straight to work yesterday — all she's wanted to do is sleep. But whatever and whenever, you always stand shoulder to shoulder with your men.

Jack Caffery, who is supposed to be the SIO on this, hasn't shown his face in all that time. Why should he? she reasons. He knows there's going to be no new find — no evidence. Maybe it was for the best — it's given her time to work through in her head what she wants to explain to him.

At five, when it's getting dark and all her men are freezing and exhausted, she takes them into a huddle, gives them hot chocolate from the giant flask she's kept in her back seat and supermarket cakes from a Tupperware container. She explains that if it was up to her, they would be paid not by the number of hours but by the difficulty and by the toll each hour takes on the spirit. Around them the RV car park is in chaos, the other support-unit teams are packing up for the night. She almost fails to notice the old

Mondeo that pulls off the road and into the far corner of the car park. But then two of the big vans drive off and the car is out in the open.

Jack Caffery. At last. She sends her team home with the truck and when she's certain they're on their way, she approaches. He rolls down the window.

'Hi. You OK?'

'I'm fine.'

'Do you want to talk?'

She shrugs and walks round to the passenger seat, rattles the door. He clicks off the locking and she opens the door and gets in. Her body is aching from the cold of the day in the field — out here play-acting trying to find Misty — and the car isn't as warm inside as she'd expected. It's not lush and easy to sit in, her breath still fogs the air. Caffery's in his work suit with a thick corded jacket over the top. He's turned in his seat, waiting for her to speak.

'Yeah.' She buckles the seat belt. Nods out of the windscreen. 'Can we just go?'

He doesn't argue. He starts the car and pulls out of the parking area.

'Take a right. Go through Monkton Farleigh.'

He does as she says. She sits with her elbow jammed against the door, her forehead against her fingers. The night countryside squirms past the car, swallowed up under the wheels.

'At the main road take a right — head towards Bath.'

He obeys her instructions without a word. She lets her eyes sneak sideways and follow his hand on the gear stick. She's watched his hands several times before. They are hard and slightly tanned, no rings. She's never seen a ring on his fingers. Not even the white mark from one that has existed there in a past life.

'OK,' she says when they are on the main road and have reached cruising speed. 'I did want to talk. And when you didn't come on site I thought about calling. I did. Just didn't know how to start.'

'Now's a good time.'

'First let me say sorry about the other night. I didn't mean to be as blunt as I was.'

He gives a grim smile. Changes gear. 'Understandable. It wasn't an everyday conversation — a coffee-morning chat.'

'To put it mildly.'

'I could have been better about it. I could have been more gentle.'

She turns her eyes away — focused on the road, because she knows he'll be trying to see her expression.

'Before you judge why I said no you need to know some of the things that happened. After Misty was . . . ' She stops. Starts again. 'After she died.'

'What things?'

'You'll see that what I did was the best thing I possibly could — the best route. It's not as simple as you think.'

'Try me.'

She takes a long, deep breath. Leans her shoulders back in the seat. She really doesn't want to go through it again. Not at all.

'OK,' she starts tentatively. 'Imagine it's late

spring. Here . . . the same road, but eighteen months ago. Thom's borrowed my car. It's eleven at night and he's off his head and . . . well, you and I both know what's happened back on that road. He's coming along here — just like we are, except he's trousered and he's going fast because he's got something awful in the boot of his car. Something he really shouldn't have — you know what I'm talking about. As he comes round this corner, he picks up a tail — '

'A traffic cop?'

'Yes. One of ours. Avon and Somerset's finest — someone you and I happen to know, but that's another story. Left here.'

Caffery swings the car to the left and they begin to wind their way down the side of the valley that leads off the escarpment.

'So he comes down here with the cop on his back, and I'm in the house — we're going to get there in a minute — you'll see — and the first I know about it is headlights and noise and Thom crashing into the house so pissed, *so* pissed he's straight into the toilet and throwing up and crying. And then the cop — minutes behind. It was a split-second decision: I couldn't even begin to go forward and guess what it would mean in the end.' She breaks off for a moment, knowing the next bit is insanity. 'But anyway — I told the cop I was driving.'

'You *what*?' His eyes go to hers and she isn't quick enough to look away. 'Say it again?'

'And I did the breathalyser for Thom.'

'What the — '

'I know, I know . . . ' She massages her temples wearily. 'But *I didn't know what had happened*. I didn't know Misty was in the boot until *four* days later. She was in my car for *four* days before I realized. My shithead brother? He's picked up her body, put it in *my* car, and doesn't even tell me — leaves me to find it. The next morning he's gone — and after that I can't contact him — he won't take my calls. I had to doorstep him to even get a word out of him.'

Caffery shakes his head. Lets out a low whistle. 'And still you protected him?'

'By then it wasn't me protecting him, it was me protecting myself. From him and his mondo-bizarro bitch of a girlfriend, who turned the whole thing around so it looked like I . . . ' She rubs her arms. She realizes she is trembling. A sweat is coming out on her forehead. 'So it looked like I did it all. Take a right here. This is it. My house.'

The Promise

When Melanie asks where AJ got to this morning, he lies. He tells her that Patience called — Stewart was acting up and needed another walk. Patience had a headache so AJ had to drive home and do it, because the dog is so nuts lately he can't be trusted to go out on his own without running away into the forest. AJ hates the lie, almost dents it, his teeth are so tight as he delivers it, but he hasn't got the balls to tell her what he's done. He dreads the moment the phone rings and Caffery's voice on the other end announces: *I'm going to have to come out to Beechway*.

He's going to be ready by then. He's made himself a promise. He'll have explained it all to Melanie by then and she'll be fine about it. She'll understand, because she will have come to her senses. He stands in the gents' and looks at himself in the mirror and makes himself repeat it.

'AJ, you are going to find the right time to tell her. Swear it now, swear it? I promise. On Stewart's life, I swear.'

At five p.m., when he's finished all the rotas and the overtime sign-offs, and checked that the care-plan reviews have been written up, he is done in. The late nights have caught up with him. He locks his office and heads home. Melanie has a board report to prepare, so she's going to follow later.

Patience has spent the day preparing another challenge for 'breakfast' — a proper English kedgeree, served with boiled eggs, chopped chives and coriander. Her disappointment when AJ walks in alone is written all over her face.

'Awww, Patience, don't make her do it again. She passed once.'

'Girl needs feeding up.'

'You'll just make her ill.'

Patience purses her lips and busies herself around the kitchen, getting a mug of coffee and cream, tomato ketchup for the kedgeree. AJ ought to be the size of a house with all the food she dishes up.

'Did your washing — it's ironed and hanging in your wardrobe. Just in case you wanted to say thank you for that.'

'Thank you, Patience.'

'And for your information . . . ' She ladles dusky yellow kedgeree on to his plate and sets it in front of him. 'The patron saint of good dress sense has paid us a visit. Your Hawaiian shirt got blown away.'

'What?'

'Off the line. Disappeared.'

'Patience,' he says warningly. 'That was my favourite shirt.'

'I know. And I'm telling the truth. I pegged it like the others. Must have been the wind. Clearly it's got better taste than some of us.'

She turns away and clucks around, tending to her jam. Lifting the lid of each saucepan and peering inside, releasing huge plumes of steam. AJ sighs and picks up his knife and fork. By the time she has finished her jam duties the windows are covered in condensation and AJ has cleaned his plate. She snatches it up, carries it to the Aga, heaps it with more kedgeree.

'Steady,' he says. 'There won't be enough for Melanie.'

'We'll see,' she says sourly. 'We'll see.'

AJ gives her a narrow, thoughtful look, wondering what's going on. He thinks he knows. He picks up the ketchup and squirts it on the kedgeree. 'So?' he says, casually clicking the bottle closed. 'What do you think?'

'What do I think about what? What do I think about your Hawaiian shirt? You know the answer to that. What do I think about your job? You know the answer to that. What do I think about the way you spoil your dog? You know the answer to that.'

'And *you* know what I'm talking about.'

Patience makes a disapproving noise at the back of her throat. She takes the kedgeree pot to the Aga and puts it on the warming plate, clunking down the heavy lid.

'Well? Come on — spit it out.'

'I like the way she eats,' she says guardedly. 'She eats like a proper human being.'

'Apart from that, what do you think?'

She doesn't answer. She picks up an oven glove and bends to check the jars sterilizing in there. 'Patience? I asked you a question.'

She slams the oven door. 'I heard your question. I did hear.'

'And your answer?'

'I'm worried.' She wipes her hands quickly on

the tea towel and drops it on the table. 'If you want God's honest truth, I think this time it's different.'

'Different?'

'Yes — this is the first time I've seen my nephew acting like a grown-up and not a twelve-year-old boy who's just worked out what his weenie is for.'

'Is there a problem with that?' AJ puts his knife and fork down. 'Being serious?'

'Hey,' Patience says gently. She sits opposite him, watching him with her kind brown eyes. 'You don't know who you are — you really don't. You don't know how precious you are to me. I never had my own children — and isn't that a blessing, because they'd be wild as boars if I had. But long before Dolly died, when you were still a little snotty kid about the size of a jelly bean and so ugly it hurt to look at you, me and Dolly both swore that whatever one of us went first, it would be the other who brought you up. She might have popped you out into the world, but as far as she and me were ever concerned you had two mothers. Maybe not perfect mothers, neither of us, but together I think we did a good job.'

'And?'

Patience gives one of her rare smiles. She's got teeth cleaner than poured milk, and when the light comes into her eyes she's the prettiest woman alive. 'I'm a mother bear, sweetheart. The first time my little boy's put his heart on the line, and I want to be sure you're going to be treated right and that the lady in question hasn't got something else in her mind.'

Boxes

Caffery has come straight from Penny Pilson's to the search site and all the way the holdall containing Handel's dolls has been making a low shuffling sound in the boot on the sharp corners. Now he knows their relevance, what they meant to Handel, he's especially conscious of them. It's tempting to stop the car and go back there to check the boot — if only to convince himself the little bastards haven't climbed out of the bag. But then Flea gets into the car and he forgets all about Isaac Handel and starts thinking about Misty again.

They stop at a place just to the north-east of Bath. She shows him where to park: in a gravelled courtyard. Ahead stands a cottage. It is long and low — two-storeyed, spindling along for nearly twenty metres. Abutting it, coming out at right angles to form the second side of the yard, is a large house with a sheer brick wall topped by chimney stacks that block out the night sky. There are lights on in the only windows, which are high up, as if it's a prison.

'That's the neighbours.' Flea waves a hand at the wall. 'And this' — she indicates the rambling cottage, lit only by an old-fashioned coaching lamp covered in dead creeper — 'is me.'

She swings out of the car, hefts her kit on her back and heads to the door. He gets out, looking around. In the moonlight he can make out the garden, which seems to be huge and unmanageable. Weed-choked and full of attempts at design that have gone wrong and been overgrown. Rose beds spill on to lawns that have grown into meadows and been defeated by the rains and the cold. What must once have been elegant terraces cascade down like jungle ledges, disappearing into the night. A wind comes up, blows straight through him. Autumn is here with a vengeance. He pulls his jacket tight and turns to follow Flea.

She dumps her kit outside the front door and uses a cast-iron boot scraper to lever off her boots. 'Come in,' she says. 'Come in.'

He stands in the hallway unlacing his walking boots, glancing at the surroundings. The house is long and ramshackle and as untidy as his place, with boxes lining the corridor. But the thing that sets this apart from his house is a sense of home his remote and unloved cottage will never have. Everything smells faintly of open fires. He looks to his left, where the cottage extends off, the floor uneven, dried flowers in the mullioned windows. He looks to his right, where Flea has disappeared. At all the coats hanging on the painted peg board.

This was where it happened. This was where she struck the deal to cover up what her brother had done. He pushes the boots to one side and follows her through the house. The boxes are in every corner, taped and stacked. She is making coffee in the kitchen. She's taken off her jacket and sweatshirt and is dressed in black combats and polo shirt with the Underwater Search Unit's badge sewn on the front. Her blonde hair is bundled up carelessly. Her arms are a mass of scratches and gouges from the day's search. As she fills the kettle she has to negotiate a taped box on the floor.

'What's happening here? You moving?'

'Not in the way you think.'

'Cryptic.'

'Yep — cryptic.'

She bangs about the place, making a lot of noise getting things out of cupboards. Slams down cups and spoons and jars of sugar.

'Your house?' Caffery says. 'You grew up here?'

'Milk? Sugar?'

'Yes to both, thanks. It must have been a good place to grow up.'

She pauses, with the kettle poised above the cup, and he realizes his mistake. Her parents. He's an idiot. 'I'm sorry,' he mutters. 'Sorry.'

She pours the water, adds some milk, mixes it quickly and hands him the cup.

'Bring it with you — I'm going to show you what I had to do.'

They go down another passageway — it seems to Caffery that the house is a warren — until they get to a door which she opens to reveal a garage.

'This,' she says, 'is where things got really nasty.'

The moon has found a niche in the clouds and has chosen this moment to scythe into the windows above the roll-up garage door. It picks out the filigree of spiders' webs, makes them sparkle like Christmas decorations. On the walls, garden tools have been hung in neat order. Here too boxes are stacked. In the centre of the garage sits a cast-iron Victorian bath.

'What happened?'

'After four days — when I worked out what Thom had left in my boot — I brought the car in here. My first thought was the freezer — ' She indicates a chest freezer in the corner. 'Then I remembered some pathologist telling me about ice-crystal artefacts. You heard of those?'

'I think so. The heart muscle or something — you can tell if a body's been frozen?'

'Yes — so I had to keep her chilled. Cold but not frozen.' She nods at the bath. 'Gallons of ice in there until I could work out what to do with her.'

'Jesus.'

'I know. And I'm supposed to be the one who's used to dealing with dead bodies. My *job*.'

She goes to the windows now and stands on tiptoe, peering at them — at the frames — as if they contain some hidden clue. It is freezing in here — her breath steams the glass. The moon slants sideways on her face. Seeing her now, next to the window, side lit by the moon, he realizes again how delicate she is. Whenever he looks at Flea the animal part of his brain lights up. His limbic system goes into overdrive. Sometimes it screams *sex*. Sometimes, like now, it screams *protect. Kill anything that threatens her . . .*

'I taped off all the windows, but my neighbour knew something was going on.' She's looking at the towering wall of the neighbouring house. 'Kept nosing around the place — I was going out of my mind. It was — ' She puts her finger to her forehead. Drops her weight back on to her heels. There's a small pause. 'Surreal. I still can't believe it.'

She turns and gives him a rueful smile.

'So that's two counts against me — the record I was driving that night, and my neighbour. And as if those two weren't enough, there's more. Do you remember that bald guy — the POLSA on that job we did, the suicide on the Strawberry Line?'

Caffery remembers him well. Flea and the POLSA — an officer trained in search management — butted up against each other like a pair of billy-goats. 'Yeah — you really didn't like him.'

'The feeling was mutual.'

'You called him a combed-over old twonk.'

'And I was right — he was a combed-over old twonk — proper jobsworth. It was a hate-hate thing from the moment we laid eyes on each other. What you *didn't* see was where our relationship started — which was the day after Misty went missing from the clinic. The POLSA twonk wanted my unit to search a lake in the grounds of the clinic. I pulled the team a little earlier than satisfied him and he made a big deal of it — said if I was so confident Misty wasn't in the lake maybe I knew something about where she was.'

'Oh, OK — OK, so not brilliant.'

'Not brilliant? I'm on record for speeding that night, my neighbour knows I was up to something at about the same time — her curiosity isn't going to burn itself out overnight, you can put money on that. And I've been told, in front of witnesses, that I'm acting like I know where Misty is.' She gives a deep, weary sigh. 'And that's before I even get started on the car.'

'The car?'

'The one that hit her. The one Thom was driving — the Ford. *My* Ford. It's a time bomb. It only has to be forensicated and I'm screwed another way.'

In answer Caffery drains his coffee. Tips the cup upside down to see if there are any last drops. 'I can make coffee too,' he says.

'Oh?' She raises an eyebrow. 'Well done you.'

'I think you should try a cup. Then you can judge.'

Ghosts

Melanie gets back to the cottage at eight. AJ is out throwing a stick for Stewart, in the front field because it's enclosed and the dog can't run away. He's checked the hedgerows for his missing shirt and found nothing. If Patience did chuck it then maybe she's got the fury out of her system. He's not sure whether to be flattered by or annoyed with her. All that her anger has really given away is exactly what's been in the back of his head: that if Mel still has feelings for Jonathan then AJ could wind up getting hurt.

The second morning at her house AJ found himself alone in her bedroom while she was taking a shower. There were so many temptations in the house — her handbag left open on the kitchen table, her phone on the bedstand. He remembers now rolling on to his side, plumping up the pillow under his head and gazing at the slim blue profile of it, his pulse tick-ticking away in his temples. Every atom of him bearing down on that sliver of rubberized polymer casing.

What information did it harbour? What windows into Melanie's head could it unlock? Something about Jonathan Keay? Would his name and photograph appear on her recents screen? Would there be text conversations, emails or even her own ruminations about him noted somewhere? AJ was eaten up with curiosity, but he hadn't acted on it. Eventually he'd turned away, picked up his own phone and started playing a mindless app to distract himself.

Now, when Melanie's car headlights sweep up the drive, he attaches Stewart's lead and comes over to the car to help with her bag. He keeps sneaking glances at her. She is so so pretty. Patience is right. He's got to be so careful here.

Inside the house is warm, condensation gathering on the windows. Melanie comes in and gives Patience a kiss that leaves AJ's aunt completely stunned. She says nothing, but turns away and spoons kedgeree on the plate she's been warming on the Aga. She doesn't go crazy with the amount of food, she keeps it civilized, and maybe the conversation she's had earlier with AJ has softened her a bit, because she's polite and even chatty, asking Melanie about work.

Everything is rolling along nicely, and AJ is so relaxed he cracks open a demijohn of the cider he made last year.

'Kingston Blacks. Proper cider apples.' He fills up three Duralex glasses taken from the wonky old cupboard above the sink. 'Scrumped from over Old Man Athey's field.'

Melanie gives the rim of her glass a quick wipe with the sleeve of her blouse and sips politely. She'd prefer vodka, but she's too much of a lady to say it. Patience downs her glass in one. Sets it on the table for AJ to refill. 'You mean where Stewart thinks he wants to go and live. With the ghosts.'

AJ shoots her a look — he doesn't want the mood spoiled, but Melanie doesn't appear to have picked up on the reference to Upton Farm.

'Does he still want to go in the woods?' she asks, smiling down at Stewart, who is dozing next to the Aga. 'He seems quieter today.'

'I've just taken him in the top field. He can't get out, but he didn't seem to be interested in going anywhere, tonight, did you, boy?'

'Well, he wanted to go somewhere this morning.' Patience knocks back her second glass of cider as if it's a thimbleful. 'Couldn't get him settled. Ended up taking him into town. He helped me shop for the haddock for the kedgeree.'

It's only when she reaches the word 'haddock' that AJ realizes what she's said. This morning, to cover for going back to DI Caffery, he told Melanie he'd walked Stewart. He checks over the rim of his glass to see if Melanie has registered this. He can't tell. Her expression is steady. So he quickly changes the subject, he finds anything to talk about, imagining a huge red light bulb flashing over his head, flashing LIAR. LIAR.

Melanie appears to be oblivious. She smiles and engages. She laughs at his stupid jokes and compliments Patience's cooking. It's only when the evening moves on and they get into the bedroom that he knows he hasn't got away with it. Instead of coming to bed she stands at the window, staring outside. There is no moon tonight and no stars, the world seems sealed shut by the clouds. The bean trellises and the potting shed are just visible in the pale electric light from the kitchen windows; beyond that almost nothing.

AJ comes to her and touches her shoulder tentatively. 'Mel?'

'You told me you came home to walk Stewart.'

'I know — I'm sorry — I'm sorry, I'm sorry.' He puts a hand on the window frame so he can lean forward and look into her face. It is stony and controlled. 'Melanie, I was so stupid. I don't usually lie — that was crazy of me. I was . . . I'm embarrassed to say why I lied.'

'You can always try.'

'I was at some stupid home-brew shop in town. They'd just got some special handles for my old screw press — difficult to find. I didn't want to miss out. Cider, you know, it can take over a man's life.'

Melanie turns her eyes to him. She studies his face shrewdly, not finding any humour. A part of him inside wants to shrink.

Liar, liar, pants on fire.

'Melanie? You think I'm a hairy old hobbit already.'

'Did I say that?'

'Well, no — but in case you'd noticed the . . . you know . . . *hairy hobbit* inclinations — I sort of didn't want to reinforce that image. That — stereotype.'

'I don't see stereotypes. I just see people.'

'And so should we all. That's what's so good about you.' He gives a sheepish smile. 'I'm sorry? Am I forgiven?'

'I don't think I can remember one relationship I had where my boyfriend didn't lie to me.'

'Jonathan, you mean?'

He's jumped in too fast. He waits for her to

react, but instead of fury she nods. Admitting it.

'It nearly destroyed me — being lied to. I know I've told lies too — the whole thing with Isaac's tribunal — so I can't really complain, but when it happens to me . . . ?' She clenches her fists helplessly. 'Somehow I've got this weak spot about it. I don't know why. Maybe my dad and his cancer — Mum never told me he was dying, she lied — said he was coming out of hospital, and of course . . . ' She shrugs. 'Well, he never did.'

The part of AJ that felt like shrinking now gives up and shrivels into a tight ball. It pulls up its knees and wraps its hands round its ears and rocks back and forward. 'I tell you what.' He clears his throat. 'How about we make a deal? If I promise never to lie to you again, will you promise not to notice my hairy-hobbit, real-ale, tree-hugging proclivities?'

There's a long silence. And then, like the sun coming out from behind a cloud, Melanie smiles. 'Oh, AJ,' she says sorrowfully. 'Can't you see — it doesn't matter to me? It's *you* I'm interested in. Not what you wear or drink or eat. I'm only interested in *you*.'

Priddy

Flea follows Caffery in her car — she can hear her pulse thumping away in her ears. She's always half wondered where Caffery lives. She's expecting a slick apartment on the Bristol Docks, one of the recycled metal-and-glass ecohouses. Instead he drives out into the Mendips, along country lanes, past barren, frost-blasted fields, finally slowing in the ghostly village of Priddy; a place she's only driven through, never stopped in. The Priddy Circles — the famous ancient earthwork enclosures — are somewhere out in the darkness to her left. On her right there's a drenched and dirty plastic children's climbing frame in the local pub garden, a solitary beer glass on the top of the slide, half full of rainwater.

She's expecting some villa or secret golf course or driveway to open itself up and is surprised when he indicates and turns left into a bedraggled cinder driveway that leads to a thatched cottage.

This is karst land, and in the headlights it is easy to make out the depressions and scars of sinkholes in the limestone caused by acid rain and the porous nature of the bedrock. It's poor land, prone to flooding, colonized by sedge grasses that can't be eaten by livestock. It's dangerous too — apt to open up and swallow a man who doesn't take care where he places his feet. This is not at all what she imagined. She should be relieved; instead she's set off balance. Once again Caffery has walked all over her expectations and prejudices.

She climbs out of the Clio, pulling on her fleece, and stares at the bowed white walls, deep-set mullioned windows and grey thatch. 'What's this?'

He slams his car door. 'This?' He eyes the place. 'This is where I live.'

It looks so small, so rundown, domesticated. So romantic. Lots of tiny comforting windows instead of what she expected: vast glass walls with water and city lights reflected in them. The biggest threat here, she decides, is how familiar it all feels.

'What?' he says across the car roof. 'What is it?'

'Nothing.'

'It's a rental.'

'Oh,' she says noncommittally. 'It's lovely. Where's the coffee?

He slaps the top of the roof twice. Beckons. 'Come on. Let's do it.'

They go into the cottage. Inside she's in for another surprise. It looks a lot like her place, with boxes everywhere and piles of notes and paper files. An iPad charging — propped on the skirting board in the hallway under the radiator. The staircase is in the living room; once it must have been walled off, now it's got open banisters. A sweater is looped over the crevice of the bottom post. She wants to stare at the sweater — suck up the clues it can give her about him. But she can't let her interest in him be that naked, so she settles for surreptitious glances, taking in everything from the empty flight bag at the bottom of the stairs to the almost-empty bottle of expensive Scotch on the windowsill. It's like being a camera. Click, and she's committed everything to memory for later analysis. Click, store. Click, store.

She goes into the kitchen where he is pulling milk out of the fridge. There's a metal espresso pot bubbling on the hob. 'So are *you* moving?' she asks.

'No — I haven't unpacked yet.'

'How long have you been here?'

'I dunno. Two years?'

'Two years and you haven't unpacked?' She isn't sure whether that impresses the hell out of her or makes her incredibly sad. 'Has to be some kind of record.'

He looks at her now. Blinks as if the comment has made him realize how stupid she is. 'It's not a record,' he says levelly. 'It's the problem. When you don't finish something it's what happens. You never settle. Not ever.'

He says it so decisively she knows what he's talking about. His brother — years ago — never found. Her own parents, whose bodies never came back after the accident. Lost for ever. Jacqui Kitson too — still wondering where Misty is. It's his attempt to chasten her. To remind her why they're here. She waits while he makes coffee, not speaking, because she can't think of anything sensible to say. When he hands her the cup, she gives a brief smile and sips politely. 'Nice,' she says. 'Very nice.'

'Thank you.'

'In fact it's lovely — but it's not going to make me change my mind. I still can't do it.'

'Can't or won't?'

'Both. Please — I'm just starting to be able to deal with life again — I can't turn back now. And I've given you the other reasons.'

'Yes — and they're all surmountable. Sit down. It's my turn.'

Resignedly she obeys — sitting at the kitchen table, with all the scars and pocks of life in its surface. He puts down sugar and the milk carton. Automatically she scans the carton, absorbing the details, the brand he's chosen. She's also noticed that on the sideboard is a stack of V-Cig cartridge refills and on the windowsill is a pile of mail, unopened. Part of her is readying itself for what he's going to say — the other part of her, the part that's always secretly found Caffery crazily sexy, is over at the window, nosing through that pile of mail. Opening anything that might give her more of a clue about him.

'Do you know what I've been doing all day?' He stirs sugar into his coffee. 'I've been talking to people about a case at Beechway High Secure Unit. Ring any bells?'

Beechway. She knows the place — she's done a job up there, but she doesn't know what he's talking about.

'Pauline Scott?' he prompts.

Pauline, if she remembers correctly, was a misper her team failed to find. To her eternal shame Pauline's body turned up months later, three metres outside their search zone.

'What about her?'

'You didn't find her for one reason: she was a few metres outside your parameters. The ones set by some combed-over old POLSA twonk. So it is all possible. And feasible.'

Flea smiles. 'Jesus,' she says. 'I wish you'd met my dad. He'd have loved arguing with you. He'd have ripped you limb from limb.'

'Nah — I'd have let him win.'

'He'd have won, whether you let him or not.'

Caffery inclines his head politely, as if to concede that possibility. 'But give me my time in the witness stand, OK? First off — your car isn't a time bomb.'

'It is. I totalled it — but the yard didn't crush it because there was too much nice stuff left on it and I couldn't exactly push the point. It's still there. Slowly being stripped down for parts.'

'Is it? When was the last time you saw it?'

She shrugs. In truth she can't recall. She knows it was before the explosion because of how little she's done since her hospitalization. Before that things are hazy.

'I'll tell you,' Caffery says. 'It's been almost a year. Since last November, it's been a cube. I watched it go through the crusher myself. No one will ever trace it and if they do they're going to have a good laugh trying to get any forensic from it.'

He raises an ironic eyebrow at her expression.

'I've been thinking about this for a long time. Don't ask questions — just take the car off your list of 'why nots'. And you can take the breathalyser off — if no one knows the car was involved then no one's going to look at its records.'

'I've got another why not: head injuries. She flew over the car — the side of her head was smashed completely.'

'We lose the head.'

'*What?*'

'OK,' he says, 'all right.' He is silent for a minute. Then he says, 'What part of the head?'

'What part? The head is the head, Jack.'

'If she was hit from behind, my guess would be here.' He touches the back of his head, just above the neck. 'If she was facing Thom — the forehead. Or maybe, if she turned at the last moment in a reflex action — ' He turns his own head. 'Here.' He traces a line with his fingertips along the side of his head, above his right ear.

Flea doesn't answer. Actually it was the left side of Misty's head, but he's still pretty damned close. Like her, he's been to his fair share of car accidents. Misty's ear was nearly torn off by the impact with the roof of the car.

'OK.' He seems to have taken her silence as agreement. 'We can leave the jawbone for IDing. If they don't find the skull, they'll think it got carried off by a fox, or a badger.'

'Jack — it *won't work*. You've got no clothes. No belongings. I burned them all.'

'So?'

'No clothes is a red rag to any pathologist. No clothes equals sex, equals someone else there, equals not putting it down to hypothermia or overdose. No belongings equals theft, equals the same thing. You'd have to be seen digging deeper if there weren't any clothes.'

'Not necessarily. Hypothermia can do that to people, can't it? Make them confused about whether they are hot or cold? With the bones pulled apart, her clothing could be anywhere — hidden in the undergrowth, lining a fox's den.'

He pushes back his chair and stands. He's still wearing his jacket. She gets a glimpse of the place his shirt is tucked into his trousers. It is creased. For the first time it strikes her that he sometimes has it hard. Living in this cottage with none of his belongings unpacked. Maybe he'd understand if she told him about boxes. And how important they are.

'Put down your cup,' he says. 'There's something you need to see.'

She gets up and follows him into the garden. It's easier to see now it's illuminated by the lights from the cottage windows. He goes to the garage. When he comes out again he's holding a spade. Flea doesn't speak as he begins to dig. He fumbles in his jacket pocket for a pair of nitrile gloves. Slips them on and begins tugging at something tough and organic-looking in the earth. Flea folds her arms. Over the years she's had the responsibility for recovering several bodies — both in and out of the water, and what Caffery is uncovering now is putting her in mind of a shallow grave. She glances right and left, checking they can't be overlooked here.

Caffery gives the material another tug and it pops out. He gives it a shake — clods of earth fall from it — and she sees what it is. A dress.

'*What the . . . ?*'

'Misty's dress.'

'No — I burned it.'

'You burned her dress — but we did a reconstruction. Remember?'

She does. A girl coming down the steps of the rehab clinic — acting stoned. Looking more like a shampoo commercial than a drug addict. She shakes her head and whistles under her breath. 'Are these the clothes the actress wore?'

'They disappeared from MCIT — must have got lost when we moved offices. Scandalous how things like this always seem to go missing.'

He pulls out a handbag and a pair of sandals and lines them up on the frozen ground. 'Even if they called in a forensics specialist to check the clothes — which I doubt, because who's going to raise that suspicion with me directing the investigation? — this is going to vaguely match the profile of the woodland. Wood or a fallow pasture with a similar soil composition to this one. Any amount of minerals the clothes have accumulated will match.'

He brushes his hands off and uses the sleeve of his jacket to wipe his brow. 'Well? Could I make it any easier?'

Her eyes go to his. 'I told you — I can't dive.'

'And is that the truth? Or is it an excuse?'

She can't answer. She can't because it would be something like — *it's an excuse. Actually I can dive, I just don't want to open up the past . . . if I do it then everything's going to come falling out and it'll all go to hell.*

And then she'd probably start crying too.

'I've got to go.' She fumbles in her pocket for the car keys.

He shakes his head, defeated. 'Again? You're going to walk out *again*?'

'I'm sorry, Jack, it's getting late.'

'No — it's really not funny any more. Really. Not funny. I'm getting tired of this — and I'm especially tired of you protecting your shit-head brother.'

'*It's not that,*' she says, shocked. 'It's not my brother.'

'Then what is it? Hmmm? What is it?'

She stands looking at him for a long time. That thing inside her that wants to give way is trembling. She's not going to cry. *Not* going to cry.

'Please, Jack — please, you don't understand.'

'Forget it.' He turns away, his hand held up to stop her speaking. 'Just forget it. I don't want to hear it.'

The Old Mill

Lying on her bed, fully dressed, a stone-like emptiness settles in Penny's head. The Old Mill is empty and silent beneath her — not a creak, not a sound. DI Caffery is long gone. Penny watched him go, through the heart holes in the shutters at the front of the house. He didn't get straight into the car, but walked through the side gate. She had to dart across to the back windows to find him again, standing on the back terrace where all her plant pots are gathered. He stood for a while, gazing across the valley at the treetops where Upton Farm is. A wind came up and flapped open his jacket, flicked up his tie and flattened the shirt and trousers against him. It seemed to break whatever spell was holding him. He headed back the way he'd come, got in the car, and was gone.

Caffery must be about her age, maybe a little younger. A lot of women would think he was sexy, but he wouldn't be the sort they'd want to marry. A lot of women need charmers, flatterers, men who spend money on Valentine's day gifts wrapped in cellophane. He's none of those things — she could see it a mile away. Instead there's something straightforward about him that Penny recognizes. An honesty. No wedding ring, she noticed. Maybe because of the gifts.

She closes her eyes. There's no point wondering what age Caffery is, whether he's single or not, because he will live in a fancy city loft apartment. He will eat at the best restaurants with loads of friends every night. He has a string of beautiful, accomplished girlfriends. He is an utterly different species from Penny. All men are. Or rather, *she* is the different species.

Penny can't read other humans — she can't decipher their moods and the layers of deception they pile on themselves. Isaac, for example. There'd been a time she actually thought he liked her — she even believed he saw in her a mother more caring than Louise, the same way she imagined Graham saw in her a wife more caring than his own. She was wrong there, as she has been so often. She's learned this lesson over and over: in this huge human jigsaw puzzle there is no mirroring piece to match her, no niche for her to slot into. She's given up hoping.

She thinks about that day — all those years ago. It was cold and damp and very still, the clouds squatting over the country like a warning. She remembers Isaac cannoning down the stairs and out of the front door, knocking down the coat stand in the hallway. He wore his school shoes and socks and nothing else — his torso and arms were smeared in blood and faeces. A stranger might have misunderstood — might have believed Isaac was being attacked, that *he* needed help, but Penny knew.

She leapt back in the car. Engaged the central locks. He raced towards her. *Penny, Penny* — his voice low and unnatural. As she started the car, he clambered on to the bonnet, his legs and genitals stained and bloody. She leaned on the horn and rammed the car into such quick reverse that he somersaulted off on to the ground. She slammed on the brakes, flicked up the headlights and sat trembling, watching him. He was already getting up, unsteady on his feet — maybe he'd been drinking — he swayed around, fumbling on the ground until he found what he'd dropped: one of his poppets. He was so hot with blood and death he was steaming in the frigid air.

He straightened and turned to look at Penny.

'No,' she hissed. 'You won't get me too.'

She floored the accelerator. The car danced and skidded forward, forcing him to scamper away into the barn. He slammed the doors closed behind him and Penny, high on fear and adrenalin, dared to leap out and run home the big latch, locking him in. It was only when she got to the first phone booth and dialled Harry's number that the shaking started.

Now, in her unlit bedroom, she curls up in the bed, the quilt over her ears. She never saw the bodies, never saw the bedroom. She pieced it all together — some from what she saw smeared on Isaac's naked body, some from later newspaper articles, but mostly from the questions Harry refused to answer. He was never the same man after what he saw in the Handels' house.

Something occurs to her. She sits up and switches on the reading light. Grabs her glasses and lifts up the quilt. The missing patch. Two mornings ago its disappearance reminded her of Isaac and his habit of stealing clothing for his poppets. She didn't know then that he was out of hospital, so she hadn't given it much thought.

Now, trembling, she inspects it feverishly. The stitching all over the quilt is loose. The piece could have easily come away from general wear and tear, nothing to suggest it's been cut out.

The thought doesn't go away though, the sudden shaky idea that Isaac has come back. She gets up and goes downstairs. The big old painted grandfather clock says eight o'clock. She rechecks all the windows and the doors. She's about to turn to the stairs when her eye is caught by the medlars in the prep room. There's a store cupboard there where she keeps boxes of citric acid and gelatine. At the back of it is a door. The door leads to the basement. It has a lock on it but she hasn't checked if it's closed.

Stupid, stupid, she tells herself, you're turning into a bundle of neuroses. Over-reacting. A doctor would say you're suffering from the curse of the female — hysteria brought on by an imbalance of hormones. When's your next period due, Miss Pilson? But she can't stop staring at that cupboard.

Under the floorboards are the skeletons of the mill. The water-wheel has long rotted away, but the huge stone troughs they used for washing the fleeces are still there, and the old maintenance hatches for the days when they'd send a child down to unlodge a branch that had entangled in the mill wheel. There's a whole labyrinth of tunnels and culverts and sluice gates — most are wadded and sealed to prevent draughts coming up through the floorboards, but if someone really wanted to come into the house — if they really wanted . . .

From the kitchen she gets her heaviest skillet. There's a torch hanging next to the back door — she loops it round her wrist and clicks it on. She creeps into the prep room and into the larder. There's a bare electric bulb in here which she switches on. Then changes her mind and switches it off. She's picturing what she will look like from the other side of the door — lit up and emblazoned like on a movie screen. A perfect target.

She steps forward. Rests her fingers on the handle. She's been through this door several times: it leads to a rickety flight of wooden stairs that creak and complain at the smallest weight. There is no electricity down there — nothing. Just moss and stone and hardened expanding foam in the cracks.

Open it. Open it. There's nothing there. Nothing.

Her hand trembles.

Open it. Open it — prove to yourself he's not standing there. Open it.

She lets all her breath out. She runs the two huge bolts at the top and the bottom, turns the old key in the lock. Then quickly she pulls boxes off the shelves and stacks them against the door. Anything heavy — anything with glass that will make a noise if disturbed. The outer door has no lock, just an old-fashioned T-hinged latch. She uses string to wrap around it several times. Then she pushes a chair against it and drops back against the wall, shivering and sweating.

Graham and Louise Handel

Caffery starts to compose a message to Flea. He gets twenty words in then changes his mind, puts the phone in his pocket and walks around the garden impatiently like something that's about to explode. This is like the man who keeps hitting himself in the face over and over. Still hoping Flea'll change her mind? What a joke that is. Whatever is stopping her isn't going to go away. His best bet is to get to the bottom of the Isaac Handel case, then take a long breath and move on to alternatives for closing the Misty Kitson case.

Eventually, for no particular reason except that he can't think what else to do with them, he re-buries Misty's clothes in the garden. Covers them with soil. He doesn't want to get the holdall with the dolls out of the car, it's the last thing he wants, but he does it anyway. The one place he can close off from the rest of the house so the smell doesn't permeate everywhere is the utility room, so he carries them in there. Then he showers and changes into an old T-shirt and sweatpants. He spends an hour printing anything he can find about voodoo dolls, then pours a large Scotch and carries the printouts through into the utility room. He puts his nitriles back on and starts picking through the dolls.

They make an ugly hotchpotch of textures — Handel seems to have used all manner of materials, from patchwork squares, to raw sheep wool, to glazed clay, to small pieces of stick or wood. Anything he can scavenge. They are crude and unsettling — having them here is like having extra people in the house.

The printouts tell him the notion of a voodoo doll is a popular myth. There's almost nothing to connect it to the Haitian strand of voodoo; the only place the dolls seem to surface is in New Orleans, where voodoo has undergone a kind of Americanized renaissance for the tourist industry. Nevertheless, in the popularized fiction of voodoo — the sort of thing a fourteen-year-old boy might read — voodoo dolls not only exist, they are objects of terror. They obey a fixed set of rules, they can be used to control the humans they represent.

Caffery fumbles two of the dolls to one side. Both are made from leather — human outlines stitched crudely together with something that looks, to Caffery's uneducated eye, like catgut from a stringed instrument. When Isaac came out of the house after the murders he was clutching two dolls. Penny only glimpsed them, and doesn't know what happened to them afterwards, but she maintains she'd seen them before and they were the ones which represented Graham and Louise Handel.

Isaac's juvenile-custody record was destroyed — as is usual — after three years, so there's no way of finding out what property was detained. But it's not a leap of faith to believe that the dolls Caffery's looking at now were the ones Isaac was holding. They are dressed in clothes strikingly similar to the ones itemized in the CSM's report as found on the Handels' bodies — jogging trousers and a T-shirt on the female doll, brown cord trousers on the male. It may be that they seemed innocuous enough to a string of custody officers and nurses to have slipped unnoticed through the system. A sectioned patient showing a particular attachment to an object? One which, when scanned, showed no traces of metal, no sharp objects — it's feasible he managed to convince people to let him keep the dolls.

Why? Caffery wonders. Graham and Louise were already dead. Why would he want to keep their effigies?

He goes into the kitchen and fetches a reading light and a magnifying glass. Studied under the glass, the dolls are even more disconcertingly ugly. They have polished shells in place of their teeth, and they differ from the other poppets in that they both have their eyes sewn shut. If the poppets symbolized whatever it was Isaac wanted to inflict on their real-life counterparts, did he stitch their eyes closed because he wanted them dead? And did he continue doing things to the dolls after his parents' murder? The dolls are covered in tiny puncture marks, the heads have been twisted repeatedly, leaving a cracked black crease in the leather delineating the neck. Maybe it wasn't enough simply to kill his parents, Caffery thinks, maybe he's kept these dolls so he can continue to torture his mother and father beyond the grave.

He sits back in the chair and stares at his

reflection in the black windowpane. There are a few stars visible above the trees — otherwise the countryside is wide and black and limitless. He imagines Handel out there somewhere — tries to picture what he's thinking. What he's planning with his Stanley knife, his pliers and his wire.

Dandelion Ward

The Maude hasn't gone. It's tricked them all. It has changed its mind and it's coming back. It's not far away, not far. Already it has done things Monster Mother can't think about. Things it never should have done.

She sits in the middle of the room in the darkness and rocks gently to and fro. She hasn't been to the day room — she doesn't like the different colours her monster children wear — or the rainbows that flash across the television set. They send her mood up and down a hundred times a second. So she stays on the floor in her room, still dressed in her lilac gown, still happy because today is a lilac day and she is going to make sure it goes on being a lilac day. In spite of everything.

AJ is the best of her children. He's getting cleverer too. Cleverer and cleverer. He doesn't have the extra eye, but maybe he's growing one. Because he is starting to get near the truth. The big truth that Monster Mother has watched in silence all these years.

AJ has found Isaac's poppets. The finished-with poppets. But he hasn't found the ones not yet finished with. The ghosts of things to come. Monster Mother has seen them — she won't tell a soul, but she's watched Handel with his busy fingers, his heart full of revenge, and his anger. She's watched him making the other poppets

— the two lady dolls — one with blonde hair, the other with short, spiky hair. Bright, bright red, the colour of a poppy. With dangly earrings and dangly bracelets and a floral dress.

A dark-haired boy poppet is holding on to this lady poppet. Holding on face to face. His arms gripping her tightly, gripping her in that special way boys sometimes hold on to girls when no one is looking.

Monster Mother lets out a small groan. She sways and sways and sways, her moon shadow splintering and leaping around her on the floor. Her lost arm is aching, as it often does when her mood changes. If it gets worse, if The Maude comes any nearer, Monster Mother is going to have to take off her skin and hide again.

Tomorrow is going to be a dark, dark-blue day. Navy-blue as midnight.

Groundhog Day

Flea wakes fully dressed on the sofa at six a.m. Her head is throbbing, her mouth is dry. The curtains are open, outside is still dark and freezing, a crystalline hush — winter on its way. She rolls on to her side, a cushion under her face, stares at the silent television. Maybe it's Groundhog Day, because on screen is Jacqui Kitson again. Different sofa, different dress, different interviewer. The expression, though, that's the same. Flea doesn't turn up the volume. She doesn't need to. She knows what Jacqui will be saying.

She looks at her watch. There's no going back to sleep — she's got to commit to the day.

She rolls off the sofa and drags on her jogging gear and makes her morning run in the dark, using her head torch and her memory to guide her. It's frosty, the trees poke their thin fingers through the sheet of white. She sees no one — no car passes, not a single light shows in the few houses she passes on the six-mile loop. The whole city of Bath is down the slope half a mile to her right — but it is silent. The only way you'd know it was there is the orange miasma in the mist.

Back at home she showers, washes her hair, gets into uniform, thermals underneath — ready for another day of searching. She snaps on the long johns and as she does feels something loose about her stomach — as if the muscles are going to split and spill. She stands for a moment in the bathroom, her hands pressed on her belly — wondering about that sensation.

Her eyes lift to the corridor, to all the boxes lined up there. They are so neat, so contained, organized and closed. It's taken for ever to pack it all away. Fuck, fuck and fuck.

She drags on her fleece, kicks on her boots and goes into the bathroom to clean her teeth. As she brushes, she keeps one hand pressed on the mirror, her eyes down on the porcelain and plug. There's no need to see her reflection. Absolutely no need.

Old Man Athey's Orchard

Damn Stewart and his crazyhead ways. He's still got that fly in his backside about something in the woods and in the morning when AJ lets him off his lead he heads straight across the field and has shuffled under the bushes and round the stile before AJ has a chance to do anything.

He is left standing there, swearing under his breath. He's tired. He hasn't slept. While Melanie eventually calmed and fell asleep, curled like a child in the crook of his arm, he lay awake, watching shadows on the ceiling, his head turning and turning. When he did sleep it was patchy. He was conscious of her there — as if her dreams and her fractured faith in him were leaping the barrier into his own nightmares.

In the end he gave up. It's six thirty and still dark, so he's put cups of fresh-brewed coffee on Patience and Melanie's nightstands and has come out here with Stewart. All Stewart seems to want to do is whine and give him pathetic looks. And now he's buggered off.

The kitchen window doesn't cast enough light to follow, so AJ goes to the garage and gets a torch — a huge thing that frightens the wildlife — and starts after the dog. He finds him about twenty metres inside the forest, his tongue out, his tail wagging eagerly to see AJ following him.

'Stewart,' AJ hisses. 'You total pain — don't give me a hard time, I've got enough to think about at the moment.'

But Stewart gives him a look of such hope and faith that AJ sighs. He might live by the maxim that what he doesn't know can't hurt him, but he's had enough of his dog and this emotional blackmail.

'Come on,' he tells him. 'We've got exactly thirty minutes, fifteen out, fifteen back — let's go see what all the fuss is about.'

They go through the forest and out the other side, over a field and up to the plateau. Though he doesn't know exactly which turnings the path goes through, he knows where it could lead eventually. The place he doesn't want to think about. The dog is beside himself with excitement. He runs with his stumpy tail high in the air, fantasizing he's some sleek high-bred gundog. AJ follows at a short distance, grumbling every inch of the way. The fields are dark and the ground crunchy with frost. His nose is cold and he wishes he'd stopped to put on gloves — his hands are like blocks of ice.

'This had better be good,' he yells to Stewart, who is waiting at the top of the path, looking back at him, his tail wagging crazily. 'Another five minutes and then we turn back.'

Stewart has taken him over the plateau, down the other side, and along the edge of the evergreen forest with the views of the village on the far side of the valley, a few lights coming on in the windows as the early risers wake. Old Man Athey's apple orchard, the place AJ scrumps for Kingston Blacks, lies to his left in a cone-shaped section that bites into the forest. Ahead is the place called The Wilds by the locals because it seems no one knows who owns it. Could be it's National Trust property, or the forgotten estate of someone decaying away in an oxygen tent on a remote Greek island. AJ has known about The Wilds all his life, but he can't recall ever having set foot in it. Upton Farm lies beyond it.

Stewart stops so suddenly that AJ almost runs into him.

'Hey, you lunatic. What the hell's going on?'

The dog doesn't move. He's as still and obdurate as a rock — his ears forward, all his attention on the path ahead. Dawn has made a wash of white in the sky overhead, and enough light is creeping down here for AJ to discern individual trees without the aid of his torch. The path stretches into the forest, greying about fifteen metres ahead, then vanishing in the poor light.

AJ is a child of the countryside and nothing scares him. There is no reason for the way the hair suddenly stands up on the back of his neck. He holds his breath, strains his senses ahead in the wood. He can't be sure, but he thought he saw something a little darker than the surroundings, a shape moving in there. Isaac Handel. AJ can't shake the thought — the certainty. His skin crawls.

Stewart suddenly gives a whine and half turns to head back in the direction they've come, as if cowed by what's in the woods. He gets a few metres behind AJ and hesitates, undecided. He turns his head back inquisitively, looking past AJ into the woods.

‘Hello?’ AJ shines the torch into the path. ‘Hello?’

His voice is thin and hollow. It is swallowed instantly by the trees. He takes three steps along the path.

‘Hello?’ he says again. ‘Don’t want to scare you, I’ve got a dog.’

Silence. Not even a crack of twig. Gathering his courage, he goes forward a few more experimental paces. He can see nothing.

‘Isaac? Is that you?’

Stewart creeps up next to him, tippy-toed and cautious, his rugged body pressed hard against AJ’s shin. Together they move further into the woods.

About five metres ahead, at the place the path seemed to disappear in the gloom, it opens instead into a wide and unexpected glade. AJ and Stewart stand at the end of the path and look around. Thready daylight creeps in, finding thin plumes of mist erupting from the forest floor, a few leaves dropping listlessly from the trees. In the centre of the glade is an object that for most would defy description. Even AJ is taken aback by it at first.

It’s a tree, but its trunk is three metres across. The branches are so thick that at seven or eight metres from the centre, bowed under their own weight, they stoop to the ground, as if the old tree at the centre was resting its elbows on the cold earth. Under the arching branches, the earth is dry and the air is silent and still, like a cathedral. And where the walking tree leans its elbows, it takes root, creeping outwards from the centre. Around it, an outer ring — a magic circle of seven trees. All identical, all cloned from the older one at the centre.

Taxus baccata: its needle-thin leaves, bark, seeds and sap are all deadly. The walking yew. A tree as old as time. As mean and still and deadly as a snake.

AJ lets out all his breath. Just a tree. Nothing to be scared of. Absolutely nothing here. He and Stewart stand for a moment longer, breathing in and out, in and out. Nope. Not a thing.

Even so, he's not going to get any closer to the damn thing — and he certainly isn't going to pass it.

'Come on, mate.' AJ clips on Stewart's lead, turns him in the direction of the house. 'Whatever you thought was there, it's not there now. Let's get breakfast.'

Inside the Poppets

In the Mendips, Caffery wakes aching in every bone and joint. He lies there with his hands over his face, feeling the pain as a death sense. Dull and ancient. It takes a long time to go, and for him to find the energy to get up.

He sits in the kitchen drinking coffee — waiting for it to work. Then, when his head starts to move a little, he realizes he feels like this because something has occurred to him overnight. Something that outside in the real world would be unspeakable, but viewed from inside Handel's skewed world order makes perfect, nasty sense. He pulls on an old sweater that's hooked over the banisters and gets his glasses. He finds his Swiss Army knife and, buoyed up by the caffeine, opens the door to the utility room.

The window has been open overnight — cracked on to the secure setting so some air can circulate — and the room is freezing. Early sunlight comes through the window. The poppets lie on the tiled surface, motionless, eyes staring at the ceiling. What is it about them that makes him sure they've only lain down like this in the last few seconds? That all night while he's been asleep they've been moving? Maybe creeping out of the window frame. Finding the nearest churchyard and lifting gravestones.

He pulls on his gloves and picks up the male doll. Graham Handel. Using the knife's tweezer head, he carefully unpicks the stitching. Underneath the outer layer is an inner layer of stained muslin. This is covered in writing, though Caffery can't immediately decipher it — or even decide which language it's written in, the ink is so smudged. He finishes stripping the outside covering, lays it out to one side, like a miniature flayed skin, and sets to work unpicking the muslin. Inside is another layer.

When both dolls are unpicked he has lined up in his utility room eight tiny skins all in different shades and fabrics. One set of four has all the characteristics of a female, with breasts and hips. The other has a penis. Scattered among the fabric wrappings are the other things he's discovered stuffed inside the dolls. The dolls' teeth, he sees, are not fashioned from polished shells as he'd thought, but human. Eight of them — yellow and old. Incisors and molars. Two tangled masses of hair — one blond, one dark — and something that looks, to his experienced eye, like the shrivelled, mummified remains of human ears.

Suki and the Snow

The recurring dream is different tonight. It starts, as always, in a room with smooth walls. There's the length of silk reaching into a hole from the ceiling, but this time it's a wire. And this time Penny knows the room is in a wood. She can hear the chatter of birds and smell the fresh air. She gets a glimpse of an opening — sees snow. She stands and turns towards it, and there is Suki, a puppy again, leaping in the snow, leaving the ground and landing on all four paws, her ears flopping. She snaps at the flakes, turns and turns, chasing one flake that evades her.

Oh, Suki, Suki.

The dog lifts her head and bounds towards her. There are wet snow and leaves in her hair — but Penny is so overjoyed to see her she scoops her up and sits down, hugging her, burying her face in her fur. She smells like a wet jumper and she is soaked, completely soaked, and so, so cold.

Come on, Penny says, *come on — let's get you dry.*

Thank you, Suki says in a deep voice. *Thank you — you've always been so kind.*

Surprised, Penny puts the puppy on the floor. Suki looks up at her. Her face is different — bigger and coarser. Her eyes are narrowed like a human's.

Suki?

In reply, Suki lifts her paw. It's a human hand — large and hairy like a man's. She takes Penny's hand and squeezes it.

You locked me in, says Suki. *You locked me in and now I want to get out*.

Penny wakes with a jolt. She is panting. The smell is real and someone is holding her hand. It's dark in the bedroom, darker than usual. But she can just make out the face on the pillow next to hers.

Not Suki's but Isaac Handel's. He is inches away from her, his mouth open in a smile.

Dirty Pink Satin

Caffery unpicks the dolls and finds they contain a grotesque array of body parts and excretions. However, aside from the dolls representing Handel's parents, the contents are things that have been taken or gleaned from people without violence: hair snippings, nail parings, scraps of clothing, numerous balled tissues stained in some unnameable secretion.

Isaac spent time in that big bedroom taking pieces of his parents and sewing them into the dolls. He didn't eat the missing parts, or throw them out of a window. He carried them out in plain view.

As for the remaining dolls . . . this is where Caffery is on less concrete ground. He's not sure who they are supposed to symbolize, but he's guessing staff and other patients at Beechway. There is a male doll with, hideously, a red boiled sweet stitched into the socket where an eye would be. Caffery hasn't forgotten AJ's conviction that Handel had somehow talked one of the patients into taking his own eye out with a spoon. Moses.

Penny said she imagined there was a doll for her too. He hasn't found anything that represents her — so maybe Isaac didn't have any long-term plans for her. Nor has he found anything that relates to AJ or to Melanie Arrow — which is surprising, given that, as head of the unit, she would have represented power and authority in Isaac's eyes. She's an attractive woman in a position of power — even someone as sick as Handel would have noticed that.

Caffery isn't sure whether he should be concerned by this absence or if it's just a distraction. A case of projecting his own thoughts into someone else. He scribbles a note on the edge of his writing block. Pushes it to one side and continues his study of the other dolls.

Two have been set aside for particular scrutiny. These are the only dolls apart from the parents that have their eyes stitched closed. Maybe they represent other people Isaac has targeted. The two dolls are female. Although they appear to be dead, they are not twisted and tortured and stabbed the way Graham and Louise's poppets are. Instead these two are cushioned on dirty pink satin, their hands folded over their chests. One is depicted as overweight, dressed in a garish red T-shirt and red socks. The other is dressed simply in crude pyjamas of blue ticking. Her hair is fashioned from strips of silk and it is the colour of soft cheese. Her body is nothing more than a wire frame draped in felt. She looks like a skin-covered skeleton.

On Caffery's phone is an ante-mortem photograph of Pauline Scott. He looks at the poppet. He looks at the photo. He stares at the poppet again.

And then he picks up the phone.

Red T-Shirt

AJ is in his office, trawling the Internet for articles on MHRT tribunals and post-care plans, wondering how the hell Isaac Handel could have disappeared with all the so-called 'safeguards' in place. The phone rings. It's DI Caffery. AJ gets up and closes the door to the office.

'Yeah — hi,' he says. 'I was about to call you. How's it going?'

'Sort of OK, sort of not. Tell me — did you look through any of this stuff you brought me?'

'Not really.'

'You weren't curious?'

'Curiosity killed the cat. Not having a sense of curiosity is the chief reason I've survived in this job.'

At the other end of the line Caffery gives a small ironic laugh. 'Strange, because curiosity is the reason I've survived in my job.'

AJ clears his throat. He goes to the window and looks out at the grounds. It's a squally day; from here he can see the windows of Myrtle Ward. Above it a little electric light comes in slices through the lowered blinds in Melanie's office. He drops his blind. Turns away from the window.

'Is there news?'

'Yes, it's good news. You've convinced me. I'm opening an investigation.'

AJ bites his lip. Thinks about the light glowing

in Melanie's office window behind him. 'Does that mean you've got to come out to the unit?'

'It does. You know we're taking this seriously, so maybe you can clear things your end.'

AJ scrunches up his face. What promise did he make himself yesterday? And has he kept it? No.

'Can you give me a day or so? Is it urgent?'

There's a tiny pause — a reticence from Caffery. 'A day or so?'

'Yes, it'll give me time to open all the — uh — channels.'

'I'd prefer it sooner. I'd like to be there this afternoon or first thing in the morning at the latest. We have to motor on this — we don't know where Handel is.'

'OK. OK, I'll do my best.'

'Please do.' AJ hears Caffery shuffling papers at the other end of the line. 'And something else, while I've got you, just so I can get some questions sorted — red T-shirt and red socks? Mean anything to you?'

AJ takes a deep breath. His heart hammers in his chest. 'Red socks, red T-shirt? Meaning?'

'The dolls — they look random, but they're not. Didn't you notice?'

'No — I mean, I didn't examine them.'

'Each one symbolizes someone in Isaac's life. Probably most are people from the unit, since those are the only people he's had contact with the last eleven years. One of the dolls is dressed in a red T-shirt and socks, that's why I'm asking.'

AJ's heart sinks. He wishes everything that has happened was just his imagination. 'Zelda,' he says. 'The red socks, the red T-shirt? We had to fight her all the time about the socks — the staff hated washing them because they turned everything pink . . . ' He trails off, his throat dry. 'Mr Caffery, do any of them look like anyone else in the unit?'

'Like you? No.'

'Ummm — how about our clinical director. Remember? Blonde?'

'Maybe you should look at them when I come to the unit. There's one I think is Moses Jackson.'

'Shit.'

'And a very thin girl in pyjamas . . . '

'Long hair? Blonde?'

'Yes.'

'Pauline,' he murmurs. 'She was wearing pyjamas when she . . . '

He stops speaking. Framed in the glass panel of his door is Melanie. She is smiling and waving through the window. He gives her a weak smile, holds up a finger. *Won't be a second,* he mouths. He turns away from the window and speaks in a rapid voice.

'I'm going to do what I can to sort things. I'll let you know as soon as I have.'

'OK. I really want to move on this so — '

'I'm going to hang up now — it's not a good time to talk.'

'Fair enough. Let me know as soon as you can. I'll be waiting.'

'Will do.' He presses his thumb on the red button. Takes a moment to calm himself. Turns and smiles at Melanie. Beckons. 'Come in.'

She comes in. 'Sorry — I didn't mean to interrupt.'

'That's OK, it was nothing.' She doesn't ask him to explain, but he finds himself doing so anyway. 'It was a sales call — I don't know who sells our damned numbers on. An urgent message about my payment-protection policy, apparently. Can I make you a coffee? It's not the best coffee, down here in the bowels of the unit, but I'll do my best.'

'That's OK — I just had one.'

AJ gives a nervous cough. He's lied. He's lied *again*. 'Did you . . . I mean, was there something you wanted to — ?'

Before he can finish the sentence the phone rings again in his hand. His heart sinks. Melanie looks at it. There's an awful awkward moment while his heart races, trying to think what he'll say if it's Caffery again.

'Go ahead,' she smiles. 'I can wait.'

'Yes, I mean, I . . . ' Resignedly he turns the phone over. Sees to his immense relief the name 'Patience' flashing on and off on the screen. He gives Melanie a pained expression. Holds it up so she can read it.

'I'm going to have to . . . ' he says.

She nods. Blows a kiss, turns for the door and leaves. He stands at the door and watches through the window, waiting for her to disappear round the turn in the corridor before he answers the phone.

'Now, AJ,' says Patience. 'Don't get upset about this . . . '

'That's *exactly* the way to break news to someone, Patience.' He turns from the door. 'Something, I dunno, so soothing about it. What is it? You been gambling with our council-tax money again?'

'No — it's Stewart.'

'Oh.' All AJ's bravado drains away. He sits down at the desk. 'Is he . . . ?'

'He's OK. He's right here with me, AJ. Fast asleep. But he hasn't been all right. I've been at the vet with him and he's had his stomach pumped and blood taken off of him, and — '

'What?'

'I know — it's cost a fortune. But I didn't have my phone with me at the vet, so I couldn't check with you, and this vet lady's yelling at me how I've got to make up my mind, just like *that,* or Stewart's liver's going to stop working and his kidneys and . . . ' She takes a few gulping breaths. 'AJ, I thought we'd lost him.'

AJ can't make sense of this. A few hours ago Stewart was running through the fields with him, his tail wagging like a mad thing. 'What the hell happened — what's wrong with him?'

There's a long silence at the end of the phone. He can pretty much hear Patience weighing her words, testing each one before she gives them voice. When she does speak, it's with the heaviness she employs whenever she wants AJ to read between the lines.

'The vet says Stewart got poisoned somehow. It's nothing *I've* given him.'

'Poisoned?' It's as if something cold and scaly has dragged itself down AJ's spine. All he can see in his mind's eye is the walk in the woods this morning. 'Poisoned how?'

'The vet doesn't know. She's on about how it

could have been lots of things, nothing obvious came out when they pumped him. But he's eaten something — a toadstool maybe. You know Stewart's not all that discriminating when it comes to eating.'

'It's OK, Patience, you did the right thing, don't get upset about it. I might be late home tonight, but don't worry about the money, OK? We're going to be fine.'

'I hope you're right,' she says drily. 'I truly hope you're right.'

'I am.' He looks out of the window as he says it — at the lights on in Myrtle — and Melanie's office window. He's got to build up his nerve to tell her about Caffery. Somehow it has to be done. 'I am right. Give Stewie a hug for me.'

The Duck

If it looks like a duck, swims like a duck and quacks like a duck, then chances are it is . . . a duck.

One of Caffery's drill sergeants at police training college in Hendon was fond of this phrase; he'd bark it at the recruits during scenario training. It must have sunk in deep, because it comes back at Caffery now, as he sits in his office, staring at the piles of paper from the Upton Farm investigation.

He's brought in Handel's poppets. The superintendent has authorized an interim forensics budget and the CSM is coming up to Caffery's office to bag and organize the dolls.

Caffery looks at the doll in the blue ticking pyjamas and the one with the red T-shirt. Both laid to rest peacefully, on a cushion of satin, not twisted and hacked into. Yet their eyes are stitched closed. The same way Isaac stitched closed the eyes on the dolls of his parents.

Zelda and Pauline . . .

If it looks, swims and quacks like a duck . . .

By late afternoon there will be a full team assembled. Someone is talking to Serious Crime about initiating a manhunt for Handel. The report on Pauline Scott's disappearance and postmortem have already been circulated around the team. People talk about the cogs of bureaucracy moving slowly, but Avon and Somerset seems to have its wheels especially well oiled just now. All he's waiting for is AJ to call him with the go-ahead to visit the unit.

That is the big problem. It's mostly Caffery being decent — out of some unexpected and inexplicable loyalty to the guy. The courtesy, however, can only be extended so far. Once the team is assembled, he's going to have to pull the plug on AJ and go into Beechway, regardless.

Time for a coffee. He inspects his chipped old cup — empty. He picks it up and stands, pausing briefly to look at the area map on his wall. It's an unprofessional map because there are places he should have put pins and hasn't — like the quarry at Elf's Grotto, the road near Farleigh Park Hall. Nevertheless, it's an aid to him. Sometimes a thought provoker when he needs the inspiration.

He looks at it for a bit longer. Then, not sure what he's looking for, he clicks on the kettle. While he's waiting for it to boil, he looks out of the window at a fog bank lifting above the high rises. What are you up to, Handel, he thinks. What is going on in your screwed-up brain?

The kettle boils. Caffery makes his coffee. He's pouring in a little milk, and is about to spoon in the sugar when something becomes clear to him. He stops what he's doing and jerks his head up, looking across the room.

The map. The fucking map.

He puts down the spoon, crosses the room, and stands, arms folded, staring at it.

There it is, plain as day. Just below Upton Farm, a tiny annotation, written in the Old English calligraphy beloved of OS maps:

The Wilds.

How to Tell the Truth

At last AJ gets up the courage to go and tell Melanie about Jack Caffery. He knocks on her door and when he goes in she is sitting at her desk, smiling up at him.

'Hi,' he says cautiously. 'Earlier — did you come to see me for something?'

'Only to give you a hug. Say hi.' She gives a sheepish smile. There's no suggestion she knows he's lied about the phone call. 'Are you OK?'

'I'm fine. I mean, sort of.'

'Sort of?'

'Yes, I . . . I need to speak to you. Something's happened.'

'Something?'

He sits down. Puts his keys and phone on the desk — looks her in the eye. He fumbles in his head for the first sentence of the speech he's prepared. But when he opens his mouth, what pops out is: 'Stewart's ill. He's been at the vet.'

Melanie's face falls. 'The vet? Is he OK?'

'Yeah — he's going to be fine. Patience dealt with it.'

'God, I'm sorry. Poor Stewart. Maybe he ate something while he was — you know . . . ' She wrinkles her brow. 'Wherever it is he keeps yomping off to.'

'Maybe. But it's OK. He's going to be fine.'

'That's good.' She smiles again, and he smiles stupidly back at her. She's waiting for him to speak, but he can't bring himself to say the words. He's a wuss. A coward. A lily-livered surrender monkey. He casts around for a way of changing the subject, a way of justifying being here. 'So.' He indicates the corridor that leads from the director's office to the kitchenette. 'So. Do you mind if I make some coffee?'

'Be my guest. I'll have a cup too.'

He can feel her eyes on him as he leaves the office. He knows she knows there's something more. He will say it. He *will*. He fills up the coffee-maker, clicks it on and starts getting the jewelled cups out, repeating under his breath: '*I've lied to you, not because I'm like the others, but because I was trying to do the right thing . . .*'

He puts milk and sugar on the tray. The coffee-maker pings, and he pours coffee into the cups. His heart is thudding.

He puts two biscuits on a plate and carries the tray through, sets it in front of her.

'Thanks.'

'You're welcome.'

She sips the coffee and he places his cup on the desk. But instead of sitting and drinking he remains standing. Not speaking. Eventually she notices. She lowers her cup and raises her eyes to him.

'AJ? What is it?'

'Zelda Lornton. Pauline. Moses. The police want to open an investigation.'

The response is instantaneous, and exactly what he'd dreaded. Her face drains of colour. 'What?' she murmurs, disbelieving. '*What?*'

The Wilds

Penny Pilson isn't answering her phone. Caffery leaves a message — 'When you have time I want to ask you something. Wonder what you meant when you said Handel would be 'off into the wilds'. Give me a call.' Then he checks his watch. The super is in a meeting at HQ and he's going to be there until lunchtime. AJ LeGrande has Caffery's mobile number. There's nothing keeping him here. He finds his keys, and at the last minute gets his North Face Triclimate jacket from the cupboard and his walking boots.

Wotton-under-Edge is named because it sits under the edge of the Cotswolds. An old market town, it retains that atmosphere of a place people gather. But at this time on a chilly late-October day it is peopled only by a few shoppers, ducking in and out of the brightly lit shops. Caffery drives through, watches the town dwindle in his rear-view mirror. Upton Farm is only two miles from here. Wotton would have been the place the Handel family shopped. He wonders if Isaac has been here more recently. Whether he's sat in that bus shelter or on that bench and watched people coming and going.

Wire and pliers. Something left unfinished?

The road winds up the escarpment until he's cresting along the summit, passing Westridge and North Nibley. Using his phone and his memory of the map, he locates a small farm track that leads through an abandoned orchard. A rusting skip lies on its side under the gnarled trees, as if some giant has got fed up apple picking and cast it aside. The grass hasn't been cut — it lies flat and bedraggled under the sodden heaps of rotting apples.

Where the track stops, Caffery parks. He pulls on the boots and jacket, and from under the driver's seat takes a torch. It is weighty and solid and feels good in his hand. He locks the car, turns up his collar, and heads off down the footpath that leads into the trees.

It takes him fifteen minutes to pick his way to the place named The Wilds. Several times his phone drops its GPS connection and finds it again. As he comes down a path and sees daylight ahead where it opens into a glade, the signal flashes to SOS, and then, in the next moment: No Service. He tucks it inside his jacket and continues.

The moment he gets to the clearing the shape leaps out at him. A mountain — a white-boned giant. It's a tree, he recognizes that immediately, but like no other tree he's ever seen: it is huge and dead in the thin light. The collapsed skeleton of an ogre.

He scans the surrounding woods, then, drawn to the tree, moves forward a few steps, approaching it slowly, his feet crunching the dead leaves. As he circles it he finds, half hidden, an arch leading to an empty chasm where its heart must have once been. One hand on the nearest root arch, he bends and shines the light inside. He sees beer cans, a soaking wet sleeping bag on an unfolded cardboard box.

'Hello?' The torch picks up the gnarled interior of the tree, pocked with sealed knots and bumps — like polished rock walls. 'Anyone home?'

Silence. He flicks the torch on from side to side — as if the movement will shake anything hiding in the tree out into the open. He switches it off and waits, his breath held. There is no noise at all. Nothing.

He sniffs. There's a strong smell of wet earth and leaf mould — and something else. A lower keynote under the damp that touches a deep nerve and makes him hold his mouth open slightly like a cat testing a scent. He's smelled it recently — it's too familiar. The uncared for, urinated-on funk of Handel's dolls.

He stoops and, bent almost double, enters. It's impossible to stand up inside. The smell is so strong it makes him cover his mouth. He finds a broken stick on the ground and uses it to poke through the items on the floor. It's like going through a recycling bin. Beer cans are squashed into bumpy discs. There are flattened plastic bottles and a few empty crisp bags. He uses the stick to lift the corner of the sleeping bag. Sees that lying on top of the cardboard, serving as a half-hearted waterproof layer, is a Wickes carrier bag.

'Hello, mate,' he murmurs under his breath. 'Nice to find you at last.'

Level Pegging

AJ badly wants to sit down next to Melanie, but he's got to stay standing, whatever. 'I had to get the police involved.' He tries to sound reasonable. 'I mean, let's face it, we've both known it for a long time. It's not just Isaac being in your garden, it's so many other things putting an arrow over his head.'

'Oh God.' Melanie covers her mouth, drops her face. 'Oh God,' she says. 'Oh God.'

'He's clever, Melanie, much cleverer than we ever realized. He knew how to manipulate people. Zelda, and maybe Moses too. Maybe even Pauline. They were all scared — so many of the witnesses say they were scared in the days leading up to . . . '

His voice peters out. Melanie is raking her hands through her hair. Digging the nails in and turning her head from side to side, like someone being tortured. He keeps up the conscious effort not to go and comfort her. Stands silent and still — feet together, hands in his pockets. He's got to see this through. He waits, watches her tearing herself apart. Shaking her head and saying 'no', over and over.

When she at last puts her face up there's a complete clarity. A couple of streaks of mascara where she's cried, but otherwise her face is completely calm. It's as if she's made the decision to wipe it clean.

'AJ?'

'Melanie?'

'AJ.'

It is half a question, half an admission. And suddenly something he hadn't even dreamed of swims into glaring, blinding focus. Melanie's been hiding something else. The muscles in his jaw loosen, because he realizes on some level he's always suspected it. Always been aware of what she wasn't saying.

'You knew,' he murmurs. 'You knew what happened. You knew it was him.'

She looks back at him steadily.

'*Melanie?* Did you know?'

Now he can't keep his stiff posture. He sinks into the chair opposite and stares at her.

'You knew — you *knew* what Isaac was doing.'

She lowers her forehead again and puts her elegant fingers to her temples.

'AJ, we've slept together, we've done things that are probably illegal together and I suppose that means we should share everything — '

'Just answer me. Did you know?'

'Not *know* as such. But if I'm honest I . . . suspected.'

'*Suspected?*'

'Everyone has the right to make up for what they've done. They all need a chance at rehabilitation. That's what my ethics have always been founded on.'

'Ethics? You bent over backwards to have Isaac fucking Handel released? Knowing what he'd been up to?'

'Not knowing. Suspecting.'

'*Suspecting*, even.' He puts his head back, opens his hands, as if he's asking God for help. 'I can't believe this.'

'That's because you've never been in *my* position. You've never had to face that pressure. I'm not blaming you, I'm not, but you cannot imagine what it's like. It's the curse of middle management, being the ham in the sandwich — which, if you're the bottom of the sandwich, probably sounds a privileged place to be, but the truth is, it's hell. The crap comes from both sides. To everyone in the unit I've got to be a figure of authority — whatever bullshit that means — but to the Trust I'm a tool. I have to take whatever they say and convert it into something that my staff can understand and respond to.'

'I'm not all that interested, to be honest. You finessed Isaac's tribunal so he'd be let out.'

'Hysteria spreading through the patient population.'

'And it still *is* spreading. Except now it's *outside* the unit — so you've really shot yourself in the foot. Isaac is missing from his placement, and you and I both know he's been in your garden. For all I know, he may have been to my place too. Maybe he even poisoned Stewart. I'm sorry, Melanie, but I'm finding it all a bit too much to take in at the moment.'

'AJ, my job was on the line. Completely on the line. You don't know the sacrifices I've made to stay in this job, the shitty things I had to do to get here in the first place. I wasn't to know he'd come back. OK, I'm an idiot — I realize that. I do.'

'It's nothing to do with Jonathan, is it? Nothing he put you up to?'

She blinks. '*What?* No, of course not. What's he got to do with this?'

'I don't know. Nothing — it's just all so . . . . You *lied* to me.'

'You lied to me too. Lots, it seems. So maybe we're level pegging?'

'*Level pegging?*' He nearly loses it then. For a man who never suspected himself of having much in the way of moral fibre, he finds it surprising how much all this bothers him. He gets up and walks from one side of the room to the other, trying to order everything in his mind in a way that makes sense.

'I'm sorry,' she says timidly. 'I really am sorry.'

He keeps walking, trying not to look at her. A detached part of him knows it's all illogical and unfair; it also knows he'll probably forgive her. Because she is Melanie and he is in love with her.

'AJ? AJ?'

He looks at her. She is standing, smiling hopefully, her hands out to him. He frowns, still uncomfortable.

'AJ? Come on? Truce?'

Eventually, grudgingly, he embraces her. Her arms go up under his, her hands crossed on his shoulder blade, her face squashed against his shirt. 'AJ, I'm sorry — I'm so sorry.'

'It's OK.' He strokes her hair, a little rigidly. 'All OK. Everything will be fine.'

'I get so insecure. At work.'

'I know. I know.' He continues stroking her

hair, still not quite sure what to think. A long silence passes while all he can feel is her heart beating fast and shallow against his arm. Out of the window the old clock on the tower ticks towards three o'clock. AJ imagines what they look like from outside. People who care about each other? Or people who are angry?

'I've got an idea.' Melanie takes a step back. She fumbles a handkerchief out of her cardigan pocket and wipes her nose. 'Let's go.'

'Go?'

'Yes. Just go.' She makes her hand into an aeroplane and directs it towards the window. 'Let's disappear until it blows over. You can tell the police you were mistaken and we can both take, I dunno, sick leave, or annual leave or whatever — and head off. I've got strings I can pull in HR. A desert island, maybe. Sun, sand and sex.' She lifts her face to him. 'I once drank six pina coladas at lunchtime and fell in the swimming pool.'

'I can picture it.'

'The lifeguard had to get me out.'

'I can picture that too. I'm jealous.'

She flashes a watery smile at him. 'Shall we? Shall we just go?'

'Oh, Melanie, Melanie.'

'What?'

'I can't go away.'

'Why?'

'We can't just pretend it's not happening.'

'OK. OK.' Deflated, she bites her lip. 'I understand.'

'And there's Stewart too — he's, well, God

only knows what's up with Stewart, but I can't leave Stewie. Not when he's ill.'

'I understand.'

She looks around herself helplessly — as if she's trying to find something to divert attention. He doesn't say anything. He knows when to keep his mouth shut. 'I um . . . AJ . . . I . . . ' She begins to gather up her belongings — her handbag, her phone, her keys. 'I think I'm just going to have a quick walk, maybe a drive. Get some fresh air, you know?'

'It's probably a good idea.'

She nods. 'Yes. A good idea.' She pulls on her cream raincoat, jams the hood down over her face and, without waiting to hear if he's going to speak, heads for the door. A moment later he sees her out of the window: she's gone through the pinch-point security gate in the stem corridor, through the admin corridor and has appeared outside — walking fast across the car park, her car keys out. The security lights on the Beetle flash on and off and she jumps in.

There is a moment where he sees her face lit by the dashboard, her honey-blonde hair hanging bedraggled around her face, and he sees she is crying again. Then she is through the security gates and gone, leaving him staring into nothing.

Eat Me Cake

Caffery leans back against the inside of the tree, in a half-sitting position, his back supported, his head contorted like Alice after the EAT ME cake. He shines the torch on the sleeping bag, thinking about what it would be like, sleeping out here. Sheltered from the wind, at least. Isaac Handel knew this area as a child — he must have, it's so close to Upton Farm. But Caffery's not sure what it means, that he's gravitated back here. Is it only because it's familiar? Or is there another reason? Some unfinished business?

The pliers and the wire and the other things Handel bought at Wickes aren't here. Maybe they're elsewhere in the woods. Caffery starts to manoeuvre himself backwards out of the cave, ticking off in his head the searches and permissions he's going to need. Surveillance. The superintendent should OK the surveillance spend, but he can't picture anyone in the Force Targeting Team relishing the prospect of staking out this place. They have a limited overtime allowance and they're not going to waste it. They want a nice warm car to sit in. Not bird watchers' gear, sou'westers and peeing in a bottle.

Something dangles near Caffery's face. He freezes, half bent over. His eyes rotate slowly, and he lifts the torch, partly as a weapon. The object is inches away from his eyes — so close it takes a moment to focus. It's the crudely stitched face of a doll. It must have been wedged between the roots overhead and Caffery has dislodged it. It hangs from its legs, upside down, swinging with the momentum of its drop.

It bears all the hallmarks of one of Isaac's poppets. The mix of textures — in this case a butterscotch-coloured fake leather for the skin, highly polished porcelain for the face, and a strange little dress made from a scrap of white lace. Caffery doesn't touch it. He scrambles his glasses out from the pocket of his North Face, crams them on his face and cants his head round so he can study it in the torchlight.

Yes, it's similar to the others. But there's more. This one is different, nastier. It's a female with long yellow strands of wool, like blonde hair, that sway as she rocks to and fro upside down. Her hair is free, but nothing else is. She is gagged with a narrow strip of duct tape and her arms are folded across her chest, stitched there. As if to secure her arms further the wrists have been bound with a delicate silver chain wrapped tightly around them.

Caffery is now sufficiently conversant with Handel's style to understand. This means a woman, a flesh-and-blood woman in the real world that Handel has plans for. She has blonde hair and in her wardrobe will be a lace dress or a blouse with a tiny, unnoticed tear in it. Missing from her jewellery box will be a silver bracelet.

An Unfortunate Dwarf

The plans of Beechway High Secure Unit are like the map of the Odyssean labyrinth. So multilayered, multifaceted you could lose yourself. A print of them has been framed and mounted in Melanie's office and now AJ stands and stares blankly at them. Maybe there is something in this place that can engulf a person. It swallowed Pauline and Moses and Zelda. Maybe it's busily swallowing him too.

He runs his hands through his hair. Scrunches up his eyes and wishes he could take a pill — some of the drugs the patients get when they go into crisis. Something just to switch his head off and sluice things out of him. He glances over his shoulder at the kitchenette. The little touches of homeliness Melanie has added. A print of a cat sleeping on a white Mediterranean wall. A teapot in two pieces, painted with the blue water and sky of the Riviera. He's sure he and Mel have touched something in each other. But this? This secret? All the openness he thought they had — after sex and laughing and their candid admission sessions — after all that, she's still hidden things. AJ is sure it's got something to do with her separation from Jonathan, he just doesn't know what. This is turning to a bleaker day than the one when his mother died — alone in the garden, with grass and earth coating her half-bitten tongue.

He washes up the coffee cups. Melanie's left an open packet of chocolate digestives, which he diligently wraps and tucks into a tin. He switches off the light and heads back through her office. At the door he stops. He stands very still, his head against it, his hand on the light switch. He breathes in and out.

Then he switches the light back on, goes to the window, lowers the blinds and sits down at Melanie's desk. It's made of functional beech — very light and honey-clear, everything organized carefully. There is an old-fashioned in-and-out-tray stacker with one or two envelopes in it. Her computer is a PC with a light-up wireless mouse on a mat that has a quote printed on it, white against a blue background: *Failures do what is tension relieving, while winners do what is goal achieving.*

* * *

AJ looks at the mat for a long time. Eventually he touches the mouse. Just his finger resting lightly on it. The computer comes to life.

It is password-locked.

Of course it is.

He sits back, almost relieved. He doesn't want to be the sneak. He really doesn't. He has no right to spy on Melanie or judge her. It's not as if he's perfect. She's had it hard, and maybe he should understand more. She didn't know where all this would lead. He's going to call her. Say he's sorry. He pulls out his phone and looks at the screen and instantly all he can picture is

Isaac Handel with his hands around Zelda's neck. He puts it back in his pocket.

He taps his fingers on his knees, undecided. Then he opens the bottom drawer of her desk. There is nothing much of interest in there — a sponge bag, a pair of purple kitten-heel shoes — maybe in case she needs to look smart for an unexpected occasion. Also some deodorant and a pair of flesh-coloured tights. In the next drawer there is a desk organizer full of paper clips and rubber bands. Wedged under it is a hefty paperback book.

He pulls the book out: *Screaming Walls — A Ghost Hunter's Guide to the UK's Most Haunted Asylums*. It must be something she's bought in the wake of The Maude's appearances. Maybe she wants to study precedents of the unit's 'haunting'. The date of publication as 1999 — long before the first manifestations of The Maude in Beechway. Out of curiosity he flicks to the index and looks for Beechway. It's not mentioned. He's about to put the book back when something else occurs to him.

The index takes up four pages, but he runs his finger down each page, just out of curiosity, his eye scanning the alphabet: *Bedlam (Bethlem); Care in the Community; Cherry Knowle Hospital, Sunderland; Denbigh Hospital; DSMV diagnosis; ectenic force; Hine, G.T. (architect); Mental Health Act, effects of; Ryhope General; St George Field, Bethlem; 'Sitting' and possession . . .*

He comes to a halt, his finger under the words. Sitting and possession?

Quickly he turns to the page number.

The text is dotted with plans and photos of a mock-Gothic building, a classic workhouse structured on the *enpeigne* or 'comb' principle, with separate units connected like the teeth of a comb to a spine. The Gothic Revival details have been shored up by some hasty council; a set of columns that would originally have been constructed of iron core covered in plaster to resemble stone have been replaced by stacked and painted breezeblocks. But the pointed arched windows and external crenels remain intact.

Hartwool Hospital. It's in the north of England near Rotherham. He races through the text, muttering the words under his breath like a reception-year child on his early reading books.

> Multiple episodes of self-abuse were attributed to the influence of the so-called 'B ward sitting demon'. Rumoured to be the ghost of a past matron, a dwarf who abused the patients . . .

AJ's pulse beats strong and loud in his ears.

> A suicide attempt in which the patient tried to cut off his own nose . . .
>
> Patient X reported an incubus crouched on her chest when she woke . . .
>
> Staff absences and resignations were occasionally blamed on the fear there was a ghost dwarf or an unknown entity that sat on the chests of patients . . .
>
> . . . hallucinations and delusions of haunting . . .

> . . . this crude image of a dwarf squatting on a patient's chest was produced by one of the patients in 1997 . . .

He stares at the image. A line drawing of a dark shape crouched on the chest of a supine patient. Next to it a photo of a gravestone in the grounds of the now-abandoned hospital.

Our sister Maude, an unfortunate dwarf,
who departed this life and was born into
the spirit life, 18 September 1893

AJ glances to the page header — Hartwool Hospital. Rotherham. His pulse is deafening now.

Hartwool Hospital is the place Melanie worked before she came here. The place she was transferred from during the Care in the Community upheaval.

The place she worked with Jonathan Keay.

Things Are Not What They Seem

Penny Pilson hasn't returned Caffery's call, so he drives carefully back down the valley, over a rickety bridge, and up to the Old Mill. The shutters are all still closed. He knocks and tries to peer through the sweetheart holes but it looks dark in there. He's getting back into his car when there's a noise — a shuffling inside the house — and the door opens a crack.

'Hi.'

'Hi.'

Penny's wearing a knitted cardigan and denim cut-offs, and has her arms crossed with her hands tucked under the armpits. Her feet are naked and her hair is ruffled and smeared as if she's been kneading it with greasy hands.

'You OK?'

'Yes.' Her face is quite clear of make-up, but as Caffery approaches he's sure it's more than just the nakedness that's different. It's not the same nervousness she had yesterday, it's different. It's a kind of new reserve. As if she's holding something back.

'You sure?'

'Of course. I was in the bath, that's all.'

He nods. He's a bit taken off guard by her. 'I left a message earlier.'

'I know — I've been so busy all day — I was

going to call when I'd had dinner.'

He assesses her carefully. She hasn't invited him in, and she's positioned herself to fill the gap in the door so he can't see past her. 'I had a question. I've been up there — ' He lifts his chin, indicating the direction of The Wilds. The old yew tree. 'And I think I've found where he's living.'

'Oh?'

'The Wilds?'

'Yes. You're right. He used to go there when he was living at the farm.' She gives a blank smile and begins to close the door.

'Wait.' Caffery puts a hand up. 'Just a minute — I've got another question.'

She hesitates. Then, almost reluctantly, she opens the door again. He gets a glimpse of the passage beyond. No lights on. A strange smell. Maybe something she's cooking. Her fingernails are bitten and raw.

'I found something I wanted you to look at.'

From inside his jacket pocket he pulls out the doll. He's wrapped it in a plastic carrier bag, and now he carefully opens it and holds it out for Penny to inspect. She stares at the doll, her throat working.

'Yes,' she says tightly. 'That's his work.'

'Do you know who it could be?'

She shakes her head. 'I don't really want to look at it any more. If you don't mind.'

He wraps the doll and returns it to the inside of his jacket. Penny is a different person from the one he met yesterday. She doesn't want to have anything to do with him. His memory flits over the affair — her dalliance with Graham Handel. Maybe that's what's happening now. Maybe she's got someone in the house she's ashamed of.

'I'll be on my way then.' He is about to turn away when she leans forward and whispers fiercely at him.

'*Mr Caffery?*'

'Yes?'

'*Things are not what they seem.*'

'I'm sorry?'

'Just that.' She straightens. 'I'll say goodbye now.'

And before he can ask her what she means she steps back inside and closes the door, leaving him standing there, bewildered, not entirely sure what has just happened.

He drives back to MCIT, wondering if he should turn round and go back. What the hell did she mean — *Things are not what they seem* . . . He parks in his usual spot under the flyover and goes upstairs. The doll in his inside pocket presses against his chest — as if it is digging its fingers into him. He hates the thing. He'll be glad to see the back of it. In his office he puts it on his desk, the plastic carrier bunching around it like a nest. While the rest of the office block hums gently as various team members come and go, as the necessary phone calls go out, as the superintendent gets on to the surveillance team, Caffery moves the vast lens of his microscope lamp and positions it over the doll.

Using one gloved finger, he lifts the chain that

has been used to bind the doll's arms. It's a bracelet — and now he has the chance to study it carefully he sees there is a silver pendant tucked inside the chain. He takes one or two photographs of the doll as it is; figuring there's nothing to lose if he pulls it out, he uses the nail of his little finger to get leverage on the object. It springs free and falls across the gagged face of the doll.

Two letters in curlicue script. The letters are M and A.

In his pocket his phone rings. He pulls it out and sees AJ LeGrande's name flash up on the display. 'AJ, hi.'

'Can you talk?'

'I can.'

'I've got a name.'

'A name for . . . ?'

'I keep thinking — whether Handel had some place he could hole up. Someone who could help him?'

This is so apposite — so like having his mind read — Caffery lets out an incredulous laugh. He stops studying the doll and sits down — pulls over a Post-it pad and finds a pen.

'Go ahead?'

'Jonathan Keay,' says AJ. 'K-E-A-Y.'

'Keay. Who is?'

'Who was an ocky-health person here — occupational therapy? Until about three weeks ago. No idea where he's gone.'

'Fine.' Caffery keeps writing, the phone jammed under his chin. 'So . . . details?'

'Out of date. I've got an address — but I've

just been told he's not renting there any more and the mobile I've got is a dud too. Just tried it.'

'DOB? National insurance number — should be on his records.'

'Yes, but that's HR and I'm not authorized to get into them. I've got an old landline — haven't tried it. Looks years old.'

Caffery scribbles down the number — some UK area codes still work off the telephone keypad where letters are assigned to numbers, so a town name beginning Adi . . . would read 0123. The number AJ gives him is local — in fact he recognizes it instantly as somewhere near Yate. Using his right hand, he drags across his keyboard and wakes his computer up. Starts tapping out an email.

As he types he talks. 'Why are we looking at Keay?'

'Um — because he was . . . I don't know. Sort of secretive. He used to talk to Isaac, in private, maybe. I'm not sure, but that's how I recall it. Also Keay was working in Hartwool Hospital.'

'Which means? To the uninitiated, i.e. me?'

'It's in Rotherham, or nearby. Handel wasn't held there, but the place is connected somehow. As I'm talking to you I'm looking at a book I've found and what happened in Hartwool is word for word what happened here in Beechway — patients had *exactly* the same delusions with *exactly* the same results. When Keay left Hartwool he came here. Less than a year later the same thing started happening to us.'

'Why did he move?'

'The place was closed down when there was

that radical shake-up in the mental-health system. He and — um — our director got moved down here at the same time. You know — Melanie.'

Caffery's hands hesitate on the keyboard. His attention shifts to the doll. The initials MA on the bracelet. The blonde hair. He pushes the keyboard aside and swivels his chair so he's facing the door and doesn't have to look at the gagged face. He takes his time — choosing his words carefully. Never alarm people unnecessarily.

'Actually,' he lies, 'you've just reminded me. I was looking for a number for your director.'

'I thought we'd agreed you wouldn't. You were going to wait,' he says, cagily.

'I know.' Caffery wants to turn and check the doll. He imagines it behind him, sitting up on its own. Reaching a hand out. 'But it can't wait any longer.'

There's silence at the end of the phone.

'Do you know where she is? I need to speak to her. Call it a matter of urgency.'

Again a silence.

'AJ?'

There's a long exhalation. 'It's been a shite hound of a day,' AJ says. Suddenly he sounds very loose, very apologetic. 'Truth is, I don't know. I've tried to call. She's not answering her phone. I think it's because she already knows what I've just told you about Keay.'

'She does?'

'They were . . . they were an item. For a few years. And now they're not. He's part of all of this. I think she knows about it — or maybe she suspects.'

Caffery keeps his tone light and noncommittal. Embryonic answers and questions are floating in his head. He still resists the urge to turn and look at the doll. 'Do you know where she's gone?'

'No. Why?'

'Why? Well, for all the reasons you just said. She might be able to give us something useful.' He injects enthusiasm into his voice. 'And I'd like to have a word with her as soon as possible. In fact, let me have her details, her number, her address — I think we'll pay her a quick courtesy call.'

Closed Road

AJ drives too fast. He knows these roads well, and usually he absorbs the colours of the trees, the flowers in the hedgerows — sometimes he's too engrossed by them to notice the important things like speed signs and other motorists. But tonight the countryside is just a flattened grey cloud on the periphery of his attention. He is eaten up by wanting to see Melanie.

He's called her maybe twenty times. Each time it's gone to voicemail. He's left three messages, with varying degrees of frustration, anger and forced patience. 'We need to talk about this.' 'Can we chat — no blame, no anger, just a chat to get things straight?'

He doesn't say, *You need to explain where Keay is in all of this. Have you covered for him? Have you been covering for something he's cooked up with Isaac?*

It's six when he arrives at her house. Nine minutes before the satnav said he would. He can tell as he pulls into her road and sees blue lights flashing from several vehicles parked in the close ahead that whatever mistakes Melanie has made she's paying for them tenfold. At the neck of the road, a uniformed cop is unravelling blue-and-white police cordon tape.

It's a closed road. Not a crime scene. To AJ the difference is immaterial.

He puts the car into neutral and lets it roll

slowly towards the cop. The officer blinks, blinded by the headlights coming at him. He stops unravelling the tape, bends his head to speak quickly into the radio attached to his hi-vis jacket, then lowers the tape reel and comes towards AJ. Batting his hands together and breathing out frosted clouds like a dragon.

'Yes, sir? Can I help?'

AJ stares past him at the house. He can see people moving in the garden. There's a van parked to the right of the driveway — white and unmarked. He can see into the kitchen: it's a mess. Food and plates smashed on the floor. Windows smashed. Someone has torn the place apart.

'I'm looking for Melanie Arrow. She's a resident here.' He licks his lips, not taking his eyes off the mayhem inside the house. 'But I guess you're not going to let me through.'

'We're carrying out a routine inquiry, sir. Are you a relative? A friend?'

'Of Melanie's? Yes — I am, very much a friend.'

'Have you any ID?'

AJ has. His NHS card is in his wallet. He holds it up. 'I work with her. DI Caffery knows me.'

'Is he MCIT? Avon and Somerset?'

'Yes.'

The cop nods. 'And you last saw Melanie . . . ?'

'A couple of hours ago. At the hospital we work in. Can you tell me what's happening?'

The cop doesn't answer. He half straightens, hands behind his back. Turns his head left and right, as if surveying the horizon. As if weighing up his response.

'We don't know. She's not here.'

AJ closes his eyes. He puts his finger to his forehead.

'Sir? Are you OK?'

He nods weakly. The cop is leaning through the window, a hand resting on his shoulder.

'Sir?'

'I'm fine. Honestly, fine.'

Monster Mother

No one has said 'kidnap' and no one has said 'abduct', but the words are there, as clear as can be, in the gaps between what the police are saying and what they're not saying. He doesn't tell them what he knows about Melanie's role in releasing Isaac. It's not ironic or deserving, the way it's backfired on her. She is going to pay for her mistake a hundred times over. He feels like throwing up. And him — a psychiatric nurse. He's supposed to be able to deal with stress. Ha fucking ha.

He gives the officer his statement, tells them as much as he can remember about Melanie's Beetle (limited — he knows it's black, but he can't recall the number plate). When they've finished with him, he doesn't know what to do with himself. He's tried calling Caffery, but he's out of signal range, and the receptionist at MCIT keeps repeating, *He's out of the office, I'll get him to call you . . .*

The idea of going home fills AJ with dread. Patience isn't going to be sympathetic. She has no idea about the weight of guilt he staggers around under daily — that he blames himself for what happened with Mum, and that it's happening again. Once again he's failed to be there at the right time.

Now without having given it any conscious thought he finds himself back in the unit

— standing outside Gabriella's room. He must be expecting some glimmer of hope or a reassuring word from her, because the moment he looks through the wire-reinforced window and sees her, his spirits sag even further. He's not going to get happy Monster Mother. He's going to get the dark heart of the storm.

She's crouching in the corner. Nursing her non-existent arm as if it hurts. Her dress is of an indigo so dark it looks black. When he knocks she doesn't answer. He understands she's taken off her skin again and is hiding.

'Gabriella?'

He steps inside. Doesn't look at her, keeps his gaze steady.

'Gabriella — where are you?'

'I'm here,' she hisses. 'AJ, over here in the corner.'

He looks at her. 'Hello,' he says, pathetically. 'Hello.'

Her smile is sorrowful. 'You can feel it, can't you, AJ? I can see it all round you — you've got the aura. It's hurting.'

AJ is almost knocked over by the tenderness in her voice. It's like being touched on the forehead by Mum when he was a kid having a nightmare.

'Yes, I'm . . . I'm . . . ' He can't get the words out. 'Can I sit down?'

She gives a gracious nod. 'But don't look at my skin. If you look at it The Maude will know.'

'And your skin is . . . ?'

'Over there, hanging on the bed. Don't look!'

AJ turns the chair so his back is to the bed,

where her skin is hanging. His hands and feet are jittery with adrenalin. Like having air pumped around his arteries and veins.

'Gabriella, things are happening. Out there — in the world — things are happening.'

'I know, AJ, I know. It's coming back.'

'What's coming back?'

'You know what I mean. I mean the one who sits.'

AJ stares at her. She's insane, he repeats to himself. She is completely insane. She doesn't know anything. She's picked up on his tension about Isaac and what he's done with Melanie and has converted it into a fantasy.

'Gabriella, do you remember the man who used to teach art in the unit? His name was Jonathan Keay? He left about a month ago.'

Monster Mother's face twists. She rubs her non-existent arm convulsively.

'Jonathan. Yes — Jonathan. I remember you all, you see, AJ. Each one of you — whatever you've done — whatever's been done to you . . . Jonathan is one of my children, but he's in pain — he isn't the person he should be.'

'What sort of person should he be?'

Monster Mother shakes her head. 'It's coming now, AJ — it's getting nearer.' She raises her hand to the door. 'It's so near it's going to come through there — this minute — it's going to come through the — '

Before she can finish the sentence, the panic alarm starts to wail. It's not the usual ward alarm — that has a different cadence. This is the unit-wide alarm — it means a serious incident.

'See?' Monster Mother says. 'I told you — it's coming back.'

AJ checks his pager. There's a message: *AJ — security central please*. He stares at it.

He doesn't want to, but he gets to his feet.

'Gabriella,' he says, in that weary monotone all the staff adopt when they have to instruct the patients. 'This is a lockdown — you'll have to stay in here for now, OK?'

Monster Mother nods solemnly. 'Good luck, AJ. Good luck.'

He opens the door. Looks from side to side. There are one or two patients with their heads out of their doors, wondering what's happening. Others are being herded from the day room into the corridor. The Big Lurch is there, helping get patients into their rooms, quickly locking doors. He sees AJ and waves frantically.

'AJ — AJ! Unit-wide alert, mate. Get to the security pod — the supervisor wants to talk to you now.'

Berrington Manor

Caffery is not enjoying the phone calls and organization required now this case has gone cross-border. The task of checking on Melanie's welfare has been passed to his oppo in the Gloucestershire force. The message that comes back isn't a happy one. The front door of her house stands wide open — there are signs of a struggle. The house has been ransacked and her car is missing. AJ — who must have known just from Caffery's tone that Melanie was in danger — has appeared at the house. According to the Gloucestershire police, he's filled them in on what he knows. The Serious Crime unit has been mobilized. Panic is mounting.

Jonathan Keay grew up in Berrington Manor. No house number, no street name. Just the house name, the village and the postcode. There can't be many psychiatric nurses who were raised in a place like this, Caffery thinks, as he pulls into the property. The driveway, flanked by tall poplars like some grand French avenue, is almost half a mile long. A bank of floodlights comes on with his arrival, illuminating a smartly kept equestrian yard with stalls the size of dining rooms and highly polished finials on the partitions. Beyond he can see the pale expanse and hand-lettered signs of an outdoor ménage — jumping poles stacked in a three-sided barn. The grey stone chimneys of a sprawling mansion rise behind a high brick wall to his left.

He drags on the handbrake, cuts the engine and opens the car door. The yard is quiet, well swept and cleaned — in fact, there's no sign of anything actually going on here. No straw bales or farm machinery or buckets or horse rugs draped over doors. No people. There are three high-end BMWs all in the same slate grey in an open car port facing the stables, but aside from that the place could be uninhabited.

He hasn't called ahead. He doesn't want the Keay family getting advance warning of his arrival. No time to dream up excuses. Maybe he should have made contact though, if only to check that someone is actually here.

The wrought-iron gate in the wall opens on to a knot garden of low boxwood hedges with a large conifer at the centre, its branches sweeping down in a dark tent shape. A stone bench encircles the trunk and a few modest pieces of statuary are dotted around, all uplit by invisible lamps. The house itself is three storeys, with an additional row of dormer windows in the roof. The trunk of an enormous wisteria winds across the entire lower half of the façade, gnarled and grey as the stone itself. The front door is closed and there are no lights on at the windows.

The heavy iron knocker echoes through the house. There's a long silence. He's about to turn and go back to the car when he hears a woman's voice on the other side of the door.

'Who is it?'

'Police.'

'Police?'

'Nothing to worry about — just a few questions I want to ask.'

The door opens to reveal a woman in her late fifties — tall and extraordinarily elegant in her lavender-grey pashmina, her tailored jeans. Her angular face is framed with carefully cut greying hair. June Keay, he thinks. Jonathan's mother.

'DI Caffery.' He hands her his card. She takes it and inspects it carefully. 'I've driven up from Bristol. Can I come in?'

She hands it back. 'My husband's not here. Is it him you want to speak to?'

'No — I want to talk about Jonathan.'

Her face falls. 'Jonathan,' she repeats woodenly. It's neither a question nor a statement.

'Yes. Jonathan.'

'My son.'

'You're June Keay?'

'Yes.'

'Can I come in?'

She stands back and opens the door to him. 'I'm sorry — so rude of me.'

They go into a flagstoned kitchen where the Aga is turned up high. There is a woollen blanket on a chaise longue next to the window, with a pair of glasses and an iPad on it. Music is playing in an adjoining room, some kind of Gregorian chant. He can make out a deer's head on the wall in there, and a boxed taxidermy scene mounted above a doorway — stuffed squirrels dressed as Victorian gentlemen gathered around a fireplace, smoking and drinking port. Lots of elegant furniture, lots of furniture polish, but no signs of life.

Mrs Keay closes the iPad. 'He's upstairs. I'll take you up there in a minute. But first, can you tell me, is this about the fight?'

'Fight?'

Mrs Keay searches his face for a long time. Then she gives a sad smile. 'No, of course not. There was no fight, was there? He's lied to me — I *knew* he was lying.' She grips the back of the chaise longue, squeezing it distractedly. Her eyes draw vaguely to her reflection in the dark window. 'He used to get the same look when he was a little boy. I said to my husband, 'He's lying again'.'

Caffery raises his eyebrows. 'Lying?'

She sees his confusion and sighs. 'He was gone for nearly twenty years — he went through one of those student things, hating our money. Paying back his debt to society. We didn't have the chance to cut him off; he cut us off. And then . . . ' She pushes the hair off her forehead. 'And then, out of nowhere, he came back.'

'It doesn't sound as if that was a good thing.'

'Well, it would have been, if he wasn't injured so badly.'

'Injured?'

'Didn't you know? He's been in hospital — he contracted septicaemia from his wounds.'

'How did he get wounded?'

She frowns for a moment. 'I thought that was what you were here to tell me.'

The Security Pod

The alarms have stopped now and the sudden silence is like a slap. AJ's ears are ringing. He is in the security control pod at the very front of the unit with the Big Lurch and the supervisor. They both stand with their arms crossed, hands tucked inside their armpits, sheepishly avoiding each other's eyes. Neither of them fully understands what has happened. More worrying still, they have no idea who is going to take control of the situation.

They have issued a unit-wide lockdown: all patients are confined to their rooms and each ward has come back with a head count. The supervisor has just finished scribbling notes of his actions in the incident log. Camera feeds have been switched so that the images they want appear on the two monitors closest to the supervisor's desk. One monitor shows Myrtle Ward. The camera is focused on the closed door of the ground-floor seclusion room. The nurses refer to it as the 'quiet room', even though everyone knows that's a euphemism for a containment cell. Any uncooperative patient is taken to the 'quiet room' to have a 'bounce around' until they calm themselves down.

Usually the patient's first action is to take their clothes off and start kicking the walls. Not this time. This time it's not a current patient in there. It's an ex-patient: Isaac Handel. And with him is Melanie Arrow.

'But the door can't be locked — not from the inside.'

The security supervisor nods gravely. 'It can if you take in the things he's taken in.'

'What things?'

'I don't know. He was carrying a holdall. We didn't get a chance to see, but the door is wedged or locked somehow. We don't know what he's used. And as you can see, there's no picture. He's sorted the camera too.'

AJ swears under his breath. He'd like to kick the shallow-minded rent-a-gorilla supervisor. This can't have happened. It just can't have happened. This is one of the country's most secure psychiatric units — it should not have been breached in this way. But then, most of their security measures focus on stopping the patients leaving, not preventing them coming in.

A third monitor shows pre-recorded footage. AJ puts his hand on the top of the monitor and peers at it closely. 'Skip to the beginning — let me see it again.'

The supervisor presses his lips together. He's trying hard not to lose his cool and his expression doesn't falter as he flips the remote control at the player, skips the video back. He lets it roll and AJ sits down, his eyes glued to the scene.

This is the footage from the camera here at central security. It starts with an image of the car park, solid pools of white cast by the security lamps. The blinding cones of approaching headlights is the first indication of anything amiss. Melanie's Beetle shears into the car park, coming to an erratic stop across two marked bays. She is at the wheel, and something is being held to her neck. AJ knows it's a Stanley knife, even from this distance, because he's seen what happens next.

The passenger door opens and Isaac gets out. It's clearly him — he's small with the distinctive pudding-basin haircut that gives him the appearance of a nervy junior monk. He's wearing his striped sweater, artificially faded jeans and trainers. His head is held back and up slightly, as if he's wearing a mask and the only way he can see anything is by squinting down.

The driver's door opens. Although Melanie is obscured by the windscreen, AJ can tell she's deciding whether or not she can make a dash for it. But before she can attempt anything, Isaac has scurried round the front of the car and is holding the Stanley knife to her neck again.

AJ has seen the footage three times — but he can't help watching it again. The next two and a half minutes are played out on three separate cameras. The time code clicks away in the top-left-hand corner as Handel pushes Melanie away from the car. They pass under a light and for a moment AJ can see their features in the fizzing glare, then they go under the lens and disappear off screen.

They are picked up by a second camera, which is mounted inside the reception corridor. A security guard can be seen from behind, slowly rising to his feet, puzzled by what is happening outside. And then Isaac Handel is at the door, banging on it. The security guard seems to freeze — he hits the panic button under the desk, but moments later he opens the door to allow Handel into the airlock.

'She told him to do what Handel said. That's why my guard let them through. He's kicking himself now.'

AJ sighs. 'OK, let's see the rest of it.'

The footage jumps to another camera's perspective. This time it's the long thin corridor — the 'stem' leading to the clinical area. The pair get to the pinch-point doors and this time Melanie can be seen giving clear instructions to the camera. 'Let us through,' she mouths. Her face is ghostly and resigned, there are shadows under her cheekbones. 'Just do what he says.'

The next camera to pick them up is on Myrtle Ward. The time code has this as happening just ten minutes ago. It shows Handel pushing Melanie in front of him. As he passes under the camera, they have a clear view of the blade he's using to control her. He pushes her into the ward seclusion room. The supervisor switches to the view inside the room just as the two enter, Melanie first, Handel behind her.

It's a strip cell — completely empty. Handel points to the floor.

'Sit,' he says.

She obeys, shakily, sinking to her haunches. Handel turns to the door, fumbling stuff from the holdall. There is the sound of a power tool, but he's too close to the door for the camera to pick up exactly what he's doing.

Melanie says something to him. There are microphones in the room, but her voice is too soft — too scared for it to be audible.

Handel doesn't answer. He sets down the holdall and straightens. He looks immediately at the camera — he knows it's there, after all he's been in this room as a patient. In fact, he knows the hospital inside out. From the holdall he pulls a long-handled tool and places a piece of duct tape on the end of it. Carefully, his tongue between his teeth, he uses the tool to fix the tape over the camera lens in the ceiling. The screen goes grey — just the canvas-like weave of the tape visible.

'What are you doing?' Melanie asks, quite clearly this time. 'Why are you doing that?'

'They don't need to see.'

'Why?' Melanie's voice is tight. 'What are you going to do?'

Handel doesn't answer. There is the sound of people knocking on the door.

'Fuck off,' he says in a level voice. 'Don't interrupt.'

Melanie begins to weep. And seconds later the sound drops out. Handel must have found a way of covering the microphone, because from that point on the noises are muffled. When the speakers are turned up high vague sounds can be heard, but they are too indistinct to make any sense.

'That was all happening, I dunno — ' The Big Lurch checks his watch. 'Five minutes ago? We were wondering whether to isolate the services inside the room.'

'Not yet. We want to be able to see if he takes that tape off. What does he want?'

'He hasn't said.'

'And when are the police getting here?'

The Big Lurch doesn't answer. AJ turns and glares at him. Then at the supervisor. 'Please tell me you've called the police?'

'We weren't sure if we . . . ' He trails off. Lowers his eyes. Even the Big Lurch finds something else in the room to stare at rather than connect with AJ.

AJ shakes his head. This must be punishment for the way he was earlier. He gave Melanie such a hard time over helping Isaac to get his discharge. She needed his support, he didn't give it, and now she's in deep shit and there's nothing he can do about it.

'OK,' he says. 'I'm the senior staff member on the floor at the moment, so I am in control here. I want' — he taps orders off on his fingers — '*one*, top priority: call the police. *Two*, we need to establish that our audio link into the room is live — I want to know if they can still hear us. If not, we have to figure out a way of communicating with them. And *three* . . . '

He hesitates. Doesn't know what three is. What he hasn't voiced to himself, and what he will never voice to anyone, is that he wants to see that footage again. He wants to watch it again and again and again. Because looking at the closed door of the containment cell, with the unearthly muffled crying coming from the mounted Bose speakers on the security-pod wall, he is afraid this footage may be the last time he sees Melanie alive.

'Three? Mr LeGrande?'

'Yes,' he says. 'I want this footage copied on to a separate drive — on the Trust's central server, not downstairs. Now.'

Jonathan Keay

Berrington Manor is turning out to be the creepiest place Caffery has ever been. Jonathan, according to his mother, is on the top storey of the house. 'He wants shelter in our home, but he doesn't want to see us or speak to us. So you'll understand if I don't come into the room with you.'

She leads Caffery up narrow wood-panelled stairwells, not saying a word. The only noise is the creaking of the steps. Her back is rigid — it's like following a prison warden, or a starchy matron in a boarding school. It crosses his mind that he won't come out of here alive, that Mrs Keay is going to open a door and push him through it — and he's going to find himself on a roller-coaster ride into the bowels of hell.

They get to the top floor — a narrow, low-ceilinged corridor with lamps set in the dormer windows. A slightly medicinal smell, mixed with the scent of saddle soap, hangs in the air. Mrs Keay stops at a door, her fingers on the handle. She turns to Caffery, giving him that sad smile again.

'I'm sorry — I'd love to come in. But he won't want me there.'

As Caffery steps through the door, Mrs Keay pulls the door closed behind him. He is left blinking in the gloom. She hasn't locked the door, but that doesn't take away the vaguest sense he's somehow been hoodwinked.

'Hello,' says a voice. 'You look like a cop.'

He turns. No greased rubbish chute to hell — instead it's an attic room with two dormer windows and shaggy flokati rugs on the bare floorboards. A tall man with a closely cropped greying beard sits at a low desk in front of an iMac.

He pushes back his chair and swivels it to face Caffery. 'You are a cop, aren't you?'

'You can tell?'

'Got used to it over the years.'

Caffery blinks. His eyes are adjusting to the light and now he can see Jonathan a little more clearly. He's in his late thirties and dressed in a black T-shirt and shorts. There's pink Kinesio tape in a star on his right biceps.

'Detective Inspector Jack Caffery.'

'Jonathan Keay.' He gets up and crosses the room. Shakes Caffery's hand.

'Are you ill?'

'That depends on your perspective.'

'Your mother said you were in a fight.'

There's a long silence. Jonathan studies Caffery closely — his eyes travelling over his face. 'Are you going to sit down?' he says.

'Am I invited?'

'Why do you think I said it?'

Caffery goes to a white leather designer chair with a steel pipe frame. He sits on the edge of it, peering at Jonathan, noting the sinewy limbs scattered in freckles. There are boxes of medication stacked on the cabinet next to the bed and the pink tape on his arm disappears up under his sleeve and emerges just out of the neck of his T-shirt.

'Mr Keay. A few things I need to ask . . . and can I start with Hartwool Hospital, Rotherham? You worked there?'

Jonathan sits down wearily, as if he's resigning himself to a long and inevitably painful process. 'That's correct.'

'And then from 2008 until last month you were working at Beechway.'

'I was.'

'I've been asked to look into some . . . *inconsistencies* at Beechway High Secure Unit.'

Jonathan clenches one hand, then opens it. Peers at it distantly. 'Yes. I guessed that was why you were here.'

'It is. Are you ready to talk?'

'I am. But it's not going to be easy.'

'It rarely is. We'll get there. Let's begin at the beginning. Take me back to Rotherham.'

Jonathan moves his jaw from side to side. Eventually he begins to talk, haltingly, as if he is having difficulty with the words. 'Yes — Rotherham. The mid-nineties.'

'Keep going.'

'One of the patients at Hartwool had a terror of being sat on at night. An anxiety disorder from childhood, something about being suffocated, I don't know. There happened to be a grave on the site of the hospital, of a dwarf who'd been there when the place was a workhouse. It got conflated with the idea of something sitting on people — and it spread round the unit. We all tried to ignore it, but the hysteria kept building and then things started to happen — things we couldn't put down to self-abuse. It escalated until finally we lost a patient. The inquest came back as suicide, but I was never convinced.'

'The same as at Beechway?'

Jonathan shakes his head. 'There never was a grave or a dwarf at Beechway — it was only at Rotherham. It was always Hartwool's story.'

'But you brought it to Beechway? Helped it take root?'

'No.'

'No? Then how did the story transplant itself down here?'

'That's what I'm going to tell you.'

Tactics

Flea gets the call as they're unpacking the van. The team has finished the day's search, but there's a dynamic situation at a secure psychiatric unit on the outskirts of Bristol. Can they go into overtime?

She talks to the men briefly, then gets back on to Control to say they'll be there in thirty. The men clamber into the van again and set about changing their kit and dragging riot gear out of the prisoner cage in the back. They are used to tactical entry and containment situations: when they're not diving, they spend a lot of time on searches or executing arrest warrants — often on drug dealers. They have every tool of the trade for forced entry, and their 'big red key' — a battering ram — is looped in netting on the van wall. They head off through the rush-hour traffic, Flea driving. She is grudgingly grateful for this distraction. She doesn't think she can stand another minute out in the countryside on this fake search.

Beechway is all lit up at night, cordoned and protected by razor wire. Some of the team recognize this place — they've been here before. The last time they came was to search for the missing patient Jack was talking about last night. Pauline Scott. Flea remembers it well.

The team aren't the first on the scene: the place is crawling with vans and marked cars, lights flashing. Inside, it's a fair approximation of pandemonium. She takes her men down to the containment area on the ward called Myrtle and, with her right-hand man, Wellard, assesses the door. It's going to take under ten seconds to get through it with the ram, but they have to wait for the nod. She agrees their radio protocol then leaves Wellard in charge and makes her way back down the glass corridor to the security centre.

The main players have congregated in the room that leads to the security pod. It's a sort of recreation area for the security staff, with a fridge, a TV and a coffee-making machine. The boss of the show — the so called 'silver' commander — is a tall, gentle-faced guy Flea has worked with before. With him is his tactical advisor and the bronze commander. Hovering in the glass-walled pod itself are the hospital security supervisor, one of his staff, and the most senior member of the nursing staff, a guy in a suit who is introduced as AJ LeGrande.

LeGrande is good-looking and he's very *nice* — Flea sees that right away. He's sweet-natured and kind, and *totally* out of his depth. He is walking around the room, swinging his arms, clapping his hands together, shooting glances at the monitor in the pod. The screen is a steady, unchanging grey-hatched pattern. The hostage taker — Isaac Handel — has covered the lens with duct tape. It's been three quarters of an hour and no one has any idea what is going on in there.

'Do you think you should be sitting down?' Flea murmurs under her breath when AJ is close enough. 'You don't look too good — no disrespect.'

He glances at her. His eyes are very dark brown.

'No,' he says. 'But thanks all the same.'

There's more to this than meets the eye. There's something personal in this for him — maybe something to do with the female hostage who is locked in the containment room. Flea can't help herself, she turns her eyes to the monitor with the blank, hatched image. AJ sees her reaction instantly.

'I know,' he says. 'Horrible, isn't it? I'd rather see anything than that.'

'Anything?'

'God, yes. I know when that comes off it's going to be like opening Pandora's box, but it has to happen eventually.'

Two trained negotiators arrive. One is the national negotiator — the senior of the two — and the other is a local Negotiator Support Officer, introduced to Flea as Linda. She has been appointed to conduct the negotiations and she shakes everyone's hands efficiently as if to say, *OK, relax, I'm in control now*. She's a small woman in her thirties with shiny chestnut hair. She wears jeans and a long striped cardigan with sleeves she keeps pulled down over her wrists as if she is cold.

All six of them stand in a huddle, discussing strategies. When it comes to Flea's turn she explains how long it will take to effect a forced entry into the seclusion room. 'But,' she says, eyeing Linda, 'I'm assuming that's our last-hope scenario.'

'Of course. And look, Sergeant, whatever steps are being taken to put containment on that room, can you *not* tell me? If the commander decides that's where it has to go, just do it — don't inform me first. If I know the team's about to storm the place it'll come out in my voice. That sort of thing can completely smash rapport — I'm better off not knowing.'

'Hear that?' the commander tells the assembled team. 'All tactical conversations stay in this room. And keep the volume to a minimum.'

'I'd like to be able to speak to them too,' AJ says suddenly. 'Would that be possible?'

Linda gives the commander a dubious look. 'A TPI?' she says. 'That OK with you?'

'What's a TPI?'

'I'm sorry, sir — that's like a third party. An intermediary. No reason he can't speak, if there's a place for him.'

'Well?' the commander asks AJ. 'Is there a place for you?'

'Definitely. I'm the senior member of staff here, I know the unit inside out. I've been here four years, and known Isaac all that time. I know him well — I really do. He's not always as straight-forward as he seems.'

Linda scrutinizes AJ. 'Uh, sir,' she addresses the commander, not taking her eyes off AJ. 'I won't argue with this, but he'll need to be properly briefed and, obviously, I want primacy.'

'She must take the lead,' the commander says. 'If she needs your input, she'll ask for it — understand?'

'I understand.'

In the security pod the senior negotiator begins arranging a workstation for Linda, complete with laptop, a microphone and a notepad. Flea stands in the lounge area, her radio at the ready. The moment she gets the nod from Silver she'll relay it to Wellard down on Myrtle Ward. Linda is talking sternly to LeGrande, reeling off a long list of what he can and cannot say. Everything has to be done with a nod from her or the senior negotiator. Then everyone withdraws into the staffroom, leaving Linda alone in the pod, seated in front of the monitors. AJ stands in the doorway between the two rooms, shoulder to shoulder with the senior negotiator, who holds a notepad — ready to convey information between Linda and the command team.

A signal from her senior and Linda begins to speak. 'Hi, Isaac. Sorry, don't want to make you jump in there, but my name's Linda and I'm a hostage negotiator.' She smiles. 'That sounds a bit grand, doesn't it, but actually my role is just to talk to you — to find out what's going on, what's brought you to where you are now.'

On her laptop a spectrogram of her voice fluctuates in one half of the screen. On the other half a stopwatch app clocks up elapsed time. Beneath it neon-blue sand runs through an egg timer.

'Isaac? Would you like that? Would you like to talk?'

Everyone bends slightly, straining their ears for a reply to come through the speakers. On a screen that has been turned so it can be viewed by the commanders, but not by Linda, Flea's men can be seen in the corridor, ready. From time to time one of them glances at the camera — sends a reassuring thumbs-up. Meanwhile, the image that Linda has in front of her doesn't change: it's the hatched greyish pattern of the tape on the lens inside the room.

The egg timer flicks itself over to show one minute has elapsed. Linda switches the mic on again. 'I'll just say that again — sometimes these microphones aren't very clear. My name is Linda and I'm here today to try to understand what's happening to you. I am here for you, Isaac. If you've got a mobile phone I can give you my number. You can call me on it. Then it'll be just you and me speaking — no one else needs to hear what's going on. Just you and me.' She pauses. 'I am here for you, Isaac — I am.'

Silence again. Nobody seems agitated. Only AJ. He keeps flicking helpless glances over his shoulder at the senior negotiator, as if to say, *Do something. Make something happen*.

Linda switches on the microphone and gives her mobile number in a very clear, calm voice. She does this three times, then says, 'Isaac, you've been without a proper place to sleep for days now. You must be tired. Wouldn't it feel better if you just had a quick chat to me? I want to help you, but I can only do that if I understand what's going on with you.'

There is still no answer.

It's been an hour now. Who knows what has happened behind that door.

Berrington Manor

Jonathan is a fragile greyish-white, and dark-brown circles have appeared like bruises under his eyes. He eases himself around to face Caffery, his face creasing with the effort.

'I'm listening,' Caffery says pointedly. 'Waiting.'

Keay takes a long, tired breath. 'Yes, yes, yes.'

'You're going to tell me how all the hallmarks of what happened in Rotherham came to be circulating Beechway unit. Ultimately resulting in two deaths and — '

'*Two?*'

'Yes. One in 2009 — '

'Pauline Scott.'

Caffery hesitates. 'Pauline Scott. Yes. You were at Beechway when it happened.'

'Yes, but what's the second death?'

'Zelda Lornton. She died almost a fortnight ago. At the moment it's an open verdict from the coroner.'

'*Zelda?*'

'Yes. You knew her, obviously.'

There's a long silence. Jonathan scans Caffery's face as if he's looking for the answer to something very painful. Then he gives a long shaky sigh and swivels the chair away. Folds his arms across his chest. At first Caffery thinks he's going to start tapping away at the computer; it takes him a while to realize Jonathan is crying. Silently, helplessly, his shoulders jerking and heaving convulsively.

Poison

It's been an hour and a half and AJ cannot, cannot, keep still. He stands in the security pod shaking, but so far only two people have noticed. One is the Big Lurch, who has put a hand on AJ's back — left it there just long enough to say: *I know, mate. I know what's happening to you. And though I'm not going to acknowledge it publicly, please believe I'm with you on it*. The other is the support-group sergeant, a woman with wiry blonde hair and very blue eyes. Although she is dressed for business in a bulletproof vest that bristles with equipment and radios, she's sensitive enough to have noticed. He's felt her eyes on him. She knows.

On screen, men in black uniforms and riot vests are trying doors, checking cameras, doing risk assessments and scrutinizing the blueprints of the building and its fire-response system. When they stand still, they do so with their legs slightly apart as if to suggest their limbs are so muscled it's impossible to close them properly. Their shoulders and noses and arms are so wide and strong that AJ feels completely inadequate.

The other screen shows the grey canvas tape. Nothing has changed. The volume of the speakers has been turned up in the team's attempts to catch every nuance of what is happening in the seclusion room. But it's just silence bearing down on them — a complete and utter lack of noise.

The egg timer flicks itself over again. And again. Maybe it helps Linda concentrate. All it reminds AJ of is the sort of thing Mum would instinctively shield her eyes from — knowing it would trigger an epileptic episode. Each time it tips over, another minute has passed in which Isaac Handel has had carte blanche to do whatever he wants to Melanie. And there will be lots of things — AJ is sure of that. He recalls the way Handel used to watch Melanie going through the corridors. His eyes narrowing to slits in his face. He'll be playing out all those things he's thought about doing.

AJ hopes and prays his imagination is better and crueller than Handel's.

DI Caffery is out of signal range. AJ would feel so much better if Caffery was here. *I am so so sorry, I'm so sorry*, he mouths to the screen with the tape on it. *Melanie, I am so sorry* . . .

Suddenly Handel removes the tape he has used to muffle the microphone. The sound is deafening, startling everyone. The security supervisor comes in and hastily leans across Linda to flick the volume down. The team hold their breath. Next to AJ, the senior negotiator lowers his face, touches his finger to his forehead. Linda puts her hand over her mic — as if she doesn't want a single whisper or movement feeding itself to the hostage and the hostage taker. AJ leans silently against the wall, hoping the people behind him haven't noticed that his legs are shaking again.

Then the tape is removed from the screen. There's a blinding glare of light as the camera adjusts to the sudden brightness. Then the image of the room flashes up.

Melanie is sitting on the floor, her back to the wall, her head bent. AJ leans forward and scans her frantically, taking in the details. She is dressed. She is wearing the clothes she was wearing when she came in. Nothing is ripped or torn. Although her shoulders are drooping, she is alive. Breathing. From this angle he can't tell if she is injured.

Handel stands in the corner of the room, his head made larger by the foreshortening effect of the lens, the holdall on the ground in front of him. He is stepping from foot to foot, convulsively wiping his hands, his eyes roving restlessly from Melanie to the door to the camera. His jeans are too big for him, they hang around his skinny frame — but they are, at least, AJ notes, zipped up. And there's no sign of blood on his clothing.

In the doorway the senior negotiator leans into the staffroom and conveys all this to the commander in a whispered voice. AJ hears snatches of what they're saying: *Give it time — see what develops — implement delivery plan*. He tries to control his breathing — keeping it silent. It takes a monumental effort of will not to make a sound.

Melanie lifts her head and looks at the camera. Her face is unharmed, there are no bruises, no blood. But her eyes are like black holes.

'Can you hear me?' she says.

Linda switches on the mic, draws close to it. 'I can hear you. My name's Linda.'

Melanie nods. 'I know. We've been listening to everything you said.'

'So,' Linda says. 'Am I talking to you or to Isaac?'

'You're talking to me,' says Melanie. 'Are you police, Linda?'

'Actually, you know what — technically, I am. But that's not my role at the moment. I'm not here as a police officer, I'm here to help you and Isaac. I know at this point we may be a long way off you coming out, but my job is just to talk to you and discuss how that will happen. So Isaac, if you were thinking about coming out, I'm the one who can discuss it with you.'

'That's OK,' Melanie says. 'It's all going to be straightforward.'

In the corner, Isaac nods fervently. He is getting more and more agitated, rubbing his hands together faster and faster.

Linda shoots a look at AJ. It was the word he used earlier. *Isaac's not always as straightforward as he seems*.

'Straightforward?' she repeats into the mic.

'That's right.'

'OK, Melanie,' Linda says slowly. 'Tell me a little more. We're all working towards you and Isaac coming out of there happy so we can put this behind us.'

'Yes.' Melanie nods slowly. 'And all you have to do is listen.'

'That's what I'm doing.'

'And who is there? Who else is listening?'

'Do you want to make this more private? I can ask them all to go, if you want.'

'No. I just want to know who's there.'

'OK, there's me and I've got a colleague here from London. There's two members of your security team. There's . . . ' She looks at the commander, who stands next to the door, arms folded. He gives his head a quick shake. 'And then,' Linda continues, passing over the commander and his tactical advisor with barely a hesitation, 'there's your ward coordinator.'

'AJ?'

'Yes. AJ.'

'Hi, AJ.' Melanie raises a hand to the camera, does a solemn little wave. 'Hi.'

AJ looks at the senior negotiator. Opens his hands to say, *What do I do? Do I answer?* The guy nods and AJ crosses the room, bends to speak into the mic. He can smell Linda's perfume he's so close — she'll probably be able to hear his heart thumping.

'Hi, Melanie. I'm here.' He pauses, his eyes on the screen. Then, instinctively, he says. 'Hi, Isaac.'

Isaac knows AJ's voice. He lifts his hand in acknowledgement. Linda moves the microphone slightly away from AJ.

'Melanie — what was that you were saying about this being straightforward?'

'That's right.' She glances at Isaac. 'Yes,' she says slowly, deliberately. 'All I have to do is admit my 'crimes'.'

'Your crimes?'

'Namely the following. That I . . . ' She pauses

and swallows — as if the words are difficult to get out. 'That I tortured my, uh, my patients. That I inflicted harm on them, which I later explained away as self-harm. That I . . . ' She sends a wavering glance in Isaac's direction, as if seeking a prompt on the rest of a script. 'That I, er — '

'Hurt them,' he says dully. 'You hurt them.'

'That's right. I hurt them.'

'You put ideas in their heads.'

'I put ideas in their heads. And ultimately, unlikely though it sounds, in two cases, ultimately I . . . ' She gives another painful swallow. Then finishes in a hurry: 'I drove them to their deaths.'

'And that's what you want to tell us?'

'Yes. It is.' She gestures to where Isaac is rummaging through the holdall. 'That's what I wore when I did it, so I wasn't recognized.'

Isaac straightens and produces a Perspex mask. It's a radiation mask — AJ recognizes it instantly. Some of the people at Mum's neurology clinic used to wear them. He thinks of the picture Zelda drew, and of what he saw in Melanie's back garden. That smooth, eerie, skittle head.

There is a long silence. Linda clicks off the mic and uses her heels to wheel her chair back so she is nearer the senior negotiator. 'Into surrender plan?'

'Yup — hold for one — I'll clear that.'

He turns to the staffroom and hisses to the commander. 'We can start on a surrender plan, it's looking good.'

The sergeant with the sweet face turns to leave the room, speaking into her radio as she goes. There's a palpable notching down of tension in the security pod. Linda and the senior negotiator go into a huddle and on screen the men in riot gear begin to move away from the seclusion room. On the second camera, Isaac is working at removing the screws and the iron rods he has used to barricade the door. AJ stares at Melanie on screen. He stares at the radiation mask.

In the room there may be a release of tension but there's something else too: a kind of disappointment that it's all come and gone so easily — that Isaac isn't the deranged man they'd prepared for but a schizophrenic effortlessly defused by Melanie's 'confession'. No heroics and no door battering and no hostage situations. Just another wacko.

Only AJ isn't happy.

'Sir?'

Everyone in the staffroom stops what they are doing and turns to AJ. He holds the commander with his eyes. 'Can I speak to him before he comes out?'

The commander cocks his head on one side. 'The situation is winding down. We're into a surrender plan, I think we know what we're dealing with now.'

'Do we? Are you sure he won't try something when that door opens?'

'The team are trained.'

'And I'm trained too. I'm trained really well with this one patient in particular. He's bluffing — I know him. I've been in this position with him before and I've known things go seriously wrong at this point.'

The commander thinks about it. Then he nods at the senior negotiator. 'Let him have a go.'

'Thanks.' AJ checks his phone in its belt holster. He's waiting for Caffery to call back. He's sent six texts and left three voice messages, updating him as the situation has unfolded — so far, no reply. He tucks the phone away and goes to the desk. Linda is frowning at him — not happy at all, but eventually she gets up and bad-naturedly pushes the chair towards him.

'Don't you cock this up for me now . . . ' she whispers. 'Please don't.'

He nods. Sits and switches on the mic. 'Isaac?' he says. 'Isaac — it's me.'

On screen Isaac stops what he's doing. He tips his head back and stares up at the camera.

'AJ?'

'Yes. It's AJ. Isaac — I've got a question for you. Did you stand outside Ms Arrow's window four nights ago?'

Isaac's eyes are wandering, the way they often do when he's stressed — the way a blind person's eyes will wander, unable to hold any sort of contact. It gives the impression Isaac is answering someone he perceives behind his own eyes. 'Yes,' he says. 'I did.'

'Why did you do that?'

'Um.' He closes his eyes and opens them. 'Because she had to be frightened like they were.'

'Like who was?'

'Like with Pauline and Zelda and Moses when she sat on their chests. I wanted her to be frightened too like they were.'

Linda clears her throat. When he turns she's hurriedly scribbled on a notepad the words: *Don't challenge. Go along with it. Collude with him is fine. Objective = get the hostage out.*

AJ nods. Then he clicks the microphone on again. This time he allows his hand to rest protectively over the button so Linda can't switch it off. 'Isaac?'

'Yes, what?'

'*Did you poison my fucking dog?*'

Linda draws in a sharp breath. She stands next to him, staring meaningfully at him.

'Answer me, Isaac,' AJ says hurriedly. 'Why did you poison my dog?'

Isaac moves his head from side to side, as if he's hearing something so surreal and inexplicable it's almost beyond wonder. 'Poison?' he murmurs. 'I don't think I did that, AJ. I wouldn't do that. I like dogs, I do.'

Berrington Manor

Eventually Jonathan calms himself. He takes sips of air, like water, swallowing over and over. Then, when the shaking has stopped, he drags his T-shirt up from the waist and wipes his face.

'OK?' Caffery asks.

He nods. He licks his lips. 'I didn't know about Zelda. If I'd known it was going to happen again I'd have — I'd have done something.'

'I'm sure you would. Let's go back to you arriving at Beechway. When did you first mention what happened in Rotherham to Isaac Handel. Was it when you — '

Jonathan shoots Caffery a quick look. 'Isaac Handel?'

'Yes. Tell me how you got talking. You worked with him on his dolls in art therapy — the poppets. You helped him with them.'

Jonathan frowns. His eyes leap all over Caffery's face as if he's trying to work out where this is going — what his strategy is going to be. 'Yes, I did. Handel's dolls were . . . his outlet.'

'You must have let him use tools?'

'Yes, and I supervised him constantly. Took the equipment away after every session. Followed the rule book.'

'You know Isaac thought he could control people with the dolls. You are aware of that, aren't you?'

'I'm aware he believed that. What's this got to do with anything?'

'And you never had any professional reservations about what he was doing? Dolls with their eyes sewn closed?'

'Reservations? Not really — I thought it was odd, him depicting death like that. But no more than some of the things that go on in places like Beechway.'

Caffery pulls out his phone and scrolls through the images of the dolls. Finds the one of Pauline in the pink satin and holds it out. Keay shifts himself forward and looks at it. He nods. 'Yes — that's Pauline. This pink satin — that was his way of making her comfortable.'

'Making her comfortable? By killing her?'

'*What?*' Jonathan blinks. '*Isaac?*'

'This doll he made — her eyes are stitched closed, same with the dolls of his parents. Showing what he wanted to happen to Pauline — what he intended doing.'

'No — no. This is all — '

'This is all what?'

'Wrong. Isaac might have stitched his parents' eyes closed before he killed them, I don't know. But with Pauline it was different — he only stitched her doll's eyes closed *after* she was found in the grounds. He was extremely upset about it. That's why she's at rest in all this pink satin. Like a coffin. And is that meant to be Zelda? See, he's closed her eyes too. That will be after she's died, not before.'

Caffery puts his phone away. 'OK,' he says calmly. 'We're talking at cross purposes, aren't we?'

Jonathan nods at him incredulously. 'Yes. I mean, you have got this so wrong.'

'Have I? Then tell me.'

Jonathan traps his hands between his knees, as if he is afraid they might do something independent of him that he will regret. 'OK,' he says eventually. 'OK. Tell me — how much do you know about domestic violence?'

Caffery did a one-day course back in the Met, years ago — he remembers the phrases: cycles of abuse; Stockholming; justification; self-blame. He remembers because he once hit a girlfriend himself and he still hasn't quite levelled that in his head.

'You do at least know the psychology of abuser and victim?' Jonathan prompts. 'And when you think 'domestic abuse', you automatically think man on woman, right?'

'Or man on man.'

Jonathan gets up and lifts the hem of his T-shirt. Caffery stares at his naked stomach. Under the pink Kinesio tape his ribs and abdomen are covered in bruises, faded to yellow or green, some merging into larger blocks of colour. He has deep scratches in several places — some at least ten inches long. One appears to have been infected at some point. He tries to lift the T-shirt above his head, but can't. 'Sorry. You'll have to help me with this.'

Caffery stands. Carefully, conscious of the intimacy of this, he raises the T-shirt from Jonathan's waist. As he lifts he sees instantly — Jonathan's chest, from armpit to armpit, has deep scratches etched across it. A patchwork of blackened scabs cling to newly growing scar tissue. Caffery squints at the scars. They're difficult to see in the low light from the computer screen.

'*Thou shalt not commit adultery*.' Jonathan sits back with a wince. 'You need a mirror to read it. My partner thought I was leaving. I was meant to see this every time I looked in the mirror. I told my parents I was in a fight — in a pub. They want me to press charges. I've said no.' He turns his head painfully so he can see Caffery's face. 'I suppose all along I've been waiting for you to turn up.'

'Your partner?'

'You're wrong when you think domestic violence is only man on woman, or man on man. A woman did this.' He sees Caffery's face and gives a dry laugh. 'I know — no one believes it when you say it. But it does happen that way, trust me. She got hold of some benzodiazepine — I never did drugs myself, so the benzos poleaxed me. Woke up ten hours later. I thought it was a bad dream until I noticed she'd dressed my wounds and bandaged me. She was crying on the floor next to the bed. Begging me to forgive her. I was so in love I think I'd have done anything rather than believe she could . . . could do some of the things she was doing.'

'Does 'she' have a name?'

He hesitates. Then he says in a low voice that is almost a whisper, 'Melanie Arrow.'

'Melanie Arrow?' Caffery lowers his chin, frowns at Jonathan. 'The unit's director?'

Jonathan nods. He presses two fingers on

either side of his Adam's apple, as if he's trying to control something in his throat. 'Nearly twenty years we worked together. She couldn't keep a relationship together — not with anyone. I sat and watched them come and go. Watched her tear herself apart over each one. Waited my turn. I'd have followed her to the ends of the earth. She was everything I wasn't. There was softy public-schoolboy me, with my Latin A levels and rich mummy and daddy, while she was born on a sink estate in Gloucester. You'd never guess it from the way she talks, would you? She dragged herself all the way up the tree — to the place she is now. I met her when I left the whole money system and become Citizen Keay and . . . well, shit — I mean, you've seen her. She was pretty and sweet and above all she was a fighter. Can you imagine how I felt about her?'

He trails off, looking again at his hands, which clench and unclench on the bed.

'Except I was a fail at supporting her — keeping her sane. It was like keeping a drowning victim's head above the water. When I worked out exactly who she was — what she was — I told her I was leaving. Leaving her, the hospital, the profession.' His mouth twists into an ironic smile. 'That's when I got my brand. Adultery.'

'What are you telling me, Jonathan?'

'Don't you know?'

He holds Jonathan's eyes steadily. 'I'd like to hear it from you.'

'A childhood like Mel had? It leaves scars. Her dad had cancer when she was a child. He survived, but she used to tell everyone he was dead. She'd cry about it to anyone who'd listen — and all the while he was alive and well. She just didn't want anything to do with them. He was a council worker — basically, he was a dustbin man — and she was too proud to admit it.'

'I repeat — what are you telling me, Jonathan?'

He clears his throat, embarrassed. 'When patients at Beechway started talking about The Maude, exactly the same as they had at Hartwool, I thought . . . ' He waves his hand in front of his face, as if to say he was blinded. 'I don't know what I thought. I was in denial, I suppose. Have you ever been so in love with someone you'd close your eyes to almost *anything*? Even something like this?'

Caffery can't answer that. Not to himself, and certainly not to Jonathan.

'Even when Pauline died I tried to pretend she'd just wandered off of her own volition. Melanie is absolutely lovely, so charming to everyone around her, you'd never think for a moment she was capable of . . . ' He breaks off to wipe his eyes again. 'It was her pattern when her relationships ended, her way of releasing her anger, frustration. You can time every appearance of The Maude by her break-ups. Pauline was attacked in her room a week after Melanie's husband filed for divorce. A couple of weeks later Moses gouged out his eye. And now you're telling me Zelda? After I left?'

Caffery folds his arms. He puts his feet out

and tips his head back, eyes closed. It's the attitude of someone having a five-minute afternoon nap, but he's not relaxing. He's slotting everything into place. He's thinking about the power cuts — effectively blocking the CCTV recordings. It's bothered him from the start, how Isaac could time his strikes so easily — as if he was ready for the blackouts. But if Melanie Arrow is AJ's Scooby ghost . . . it all fits. As clinical director, she would have access to all areas, she could come and go at will, interfere with security settings and fuses and locks. And the victims were always the patients that weren't well liked by the staff. Did Arrow think they'd be missed less? Or were they the ones who irritated her the most?

Caffery opens one eye. Jonathan is staring at him. 'What?' Caffery says. 'What?'

'You have to believe me when I tell you this. She is more insane, more dangerous, than any of the patients in that place.'

X-Ray Vision

'What's going on?' In the containment cell, Melanie is puzzled by the delay AJ is causing. 'Shall we just get on with it?'

Isaac's eyes flicker to and fro in confusion — trying to understand this change of mood. Because, intelligent as he is, he isn't a liar. He may be manipulative and capable of violence, but he can't lie. He said he didn't poison Stewart and AJ believes him. Scales have fallen from his eyes and he can see more clearly, as if he's been granted X-ray vision. Earlier, when he told Melanie that Stewart was ill, she immediately assumed it was something he'd eaten. He'd never said Stewart was poisoned, just that he'd been ill. And the mask — the radiation mask — it is the one her father used in treatment.

AJ looks at her pretty face, her wide-set eyes, her pale-blonde hair. He thinks about Stewart barking at her when she first arrived at Eden Hole Cottages.

Stewart knew. And now AJ does too.

'Hello?' Melanie repeats. 'I said, shall we get on with it?'

AJ has thrown the security room into uproar. The Big Lurch is staring at him, his eyes bulging, and Linda and her senior are having a long, angry conversation with the commander. She keeps shooting AJ hostile looks through the doorway. Eventually the conversation breaks up.

Linda fires AJ a resentful scowl and steps aside, shaking her head. She tucks her shirt back into her belt, glancing around the room for some confirmation that this is all out of order. The commander comes into the pod and stands next to AJ, one hand on the desk, the other on the back of the chair, leaning in so he can speak to AJ in a low voice. 'The language you were using wasn't very helpful. I thought we'd reached an agreement about what you would and wouldn't say?'

'I promise — no more swearing. I promise.'

'I'm giving you the benefit of the doubt because this is your environment — please don't let me down.'

'I won't.'

'One more chance.' He raises his eyebrows. 'OK?'

AJ nods.

'Can we get this over with?' Melanie repeats from the seclusion room. 'Please?'

The commander retreats to the doorway. AJ keeps him on the edge of his vision, where he can monitor him. He flicks the mic on again. 'Yes,' he says steadily. 'We'll get it over with, Melanie, when you tell the truth — the real truth.'

'I'm sorry?'

'You heard me. Explain why you've confessed all of a sudden.'

'*AJ*,' Melanie says, with a meaningful glance at Isaac. 'Do you have to ask me that question? Isn't it *clear*?'

In the staffroom Linda has turned furiously

— her hands out in disbelief. But the commander hasn't moved — yet. His arms are folded, and he is watching AJ like a hawk.

'Melanie,' AJ says quickly, before the commander changes his mind, 'what I'm confused about is why Isaac would think it in the first place. Why would Isaac come up with something like that?'

'You are joking, aren't you?'

'You tell me.'

Melanie's eyes flicker from Isaac to the camera and back. She points her toes and knees together — like a child who doesn't know the answer to a question.

'Melanie?'

'AJ, I've explained. Isaac *thinks* it because, naturally, I *did* it.' Her chin is down, her eyes are locked on the camera, sending the clear message: *This is a game we're playing — now for God's sake do your bit*. 'I *did* drive them to their deaths. I *did* hurt them and I *did* try to pass it off as self-harm and I did — '

'Say it again,' AJ cuts in. 'But this time, don't act it.'

Melanie's mouth opens in disbelief.

'AJ,' she says in a hurt tone. 'Tell me — why aren't you getting me out of here?'

'Tell me,' he replies. 'Why are you being so theatrical?'

She falters. Then her face hardens. Her feet turn outwards. She sits back and drops her hands at her sides. 'I don't know what you're talking about.'

'Yes, you do.'

'You're insane. Is there anyone else there? Who's in charge? Where's Linda?'

AJ glances at Linda, who glares at the commander. But he is standing with his back against the wall, one hand pinching his mouth ruminatively.

'I want to know who's in charge,' Melanie says. 'Put him on. Or get Linda back on.'

The commander taps his lips thoughtfully, considering his response. At length he pushes himself from the wall. He comes to the desk, leans over to the mic. 'Yes, Melanie. I'm the most senior police officer here, the commander on this incident. *And*,' he continues before she can cut in, 'I'm listening. It's all yours.'

'*Wha —* '

'You heard him,' says AJ. 'Now answer my question.'

There is a long pause. Melanie's eyes seem to get bigger and bigger by the second. She cannot believe this is happening. Everyone in the control room is absolutely motionless. Linda's egg timer turns itself over.

Eventually Melanie smoothes her hair back from her face. She takes a deep breath. 'Sometimes, AJ,' she says, in a soft voice. 'Sometimes when we lose someone — the way you lost your mother — sometimes we look around ourselves and all we can see is pain.'

AJ goes cold. 'This has nothing to do with my mother.'

'Sometimes when people carry around the sort of pain and the guilt you're feeling about your mother's death, it can occasionally get transferred to others. So easy to assume that if we feel guilt, others must too. Maybe that guilt is there because, what . . . ? Because secretly you wanted her to die? Maybe you'd been a little careless with her medi — '

'Melanie — '

'*Careless* with her medication. Only you — '

'Shut up, please.'

'*Only you* know the truth, AJ. What actually happened. But one thing is sure: you've attached the guilt you feel about your mother's death to me, which is why you're doing this.' She shakes her head, bites her lip. 'I'm so sorry. I think you know what I've been trying to tell you for a while now.'

AJ is silent for a moment — awestruck by her. She is good, but not quite good enough. She's a cartoon villainess.

'I'm not sure I do know,' he says. 'What have you been trying to tell me?'

'I hate to say it like this — it's too public. I can't say something that hurtful in a place like this.'

'Oh, I think you can.'

She sighs. 'OK — you're doing this because you know it's over between us. You know it was never going to be a reality. I mean, *me*? With you?' She makes a face as if she's seen something particularly noxious which, out of decency, she can't specify. 'Especially you know, the earth that didn't move when we got between the sheets. I can sort of see your point of view — and I can understand why you'd hit back at me like this. It might seem, from an onlooker's perspective, a particularly hurtful and childish way of doing it — but it's probably understandable. You have your problems and I can't pass judgement on that. Now,' she says calmly, 'please pass the microphone back to the inspector.'

'I think I'll decline that.'

'No, you won't.'

'I will.'

'I don't think you fucking will,' she says. 'Dick.'

In the security pod an icy silence descends. Every person is transfixed by Melanie's face. The hardening angles.

AJ swallows. He's almost got her. 'Yes,' he says softly. 'I will.'

There is a pause. Melanie breathes in and out. She is shaking. Eventually she says in a voice so low it's barely audible, 'You wet dick. Get the commander back on the microphone *now*.'

In AJ's holster his phone is ringing. He looks down. It's Jack Caffery's number flashing on and off.

Timing, he thinks. Sometimes life is about little more than good timing.

How to Make an Arrest

Beechway High Secure Unit is visible from miles away — blazing like a beacon with the blue emergency lights flashing on and off, strobing through the trees like lightning. As Caffery winds his way up the drive the usual faces emerge in his head-lights: the divisional first-response cars, ambulances, three plain cars he takes to be local CID — and a support-unit armoured Sprinter van.

He's not sure what to expect. He has sent through a directive not to arrest Melanie Arrow until he arrives — he wants to be there when that happens. She's currently in a containment cell.

'Jack,' a voice says as he comes up the drive. He stops. Leaning against the van at the top of the drive is Flea Marley. She has one foot up against the van and is holding coffee in a Thermos cup. She's in personal protective gear — covered in radios and gizmos — and she looks tired. Her hair is scraped back off her face and she wears no make-up.

He's reached the end of her jerking him around. He thinks of Jonathan Keay and his confusion and embarrassment that he'd protected Melanie so long. When is he, Caffery, going to wake up to his own blinkered breed of denial? He's not going to talk to her. Instead he gives her his professional face.

'Yeah, hi — how's it looking up there? Easy?'

She pauses. Caught by the hard edge in his voice. 'Yeah — I . . . uh.' She brushes a strand of hair from her face, using her hand to shield her expression. When she drops her hand the look has passed and her manner is all business. 'Simples,' she says lightly, gesturing at the hospital. 'We've piled in here tooled up to the ears and it turns out to be nothing. Damp firework. The bronze and silver commanders are in there arguing the small print. Both hostage and the target are compliants, so it makes our job easier.' She takes a deep, deep breath. 'Before you go . . . ?'

'Yes?' he says impatiently. 'What?'

She's silent for a moment. Then she lowers her face and sips from her Thermos cup. 'Nothing,' she mumbles. 'Nothing. Good luck.'

Caffery knows for sure that 'nothing' doesn't mean 'nothing', but he's a stubborn bastard when he wants to be. He's not going to forget the way she's jerked him around this week. He holds a hand up as goodbye, turns and heads up the drive. He doesn't turn to look at her, though he assumes she'll be watching him. Hating him.

He goes through security — running the gauntlet of the local uniforms, the security staff puffing themselves up and acting big because the real cops are here. Some of the patients in one of the wards have come to the window to peer out — wondering what has come to pieces in the unit. He can hear them wailing and giggling.

A face appears at the window, grinning at him. A white woman in her thirties who's been eating something red and sticky which is now smeared across her face, giving her the appearance of a lioness after a kill. She lolls her tongue lasciviously at him. Makes a kissy face. He continues across the central domed area towards the place called Myrtle Ward, following the two uniformed cops who are escorting him.

The place smells like a slaughterhouse toilet. The walls are covered in hand — and footprints, and every wall corner has a padded strip — like in a boxing ring. There's an overlying fug of dismay and sadness and fear in the place. It makes him feel even emptier than he did before.

Handel has been arrested — there was a scuffle, but he's been moved to an empty bedroom on Myrtle where he is waiting for a consultant to give him a psychiatric evaluation before he can be interviewed and charged. Caffery looks through a window and sees him sitting on his bunk, his hands in cuffs. His nose has bled all over the baggy jeans he's wearing. He's refused a medical exam, insisting he's OK.

Melanie Arrow, meanwhile, is still in the seclusion room. Four members of Flea's team stand at the door, the visors on their riot gear lifted. At their feet is a Stanley knife, bagged.

'There's blood,' Caffery says, looking at it.

'Yeah, but it hasn't been used,' replies one of the cops. 'It just got in the way. Handel had a clout on the nose when we went in — there was a bit of claret floating around, got on to everything. Including this.'

'How about her?'

'Quiet. Compliant. She's been asked if she

wants to come out but says no, so I guess it's an arrest sitch.'

'Yes. Yes.' All the way here Caffery's been trying to work out what he can arrest her with. Usually in a case like this they'll start with something easy to prove, then up the charge when the dust has settled and they've had time to think. He looks through the window. Melanie is sitting with her head lowered, as if she's studying her hands. There are one or two spots of blood on her white blouse. More on the floor. It's still a leap to believe what Jonathan Keay and AJ are telling him about her.

He opens the door. She raises her eyes calmly.

'Hello,' she says. 'It's been a while.'

'Melanie.'

'Bit of a mess, isn't it?'

'Do you want to talk about it?'

She lifts her face — a bright smile pasted there. Her eyes are blank. 'You're so kind. But I think on this occasion I'll decline, if it's all the same to you. I think I'll just go home now.'

She gets to her feet and walks towards him as if it hasn't even occurred to her that he might object. He puts a bit of width into his shoulders and moves his foot so he is blocking the door.

She stops a pace away from him and drops her head again. Studying his feet — trying to decide how on earth this obstacle came to be in her path.

'I'd rather you came to the station,' Caffery says. 'I don't think home is a good idea — under the circumstances.'

There's a long pause. It is so quiet he can hear

the breath whistling in and out of her nose. Then she says, in a voice straight from the Gloucester sink estate she grew up on: 'And you don't have any fucking right to be speaking to me like that.'

'I'm being civil. Do you want to extend the same courtesy to me?'

'This is my unit.'

'You haven't answered my question. Are you going to be civil?'

Melanie lifts her chin and spits at Caffery. It hits him on the eyebrow. Drips into his eye, stinging. He wants to wipe it off, but he doesn't. He smiles.

'Thank you for that. I've been trying to decide what I was going to arrest you for.'

Teeth

It's kind of fitting that Halloween is coming — the time when pumpkins get scooped out and displayed — because that's the way AJ feels just now. Like someone has ladled out every piece of hope and light and love his body could contain. What's left in the place he was holding Melanie is nothing.

When Jack Caffery has accompanied her, cuffed and escorted by two cops, to a waiting car, the Big Lurch comes by and puts a hand on AJ's arm. He squeezes it. Doesn't say anything, but AJ gets the message. *I understand. When you're ready to talk, I'm here.*

AJ nods. Mutters a 'thank you'. The Big Lurch wanders off, leaving AJ standing helplessly in the corridor — not knowing what to do with himself, wishing he could sit down somewhere. He thinks about calling Patience. Then he imagines telling her what has happened. She'll be sympathetic, but there will be an undernote of *I told you* so in her voice — and he can't face that. Instead he finds himself back in his office, holding the crude picture Zelda drew — the first thing that sent him on the hunt for Isaac. And now he sees, as he runs his fingers over it, that it has been added to after the original drawing. The paint is higher and fresher than the rest.

He shakes his head. It's like holding a kaleidoscope to your eye — growing more and more conscious of the intricate possibilities presented. Melanie — sweet, funny Melanie — is like a million different-coloured pieces of glass, reflecting back the colours the observer wants to see. She worked hard to get Handel's tribunal to release him — hoping he'd walk out of the unit carrying all the stigma of The Maude with him. It never dawned on her that Isaac knew what she was doing.

AJ goes back to Myrtle Ward. Down the corridor to the room where Isaac Handel is sitting, waiting for a psychiatric appraisal before he can be taken into custody. AJ nods at the cop sitting outside, unlocks the door and enters.

Isaac is sitting dejectedly on the bed. He looks up when AJ comes in, but doesn't speak. He is deathly pale. His jeans are covered in blood and there are twin lines of blood coming from his nostrils. He's a mess. After they've cleaned him up, they're going to put him through the wringer — drag him in front of a hundred courts and then the system is going to end up putting Handel back in a place just like Beechway. Except this time he'll be at the head of the chain — in high-dependency Acute, with a very very long wait until he cycles back to discharge. Years, probably.

AJ doesn't speak at first. Instead he drops back against the wall, his chin lifted, and slides down until he's sitting on the floor opposite Isaac. He rubs his face a few times. He's known the guy for years and yet never noticed that actually Isaac is the strangest guy on the planet. He's tiny. The pudding-basin haircut is freaky and ridiculous.

Unbelievable that AJ's been so nervous about him.

'Isaac,' AJ says, 'tell me something . . . '

Isaac lifts his head. His eyes aren't on AJ — they are somewhere on the ceiling, as if AJ's voice is being projected from up there. His hands are clenched. There is so much blood. Everywhere.

'Yes, AJ?'

'The dolls,' he says, almost not wanting to hear the answer. Because he thinks he can answer this himself. 'Tell me about the poppets.'

'I lost my poppets. I did lose them. From being bad.'

'You were bad?'

He nods. His face is so pale it's almost blue. He is shivering. 'And so she took them off of me. The Maude.'

AJ stares at the side of Isaac's face. He flashes back to Melanie's bathroom. The broken panel. The missing bracelet. Could she have planted the notion of the broken panel as a way to focus AJ's attention on the bath — just so he'd find the dolls in Handel's room? The biblical scripts — she could have written them out herself. She's been so clever pinning this on Isaac — looking back it's been as dizzying as watching a circus acrobat.

'OK. And something else. Why did you do what you did to your parents? To your mother and father?'

Isaac answers the question as automatically as a child answering the question *What's one plus one?* 'I didn't like them biting. Didn't like their teeth.'

'Biting?'

'Uh hmmm,' he says, nodding. 'Used to get teeth when I didn't play the games they wanted.'

AJ is silent for a long time, picturing this. What other cruelty is locked away in Isaac's head? He wants to say sorry — he wants to touch Isaac, but before he can, Isaac draws in a long, shaky breath. His voice is very small, very distant. 'Something else, AJ,' he murmurs. 'One more thing.'

'What?'

'It's only going to last another few minutes. That's all it's going to last. You are going to think it's finished then. But it hasn't. The end isn't here yet.'

'Isaac?' AJ tilts his head on one side. Frowns. 'The end? What are you talking about?'

Isaac doesn't answer. He's smiling, but his eyes are glassy. His expression fixed. AJ levers himself up and away from the wall. Stands and crosses to the bunk.

'Isaac?'

AJ is long experienced. He should have picked up on this like an eagle. But it's passed him right by. Blood bubbles from Isaac's mouth. His lips are grey.

'Isaac.' He grabs him, but Isaac falls against him, suddenly heavy. His eyes roll back. '*Isaac — Jesus*. HELP!' he yells. He fumbles for the alarm cylinder on his belt. '*Paramedics* — get the fucking paramedics in here now.'

2 November

Monster Mother has given birth to some of the worst beings, yet each and every one is her offspring. She has responsibility for them all, good or bad. The Day of the Dead is here — All Souls' Day — the day when the souls of the departed come back to visit their loved ones. It is a time of turmoil for Monster Mother. She is pulled to and fro by the voices of her departed children.

Dressing is a particularly confusing problem. How can she put a colour to a day which is so varied — so striped with good and bad — peppered with sadness and happiness? She has the overhead light on as she goes through her wardrobe, choosing what to wear. The curtains are closed — the spirits are all out there, wanting to be let in — zipping back and forth outside the window. She doesn't dare look yet — if she does, her head will be pulled from one side to the other, so fast it will come loose from her neck.

Her missing arm has a spirit — a spirit that is dark pink. Crimson. Like the sex and the anger that made her cut it away. So for her dead arm she chooses crimson shoes. Pauline, poor Pauline — her spirit is so thin it can't be heard above the others. She is the pale, leached-out yellow of the camisole that Monster Mother chooses. Zelda was a bad girl — so bad and so alive — she was a firecracker and the red headband at the back of the wardrobe is for her.

Next to consider is Ms Arrow. The Maude.

What colour for her? She is patchwork, light on dark. When she was happy the hospital was a safe place. When she was unhappy, The Maude slid along the corridors. Found ways through locked doors in the dark. Goosebumps pop along Monster Mother's arms just thinking about The Maude. The greed and the anger, the cleverness. Melanie Arrow is gone from the hospital — but her anger, her power and her need reach out from the police cell like radio waves and search for Monster Mother. She plucks out a pair of gloves. They are of a purple velvet that appears almost black in some lights. From other angles it's a radiant violet. As pretty and deceptive as deadly nightshade.

Lastly she chooses her skirt. It takes some time, because the skirt represents Isaac and Isaac is so many things. So so many things. So clever and so sad. So unpredictable.

The skirt she chooses is flesh-coloured crepe under a white net into which have been stitched a million silver sequins. Isaac was the colour of nothing — no one noticed him. But for those who saw him in the right way he was also a million points of light. From the moment he was discharged from the hospital, Monster Mother knew he'd be the one to deliver justice to Melanie Arrow.

She holds the skirt up to her face, the sequins rough nubbles on her skin. Isaac is dead but he isn't gone. He isn't finished. He is clever and he is a universe of stars.

She slips the clothes on. And when she is quite sure she is ready she opens the curtains. The spirits see her and they are cowed. They bow, lamb-like. They sit obediently on the grass. She smiles at them, blows kisses to some, shoots fond but warning looks at others.

'Gabriella?'

She startles. Someone is knocking at the door. Lately there have been strange people in the hospital, asking questions. Making notes. People she doesn't recognize, all wearing suits, carrying clipboards. She doesn't want one in here. She searches the room for a place to scuttle to.

'Gabriella? It's me — it's AJ. Can I come in?'

AJ. The finest of her children. She relaxes. She floats to the door and opens it. There he stands. She loves him so.

'Dear AJ,' she says. 'Dear son.'

'I'm knocking off shift now, Gabriella. Thought I'd come in and say . . . ' He trails off, taking in her clothes. 'Nice. You look . . . nice. Are you OK?'

'Yes. I am, thank you. And I am here — inside my skin.' She smiles. 'Today is an important day. Today is the day I care for my children. And you, AJ? You need caring for. I can see.'

'Do I?'

'You do. No one else knows, but I do. I know you so well, I gave birth to you, and I know. There's a hole in you now. A giant hole and you think it can't be filled.'

AJ lowers his head and touches a finger to his forehead. 'I'll be going,' he says, his voice tight. He turns hurriedly for the door. 'Have a lovely day, Gabriella, you look wonderful.'

'AJ?'

'What?'

'Be careful, AJ. Be careful. We all love you.'

Eden Hole Cottages

A consultancy team from the Trust is busily reviewing care procedures at Beechway and several of the security staff have been suspended pending investigation. Some of the patients have been moved to a secure intensive-therapy unit outside Bath.

Beechway is already getting back on its feet — but AJ isn't.

A hole. That's what Gabriella called it. She couldn't have described it any better if she tried. As he drives home that day, slowly down the windy lanes, he pictures himself as a carcass. A grey shell, dressed in a tired suit, driving a beat-up old Astra with mismatched tyres.

AJ and Patience are now sure Melanie poisoned Stewart. AJ found a packet of rat poison in the cellar that had been opened. But Melanie poisoned more than just animals — she poisoned minds. He wouldn't have her back if his life depended on it — he'd rather be dead. What he would have back, however, in the blink of an eye, is the peace of mind he had before she arrived. He'd guarded that for a million hours and he only let it go to her with reluctance. He thought he was getting into an adult relationship — he hadn't realized that he was the only mature person in it. Melanie has cracked him open in the place he'd healed so well and hard — and now he's got an open wound that won't go away.

'AJ, will you stop this?' For his breakfast Patience has made fried pumpkin fingers and an omelette with handfuls of dried mushrooms and cheese. She throws the plate down impatiently. 'I'm getting tired. You chose the wrong one — I tried to tell you, but you didn't listen.'

'I'm not missing her. I'm just . . . ' He shakes his head, staring down at the omelette. He can't eat. It is insanity. All insanity. 'I'm just tired.'

'And I'm tired too. I'm tired of you and I'm tired of our damned dog — who thinks I'm named after my nature — which I'm not.'

'We all know that.'

'Well, tell the dog that, will you?'

AJ draws his hands down his face. Stewart is in the corner — not in his usual place next to the Aga, but by the back door, his eyes hopeful.

'I've walked him and walked him — and look at the animal's face. The dog won't be told.'

AJ sighs. He pushes back his chair, leaving the omelette untouched. 'Come on,' he tells Stewart. 'Let's go.'

He pulls his fleece and walking boots on and opens the back door. He ignores Patience's outrage — to scorn her food offerings is to dice with death. The omelette will probably end up in his bed, under his pillow maybe. So what? Life is different now. He's ready to be taken wherever the tide goes.

'Come on, mate. Let's do it.'

The daylight is filtered through a cloying mist. It hangs low on every field. AJ hasn't brought Stewart's lead and the dog is half ecstatic with joy. He runs, nose down across the garden, stops and puts his head up to check this isn't a trick, that he's actually being allowed to do this.

'It's OK.' AJ waves a hand. 'Just let me know where you are.'

Stewart runs on ahead — and it's no surprise the direction he takes. He crosses the field and makes a beeline to the stile which leads into the forest. AJ pulls his fleece closer around him and sets out to follow. Stewart seems to have an inbuilt safety instinct, because now that AJ isn't yelling at him and chasing him to come back, he doesn't head for the hills. He actually stops and waits for AJ to acknowledge him and his position, waits for him to cover enough ground, before he races off again.

Nothing much in the woods has changed — everything is a little damper, a little colder. His trousers are covered in drops of melting frost where he brushes against hedges and stiles. The trees have lost a few more leaves; otherwise it's exactly as it was a week ago — including Stewart's trajectory, which, unsurprisingly, leads them back into the wooded crest of land where Old Man Athey's orchard is. They pass the rusting disused skip and move down the path.

Last time AJ was here he was nervous. This time weariness and sadness weigh down and muffle his fear. His hands and face are cold, but apart from that he feels very little. He trudges along obligingly until they enter the clearing.

Only now does Stewart hesitate. He hovers at the edge of the clearing, a line of fur rising like a brush along his spine. The old walking yew is there — bone-white. Stewart stares at it, but he doesn't back off.

'Jesus, Stewart. If this is a prolonged dating game — I mean, if this is you on the hunt for some skirt you haven't got the cojones to face up to alone, then I'm going to have a sense-of-humour failure. And it's going to happen pretty soon.' He checks his watch. 'Like in about twenty seconds.'

The dog trots forward. AJ lowers his hand and watches him. Stewart has his head low, his ears pinned back. AJ's never seen his dog like this before.

He follows, squelching heavily through the wet leaves. Now he sees the core of the tree has rotted, hollowing out the centre to a deep black cave. It should be dead, but it isn't. Stewart has ducked inside. AJ pulls his phone out and checks the signal — nothing — so he switches the phone light on, rests his hand on the arch at the entrance and shines the light inside.

It's an amazing, natural cave. There are crenellations and smooth, wavelike formations, polished and glowing. It goes back and back and back. He wonders where he's seen this before, then remembers — it's the dream — the recurring dream that seems to be linked to not being able to breathe. The dream of an all-consuming creature. Something that means life and death. Something that has no end and no beginning.

Stop it, he tells himself. Stop it.

He takes long slow breaths until the tightness in his ribs goes away. He opens his eyes and finds his sight has adjusted — there's enough light in here to see. He turns the phone off and pockets it. Crouches to get through the opening. Stewart is running around inside, busily sniffing every nook and cranny. Someone has been here — there are things on the floor AJ doesn't want to look at too closely. It smells too — like Beechway on a bad day.

'Hey,' AJ hisses. 'What's in here? Doggy Viagra or something?'

Stewart ignores him and heads further into the bole. Now AJ notices there's another arched entrance. You wouldn't see it if you weren't a damned dog. AJ follows, fighting off cobwebs. He has to get down on his hands and commando crawl to get through the next gap, and when he's through his eyes won't adjust to the light at all. He needs the phone again. He clicks it on and shines it around.

They are in a second natural bole. An interconnecting chamber in the skeleton tree. The phone light falls on an odd tree stump in the centre of the ground. It hasn't grown there, it's been placed. Centrally — almost symbolically. He is about to move towards it when he realizes his route is impeded by a wire.

'Ah.' He is brought up short. 'That's interesting.'

He shines the light along the length of the wire. It is tough and relatively wide bore. It originates in an eyebolt embedded in the underside of the tree and extends across the opening to the tree stump. Moving closer, AJ sees its lower extremity is attached to what appears — unless he has completely lost touch with reality — to be a small doorway, cut out of the trunk with a hacksaw.

His dream. Alice in Wonderland. A hole he can fall down. A hole that opens into heaven.

Stewart lets out a low, anxious whine. He comes and sits next to AJ, his eyes flicking nervously up at him. His tail wags warily.

AJ puts his forefinger on the wire. Crooks it so it's got control and can pull the hatch open with a simple twitch. 'What do you say, eh, Stewart? Is it a yes? Or is it a no?'

Stewart opens his mouth. Lets his tongue out.

'I'll take that as a yes.'

He pulls.

MCIT

Isaac Handel died from a wound to the liver where the Stanley knife entered. He didn't draw anyone's attention to it at the scene and it wasn't picked up by the police officers. Any blood was attributed to the thump he got on the nose in the scuffle. No matter how often they replay the tapes of what happened in the secure cell that day, no one can be sure how he got the wound.

Melanie insists it was self-inflicted. Her prints are on the knife, but she insists that happened in the scuffle and that she had nothing to do with Isaac's death.

This is the part that Caffery can't square up — because he is reasonably sure Isaac had something else planned. He is nagged by the sense there's something he hasn't seen, hasn't attended to. The missing pliers and wire Isaac Handel bought at Wickes? What was he planning to use those for? A wire. To do what? Ignite a chemical fire somewhere, the way he did with his parents? If so — where? When there's time, Caffery's going to call Penny Pilson — ask her what she makes of it. Did Isaac leave the trip wire for the police — or was it really a way of setting fire to his parents' bodies without having to be there? He'll tell her that now he understands what she meant when she said . . . *Things are not what they seem*.

For now, though, he's too busy with Melanie

Arrow and the long, untidy string of deceptions and untruths she trails behind her.

Isaac's doll of her — shiny face, slightly feline eyes — doesn't do justice to her true nastiness. He can't recall the last time he felt so contemptuous of a person. She continues — even in custody at Trinity Road — to argue her case. To lie and lie. When the CSI start coming back with hard proof of her involvement: her DNA on a pen in Zelda's room, Zelda's DNA on her father's radiation mask, she changes tack. She admits the charges but pleads insanity. She blames the system, her childhood, her ex-husband. She even blames Caffery. When, during an interview, she unbuttons the top of her blouse, subtly, so that no one in the room aside from him notices, he tells the PACE officer to stop the recording because he's leaving. He tells him to carry on without him. He'd prefer never to see Melanie's face again.

The superintendent has largely kept off Caffery's back, but now that the Beechway case has moved down to interviewing and statement-taking and debriefings and liaising with the CPS, he wants to know what Caffery intends doing with the teams out in the cold at the Farleigh Park rehab clinic. They've got one or two more days until they complete the search; the staff hours spend on this is astronomical. Caffery's time is nearly up — next week the case gets moved down to one of the detective sergeants. He hasn't had a chance to get to the search site for three days and that's fine — he isn't going to deal with Flea Marley again, no matter how he's felt about her for the last eighteen months. She's missed their biggest chance to resolve Misty's disappearance, she's wasted all the effort and intricate planning he'd put into motion. He doesn't know if he'll ever forgive her. Eventually he'll decide how to go about giving Jacqui Kitson what she wants, but he'll have to start from scratch. Misty, meanwhile, stares at him from the wall. That constant, unspoken, disappointment in her expression.

Enough is enough. He's been living on four hours' sleep and coffee for the last seventy-six hours. He shuts down the computer, gets his jacket, and heads for the door. He's crossing the car park to his Mondeo when he notes a little Renault parked next to the barrier. As he gets closer he sees Flea Marley is sitting at the wheel, the window open, watching him steadily.

He hesitates, looks left and right, half wondering if he can vanish, or find a distraction so he won't have to speak to her. Then, resignedly, he heads over to the car.

'Yes, what?'

She doesn't answer. She is dressed in her regulation black combats and polo shirt. Her hair is tucked under a cap and she wears no make-up. She's got a faint winter suntan from the long days of fruitless searching around the clinic.

'Jack, we need to speak.'

'Here we go again.'

'Come with me?'

'What, for another mystery tour that ends nowhere?'

'Give me a chance.'

He glances all around the car park again. Half hoping for a reason to say no. There isn't one. He pockets the keys, walks around to the passenger seat, throws his waterproof on the back seat and gets in. The car is tidy, her kit in the back, an iPod on a stand but no music playing. He fastens his seat belt. 'Where are we going?'

She starts the car and begins to drive. They go out of the security gates and turn on to the feeder canal road, then head over the Lawrence Hill roundabout and on to the motorway. She's got such a look of purposefulness that Caffery keeps quiet. If she's going to drive off a cliff in her fury, part of him feels so weary he doesn't know whether he'd fight. He doesn't even reach into his pocket for his V-Cigs. Fighting is for those who have something to gain.

On the M4 the sun comes out behind them. He can see in the rear-view mirror the clouds stalling in the west, in a towering bank — almost as if they've given up chasing the little Clio and are content just to watch it make its escape. Flea takes the A46 exit, heading south in the direction of Bath. At first Caffery assumes she's taking him to her house, but she doesn't. She sails past the turning and continues on the bypass towards Chippenham. Then she takes a sudden left and a right and loses him in a morass of lanes he doesn't recognize.

He fishes his phone out and tries to keep track of where they are, using his free hand to brace himself against the car frame as she throws the

Clio around corners. Are they going to the clinic? If so, it's not a route he's taken before. But Flea knows this countryside well — she grew up here. Caffery's only been here for three years and he is lost — the GPS signal ducks in and out, struggling to keep up. Eventually he gives up and sits in silence, the phone resting on his thigh.

After a quarter of an hour she pulls off the road on to a rutted, rain-soaked track which leads into a forest. It is so rarely used that the trees bend inwards over the car. Branches scrape the roof and brown autumn leaves stick to the windscreen as they bounce over the uneven ground.

About a hundred metres down, the track comes to an end and Flea stops, cuts the engine. Ahead is a stile — mossed and almost invisible with the amount of bramble that covers it. The woods are silent. Just the distant caw of rooks.

'Right,' Caffery says, looking around. 'You want me on my own — probably to explain again why you won't do it. Because there's only one other thing you can want privacy for — and I'm guessing from the atmosphere that's not on the cards.'

She ignores him. Throws the door open and gets out — goes to the back of the car. He doesn't twist to watch her, he can monitor her in the mirror. Her face is fixed as she opens the boot, pulls something out, and returns to his side of the car. She stands next to his window and drops it at her feet.

He opens the door and peers down at it. It's a

giant holdall — blue and white with a logo on it.

'Game of tennis?'

She narrows her eyes at him. She loops a GPS unit around her neck, shoulders the bag and heads off towards the stile. She's wearing black walking boots and she pushes through the brambles as if they're not there. Caffery is dressed in office shoes and his suit, but he does have his Triclimate jacket on the back seat. He grabs it, and jumps out of the car — follows before he can lose sight of her.

Into the Wild

In the entrance to the dead skeleton tree, AJ LeGrande sits on the ground staring at what is in his hands. Stewart stands next to him, attentive, uncertain. He keeps lifting his face to AJ's as if asking to be reassured everything is OK.

'I don't know, do I?' AJ says. 'You're the one who wanted to come here.'

Inside the tree trunk, behind the door, was a small hollow packed with feathers. In it were lying the two dolls he holds now. If Isaac Handel hasn't made them, then someone is doing a good job of aping him, because they have his style stamped all over them. They even smell of him. AJ turns them over and over — studying them in the thin white light coming through the branches.

They have been constructed using scraps of fabric; twists of foil and bottle caps — they aren't as ugly as some of the other things Isaac used to make. Isaac was never shy about depicting the gender of his dolls — he makes that part abundantly clear — one is a male and one is a female. They are depicted embracing. It's not sex — it's an affectionate embrace. AJ's not sure how Isaac has achieved the sense of attachment and love between them. When he tries to untangle them it takes a while. He has to use his keys to snap the cotton that has been used to stitch them together.

He recognizes the male doll. It's him. AJ.

'OK,' he says, shaken. He puts the doll down, takes off his jacket, in spite of the cold, lays it on the wet ground, kneels and lies the dolls carefully on the jacket. 'OK.'

His hair is made of scraps of wool, and the front of the T-shirt is made from a scrap of the Hawaiian shirt that Patience says is a danger to all people of taste. The female doll means nothing to him. It has bright-red wool for hair and is dressed in a skirt covered in lilac-sprigged flowers. Tiny bangles made of twisted wire cover its arms.

'Isaac, old mate,' he whispers. 'Isaac? What's all this about?'

He raises his head to survey the clearing, wondering what Isaac wanted from this place. This place that has been in his dreams all these years — just a few miles from his home. With a jolt he sees he's not alone. On the edge of the trees, about four metres away, a woman stands silently watching him.

'Jesus.' He gets up hurriedly. 'Didn't see you there.'

She smiles. She is petite and pretty — with a neat elfin helmet of vibrant red hair. She's wearing wellingtons and a duffle coat — a floral skirt peeping out from under it. Stewart instantly trots over to her, as if he knows her, sits at her feet. She bends and scratches him behind the ears. 'Are you Stewart?' she says. 'Are you? You're lovely.'

'Stewart,' AJ says warningly. 'Stewart . . . ' He wants to order the dog away, the way he'd warn him away from any stranger — but this woman doesn't appear to be a threat. In fact she's so gentle with Stewart that he actually rolls on to his back like a soppy puppy so she can rub his belly.

'Hey, you like that!' She crouches and scratches him hard. Stewart's ears flop back and his head turns from side to side in doggie ecstasy. 'You are an attention sponge,' she laughs. 'My old Suki would have fallen in love with you.'

AJ stands slowly. He is frowning. 'Do you know my dog?'

She shakes her head, happily scratching away at Stewart, whose legs are twitching with pleasure.

'I said, do you know my dog? You know his name.'

'Yes, I know his name. He's just as lovely as I expected.'

'As you expected?'

She stops scratching and raises her eyes to him. She must be about his age, but her skin is as smooth and clear as cream. Her eyes are a muddy green. 'That's what I said.'

'Are you going to explain?'

'That's why I'm here, AJ.'

He stares at her. 'I *beg* your pardon? Say that again.'

She smiles. 'That's why I'm here, *AJ*.'

'OK — stop now. This is too random.'

'No. It's not.' She points to his jacket on the ground. 'Look at the dolls.'

He glances down. Sees the red wool of the doll's hair. The dress it is wearing is similar to the woman's. A muted floral print.

'I'm Penny, and you don't know me. But I know who you are. You were Isaac's friend in the hospital.'

'Who *are* you?'

'I told you — I'm Penny. And I'm a hippy.'

'Yes — you look like one.'

'You're not exactly David Beckham. Has anyone ever told you that?'

'Not in so many words. How do you know Isaac?'

She smiles. 'I'm his mother. No — not his mother, of course I'm not *really* his mother. I'm his dream mother. I'm the one he wanted as his mother. Do you know some of the things his real mother did to him?'

'Yes.'

'Well — you probably don't know them all. You don't want to know. *I* didn't know until last week — I didn't understand him. I thought he hated me. That was Isaac's problem. Everyone ran away from him.'

'I didn't run away. Or did I?'

'No. You didn't. And he loved you for that. He really loved you. If I was his mother in his dreams, then you were his father. Did you know that?'

AJ stares at her — speechless. He wants to argue, to tell her she's insane, and that he should know about insanity, given his profession. But he glances down at the dolls and it crosses his mind that maybe he has been guided by an unseen hand. For a long time he's thought he'd lost his way, but maybe that was all part of the path. His destiny.

A Distant Fire

The woods are thick — still dripping with the earlier rain, soaking Caffery's shoes and throwing mud and leaf litter over the hems of his trousers. Flea doesn't check he's following, she only stops every so often, to check her GPS unit. They go up and up and up, until they are on the edge of a hill — the land dropping away on their right. The density of the forest gives way to glimpses of sky between the branches. He can see snatches of surrounding farmland. But no hamlets or houses or electricity pylons. No sign of civilization at all.

She steps off the track, crashes through an impossible tangle of brambles and branches. His trousers are going to be shredded, but he follows. Ten metres in, she stops and turns to him. She drops the holdall and stoops, unzipping the side pocket. Pulls out two pairs of nitrile gloves and two pairs of bootees — the type the forensics team dole out to anyone visiting a crime scene.

'Do you know where we are?'

'You're kidding,' Caffery laughs sourly. 'This is pin the tail on the donkey — you've been spinning me round blindfold for the last hour.' He'd like to add she's been doing it for months and months. Instead he says, 'A clue?'

'Farleigh Park Lake.' She points to the north. 'See?'

Sure enough, between the trees in the direction she's indicating, there is a mirrored, grey coin of water nestling in the green. And suddenly he understands where they are. Hands on the trunks of two trees, he leans himself out over the drop, so he can survey the land. Familiar hills and sweeps of land are emerging out of the anonymous landscape.

'Shit,' he murmurs. He points his finger to the west. 'The clinic must be over there . . . somewhere . . . '

'The RV point is just beyond that clump of trees. This hillside is the last part of the search. We start here at eight tomorrow morning. Here.' She holds out a pair of gloves. 'You're going to need them.'

Slowly, slowly, Caffery lowers his eyes to the holdall.

'Yes,' she says. 'It is what you think it is.'

He stares at the holdall, not moving for a long, long time.

'And by the way, Jack, the security at your house is shite — you need a dog. I walked in there this morning and spent an hour digging up your garden. No one stopped me. The clothes are in the bag too.'

He raises his eyes to her. If he ever suspected himself of being in love with this woman now he is one hundred per cent sure.

She shrugs. 'Boxes,' she says, although he hasn't asked the question. 'Keeping things in boxes. Being scared that if you open them to take one thing out everything else will come tumbling out too.'

'Everything else?'

'Yes. All the things that it's easier not to think about. Like brothers and dead parents, and like . . . '

She trails off. Bites her lip, her eyes going over his face. Behind her the countryside stretches away — the winter landscape of Somerset. A line of smoke from a distant fire rises into the sky. Her face is lit by the dying sun.

'And?'

She gives a tiny smile. As if something has made her shy and sad and hopeful all at once. 'Oh nothing. Just 'and'.'

Acknowledgements

Many people spend a lifetime building their knowledge and skill bases, only to have a fly-by-night novelist come along and steal it all to make into a story. Why they tolerate this daylight robbery I have no idea, I can only be grateful and humbled by their generosity. Those people include: Patrick Knowles, who filled in the details of the UK's mental-health system; Hugh White, genius pathologist; Simon Gerard; DCI Gareth Bevan of Avon and Somerset MCIT (the real-life Jack Caffery); Inspector Zoe Chegwyn, who taught me what I needed to know about hostage situations. To you all — I apologize if I have skewed the truth you gave me for the purposes of fiction, but thank you, thank you, and thank you, again.

As always, the debt I owe to the wonderful folk at my publisher's and agent's offices is immeasurable. To you all, a huge hats-off for your hard work and patience. Also to Steve Bennett, for tolerating my adversity to social networking. It amazes me how you manage to run a website for someone who is so phobic about sharing.

Jonathan Keay — the real-life Jonathan Keay — made a large donation to the DeKalb Libraries in Atlanta, Georgia, and for that he has had a character named after him in *Poppet*. Jonathan, I know you are far more interesting in real life than you appear in this novel, nevertheless I thank you. And as for Karin Slaughter — who was in the background of this arrangement — you continue to outrage, inspire and amaze me. Keep it up, girl!

Lastly, I want to thank my dear friends and family — supportive and quiet and constant: Bob Randall; Margaret OWO Murphy; Mairi Hitomi; Lotte GQ; Sue and Donald Hollins. What would I do without you?